DAWN OF
THE DRAGONS

JAMES A. OWEN

DAWN OF THE DRAGONS

SAGA PRESS

LONDON SYDNEY **NEW YORK** TORONTO NEW DELHI

TO ALL OF MY READERS OF EVERY AGE WHO BELIEVE
THAT MAGIC IS REAL, AND WORTH LOOKING FOR —
BECAUSE IT IS, AND ALWAYS WILL BE.

SAGA PRESS
AN IMPRINT OF SIMON & SCHUSTER, INC.

1230 AVENUE OF THE AMERICAS, NEW YORK, NEW YORK 10020

This book is a work of fiction. Any references to historical events, real people, or real places are used fictitiously. Other names, characters, places, and events are products of the author's imagination, and any resemblance to actual events or places or persons, living or dead, is entirely coincidental. • *Here, There Be Dragons* copyright © 2006 by James A. Owen • *The Search for the Red Dragon* copyright © 2007 by James A. Owen • All rights reserved, including the right of reproduction in whole or in part in any form. • Saga Press is a trademark of Simon & Schuster, Inc. • For information about special discounts for bulk purchases, please contact Simon & Schuster Special Sales at 1-866-506-1949 or business@simonandschuster.com. • The Simon & Schuster Speakers Bureau can bring authors to your live event. For more information or to book an event, contact the Simon & Schuster Speakers Bureau at 1-866-248-3049 or visit our website at www.simonspeakers.com. • The text for this book is set in Adobe Jenson Pro. • Manufactured in the United States of America • First Saga Press paperback edition June 2015 • 10 9 8 7 6 5 4 3 2 1 • CIP data for this book is available from the Library of Congress. • ISBN 978-1-4814-2996-2 (pbk) • ISBN 978-1-4814-4143-8 (eBook)

II. THE SEARCH FOR THE RED DRAGON

HERE, THERE BE DRAGONS

PROLOGUE

IT WAS A very distinct sound, the quiet scraping of steel on stone, that first told him that his visitors had arrived, followed by a strange sort of tapping and the shuffling of feet.

The tapping outside in the alleyway became more pronounced, and he suddenly realized it was less the sound of tapping than it was a soft cacophony of claws, snapping together in anticipation. He set aside his pen and notebook and settled back in his chair. There was no denying it. It was time.

The strained amber light of an English afternoon streamed through the greasy windows of the door as it slowly opened into the study.

He refilled his pipe with his special cinnamon tobacco mix and noted with passing interest that clouds were beginning to gather on the far horizon.

A storm was coming.

It didn't matter, he thought to himself with some satisfaction. He had said the things he needed to say to the person who needed to hear them. He had protected that precious stewardship that needed protecting, and passed it to those who would use it wisely and well.

There was, he concluded, not much more that could be asked of an old scholar, in this world, in this lifetime.

The silhouette in the doorway gestured to him, and he caught a glimpse of wickedly sharp steel, which curved to a point, as the visitor's arm rose and fell. The clicking noises in the alley grew louder.

"Greetings, Professor," the shadowy figure said. "Might I have a word with you?"

"It's not here," the professor said, lighting his pipe and drawing deeply on it. "You're too late."

His visitor appraised him for a moment before concluding that the professor was speaking the truth. "I'm very sorry to hear that," he said. "That does not bode well for you."

The professor shrugged. "What happens to me is no longer important. You may claim my life, but I've put an empire forever out of your reach—and when all is said and done, which of the two matters more?"

The visitor gestured again, and the tapping noises outside gave way to snarls and animal howling.

There was a rush of bodies, and in seconds the small study was filled with ancient steel, and pain, and blood.

When the noises again faded to silence, the visitors left the study as they had found it, with one exception.

It would be several hours before the first raindrops from the approaching storm would begin to freckle the paving stones in the street, but the professor would not see them fall.

PART ONE

THE IMAGINARIUM
GEOGRAPHICA

CHAPTER ONE
THE ADVENTURE BEGINS

THE SLIM, CREAM-COLORED note may just as well have been inserted into a bottle and tossed into the ocean rather than sent by post, for by the time John received it, the professor was already dead.

For perhaps the hundredth time, John took the note out of his pocket.

> *My Dear John,*
>
> *Please make all haste to London. There is much, too much I'm afraid, that should have been explained to you well before now. I only pray that this letter finds you well enough to travel, and that you will bear me no ill will for what is to come. I do not know if you are ready, and that is my own burden to bear. But I believe you are able, and mayhap that is enough. I hope it is.*
>
> *Professor Sigurdsson*

The letter had been dated a week earlier, the ninth of March, 1917, and had reached him at the hospital in Great Haywood the day before. John cabled a reply to his mentor, requested a temporary leave, dispatched a note to his wife of less than a year at their home in Oxford, explaining that he would be absent for perhaps several days, and immediately arranged passage to London.

It was the messenger who delivered the cable who found that a murder had occurred and notified the police. John knew without asking that the officer waiting at the platform in London was there to speak with him, and why.

The train from Staffordshire had run late, but this was not unexpected, nor was it any longer even an inconvenience. It was simply one of the erosions of normality that came with a constant state of war.

John had been on leave from the Second Battalion for several months now, since before the holidays. To the doctors, he had pyrexia; it was "trench fever" to the enlisted men. In simpler parlance, his body had grown weary of the war and manifested its protest with a general weakness of the limbs and a constant fever.

On the train John fell immediately asleep, and his fever coalesced into a dream of a mountain of fire, spewing hot ash and lava into the trenches of the French countryside, consuming his comrades as they held fast against the German offensive. John watched in horror as those who fled the trenches were cut down by gunfire. Those who remained, crouched in fear, were swallowed up, the sons of England become children of Pompeii as they died in flame and smoke. . . .

He awoke to the shrill whistle of the train, signaling their arrival at the station in London. He was flushed and sweating and looked for all the world to the awaiting constable as if he was complicit in the murder of the man he had come to see. John wiped his brow with a kerchief, shouldered his backpack out of the luggage racks, and stepped off the train.

His arrival, and his subsequent departure with the policeman, were noted by no less than four individuals, mingling invisibly within the crowds exchanging places between the platform and the trains. Three of them were cloaked and walked a bit awkwardly, due to the inverted joint in their lower legs that made them walk as if they were dogs, striding upright on two legs.

Exactly as if they were dogs.

The strange figures disappeared into the throng to report what they had seen to their master. The fourth, which had been sitting alongside John on the train, slipped out of the station and turned down the street taken minutes before by the constable and the young soldier from Staffordshire.

"I'm just saying that there are a number of uses for an English night far superior to investigating a murder," said the inspector in charge of the murder scene, a stout, affable fellow called Clowes. "You can bet the killer, whoever he may be, isn't out traipsing about in this muck. No, he's home by now, having done his business for the day, warming his toes by the hearth and sipping a nice mulled brandy, while I have to be out here on the verge of catching my death. . . ."

Clowes caught himself mid-complaint and gestured in apology. "Not that talking with you lot is all that bad, mind you. Circumstances."

It took John a few moments to realize that he was not the only one being interviewed that evening about the professor's murder. For the first time, he noticed the other two cuckoos, shivering, nodding at the questioning police, wondering how they'd come to be in this particular dreadful nest.

Shaking hands, they introduced themselves. The younger one, called Jack, was straw-haired and fidgety; the older, Charles, was bespectacled and efficient. He was answering the constable's queries as if he were tallying an account at Barclays. "Yes. I arrived in London promptly at four forty. No, I did not vary from my planned agenda. Yes, I realized he was dead right away."

"And your reason for the visit?" asked Clowes.

"Delivery of a manuscript," said Charles. "I'm employed as an editor at the Oxford University Press, and Professor Sigurdsson was to add annotations to one of our publications."

"Really?" said Jack. "I've just been accepted there."

"Well done, Jack," said Charles.

"Thanks," said Jack.

"So, boy," said Clowes. "Your name is Jack, is it?"

"Yes sir," Jack said, nodding.

"Ah. Not the Jack from up Whitechapel way, are you?" asked Clowes.

"No," Jack replied before he had time to realize that the inspector was making a joke. "Oxford."

"Two of you at Oxford, eh?" said Clowes. "That's an interesting coincidence."

"Not coincidence," said Charles. "Selective association is a privilege, not a right."

"I'm a Cambridge man myself," said Clowes.

"Oh, uh, sorry," stammered Charles.

"Never actually did go to university myself, mind you," Clowes said to John behind his hand. "But he looked like I'd seen him in the Queen's knickers, didn't he? By the way—where are you from, ah, John, is it?"

"Birmingham, although I'm billeted at the hospital in Great Hayward at present."

This was not entirely correct, but John thought that pointing out that all three of them were actually from Oxford might not make his evening any easier, nor theirs, for that matter.

There was a certain kind of brotherhood that arose from the shared experiences of warfare, particularly among young men who had shared a trench for a fortnight. It was a different kind of fraternal experience to have been brought together as strangers, who otherwise had very little in common, united only by a murder.

"Never met him," Jack said of his affiliation to the corpse. "In fact, I had just arrived here in London for the evening, to deliver papers for a solicitor in Kent."

The inspector blinked, then blinked again and turned to Charles.

"My story is not much different from his, I'm afraid," Charles said, adjusting his glasses. "I was only here on university business."

"That leaves you, John," said Clowes. "I suppose you didn't know him either."

"No," said John. "I knew him quite well. He was my tutor."

"Really?" said Clowes. "In what studies?"

"Ancient languages, primarily," said John. "That was the bulk of it, with additional coursework in mythology, etymology, history, and prehistoric cultures. Although," he added, "in point of fact, I was a rather less than diligent student."

"Aha," murmured Clowes. "And why is that? Was he not a good teacher?"

"An excellent one, to be precise," said John. "But the priest who helped to raise me when my father passed, who paid for the bulk of my schooling, in fact, believes that this kind of study is, ah . . . not practical."

"I see," said Clowes as he scribbled on his notepad with a stubby piece of graphite. "And just what is 'practical'?"

"Banking," replied John. "Commerce. That sort of thing."

"Humph," snorted Clowes. "And you disagree?"

John didn't reply, but merely shrugged as if to say, *What can one do?*

"Well," said Clowes, "I'm just about done here. But as you seem to be the closest thing Sigurdsson had to family, would you mind taking a look at the scene of the murder? It may be that you can spot whether something is amiss, where another could not."

"Certainly," said John.

Jack and Charles waited with the constable in the foyer while John and the inspector proceeded to the library. The smell hit John first—burned leather, accented by the cinnamon-tinged tobacco that only the professor smoked—but the room itself was a disaster.

Books were strewn about everywhere, and the backs of the shelves had been hacked to pieces. There was not a single piece of furniture unbroken. A number of books had been placed in the hearth to burn, with limited success.

"It was the bindings what done it," said Clowes. "Leather, with metal clasps. Thick, holds moisture. Made a stench like the devil, and smoke black as his beard. That's what drew the attention of the messenger when he got no reply at the door."

John glanced around the room, settling his gaze on a dark,

crescent-shaped stain on the rug near the partners desk where the professor worked.

"Yes," said Clowes. "That's where he was found. Bled out quick—he didn't suffer, lad."

John thought this was a lie, but he appreciated the gesture nevertheless. "I couldn't tell you if anything's missing, inspector. It seems that everything that isn't chopped to bits or burned is . . . well, nothing worth noting. The books have some value, but only to persons like myself—and there's nothing here worth killing for."

Clowes sighed. "That's what we were afraid of. Well," he concluded, snapping his notebook closed, "I appreciate your time and cooperation. And I'm sorry for your loss."

"Thank you," said John. He turned to leave, then stopped. "Inspector? If I might ask, just how was the professor killed?"

"That's the other thing," said Clowes. "He was stabbed, of that there's no doubt. But the point of the weapon broke off against a rib, and so we got a good look.

"As far as we can tell, he was killed with a Roman spear. A Roman spear of a make and composition that hasn't been forged in over a thousand years."

The gray drizzle of the evening had become a truly miserable English night, and the business of the murder investigation had kept the three newfound companions out past the last scheduled trains.

"I know a club just a few streets over," Charles offered. "Shall we repair there and remove ourselves from this dismal, damp night? We can catch our trains in the morning, after we've had a bit of warmth and a nip of something to settle our nerves."

Jack and John concurred, and they let Charles lead the way through the labyrinth of streets.

"Funny that he was a book collector," Jack said after they had gone a few blocks. "A Shakespeare scholar, even."

"Funny? In what way?" asked John.

Jack shrugged. "Because—he was killed yesterday, on the fifteenth."

Slowly it dawned on John, then Charles. "Julius Caesar," John said.

"Yes," said Jack. "It may not have meant much in Caesar's time, or even in Shakespeare's, but it would've been a warning well heeded last night, if anyone had been around to sound it.

"Beware the Ides of March."

As it turned out, the club to which Charles led them had literary allusions of its own. It had been a privately rented flat not two decades earlier, and had since been transformed into a club accessible to a private group from Oxford, of which Charles was a member.

"221B Baker Street?" John said with a hint of incredulity. "Are you quite serious, Charles?"

"Completely," Charles replied. "Oxford paid for its conversion, and it's very useful to have such a retreat when on business in London."

He opened the door and ushered his two companions into the entry hall. The main establishment consisted of a couple of private meeting rooms and a single large, airy sitting room, with adjacent entryways to what John assumed were the neighboring flats, converted to a similar use. The large room was cheerfully furnished, and illuminated by two broad windows that looked out onto a solitary gas lamp and the worsening gloom of night and storm. The fireplace, attended to by an inconspicuous manservant, was at full roar and brightened their spirits considerably as they moved toward it, their clothes exchanging dampness for a light draping of steam.

"Much better," said Jack.

Jack took up residence in an immense Edwardian wingback chair and made himself quite at home. John preferred to lean on the hearth, the better to warm himself and dry his clothes, while Charles, with an ease born of familiarity, opened the liquor cabinet at the far side of the room and began pouring drinks.

"I've let the manservant go for the night," said Charles. "I don't expect any other members will be turning out on a night such as this, and to be candid, after our adventure with inspector Clowes, I rather appreciate the privacy."

"I'm looking forward to doing as you have, John, and joining the war effort," said Jack. "I was hoping to get in a term or two at school, but it seems the chancellor has other plans."

"You're young," said Charles. "You may find time and experience curb your taste for adventure."

"That was a bit of an adventure tonight, wasn't it?" Jack continued. "Imagine getting mistaken for the student of a dead professor. . . ."

Charles's scowl wasn't quick enough to cut off the younger man before a pained look crossed John's features.

"Oh, dear—Look, John, I'm sorry," said Jack. "I wasn't thinking."

"It's all right," John said, staring into the fire. "If the professor had been here, he'd have thought it was funny."

"You must mind your decorum," Charles admonished Jack. "Especially once you've begun your courses at . . . Jack—I say, are you listening to me?"

The younger man shook his head, stood, and crossed the room.

"There's a very strange man outside," said Jack. "He was standing across the street under the lamp for several minutes, and then he crossed to the corner, where he stood for several minutes more, and he is now standing outside with his face pressed to the window. . . ."

As one the three companions swung around to meet the surprised gaze of a strange apparition: a smallish man, seemingly cloaked in rags and wearing an outlandishly tall pointed hat. He was indeed pressed to the window, his nose pushed flat and his handlebar mustache askew with dampness.

The tatterdemalion at the window abruptly disappeared. Almost immediately came a solid rapping on the door.

". . . and now he's at the door," finished Jack.

"Bother," said Charles. "This is a members-only club. We can't simply be catering to every vagrant who hasn't the sense to be home on such a night."

"Oh, come now, Charles," said John, rising to answer the door. "If it wasn't for you, Jack and I would be in the same boat, and we've only just met."

"That's different," Charles sniffed. "You're Oxford men."

"I haven't actually begun yet," admitted Jack.

"A technicality," said Charles.

John opened the door and the strangest little man any of them had ever seen stepped inside and shook himself like a mongrel, spraying water all throughout the entry hall.

His appearance was what might result if you shredded an illustrated edition of the works of Jacob and Wilhelm Grimm, then
pasted the pieces back together in random order. His coat and
trousers were equal parts *Old Sultan*, *Rumpelstiltskin*, and *Hans-
My-Hedgehog*; his shoes, the unfulfilled aspiration of a hundred
cobbler tales. And his hat was some ruthless combination of *The
King of the Golden Mountain* and *The Shroud*. His eyes twinkled,
but his hair and mustache were sopping, and he looked as if he'd
been beaten about the head and shoulders with some sort of shed-
ding forest mammal. The only organized aspect of his appearance
was a large parcel wrapped in oilskin, which he clutched tightly
under one arm.

"Dreadful night," said the man, still dripping. "Dreadful.
Twenty pounds of misery in a ten-pound sack. If I'd ever known
such a night was going to come about, I'd have told my own
grandmother not to bother having my father, just to avoid the
trouble."

"Well, once you've dried off a bit, you'll have to leave," said
Charles, covertly hiding the good bottle of brandy behind the
inferior brands. "This is a private club. What were you doing
watching us?"

"Is this a question for a question?" asked the man. "I answer
yours, then you answer mine?"

"Can't say that isn't fair, Charles," said Jack.

"All right," said Charles.

"Good," said the strange visitor. "I was watching to make sure
no one else was."

"What kind of answer is that?" sputtered Charles. "That's not
a proper answer."

"Oh, come on," said John. "Be a sport." He turned to the little man. "Your turn. So what's your question?"

"I thank the gentleman," the man said with a slight bow. "And now my question:

"Which one of you is John? And do you know that Professor Sigurdsson is dead?"

CHAPTER TWO
AN UNUSUAL TALE

AFTER A BRIEF, stunned silence, John regained his composure. "That would be me," John said, standing and proffering his hand.

The apparition grasped his hand in return, pumping it frenetically. "At last, at last!" he exclaimed. "So happy to make your acquaintance, John, my dear, dear boy. And what better place than here at Sir Arthur's home-away-from, eh? So grand, so grand. Yes . . ."

Jack and Charles exchanged skeptical glances, and Jack twirled a finger at his temple.

The little man continued undeterred. "I trust you can take it from here, correct?" he said, thrusting the oilskin-wrapped parcel in John's direction. "You know what must be done. The professor would not have left you unprepared for this."

John waved the parcel away. "I haven't the slightest idea what you are talking about. We've only just ourselves come from the professor's house, and I haven't known of his death for but the last day."

"I see. Well then, if your apprentices might help me unwrap the *Geographica*, we can get down to business."

"Assistants?" said Charles. "I'm not—we're not—sorry, Jack— his assistants—apprentices," he sputtered. "I'm an editor for the—"

"Yes, I'm sure you are, and a fine one at that," the little man interrupted. "But that can only mean . . . John, tell me, are you—were you—the professor's only student? Were there others?"

John shook his head. "Not with the war going on. We had to prepare well in advance just to meet. I don't think he had the time for much correspondence and private tutoring with anyone else."

"Interesting," said Charles. "How did you come to such an unusual arrangement?"

"Hard to say, really," said John. "He came upon a few stories I'd written—trifles, really—and took a liking to them. He found I'd been billeted in Great Haywood after my return from France and came to see me with a proposal that he tutor me."

The little man did not respond to this but simply nodded, watching.

"It is a terrible loss for you, I'm sure," said Charles. "I now regret even more the lost opportunity to meet him. He sounds like an extraordinary man."

"He was," said the strange visitor.

"We only came here tonight because of Charles's membership in the club," said Jack, "but you came specifically seeking John. How is that?"

"Happenstance. Turned the wrong way and saw you enter. I can't keep these streets in order any more. Always lose my way. But even that is providence, for if I'd found the harbor earlier, when I was supposed to, I'd never have found *you*."

"What's at the harbor?" asked Charles.

"My ship is anchored there. Now, we must—"

"One moment," John said. "For all we know, this could be the murderer. He knew of Professor Sigurdsson well enough to know of me, but we know nothing of him."

In response, the little man rooted around inside his threadbare cloak for a moment before locating a crumpled note, which he proffered to John. It was, save for the person to whom it was addressed, identical to the one John had received from the professor.

"I trust that will suffice as evidence?" he asked. "I arrived from my travels abroad just yesterday and removed the *Geographica* from the house for safekeeping. The professor insisted on remaining there to wait for you. We were to reconvene in his library, this evening."

"This is the *Geographica*, then?" asked Jack, gesturing at the parcel.

"It is."

"What is it?" John asked.

The little man blinked and arched an eyebrow. "It is the world, my boy," he said. "All the world, in ink and blood, vellum and parchment, leather and hide. It is the world, and it is yours to save or lose."

Without waiting for a further response, the man carefully hefted the large parcel onto a table and began to unwrap the layers of oilcloth.

"It looks like a book," said Jack.

"I can see you're the smart one of the group," said the little man.

"Thanks," said Jack, beaming. "I'm Jack."

"Pleased to meet you, Jack," said the little man. "Call me Bert."

"Okay, Bert," Jack said, stepping forward to help uncover the parcel.

Under the oilcloth lay a largish leatherbound volume, worn

smooth with use—or great age. It was tied at the open edge with cloth straps, and debossed on the front, its letters still bearing glittering traces of golden embellishments, were the words *Imaginarium Geographica.*

"Hmm. 'Geography of the Imagination,' is it?" said Charles. "Interesting."

"Close," said Bert. "A better translation would be less literal: 'Imaginary Geography.'"

"Imaginary?" said John, peering at the large book. "Of what use is an atlas of imaginary geographies?"

The quick smile almost hid the shadow that passed over Bert's features before he answered. "Why, you are of course having a game at our expense, young John. It serves exactly the use one would think: to guide one to, from, and across imaginary lands.

"All the lands that have ever existed in myth and legend, fable and fairy tale, can be found within," continued Bert. "Ouroboros, Schlaraffenland and Poictesme, Lilliput and Mongo and Islandia and Thule, Pellucidar and Prydain; they are all there.

"Collectively, the place where these lands exist is called the Archipelago of Dreams—and it was for this book, this guide to the Archipelago, that the professor was killed."

"This looks like Greek," said Jack, his nose an inch from the open spread of the first map.

"Smart lad, Jack," said Bert. "There are a number of such maps at the beginning, but as you can see, several have been annotated in other languages, including English—although most of them are still untranslated," he finished, elbowing John. "Lucky we have you here, eh, my lad?"

"Wait a moment, just wait," said John, backing away. "I don't understand what this has to do with me, or how you even knew who I was, for that matter."

"I knew who you were, John, because I was the one who read your writings first. I was the one who sought you out and advised the professor that you were the ideal man to become his successor. I was the one who saw within you the potential to become the greatest Caretaker of them all.

"I had assumed that your companions were in turn *your* apprentices—no offense, Charles—but only because there have always been three."

"Three? Three what?" asked Jack.

"Caretakers of the *Geographica*," said Bert. "Now, we don't have time to dawdle," he continued. "The race has already begun."

"What race?" asked Charles.

"The race," said Bert, "to avoid catastrophe, my boy—with the whole of human history as the stakes. We can only hope the education you have had thus far has been enough."

"My *education?*" John said, incredulous. "But why is—"

Before he could continue, the night air was split with the long howl of a hound. It rang deeply and loud, finally fading into profound silence. Then the howl came again, joined by another, and another.

And another.

But this time, it was closer. Much closer.

Behind the horrible harmonies of the howling was a faint staccato—the shouts of men, angry, seeking. The sounds of a mob.

For the first time since he had entered 221B Baker Street, Bert's face became drawn and somber, and tinged with fear.

"That's it then, lads. We have to go."

"We?" sputtered Charles. "I'm not going out in this! Especially with some kind of . . . of *beasts* running amok in the streets!"

"You have no choice, I'm afraid," said Bert. "They're coming for John and me, so we *must* leave—but if they come here to find we've gone, you would fare the worse for it."

"Coming for me?" said John. "Why?"

"Did you think they would stop with the professor?" asked Bert. "They can't—won't. They haven't gotten what they're seeking— this," he said, slapping his hand on the *Imaginarium Geographica*. "And as it is now yours, I'm sure they'll have no problem cutting you down as easily as they did him."

Bert began to wrap the atlas in the oilcloth, and Jack stepped in to help him. "Quickly, now," he said to the three young men. "We must fly!"

"Fly where?" said Charles.

"To the harbor, of course," said Bert. "To my ship. My crew is waiting for us now, and they are beginning to worry, no doubt."

Charles began to protest, but Bert cut him short.

"These are not rioters coming for us. They are not soldiers. They are not even, in point of fact, *men* as you know them. But whether or not you believe my warnings, or that I have a ship awaiting us in the harbor, or that anything I have told you tonight is true, believe this: If we stay here a minute longer, we shall all be dead."

If Bert's appeal was not convincing enough, the shadows that appeared on the opposite street corner pushed the companions' motivation to the fore.

The band hunting them brandished swords and spears of an unusual make. But stranger still was the fact that they appeared to walk on all fours, claws clicking on the cobblestones, only occa-sionally standing upright to sniff at the air before rending the night with more earsplitting howls.

"Wendigo," Bert murmured to himself. "He's pulling out all the stops—and it can only get worse. Charles," he asked, turning quickly, "did Sir Arthur have a back exit to this place?"

"Yes," said Charles. "This way. Hurry."

Bert, Jack, and John followed Charles through a warren of small rooms to a door at the end of the apartment. "Here," said Charles. "They expanded into the adjacent flat, and it has a door that opens onto an alleyway."

As they entered the hallway, there was a crash and a splinter-ing of wood from the foyer behind them.

"Hurry, lads!" said Bert. "Hurry!"

Finding the exit, the four companions moved quickly but cautiously into the alley, which was empty. Heading for the inter-secting street, their steps became more and more hurried, real-izing that it would only be a matter of time. . . .

When they were a block distant, the angry howls of their pur-suers told them their path away from the club had been discovered. The hunt had ended. It was now a race.

In moments the companions were running at full speed toward the harbor.

CHAPTER THREE

FLIGHT TO THE HARBOR

BY DAYLIGHT THE streets and alleyways of London were a conundrum; at night, in the middle of a rainstorm, the maze became an impossible labyrinth to the four men running for their lives from a pack of hunters that could, apparently, pursue them by smell.

"What are they?" said Jack. "You called them 'Wendigo.'"

"Our enemy's huntsmen," puffed Bert. "They are his bloodhounds, and if not the worst abominations under the sight of Heaven, they are easily contenders for the crown."

"Are they men, or beasts?" asked Jack.

"Both, I'm afraid. When it's required, they may comport themselves as men—but they become more lupine with every kill. Their bodies have been misshapen by the evil they do, and thus they have gained the senses of hounds, as well as their agility and speed."

"How do they become this way?" asked John.

"By terrible means," said Bert. "To begin with, they must be black-hearted men. But to become Wendigo, they must eat the flesh of another man."

"Cannibals," breathed John.

"Yes," said Bert, "but not just. It is rumored that to truly become Wendigo, the first flesh they taste must be that of their best friend or a loved one. After that, it doesn't really matter."

A horrified expression crossed John's features as the implications of this settled in. "Do you think they . . . the professor's body?"

"No," said Bert. "I believe he was killed while they interrogated him as to the whereabouts of the *Geographica*. Killed, but not eaten. Wendigo . . . Wendigo like their meals *alive*."

"Do you really think there's a boat?" Jack said some minutes later, panting.

"I doubt it," Charles replied, "but I'm not of a mind to stand around and debate it."

"Shilling that there is," said Jack.

"Done."

The cobblestones were slick, and the companions had to measure their steps so as not to fall and risk twisting an ankle. Bert led the way. His admitted memory lapses of the geography of London streets seemed not to affect his pace—he moved from corner to corner under the gaslight with a speed and agility that belied his appearance.

"Almost there, lads," Bert said. "You can smell it, can't you?"

"Ew," said Jack. "That's really rank. What is it?"

"Fish and offal, offal and fish," said Charles. "Commerce. You know—like the kind of work John doesn't know if he wants to get into."

"Clever," said John as Bert disappeared around the corner ahead, whooping in triumph.

Turning the corner himself an instant later, John stopped in his tracks, which caused Charles and Jack to crash into him in turn.

Bert had spoken the truth. There was indeed a ship moored and floating in the harbor. A ship unlike any they had ever seen.

Jack held out his hand. "Shilling."

"Drat," said Charles, dropping a coin into Jack's hand.

"The *Indigo Dragon*," Bert said proudly. "My ship."

"Is it a galleon?" asked Charles. "It seems Spanish, but—old."

"Sixteenth century," said Bert. "At least, the newer parts. I believe the oldest parts of the hull are Greek, but I can't really be sure. There's a little of everything in her, I think. But she gets the job done and always takes me safely to home port."

"And where is home port, exactly?" asked Jack.

"Later, later," said Bert, eyeing the shadows of their pursuers stretched tall in the gaslight behind them. "Let's to safety first—there will be time to talk later."

None of the companions paused to ask what Bert meant by "later," or the broader insinuation that the dialogue was meant to continue after the danger had passed.

Bert broke into a trot and moved swiftly across the dock to the gangplank that connected to the ship. Standing at the fore of the gangplank was a young woman—tall, dressed like a pirate out of Stevenson, and displaying a commanding appearance that belied her obvious youth.

"Father, you're late," the woman scolded. "We were preparing a landing party to go in and retrieve you."

"Not necessary, Aven," said Bert. "As you can see, my young friends and I have everything running well according to plan."

From the dock, a sleek Egyptian spear flew through the night air and pinned Bert's cloak to the prow, narrowly missing his shoulder. "Oh, ah—well," said Bert, slipping out of the garment and wincing. "That's not to say that we shouldn't, ah, accelerate our departure."

As the companions scrambled aboard, Aven stood at the aft of the ship, arms crossed in defiance of the spears being flung at her by the huntsmen.

"Enough of this," she said tersely. "Take us out."

No oars were lowered into the water, and strangely, the sails were billowed in precisely the *opposite* direction of the wind—but the instant Aven gave the order, the ship pulled away from the dock and began to pick up speed.

A howl behind them scored the chill harbor air, and the young woman's eyes widened. "Wendigo? He sent Wendigo after you?"

"Yes," Bert nodded. "Stellan—the professor—was dead before anything could be done."

"You had the *Geographica*," said Aven, casting a wan glance at the companions. "He needn't have waited, only to be killed."

"His choice, Aven," Bert admonished her. "I could just as easily blame myself, for having left it solely to him while I traveled. . . ."

"Or Jamie," she shot back. "If he hadn't given it up just for that woman and her children . . . He's even in London! Why aren't the Wendigo chasing *him?*"

"They don't want him," said Bert. "They want this," he finished, patting the *Geographica*. "That's why we're here. That's why we came. And now, that's why we have to leave."

"Also," said Charles, "we're being chased by creatures that want to kill us—"

"—eat us," interjected Jack.

"Kill us and eat us," Charles corrected. "So, might I suggest we finish this discussion somewhere farther out of range?"

"Yes," said Jack, whose eyes had not left Aven since they'd stepped onto the ship. "And, ah, perhaps an introduction is in order."

"Of course," said Bert. "Lads, may I present the captain of the *Indigo Dragon*—my daughter, Aven."

Charles stepped forward, bowing slightly. "A pleasure. I'm Charles."

She nodded, eyebrow still arched.

"I'm Jack," said Jack, pushing past his companion and offering his hand. "If there's anything you need a hand with, please don't hesitate to ask."

"Do you know how to work aboard a ship?"

"Ah, well, no, not exactly," admitted Jack. "I'm a scholar."

Aven rolled her eyes and sighed in exasperation. "Another scholar. Heaven spare us from fools and their books."

She looked at John. "And you?"

"I'm John. Pleased to meet you."

She didn't respond, but held his gaze a long moment before turning abruptly and saying something just softly enough for him to hear.

"You had better be worth this."

For the first time, the companions got to have a direct look at their pursuers, who were amassing on the dock, howling and flailing their weapons about in a rage.

The Wendigo were not unlike men. Only those that crouched,

showing their disfigured, animalian hindquarters, were obviously something more. They were hairy; rough at the edges. Indistinct, as if they were part of an improperly processed photograph.

The cloaks they wore to disguise their bodies and to conceal weapons were now being flung aside to reveal strange dress from a dozen cultures.

"How unusual," said John. "I count several different costumes among them—Egyptian, Indian . . . Is that one Norse?"

"Not costumes," said Aven. "Did you think a man who turns evil and eats the flesh of his friends had to have a Cockney accent?"

John and the others shuddered and were turning away when he caught sight of another figure on the dock, passing among the furious Wendigo. He was not certain, but the man looked like one of the passengers who had been on the train with him earlier that day. If he was, it was further proof of Bert's claim that John was more deeply involved in the events of the evening than he had realized.

The *Indigo Dragon* continued to accelerate, and in moments the dock and their pursuers had receded into the dark behind them.

Given time to catch their breath, the companions now turned their attention to the strange vessel they had boarded. It was indeed a galleon, but of a most unusual design. It was a bit dirty, a bit creaky, but there was no question—it was a ship crafted for grand adventure.

At the fore of the ship was the masthead, a great head and torso of a dragon. It had eyes of gold and was colored a deep, rich purple. "Indigo," Bert corrected, hearing Jack suggest the color. "We don't want to offend her."

John thought, but couldn't be certain, that he saw the dragon breathe.

There was a cabin in the aft of the ship, and cargo holds below with a most unusual feature: They were much larger on the inside than they appeared to be on the outside.

Around them the ship's complement of some twenty sailors, all thickly clothed against the moist night air, busied themselves at their tasks under Aven's orders.

"Have you noticed," Jack ventured to the others, "that we're each and all a good two feet taller than every member of the crew?"

John had processed all of the goings-on in the background as the usual ship's business, but now that it was pointed out, he realized Jack was right. Not a single crewman stood taller than four feet, and the bulk of them were smaller than that.

"I say," said Jack to one of the passing crew, "would you happen to—"

He froze, eyes wide.

"Jack?" said Charles. "What is it?"

The crewman, eyes glittering, ignored him and went about his task. But Jack managed to lift his arm and point at the departing sailor's feet, which were not feet at all.

They were cloven hooves.

The crewmen gave no notice that they even cared if they were being observed, and Aven and Bert were deep in discussion over the *Imaginarium Geographica*. Charles, John, and Jack drew closer together and moved to the opposite side of the cabin.

"Did you see that?" said Jack, finally able to speak. "Did you see . . . ?"

"Quiet," said Charles. "I did. There is something strange about all of this, and I for one am about to be done with the whole matter."

"Agreed," said John. "We've gone a good distance from that row with the—whatever it was hunting us. We should be able to stop here along the river somewhere and contact the authorities— perhaps inspector Clowes can deal with all this. Anyroad, it's not our job."

"Right," said Jack, shivering. "We're just about to pass the bridge. They'll have to slow up at the shallows, and we can ask them to let us off at the docks just beyond."

"We have a plan, then," said Charles. "I'll speak to them."

In moments the *Indigo Dragon* had passed beneath the bridge, but instead of slowing as Jack had predicted, it began to fly across the water with an even greater velocity. The ever-present fog of the river began to coalesce and draw close to the ship. Even the rain had ceased. Something more was beginning to happen.

In the distance behind them, from beneath the shadows of London Bridge, a second ship, dark-masted and black as a nightmare, lifted anchor and silently began to follow.

Charles hastened to make his point. "We seem to have lost our pursuers," he said to Aven. "And I for one am most grateful for your assistance and intervention. Now that the danger is past, can you tell me at what part of the city you intend to leave us?"

"Yes," Jack agreed, looking askew at the ship's crewmen. "We'd like to get off, please."

Aven gave her father a knowing look before answering. "I'm sorry, but that's just not possible."

"Why not?" asked John.

In answer, Aven gestured at the glowing city lights on the not-distant shore, now dim and hazy through the fog.

As they watched, the mists drew closer, thickening around the ship, until in mere moments the lights of London had vanished. When the fog began to clear, the city was gone, and the storm had stopped. Above a thousand stars were shining, unfettered by the clouds that had blanketed them just minutes before. And around them, open ocean, no sign of shore in sight.

"B-but that can't possibly be!" Charles said, stammering in disbelief and no small amount of fear. "We haven't been at sail for more than a few minutes! There is no possible way we could be in open waters!"

"Right," said Jack. "I've been down the river plenty of times. We still have—had—at least twenty miles to go before reaching the Channel."

"Oh, I see," said Bert. "You misunderstand—we left England the minute the ship pulled away from the dock. We're nowhere near the Channel, or London, or even Europe, for that matter. In fact, we are not even sailing in the same ocean any longer."

"Then where are we?" said Charles. "Where are you taking us?"

Aven tilted her head at John. "Ask *him*. He knows."

John stood at the railing, looking out into the darkness as they let the question hang in the air, shimmering with the promise they all knew would be fulfilled if he would just speak the words. Finally, he answered.

"The Archipelago," John said, his voice muted with a mix of disbelief and wonder. "That's where we're going, isn't it? We're going to the Archipelago of Dreams."

CHAPTER FOUR
AVALON

WHATEVER PERSONAL MISGIVINGS they may have had, John, Jack, and Charles had to accept the evidence of their senses. Like it or not, they were at sea. And until a destination was named, traveled to, and safely arrived at, they were fully at the mercy of the captain and her unusual crew.

"This is all your fault," Charles said to Bert, his voice shaking with anger. "If you hadn't convinced us to leave the club—"

"If he hadn't convinced you to leave the club," Aven interrupted, "you'd be three kinds of dead. Or didn't you notice those weren't accountants and bankers chasing you?"

"She's right," said Jack, kicking at one of the spears on the deck. "Those things weren't for show. They're crusted with layers of dried blood. I think they really would have killed us, Charles."

"I agree," said John. "Whatever situation we're in now, it's better than if we'd remained in London. Although," he added, looking askance at Bert, "it would be nice if we had an idea when it would be safe to return."

"That is the question, isn't it?" said Bert. "One of several that I suspect you have. And as I have questions of my own, then perhaps we should make landfall and discuss our next course of action."

"Landfall?" asked Charles. "Is there a place to land if we're in fact sailing toward your 'Imaginary Geography'?"

"There is indeed," said Bert. "It's an island that actually straddles the border between the waters of the world you know and those of the Archipelago.

"I don't know what it was originally called—the professor could have told you, John—but for the past thousand years, it has been known as Avalon."

Aven estimated that they were still at least an hour out from Avalon, and she suggested that her reluctant passengers try to settle in and enjoy the ride. The night air was cool but not chill, and the calm waters made for mellow sailing.

Bert noticed that John seemed to be avoiding going anywhere near the *Imaginarium Geographica*, choosing instead to observe the others from the foredeck, where he could watch for the island. Charles was shaking his head every few moments, as if doing so might wake him from the undigested-mustard-and-cheese nightmare in which he found himself. And Jack acted as if whatever danger or inconvenience he had to endure would be worth the trouble, as long as he could remain in close proximity to Aven.

The crew of the *Indigo Dragon* were, as it turned out, fauns: the half-men, half-goat creatures of myth. Aven explained that while their short stature made them rather disagreeable, their inborn ability—from the goat half of their heritage, John had no doubt—to scale mountainous terrain also came in handy on a tempest-tossed deck.

"It's an amazing sight," Aven said. "Twenty-foot waves, decks as slick as ice, rain all but blinding, and these fellows walk about as if they were strolling in the park."

"Actually," said Jack, "I would've thought satyrs would be better—larger and stronger, you know?"

"Satyrs, fft," Aven hissed. "Stronger, sure—but they spend all their time drinking, and when they're not drinking, they're chasing women. More trouble than help."

"Fauns don't drink?" asked Jack.

"Not like satyrs," said Aven. "The strongest thing fauns drink is a flaming rum punch. Usually it's nothing more potent than a nice mulled wine."

"You do realize you're arguing about mythological creatures that can't possibly exist," said Charles, waving his arms. "There are no such things as fauns and satyrs!"

As if in answer, one of the crew dropped a heavy spare mast bracing on Charles's foot, then picked it up and tipped his hat in mock apology before passing through to the cabin.

Charles howled and sat on the deck, massaging his injured foot.

"I think that nonexistent mythological creature just broke some of your toes," Jack said.

"Oh, shut up," said Charles.

It was not long before the crewman in the crow's nest signaled to the captain that land was in sight. On the near horizon, shrouded in fine mist and standing in high relief against the darker thunderheads beyond, was Avalon.

The *Indigo Dragon* slowed and made its way through the shallows to rest against a tumbledown dock. There, a pebbled beach slowly gave way to a grassy slope and a tangled thicket of growth around what had once been a grand and eloquent structure.

John, Jack, Charles, and Bert disembarked, with Jack taking the lead ahead of his more cautious and reluctant companions. Aven stayed behind, occasionally casting suspicious glances back in the direction from which they had come.

Atop the slope were ruined pilasters all about; broken arches, shattered foundations, crumbling stone. In the dim twilight, the young men could almost imagine the great cathedrals that may have once stood on the island—but that age was long past, and nature had since reclaimed it for herself.

Ruined though it was, there was an undeniable atmosphere of magic and mystery about the island that permeated the ground, the trees, the very air itself. None of them had truly thought for an instant that they were actually traveling to King Arthur's Avalon of legend, but there, in that moment, they could almost believe.

Scattered throughout the ruins were several marble pedestals, and here and there they could see the occasional intact statue. A tallish one stood on the pedestal nearest what was once an entry hall. The statue was wrapped in vines and overgrowth, almost as if it were a shrub that had grown up in the form of a knight-at-arms.

Jack squinted at it and was startled to see it squint back. "That statue," he said, turning to summon the others. "I think I saw it move."

"Ah," said Bert, who had anchored the group and was still some yards back, "I meant to tell you . . ."

Before he could finish the thought, the object of Jack's attention stepped off the pedestal and with a creaking of joints and metal swung his sword directly at the young man's head.

"Jack, get down!" John yelled, diving to pull his friend out of harm's way. The sword passed in a sharp arc through the space where Jack had been standing as he and John collapsed in a tumble. They rolled to their feet some distance away, fists at the ready.

They needn't have worried. The statue—actually a knight in armor that had gone mottled green with rust and decay—could not lift the sword again for a second swing. Even stepping closer into the soft light was an effort, and they saw that his face was deeply creased with age. Age, and something more. . . .

"Speak," the knight said, rasping. "Speak and be recognized."

Bert hurried forward and spoke for all three of them. "It's just me, old friend—it's Bert, and company."

A glint of recognition flashed in the knight's eyes. He lowered his sword and lifted his head, peering at the intruders.

It was plainly evident that the old sentinel was no danger. John, Jack, and Charles moved closer, but John was the first to realize what was odd about their assailant.

"Your flesh," he said, amazed. "It's wood, isn't it?"

"Lads," said Bert, who stepped aside and put a supporting arm around the old knight's midriff, "I'd like you to meet the Green Knight. The Guardian of Avalon."

The Green Knight's limbs and torso were hardwood—stout oaks and maples; his joints and face, soft, lined pine. His hair was a bird's-nest tangle of bark and leafy twigs. When he spoke, it was with the creaking susurrations of an ancient willow swaying in a night breeze.

"Forgive my hasty estimation," he said to Jack. "If I had but known you were friend, I would not have tried to remove your head from your shoulders."

"He understands," Bert interjected. "You were simply doing your job."

"You were French, if I am to judge by your accent," said Jack.

"*Are* French," Charles said, underscoring the correction with a scowl at Jack.

The knight responded with a deep, respectful bow. "*A votre service, monsieur,*" he said. "My strength, such as it is, is yours to command."

"Call me Charles—and thank you," Charles said.

"Charles?" the knight said with a spark of surprise in his eyes. "I was called as such, once upon a time, in another life."

"Pleased to make your acquaintance," said Charles. "These are my friends, Jack . . ."

"Hello," said Jack, offering his hand, then examining it briefly after the knight took it in his barklike grip.

". . . and John," finished Charles.

"Ah," said the knight. "The Caretaker."

John blinked back his surprise. "So Bert tells me," he said. "But how would you have known?"

"The Morgaine," said the knight, as if that explained everything. "The Three Who Are One foretold your coming, and the dark troubles that are to follow."

In answer to the others' questioning looks, Bert rubbed his chin and sighed. "This bodes ill," he said, morose. "This bodes not well at all."

He turned to the Green Knight. "Take us to the Morgaine. We must know what they know—or at least, what they are willing to tell us."

◆　　◆　　◆

"The Green Knights are compelled to service," Bert said as they followed the knight's lead and began walking counterclockwise around the perimeter of the island. "The first of them was a Crusader, who assumed the duty in exchange for a gift of great value. Others were summoned as a means of penance, or to avenge a wrongdoing. Of the twenty-five Guardians of Avalon that have served, only our friend here and one other have chosen to do so of their own will."

"I'll not argue with you, old friend," said the knight, nodding back at Bert, "but one might say I was as compelled as all the rest."

"How so?" asked Charles.

"What year is it," the knight asked in response, "back in the world?"

"You refer to 'the world' as if it were a different place," said Jack. "But it isn't really, is it? After all, despite what Aven claims, we did set sail in the waters of London, and as far as my senses can tell, we never left them. Surely an ocean of the world is still an ocean of the world, regardless of the strange nature of some of the lands that reside upon it."

"Ah, my young friend, but this world *is* a different place," said the knight. "The fields you know are those of Adam and Eve, and the children who followed. The fields we walk now are far, far older."

"It's 1917," Charles put in, answering the knight's question.

"Ah," the knight sighed. "Has it truly been so long, then?" He sighed again, a deep, regretful sound. For a few moments they walked along in silence before he spoke again.

"I chose to serve as Guardian of Avalon," the knight began, "to repay a debt I could not otherwise settle. A place in Death's realm had been reserved for me—and another man took it in my stead."

"A relative, perhaps?" asked John. "Or a close friend?"

"He was an Englishman," the knight said. "A commoner, of humble birth, and he sacrificed himself for a matter of principle.

"I believed, having escaped my fate, that my life would be a happy one. But his sacrifice plagued me. I was restless, unsettled. My wife and daughter, delights both, brought me no joy, for I felt it was not I who had paid the price to live in their world.

"Then, one day, I became acquainted with one of your predecessors—a Caretaker of the *Geographica*. And as I told him my story, he shared one in return: that of the last Green Knight, who had grown weary of the job, weary of guarding this place, and yet had seen no relief in the offing."

"Not much to guard here, is there?" said Jack, glancing around at the ruined heaps of stone they seemed to be constantly passing. "Someone obviously wasn't up to the task."

"Jack!" Charles chided. "That's quite rude."

"Sorry," said Jack, reddening. "But, to be fair . . ."

"No, the young man is right," said the knight. "On the surface of things, it seems there is little here of value. But sometimes, it is not about guarding something of value that is important, but rather, being a valuable guard, so that when that thing comes along that needs guarding, there is no question."

"And did that thing ever come along?" asked John.

But the knight did not reply; or if he did, it was lost to the wind rushing in from the west.

The western side of the island was a stark contrast to the spot where the *Indigo Dragon* had landed. Steep, sharp crags of porous volcanic rock jutted up into the side of the hills from the pounding surf below. The spray of saltwater filled their nostrils and dampened their clothes.

"This part of Avalon lies on the Frontier," said Bert, gesturing to the thunderheads that lined the horizon. "The actual boundary of the Archipelago. Many a ship has been lost to the storms and tidal forces here."

The knight led them along a winding path worn through the scrubby grasses that had taken root among the riddled stone, at points coming dangerously close to the steep dropoff to their right.

Ahead in the gloom, nestled within the crags, was the reddish glow of a fire. On it sat an immense black cauldron, around which were seated three old women who were chanting loudly as the group approached.

"Witches," breathed John.

"The Morgaine," the knight said, nodding.

Each witch spoke in turn, as if singing a refrain.

"By the pricking in my breast—"

"They come o'er East, into the West—"

"Though tempest bar and block the way—"

"The Mapmaker's heir shall seek the day—"

"'gainst evil's might, he will persist—"

"To restore th' power of Arthur's throne—"

"Twine Paralon with the World of men—"

"If here be dragons once again."

Bert and the Green Knight exchanged curious glances. Had they overheard a prophecy? Or was it simple coincidence?

"Boy!" the third witch screeched, having finished the chant. She wore a heavy cloak and cowl, and she motioned for the companions to come closer to the fire. "Boy! Where are you? Ah there you are. Bring that over here. Quickly, quickly now!"

A young man—or a tall boy on the verge of manhood—appeared at the mouth of the cave on the far side of the firelight, copper pot in tow.

He was sandy-haired, dressed in simple clothes, and his face was smudged with soot, but his mouth was screwed up in an expression of determination. He may have been a servant, but it was obvious he was a good worker.

"Boy, bring the kettle—we have visitors, rare enough to be sure, but if we don't feed them proper and true, then they're not likely to return," said the first witch.

"Right," Jack whispered to Charles. "As if not feeding us would be the only reason."

"Perhaps not the only reason," said the second witch, who had long white hair tied neatly under a scarf and a wicked grin that indicated she could hear better than Jack gave her credit for. "But perhaps our hospitality is not what you should be seeking."

"Uh, pleased to meet you," said John. "And how should I address you, ah, ladies?"

"Now there's a question, if ever I heard one," said the first witch, who wore dozens of ornate necklaces and had bright eyes that flashed with intelligence. "We haven't been asked our names since . . ." She scratched her head with a bird skull on a stick. "How long *has* it been?"

"Since *he* came to Avalon," said the second witch, hooking her thumb at the knight. "Seventy, eighty years, maybe?"

"Yes," the third witch nodded in agreement. "I remember. It was a Tuesday."

"Today is Tuesday," offered Jack.

"Well, that makes things easier, doesn't it, my duck?" said the first witch. "On Tuesdays I am Ceridwen. She's Celedriel," Ceridwen said, gesturing at the second witch, "and she," she continued, pointing at the sullen third witch, "is called Cul."

"Don't want to be Cul," the third witch pouted. "Want to be Gwynhfar."

"Now, Cul dear," Ceridwen admonished. "For one thing, you could only be Gwynhfar on a Sunday, and it's Tuesday. And for another, she left us long ago to marry that Wart fellow, so you wouldn't be Gwynhfar anyway. Besides, one of us has to be Cul."

"Well," Cul grumbled, "why does it have to be me?"

"You are the youngest," Celedriel clucked. "Can't be a Ceridwen until you've been a Cul for at least another century or three."

"This is all very confusing," said Charles.

"I just call them all 'milady,'" the knight offered. "I don't think it matters which one answers you."

Jack stepped to the fire and helped the boy lift the kettle atop the cooking stones. The boy nodded, grateful, then returned to the cave.

"Good errand boy, that Bug is," said Ceridwen. "So glad we decided not to eat him."

Charles couldn't suppress a shudder. "Is that what the, er, big cauldron is for?"

"Oh, no, my dear," said Celedriel. "Can't put a living being in that one—not if you want to use them afterward."

"You're thinking of the other one, dear," Ceridwen corrected. "The pot with the ravens and writings on it—the one that was stolen by that Maggot fellow, remember? It was just a year or three before we got our Bug."

"Maggot," said Cul. "Heh. Have to pay the price for that some-day. That was my favorite kettle."

"That's just because you could keep all sorts of unusual things in it," said Ceridwen. "Misfortune and spirits, specters and shadows."

"Putting things into it was easy," said Celedriel. "It was taking them out again that was hard—because once it was open, there was no telling what would escape.

"But—forgive me!" she exclaimed. "We're neglecting our guests!"

"The chant you were singing as we approached," Bert began. "You mentioned Paralon. . . ."

"Paralon!" exclaimed Bug, who had been listening at the mouth of the cave. "That's where the king lives! And his knights!"

"Now you've gone and done it," grumbled Cul. "Once you get him started on knights and chivalry and whatnot, can't shut him up for days."

"I'm going to *be* a knight," the boy stated proudly. "A *real* knight—not like, um, you know."

The Green Knight scowled affectionately. "Brat."

John smiled and tousled the young man's hair. "I'm sure you will, Bug."

"If miladies can spare him," said the knight, "I would like the young squire"—Bug beamed at hearing this—"to resupply the *Indigo Dragon* with fresh water for its long journey to come."

Bert began to say that they had no need of additional supplies, but the knight cut him off. "A caution is better before than after." He turned to the boy. "Well? What are you waiting for?"

Without another word Bug took off down the path at a full run, and an odd expression of contentment came over the knight's face. Bert gave the knight and the departing Bug a curious look, but said nothing.

The Green Knight turned back to the Morgaine. "We have come to seek your counsel," he said.

"We've already given it," said Cul. "Or weren't you listening?"

"No hand is at the rudder in Paralon," said Celedriel. "No human hand, at least. What was lost, must be found; what was cloven, must be mended."

"But without the Mapmaker's heir, all is lost," said Ceridwen.

"Then it's not too late," Bert said with obvious relief. "I've brought John just in time."

To this the Morgaine did not reply, but merely stared into the fire. After a moment the Green Knight motioned for the companions to leave, and they began to make their way back to the ship.

While Bert made his good-byes to the knight, John climbed aboard the *Indigo Dragon* and looked around for Bug. "So, Aven," he said. "Are we all stocked up on water, then?"

Aven fixed him with a puzzled look. "Of course. Why should you ask?"

John waved it off. "Never mind. Forget I asked."

As the crew readied the ship to depart, Jack and Charles (who was somewhat more reluctant than his younger friend) took up their usual post near the cabin. Bert gave Aven a report on what had transpired with the knight and the Morgaine. Her expression darkened, but she said nothing.

"We're not returning to London, are we?" Charles said to his companions. "We've been drafted, whether we like it or not."

"I think *he's* been drafted," Jack said, referring to John. "We get to come along for the adventure. Cheer up, Charles. This could be great fun."

"Someone's got to be an anchor to reality here," Charles said as the ship began to pull out of the small harbor. "It's not that I mind falling down the rabbit hole—I just don't want to lose sight of the door."

The Green Knight kept his arm raised long after the *Indigo Dragon* had passed from sight. Eventually, he lowered it, his breathing gone quick and shallow.

"At last," he murmured to no one in particular. "At last my duties have been dispensed. And perhaps my soul can be at peace."

Sitting at the shore, the knight passed the final hours of his last night of service in meditation, until finally the sun began to rise. He raised his eyes to the shimmering sky of the Archipelago's dawn and drew a deep, final breath. "Ah, my Lucie . . . Finally, I come to join you in that far better place, that far better rest. . . ."

The knight's last words faded into the mist as eddies of dust began to swirl about his limbs. Slowly, gently, his aged body began to fragment into ash as he folded in upon himself, leaving nothing but the helmet and breastplate to settle into the grass. In moments he was gone.

PART TWO

THE ARCHIPELAGO
OF DREAMS

CHAPTER FIVE
THE CORSAIR

THE STORM LINE past Avalon was more roiling clouds and ominous thunder than rain and wind, although there was enough fury in it to push the *Indigo Dragon* across the waves like a toy. The crew was experienced, and it was obvious they had traversed this passage before. They went about their duties as usual, occasionally checking to make sure none of their passengers had been flung overboard, and in a matter of minutes they were once more through to calmer waters.

On the formal crossing to the Archipelago, there was a different timbre in the atmosphere. They still appeared to be on open ocean, with no land in sight, but the gray morning light revealed a number of varying depths in the water below. Shallows, where there should be none.

"Is it a reef?" John asked. "Like those in Australia?"

"It doesn't appear to be," said Charles. "More like submerged islands."

"These are the Drowned Lands, called by some the Lost Lands of the West," said Bert. "You'll not find them in the *Imaginarium Geographica*, for as old as it is, there are lands older still."

"I wouldn't do that, if I were you," Aven said to Jack as he leaned over the railing to catch some of the spray in his hands. "Not here, anyway—not if you want to keep your hands."

Jack quickly leaned back and looked at Bert, puzzled.

"Look into the deeps," said Bert. "You can still see the shapes of noble towers and cities that once adorned the islands here. Legend says that these islands were the proudest of the world once, when the lands of Man and those of the Archipelago were not divided as they are now."

"What happened to them?" asked Jack. "And what does that have to do with my putting my hands in the water?"

"No one knows," said Bert. "Some think they destroyed themselves by seeking too deeply into the mysteries of life itself. Some say they were destroyed by the gods for the same reason. One theory is that it was the fault of an inattentive angel who had been assigned by Heaven to watch the developing civilization. For all we know, it was simply a natural disaster.

"Regardless, my boy," Bert concluded, clapping Jack on the back, "it was not a gentle passing, nor one of good portents. And some say that when the lands were destroyed, not all of the inhabitants perished with them. Those drowned children of a great culture may still live in the murky deep, and they would be human no longer. Their hearts would be blackened, their limbs transformed to fins, their lungs gone to gills . . .

". . . and their teeth, razor sharp."

Jack's eyes widened, and Aven suppressed a grin as he moved squarely to the middle of the deck.

Charles and John peered over the side, and in fact it did seem as if they could see the outlines of what may have been cities once, a long, long time ago.

"Bert," John said, overcome with a sudden clarity, "could this be . . ." He paused, biting his lip. "Is this Atlantis?"

Bert took a breath before replying, his expression more wistful than remorseful. "It was, my boy. It was."

"Paralon is the seat of government here," Bert began, in explanation of the Morgaine's prophecy. "It has ever been so, since the reign of the first king to unite both worlds: the High King—Arthur Pendragon.

"The descendants of his bloodline ruled justly and well for centuries, until the last king was murdered nearly two decades ago. Ever since, the leadership of the Archipelago has been in question. That's one of the reasons you are needed now, John. A crisis is at hand—and the resolution will have repercussions both in this world and in your own."

"Why is it only now that I'm needed?" said John. "Surely Professor Sigurdsson could have done whatever was needed years ago, if the situation is as dire as you say."

"He could have, true," said Bert, "save for two conditions that have never before been present. To start, this is not the first time a king has been killed. As in your world, it does happen—usually by a relative who aspires to ascend to the throne. But in this case, the rest of his family was murdered as well. There *are* no heirs."

"What's the second point?" asked Charles.

"You already know, after a fashion," said Bert. "His minions tried to kill you last night.

"What his true name is, no one knows. But in the Archipelago, he is known as the Winter King.

"In the absence of a High King, a Parliament of minor kings and queens govern Paralon," said Bert, "while a successor is determined. But with no apparent heir, it has been an ongoing debate—one that the Winter King is determined to end by eliminating all other challengers to the throne.

"There are kings of other races who could assume the Silver Throne of Paralon—but tradition is not easily dismissed. The Winter King is human and is still subject to the ruling of the Parliament. What is occurring today is a Great Council—all the kings of all the races of the Archipelago are coming together with the Parliament to determine who should assume the throne."

"Well, then," said Charles, "you ought to trust the Parliament. They've held him off this long—can't they continue to do so, until a successor can be chosen?"

"No," said Bert. "They can't wait any longer, because of *that*," he said, pointing at the southern horizon. There was a black smudge against the water, below the cloud line. It was as if someone had taken a paintbrush to the landscape and obliterated some of the scenery.

Jack said as much, and Bert nodded in agreement. "More true than you know, young Jack.

"We call them the Shadowed Lands—the islands conquered by the Winter King. When he and his armies take them, they disappear from the cycle of life in the Archipelago—and then they disappear from the *Geographica* as well."

"If he's in the process of erasing it," said John, "then why is he willing to kill us for it?"

"No one knows," said Bert. "It is the greatest mystery of the Archipelago. But we do know that he is amassing power—power that would give him greater influence than any other king or ruler in this land, or," he added, "in others."

"Do you mean . . ." Charles began.

"The worlds are separate, but what happens in one affects the other," said Bert. "Arthur knew this, and established a throne to rule them both. Do you think it coincidence that in the time the Silver Throne of Paralon has been empty, your world has erupted in war?"

"Speaking of Paralon," said Aven, "it's about time our 'Caretaker' gave us some direction. The morning light is coming up, and while the *Indigo Dragon* can find the way, it'll be easier to navigate if she can be given a few specifics."

"Oh, uh, yes, of course," said John when he realized she was talking about him. At Bert's urging he unwrapped the *Geographica* and began thumbing through the pages. After a few minutes, he came to a large page of parchment with a heading that translated roughly to "Paralon," along with extensive annotations that included nautical instructions. He furrowed his brow in concentration. "It's, ah—it's all in Old Saxon."

"Is that a problem?" asked Aven.

"Ah—no, no, not really," said John. He examined the annotations for a few moments more, then looked around at the expectant faces. "It says, ah—it says we should be going, ah, that way," he finished, waving vaguely to the starboard side of the ship.

Aven raised an eyebrow in surprise, but Bert nodded to her, and she began instructing the crew to turn the *Indigo Dragon* in that direction.

Nervously, John wrapped up the *Geographica* and tucked it under his arm.

✦ ✦ ✦

"You're one of the three Caretakers," Charles said to Bert. "So why did you need John? Why couldn't you simply have left London once you had it?"

"Being the Caretaker Principia requires a lifetime of study," said Bert. "I myself have some skill and knowledge, but honestly, I simply don't have the training—which is why Professor Sigurdsson retired, so that he could begin to train his eventual replacement. You, John."

"What about the third Caretaker?" said Charles. "You said there were always three."

Aven cursed and spit. "Useless as a buck centaur in a dairy, that one. If he had taken his responsibilities more seriously, then *you*"—she pointed at her father—"wouldn't be in danger, and *your* mentor"—pointing at John—"wouldn't be dead, and you"—again jabbing a finger at John—"would still be doing whatever it is you do."

"Now, Aven," Bert chided, "Jamie has his own life to lead, and we can't begrudge him that. Not everyone is made for this sort of adventure."

"That's what makes me angry," she said. "Jamie *was*. He *was* suited to this, father. And he gave up a lifetime in the Archipelago for playacting in Kensington Gardens."

"Is it me," Jack confided to Charles, "or do I sense a hint of spurned romance in her anger?"

Jack wasn't quiet enough; Aven overheard him and shot him a venomous look before flinging her father's arm off her shoulders and storming into the cabin.

An instant later they heard her curse loudly, followed by a

flurry of shouting and banging. Before anyone could move, she reemerged from the cabin, breathing hard and red faced from exertion.

"Some men weren't made for adventure," Aven snorted, "and some boys don't know when they've had too much."

Under her arm, face purpling from the headlock in which she had him, was Bug.

They had a stowaway.

Having an extra person on board did not present any particular problems, although Aven did suggest throwing him overboard, just to save the debate. Bert suspected that the errand to fetch fresh water had been a ruse to allow the boy to sneak on board, and said so.

Charles shook his head. "Frenchmen."

"To what end?" said John. "If the knight thought Bug should go with us, why not simply ask?"

"I beg your pardon," said Aven. "I don't recall giving you any authority to say what does or doesn't happen aboard *my* ship."

"Well, he's here now," said Charles. "What do we do with him?"

"Just what we need," grumbled Jack. "A child to look after."

Bug's eyes narrowed. "I'm no younger than you."

"Young enough, potboy," Jack shot back.

"That's enough," said John. "I'll take him on as my, uh . . ."

"Squire?" offered Charles.

"Whatever," said Aven. "Just keep him out of the way." She leaned down as one of the fauns whispered something in her ear. "No," she said, straightening up and looking at Bug. "You can't feed him to the mermaids. Yet."

Bug looked at John. "She's joking, surely?"

"Probably," said John. "But keep close to me anyway."

A shout from the crew brought them all to the port side of the ship, as the water began to roil with activity. Something large was rising from under the sea.

"A whale?" asked Jack.

"Too big," said Charles.

"Just watch," Bert said, smiling, as the shape, now obvious as some kind of construct, rose from the water.

Jack and Charles stood speechless in the embrace of the growing shadow. Rising alongside the *Indigo Dragon* was the magnificent, gleaming, golden hull of a ship that was unlike anything they had ever seen. It had no masts or sails and seemed enclosed, like the submarines they'd heard of from the American Civil War. There were huge fortified portholes along the sides, and various openings below the waterline that both drew in and expelled water. And fore, on the hull, was the upper body and head of a dragon. A metallic gangplank slid seamlessly from an opening in the hull and attached itself to the railing of the *Indigo Dragon*. Above, a panel slid silently open and an impressive figure filled the open doorway.

"Dear God in Heaven," John said as he tried to take in the remarkable sight before them. "Is that what I think it is?"

"It is indeed," said Bert. "Boys, I would like to introduce you to the captain of the greatest ship to sail on the oceans of any world— the *Nautilus*."

A swarthy, bearded man with glistening, dark skin stepped off the gangplank and put his hands together, inclining his head in the Hindu fashion.

He smiled, and while not unfriendly, it was undoubtedly the smile of a predator. "Captain Nemo, at your service."

Everyone was introduced, including Bug, who got a long, curious look from Nemo.

"We're going to the council at Paralon," said Bert.

"As am I," Nemo replied. "There are restless forces growing in the lands to the north and the south, which must be quelled if we're to unite against the Winter King.

"A caution, though—you're going to catch the currents off the Shadowed Lands if you keep heading in this direction, and you'll miss Paralon altogether. I thought your captain was better trained than that."

Aven blushed and scowled at John and her father in turn. "How far off are we?"

"Five degrees to the south should correct your course."

Aven withdrew to change the course of the ship, and Nemo's eye caught sight of the *Geographica* under John's arm.

"Would that parcel hold the *Geographica*?" he asked.

"The *Imaginarium Geographica*, yes," said John.

For the first time, Nemo spoke with a slight hesitation in his voice. "May I—may I touch it, Master John?"

"Certainly."

John again unwrapped the *Geographica* and proffered it to Nemo, who accepted it as if he were holding a fragile parchment that would crumble if he breathed on it the wrong way.

"It's been through a lot," Charles said. "It's sturdy. Won't break, I assure you."

"You misunderstand my care," said Nemo. "To those of us in the Archipelago, it is a holy book. Here in these lands there are a thousand different worlds, a thousand cultures. Some are united by fealty, some by commerce. But the only thing that unites us all, the only Grail that can strengthen us by drawing the disparities closer, is the *Imaginarium Geographica*."

"Then every time the Winter King conquers a land . . . ," Charles began.

"Yes," Nemo said, nodding. "The corresponding map vanishes, and we take another step backward to the barbarian cultures that gave birth to us."

"You could always just destroy it," Bug offered, before being silenced by Jack with a poke in the ribs.

Instead of responding in anger to the suggestion, Nemo nodded his assent. "It's been suggested, boy, and tried. As valuable as it is, it may be better for the lands to lose it, if it means the Winter King cannot have it."

To underscore his answer, Nemo suddenly stepped in front of Aven and dropped the *Geographica* on the hot brazier that sat mid-deck.

There were shouts of dismay and disbelief, and John leaped forward to retrieve it before it burned.

But there was no need to worry. The coals were blazing, but they did no more than singe the outer layer of oilcloth.

"Magic," breathed Jack.

"Yes," said Nemo. "The *Imaginarium Geographica* cannot be destroyed—which makes proper stewardship of it both a blessing and a burden.

"Guard it well, lad," Nemo continued, dusting off the ash and returning the book to John. "It is a great responsibility to be the heart of the compass. But I knew your teacher, and while I mourn his passing, I sense that he chose his successor wisely and well."

Nemo turned to Bert and gripped his forearms, then kissed Aven on the cheek before leaping back to the gangplank.

"Be well, my friends," he said as the ship pulled away. "I'll see you soon."

As the *Nautilus* departed, Aven cornered John and demanded an explanation. "We're lucky he came along," she said, eyes flashing with anger. "Five degrees would have put us in the North Sea. We would have lost an entire day and missed the Council at Paralon altogether."

She gestured brusquely at the *Geographica*. "Can you read that thing or not?"

"Of course he can," Bug said. "He just needs some practice, right, Sir John?"

Aven snorted at the honorarium, but Bert voiced his agreement with the boy. "He's had a rough time of it, daughter. But he'll be up to the task in short order, of that we can be sure."

Wordless, Aven went back about her work, followed eagerly by Jack.

"Perhaps you should spend some time in the cabin studying the *Geographica*," Bert suggested to John. "Just to become better acquainted with it."

John nodded. "That's not a bad idea. At least then maybe then I'll look smarter if Phileas Fogg stops by to correct my navigation."

"Never happen," said Bert. "Fogg hates sailing."

"Speaking of which," said Charles, who was looking aft, "I daresay Nemo must have forgotten something—he's coming back."

"What?" Aven said. "He's ahead of us. He wouldn't be

approaching from the east." She shoved Charles roughly aside and peered through a spyglass toward where he'd been pointing.

"That's not the *Nautilus*," Aven said. "It seems our enemy has decided to step out of the shadows and make his intentions clear."

The fog parted, and a massive hull, broader and more forbidding than the *Nautilus* came into view.

It was the *Black Dragon*—the ship of the Winter King. And it was pointed at the *Indigo Dragon* at ramming speed.

"What do we do?" said Charles.

"Find something that's bolted down and hold on," said Bert. "Let Aven do her job—there's nothing the rest of us can do now."

"In London the ship pulled away from the docks against the wind," said Charles. "Can't it just, ah, twist out of the way and avoid being struck?"

"She's a ship, not a cat," said Bert, "and the fact that she has a will of her own doesn't mean she can pirouette on demand."

Aven was running back and forth across the deck and shouting orders, a frantic note in her voice. The ship of the Winter King was five times the size of the *Indigo Dragon*. The smaller craft would not survive a collision. But that, John surmised as he wrapped his arms around a section of rigging, was the point.

The only chance to even survive the initial impact would be to turn the ship as the *Black Dragon* reached them—but there was no way to reorient the sails to do so. Not in the seconds that remained.

This was apparent to everyone but Jack.

In his youth he'd spent a summer with a tutor who sailed, and who loved to play just such a game of daring, only to tack into the wind at the last instant and avoid the collision.

Easy with a skiff—not so easy with a galleon. Still, Jack thought it was worth a try.

Leaping atop the cabin, he grabbed a short cutlass from a surprised crewman and began severing the lines that held down the starboard side of the sails.

Aven looked on, incredulous. "Are you insane? If you cut those, the sails will . . ."

She realized suddenly what he was doing and ordered all of the crewmen to help him.

The gleaming black hull was bearing down on them with terrifying speed, but in seconds all the lines had been severed and the sails snapped around from the force of the wind. "Now!" Jack screamed. "Tack into it! Hit the rudder, hard as you can!"

At once Aven, John, and Charles threw themselves onto the wheel and yanked it around. With a horrible groan of straining wood and metal, the ship wrenched around to face the *Black Dragon* just as it reached them—and passed by, with only inches to spare.

"That was the stupidest thing I've ever seen in my life," Aven called out to Jack. But while her tone was harsh, she was smiling as she said it, and his heart soared.

The companions looked up as the nightmare ship glided by, its deck populated with the worst sort of brigands and scoundrels—including Wendigo—all too surprised that the ship was still there to sling spears and fire arrows.

As it passed, Aven's stern countenance returned. "Jack saved us for the moment, but it's going to take time to repair the riggings, and they'll have wheeled about by then, even at that speed. Then they'll have us."

"I'd hate to be wrong about this twice," said Charles, "but now I'm quite certain that the *Nautilus* has indeed come back."

Approaching at a speed greater than that of the *Black Dragon*, Nemo's ship had in fact reappeared to the north of them and was swiftly drawing alongside the *Indigo Dragon*.

"I will never again disparage the work of Jules Verne," said Charles.

"Right there with you," said John.

"Were you this much trouble when you were first mate aboard the *Nautilus*?" Nemo called out to Aven, grinning.

"No," Aven shouted in response. "But it was only called the *Yellow Dragon* then, and neither of us had developed our delusions of grandeur."

"Get your crew working on the riggings. What happened to them, anyway?"

Aven gestured at Jack. "That idiot cut the lines. It never would have occurred to me, but it saved the ship."

Nemo tipped his head at Jack. "Well done, young warrior. And now," he concluded as, in the distance, the *Black Dragon* had turned and was regaining speed, "it seems I have a battle to fight."

"Nemo," Aven began.

"No," he said, cutting her off. "You carry the *Geographica*. Get it and the Caretaker to Paralon. I'll keep the Winter King occupied long enough to let you escape."

Nemo held a clenched fist across his chest—a gesture of respect, captain to captain.

Aven returned the gesture and, shouting orders to her crew, turned the *Indigo Dragon* back with the wind. The ship, intuitive as ever, called upon her unique motive power and made full speed away from the fray.

◆ ◆ ◆

Several leagues away from the battle, the damage to the ship had been assessed, and to everyone's relief, it was minimal. With the repairs underway, Aven turned her attention, and her fury, to John.

"Enough of this! This is the second time I've risked my ship for you, and I've yet to see the reason why."

Bert tried to intercede, but she was having none of it. "Not this time, Father. You've made all the excuses for him I can stomach.

"Every captain has maps of their own lands in the Archipelago, as well as of adjacent islands. Every captain, including the Winter King, can find their way around by trial and error. But only one atlas exists that contains them all, and only it can get us to where we need to be, when we need to be there. And only one person alive has been schooled and trained in the ancient languages and cultures that will allow him to interpret the directions in that atlas.

"Well," she said, thumping a fist on the *Geographica*, "*this* is that atlas. And *you*," she said jabbing a finger at John, "are the Caretaker. So can you read it or not?"

Defeated, John lowered his eyes in shame. "I can't. I don't know how."

CHAPTER SIX
THE TICK-TOCK PARLIAMENT

"IF THAT IS true, then we may be lost," said Bert. "Only a trained Caretaker can properly navigate a ship through the Archipelago of Dreams. The maps and notations are in a dozen languages, many of them long dead. There are very few people living who could make any sense of it at all."

The lines could not have been more clearly drawn: Aven, Bert, and, and surprisingly, Jack on one side; John, Charles, and Bug on the other.

"Jack?" Charles said, a note of astonished surprise in his voice. "You can't be siding with them. After all . . ." He began to say something, then seemed to reconsider, adding only a soft admonishment. "Bad form, Jack."

"But Aven's right," said Jack. "We were chased out of London, running for our very lives, all because of him and that book. His teacher was killed for it. The entire *Indigo Dragon* was nearly just destroyed for it. And this entire . . . wherever we are, may be going to war over it. And he's supposed to be the only one alive who can read it, and he's failed."

"Jack!" Charles said. "That's quite enough."

"But he's right," said John. "I have failed."

Aven swore and reached for her broadsword, but Bert interceded and held her arm. "There has to be an explanation, Aven. I'm the one who chose him.

"John," Bert said, unable to hide the pleading in his voice, "I have read your work. You have the gift, I know it. And Stellan knew it too. That's why he agreed to take you on. Why, I've seen the correspondence myself—he *was* training you."

"Yes," John said, "he was. But I wasn't learning—not as I should have, at any rate."

He turned to Charles and Jack, resigned. "It never seemed to be important," he explained. "Ancient languages that no one else could read . . . Who could have imagined there would ever be a need? My friends at home, even my wife—they all questioned the wisdom of spending so much time on what seemed to be impractical pursuits."

"Not so impractical now, is it?" Jack said.

"For God's sake, Jack," said John. "There is a war on! I could hardly be expected to spend what little free time I had reading and translating manuscripts in Old Teutonic."

"Men will die because you didn't," Aven said. "And perhaps already have."

"He doesn't care," Jack said.

"Yes, I do!" John shouted, grabbing Jack by the coat. "I do care, you fool! I have seen men die! I have felt the spray of their blood on my face as men I laughed with, ate with, sheltered with, died in front of me! Can you say the same?"

They were both shaking. John's face had broken out in a sweat, and his breathing was fast and shallow. After a moment he released Jack and dropped his head into his hands.

"I'm sorry, Jack," John said after a time. "I do feel as if I've failed all of you—but the professor most of all. Believe me, I didn't know . . . I never knew what—"

"Enough, John," said Charles, putting his arm around his companion's shoulder. "Let's all take a little while to compose ourselves, and then maybe we can have a look and decipher it together. Three heads are better than one, and all that. What do you say, Jack?"

But when they looked up, Jack and Aven had already moved to another part of the ship, commiserating. Bert stood in the doorway of the cabin, eyes downcast, caught in the middle of his hope and his fear. Only Bug remained with them, wanting to help, but obviously swept up in something bigger than his experience could provide for.

The fellowship had been broken. And there was nothing any of them could do but continue sailing toward Paralon.

Despite his positive demeanor, after an hour with the *Geographica* even Charles had to admit he was at a loggerheads with it. His editorial position at the Oxford University Press had allowed him a great deal of experience with Latin, so those passages and some of the Greek phrases were not totally undecipherable—not that it helped much.

"I also get a smattering of Old English, and a few words of Hebrew, but the rest is dead impossible," said Charles. "There are a great deal of annotations in modern English, but there's no hierarchy to it, no order, other than a rough chronological one."

This pronouncement did little to assuage John's melancholy mood, or Jack's defiant one. Bert was still subdued, but hopeful.

"Look," he said, "since Paralon is the 'capital' of the Archipelago, its map has been extensively annotated in English.

"I myself have added to the listing, so I can read most of it myself from past experience. Besides," he added, "we're already pointed in the right direction, so we should make it that far without incident. After we're there, then perhaps we can locate a scholar, or appeal to the Parliament for access to the king's archives and library for help.

"Cheer up lad," he finished. "We still have options."

"Maybe," Bug offered from the nook in the cabin where he'd been observing, "the Council will decide on a new king, and you won't have to worry about it anymore."

"Think good thoughts, lad," Bert said as he left the cabin, closing the door behind him.

The sun was nearing the apex of its arc across the sky when the crewman in the crow's nest called out, "Land, ho!"

They had arrived at Paralon.

The island was far larger than Avalon, or any of the Shadowed Lands they had passed. In the distance a mountain range could be made out, as well as the dark greens of what could only be great forests. The vista was stunning enough that even the taciturn fauns paused in their labors to watch as they approached.

The harbor toward which they sailed was formed around a natural river basin that emptied into the sea, just deep enough for ships to moor. The ground beyond sloped up gently to a landscape of low rolling hills and fields, then abruptly shifted to a domineering ridge of plateaus that rose straight up from the valley floor.

On the tallest of these stood a massive stone fortress, gray and forbidding: the Castle of Paralon, wherein sat the Silver Throne of the High King of the Archipelago.

This was not Camelot, as they had suspected it might resemble, but something far more primal, which shimmered with the raw energies of living myth. It was the archetype of archetypes; Paralon was the reality that the legend of Camelot aspired to be.

"Dear Lord," Charles breathed. "It's magnificent."

John and Jack both nodded in agreement. Even Mad King Ludwig had never imagined a castle such as this.

"There are a number of ships in the harbor," Aven noted. "The council may already have begun."

"So this Paralon," Charles said as they began to disembark, "is the largest military power in the Archipelago?"

"Why would you think that?" Bert said in surprise.

"How else would it become the locus of power?"

"See those forests in the distance?" Bert asked. "Apple orchards—hundreds, if not thousands, of years old. Military might is transferable, losable, comes and goes. But good produce," he finished with a wink, "good produce is very difficult to attain."

Jack busied himself trying to be helpful to Aven, who did her best to ignore him without seeming to. His reckless but successful move during the encounter with the Winter King, as well as his sympathetic distancing from John, had emboldened him, much to her dismay.

Bert helped a still downcast John secure the *Geographica* inside a sturdy leather case with straps that could be slung over his shoulders for easier carrying, which Bug offered to do. He took his role as John's squire seriously and was attentive to any ways he might be helpful. Besides, there was no way to suggest that he stay behind—not when the prospect of seeing real knights and kings lay before him.

Charles was already at the far end of the dock, where a small figure was cursing and banging at the insides of an odd contraption that appeared to be the offspring of a clockwork automobile and Cinderella's pumpkin carriage.

"Keep at it," Charles said. "I'm sure you'll get whatever the trouble is sorted out."

"I'll do my best, which is all any of us can do, in't it?" came the reply.

Charles yelped and jumped back as he realized the creature that had answered him was not a man, or even one of the fauns.

It was a badger. In a vest and waistcoat, walking upright, with a pince-nez in one eye and spats on both furred feet.

Charles was still stammering in disbelief as the others came up behind.

"A waistcoat, but no trousers?" John asked.

"It's very impolite to take notice," said Bert.

"Be ye royalty types, or officious emissaries?" the badger asked.

"Scholars," said Charles. "We be ... ah, that is, we *are* scholars."

"Scowlers, are ye?" said the badger. "And whereabouts do you do yer scowlerin'?"

"Ah, Oxford, actually," Charles said.

The animal seemed to take this as a matter of course. "Oh yes, Oxford. A place of scowlerly knowledge and Druidcraft. Lord Pryderi of the race of Man was an Oxford scowler."

"And you," said Jack. "What's your name?"

"Pardon my manners, young scowler," said the badger with a gesture that was halfway between a squat and a bow. "I be called Tummeler, and Tummeler is me."

"Pleased to meet you, Mr. Tummeler," said Jack, who, to the badger's delight, shook his proffered paw. "I'm Jack. These lot are my friends and fellow, ah, 'scowlers,' John, and Charles, and our captain, Aven. The fellow with the hat is Bert."

"Welcome, scowler Jack and all," said Tummeler. "Be ye here for the Council?"

"We are," said Bert. "Has it begun?"

"Not yet," said Tummeler, "as a number of designates such as y'rselves are only just arrived, and the Council at Paralon asked ol' Tummeler to escort any last-minute princely sorts and emissaries as may be expectin' to attend."

He beckoned at them with a paw and turned away. "This way, if you please, young scowlers and company. The Council awaits."

In short order Tummeler had the vehicle running (with a discreet assist from Aven, who didn't want to embarrass the small mammal in front of visitors by pointing out that a clump of badger fur was obscuring one of the contacts in the engine) and they started across the valley to the castle.

"We calls 'em principles," said Tummeler, referring to the steam-belching vehicle in which they traveled. "As in, 'you can get from here to there, but it's easier to do it with principles.' That's in general. This 'un," he continued proudly, "I calls the Curious Diversity."

"Fascinating," said Charles. "How does it run?"

"Well enough for all practical porpoises," said Tummeler.

"No—I mean, what gives it motive power?"

"We gots to go somewheres," Tummeler replied. "What gives *you* motive power?"

"I—I just decide to go where I need to, and then I do," Charles stammered.

"Well, it's the same with principles," said Tummeler, "'cept I do the decidin'."

Aven smiled. "It's a design manufactured by one of *his* predecessors," she said, tilting her chin at John. "There is an element of steam involved, and often electricity, but no one truly knows how they run. Bacon only passed on the secret of their construction to certain animals and to Nemo. The animals can't explain it well enough, and Nemo has never shared."

"Bacon?" said John. "Do you mean Roger Bacon, the Franciscan friar? He was a Caretaker too?"

Tummeler nodded. "As I be telling you—always good eggs they be, those Oxford scowlers."

The Curious Diversity passed through an immense stone gate, bracketed by two equally massive statues. The statues' left hands were outstretched in a gesture of warding; their right hands were held closer to the breast in a gesture of beckoning.

"Th' Great Kings of Paralon," said Tummeler. "There be two outside each of the gates as th' compass spins—east, west, north, and south."

"Incredible," said John.

"Hah!" said Tummeler. "Wait'll y' see th' Great Hall."

When the Silver Throne was first established, Bert explained as they traveled, Arthur ruled from a modest castle on the island of Avalon. It was his eldest son, Artigel, who moved the seat of rule to Paralon, where he enlisted the Dwarves to build a great city.

The streets were paved, and as they entered they saw a number of other principles, each of their own unique make, chugging along the roadways. The buildings they passed were white stone and glass, and all were topped with soaring roofs and towers.

The main castle, which they had sighted from the harbor, was not built atop the plateau, but carved from it, into it, through it. It was a remarkable feat of engineering. Tummeler parked the Curious Diversity on a broad avenue at the intersection of streets below the towering edifice and motioned them to a bridge that led to two great applewood doors.

"Here," he said, gesturing with a paw. "I'll be waitin' here f'r when all's said an' all's done. One word of warning," the badger added. "Watch out for one in partic'lar. Th' one called Arawn, that is. Eldest son of the old Troll King Sarum. He's a bad 'un. Bad from the get-go, and bad to the core. He's been calling for a full council for several years, and he has made it no secret that he thinks the time of Men is past, and a new High King should be chosen from one of the other races.

"It don't take a scowler," Tummeler finished, "to guess who he thinks should get the job. Good luck to you all, master scowlers."

There were a thousand different races in the Archipelago, Bert explained—more if you included the animals. But only the four great races were allowed to send formal emissaries to the Council: the Trolls, the Goblins, the Elves, and the Dwarves.

The fifth race, Men, convened the council out of sheer tradition. Despite the occasional conflicts that arose, all of the races respected Arthur's lineage, and had accorded that respect to the Parliament during the years since the murder of the old king and his family. But they had grown restless, and each race wanted to claim the Silver Throne for their own.

"Are we going to be allowed?" Charles asked. "We are neither royalty nor emissaries."

"We'll be allowed," said Bert. "I have some standing with the Parliament, and *he*, after all," he said, tapping John on the shoulder, "is the Caretaker."

Aven rolled her eyes and cursed under her breath.

"At least," Bert added, "he is the bearer of the *Imaginarium Geographica*. That alone gives him, and you all, a degree of status."

John sighed and looked at Bug, who smiled supportively.

Together, they entered the Great Hall of Paralon.

Tummeler had not overspoken. The Great Hall was a sight stunning in its grandeur.

Each entry from the four points of the compass opened through arches a hundred feet high, bracketing a great gallery of boxfront seats. Far, far above, the ceiling ended in a crystal window that may have been set atop the plateau itself. Carved into all of the pillars were alcoves bearing torches, illuminating the entire hall in a brilliant white light. It was, in a word, spectacular.

"The Winter King will never get the throne," Jack murmured to Charles.

"Why not?"

"Because," said Jack, "he'd have to repaint everything *black*."

About half of the seats in the gallery were taken. Bert led the companions to a staircase behind one of the pillars on the left, and they climbed to an open cluster of seats about a third of the way up.

"The central seating is reserved for the human Parliament," Bert explained. "They've yet to arrive, which is good—we've not come too late."

The elves took up the seats to the right of center; they represented the largest number of delegates from any race. They were slender, fair-haired, and fair-skinned, and they bore the aloof demeanor of a race that rarely saw death.

The dwarves sat to the left, above and around the companions. They were shorter and stocky, and well armed. Not a single delegate carried less than two short swords, as well as bows and braces of arrows.

"Keep on their good side," Bert warned. "They're a testy lot. Like to pick fights—mostly with elves, though. It's a height thing."

"So, uh, you lot built this place, eh?" Jack said to the dwarf sitting three seats over.

"Yes," said the dwarf.

"Uh, nice work," said Jack.

"Humph," snorted the dwarf.

Bert raised a hand in greeting and saw the gesture returned by a greasy, gnarled man dressed in elaborate silken robes sitting high in the center of the gallery.

"Uruk Ko, the Goblin King," said Bert in explanation. "And entourage."

"A Goblin King?" John whispered in distaste.

"Oh, he's an affable enough sort," said Bert. "Stellan—Professor Sigurdsson—and I once shared a long voyage with him in the southern isles on a ship called the *Aurora*. It was meant to be an exploratory expedition—mapping for the *Geographica* and whatnot—that somehow turned into an adventure all of its own.

"But," he concluded, shrugging, "that's the sort of thing that happens when the captain is a talking mouse."

Directly opposite the goblins in the great hall, sitting low in the gallery, was a bulky, dark-visaged personage that could only have been a troll. Thick, corded arms were folded against a massive chest, which was further plated with heavy leather armor. His bearing and manner, as well as the number of supplicants crowded around his elevated chair, indicated that he was in all likelihood a creature of high status, if not the Troll King himself.

"I don't know him," Bert said. "Those of the Troll race tend to keep to themselves in the eastern isles of the Archipelago."

"One guess," said John. "I'll bet that's Tummeler's Arawn."

"Quiet," said Bert. "The Parliament is arriving."

Entering from a fifth entrance between the east and north gates, the representatives of the Parliament were dressed according to the suits in a deck of cards: clubs, spades, diamonds, and hearts. Somberly, they marched in, looking neither right nor left.

Bert's brow furrowed as the members of the Parliament filed in and took their seats with the rest of the Council.

"What is it?" John whispered.

"Can't say," Bert replied. "Something is amiss, although I can't quite put my finger on it."

They watched in silence as the elaborately dressed men and women settled into their places in the gallery. At length a shifty yet officious-looking man—the Steward of Paralon, Bert said—strode to the center of the hall and called for order.

"As Steward of Paralon, I shall oversee these proceedings," he began. "In the absence of a legitimate heir to the Silver Throne, the Parliament, under my guidance, has ruled Paralon and with it, the Archipelago.

"Now a claim has been made on the throne. A claim of birth-right and blood."

At this there was a great deal of murmuring from the gallery. "What's that about?" John whispered. "I thought all the heirs were dead."

"I don't know," said Bert. "Listen."

"The claim," the Steward continued, "has been approved by the Parliament. If none dissent, by the end of the day we shall have a new High King."

Calls rang out to the Steward, who waited for the cacophony to die down before addressing them again.

"The claim," he said, "has been made by one of Arthur's own kinsmen, and as such ought not to be disputed. While he has had no previous standing with this body, he has nevertheless come to be known by most of you . . .

". . . as the Winter King."

"Wait," boomed a voice. It was Bert. "May I speak?"

The Steward grimaced. "The Parliament . . . ," he began.

"The Parliament," said Bert, "called a council to debate the matter of succession. Whether or not there is an heir, as you say, we should be allowed to address them."

"By what right," asked the Steward, "do you speak?"

"I am one of the Caretakers of the *Imaginarium Geographica*," said Bert, "and the other sits beside me."

This brought many nods, mostly friendly, from the throng. The Steward shook his head. "I appreciate your desire to partici-pate," he began to say.

"Let him speak," came a gruff voice. It was Uruk Ko, the Goblin King.

The Steward could bluff and bluster past most of those assembled; he could not, however, stare down an actual king of an entire race. Reluctantly, he bowed and stepped to the side of the hall, casting nervous glances up at the Parliament members.

Bert stood in the center of the Great Hall and faced the gallery. "Ladies and gentlemen of the Parliament," he began, "I have had direct and recent experience with the man called the Winter King. . . ." But before he could continue, he was cut off by the King of Diamonds, who stood and shook his fist at the other man.

"Unacceptable," said the king. "The Parliament cannot accept the proposal."

"Did he make a proposal?" John whispered to Charles. "If so, I missed it."

Bert seemed similarly puzzled. "Your Majesty, if I have presumed too much—"

"Yes, entirely out of the question," the king continued, as if he had not heard Bert at all. "A Walrus as High King is preposterous. And everyone knows a Carpenter cannot be High Queen—if we allowed that, then who would organize all of the dances?"

"This is very strange," said Charles.

"Shush," said Jack. "Look—another king is rising to speak."

The King of Spades raised a hand. "Please don't fire the cannons," he said, "or I shall never be able to remove the potatoes from my ears."

The dwarves had begun to murmur, as if they too sensed all was not well.

"They're all mad," said Jack. "What is this?"

"I don't know," said Aven. "Something is very wrong."

The Steward was about to escort Bert off the floor, when the Queen of Clubs's head caught fire. The flames shot high into the air, and yet she remained seated, hands folded, a gentle smile on her face, as if nothing were amiss.

The murmuring that began with the dwarves had now spread to the elves and goblins. And the trolls were beginning to unsheathe their weapons.

The Queen of Hearts, a portly, dark-haired woman, picked up a croquet mallet from under her seat and smashed the King of Hearts in the chest. "I hate roses," she said. "They never speak when spoken to."

Bert looked around, but the Steward had disappeared. All throughout the seats, the delegates were rising to their feet, shouting.

One of the trolls overcame his forced decorum and threw a mace directly at the Queen of Hearts. With the impact, her chest split open and spilled a cascade of wheels and cogs onto the floor of the hall, showering the nearby delegates in an explosion of sparks.

The Parliament members were not human at all. They were clockwork constructs.

"A fraud!" boomed the Troll Prince Arawn, standing and shaking his armored fist. "The Council is a fraud!"

In moments the entire Great Hall of Paralon had erupted in chaos.

CHAPTER SEVEN
THE FORBIDDEN PATH

THE SMOKE WAS acrid, and it filled John's nose, mouth, and lungs. Desperately, he covered his head with his arms and burrowed more deeply into the muddy French soil.

The shelling had been relentless. And just as it seemed the travails could grow no worse, the telltale fog of the Gas came wafting malevolently through the shattered trees.

Screaming, John leaped to his feet and began to run, only to be caught up in the rolls of concertina wire that had been strung along the rear trenches. All around him were bloated bodies of the dead, lying in a landscape blackened, stripped bare of life. Helplessly, he could only watch as the Gas crept closer, accompanied by the increasingly thunderous sound of the artillery: *Boom. Boom. Boom . . .*

Boom.

"John!" said a voice he knew, but it was not that of any soldier in his battalion. "John, for God's sake, pull yourself together!"

John shook his head, blinking, as he came to his senses and his vision cleared. Charles was grasping him by the shoulders, shaking him and shouting his name. His other companions were making their way to the exit under the sparse cover of the boxfronts of the seats. Incredulous, he looked around at the maelstrom of weapon play, flames, grappling bodies, and furious shouting that had moments before been the Grand Council.

There was no sign of the goblins; and the last of the elves were just departing under the cover of the northern arch. The dwarves had spread across the gallery and had begun hurling explosive bundles at the troll delegates, as more and more trolls flooded through the southern and eastern entrances. The trolls had clambered into the center seats and had smashed the members of the Clockwork Parliament to pieces. In the uppermost part of the gallery, bellowing directions to his arriving reinforcements, was the Troll Prince Arawn.

More than one treachery had been planned for that day, it seemed.

"That's why there were so many ships in the harbor," Aven said to Bert. "The Trolls planned a revolt no matter what happened in the Council."

Bert nodded in agreement, as he and Charles supported the dazed John under his shoulders and moved lower toward the western arch. "The Steward of Paralon just beat them to the punch," he said. "This may be the Archipelago's undoing."

"What's wrong with *him*?" Jack said, scowling at John.

"The explosions," Charles said. "He's gone into a bit of battle shock."

"I'll be all right," John said, attempting to regain his footing. "Really."

Aven glared and Jack's eyes narrowed in disgust as John shook off Charles and Bert's assistance. "Let's get out of here," Aven hissed through gritted teeth, "before the whole place comes down around our ears."

◆   ◆   ◆

The companions raced down the corridor toward the avenue where they'd left Tummeler and his vehicle. Around them members of all the races ran about, trying to ascertain what had happened. Behind them, in the Great Hall, there were more explosions, and the smell of smoke.

"The trolls will almost certainly have blockaded the harbor," said Aven. "Our best bet is to try to get out of the city proper, and then circle back when the tumult's died down."

"*If* it dies down," said Jack.

"What of the *Indigo Dragon?*" asked Charles, panting. "Will it be torched?"

"No," said Aven. "She can take care of herself. She'll already be out of harm's way."

They reached the end of the corridor, bursting through the doors and into the open, where Tummeler already had the Curious Diversity waiting, its engine running.

"Quickly!" Tummeler shouted. "Master scowlers! Get in, get in!"

In a confusion of limbs the companions threw themselves into the seats of the principle. "North!" Aven shouted. "Take us north!"

Tires squealing, Tummeler pulled onto the northern thoroughfare and sped away from the towers.

It took several minutes to actually escape the confines of the walled city, and several minutes more to pass the last of the outposts where they might have been stopped. As luck would have it, all of the guards and sentries that might have held them in their flight had gone toward the heart of the conflict at the Great Hall.

John's earlier panic had subsided into a feverish slumber, interrupted only by occasional shakes of his limbs.

"Fever dreams, that is," Tummeler said, looking over his shoulder and clucking his tongue. "What ails master John?"

Talking in turns, Bert and Aven explained to Tummeler what had taken place at the Grand Council. When they got to the part about the Parliament, the small mammal cut in and changed the subject.

"Ah, I knowed there be trouble afoot, once I heard it wuz Arawn come t' speak fer th' Trolls," said Tummeler. "But enough of th' worries. I be taking you somewheres calmer, somewheres safe."

As he said this, he steered the Curious Diversity off of the main road and onto an unpaved tributary that sprouted off to the west. It led to the mouth of a canyon that creased the upper part of the plateau line, and was, Bert pointed out, supposed to be off limits to everyone.

"Not t' th' animals," said Tummeler. "This be a road known to us and few others, and since the royal family was kilt, only to us."

"A forbidden path?" said Charles. "Why is it forbidden?"

"Because," said Bert, "it leads to the remnants of the old city, the first city, which was built when Artigel sat upon the Silver Throne. The greater city was expanded upon and through the mountain when the first alliance with the Dwarves was made, but the original still exists—in fact, it houses the royal archive and library, unless I'm mistaken."

"But," said Charles, "won't we get into trouble?"

"Heh," Aven snorted. "More trouble than what we just left? I doubt it. Besides, I don't think there is anyone left in power who will care, forbidden or not."

"The advantage of following forbidden paths," Tummeler said, nodding, "is that no one will follow after."

"That's terrible logic," said Charles.

"No," said Tummeler. "That's animal logic."

John awoke to the sound of something snuffling loudly around his face, and he sat up with a start. The snuffling was Tummeler, who was kneading his small paws and peering closely at him.

"Master John, be ye awake?" the animal said, a note of genuine concern in his voice. "Be ye all right, master scowler?"

"I be, ah, that is, I'm all right," said John, attempting to lift himself up on his elbows. He was lying across the rear seats of the Curious Diversity. Nearby, Bert and Charles were talking closely, and Aven and Jack were also keeping counsel of their own a little farther on.

They had stopped near a spring, in a clearing that was sparsely wooded with thin, scraggly trees, at the cleft of the canyon. The sun was still high in the sky. The entire fiasco of the Grand Council and their flight from the city had taken scarcely an hour.

Bug sat in the front seat of the principle, face tense with concentration.

"The others," he said without turning. "They said you were a knight, back in the world you come from? That you saw battle, and that's what's making you sick?"

"I'm a soldier," John said, sitting upright. "That's like a knight, I suppose. And yes, I became sick during the war. It still troubles me at times."

Bug turned to look at him. "They said the memory made you ill. How can a memory make you sick?"

John paused, unsure how to answer. "I had friends," he said finally. "Friends who died, right before my eyes. And I feared for my own life. That kind of fear, once a man has experienced it, never fully goes away. Do you understand?"

Bug didn't reply, but swallowed hard and turned away. John got the feeling that yes, the boy did understand—perhaps more than any of them could know.

At Tummeler's direction, the companions began to walk through the canyon, heading west. "This is a continuation of th' road," Tummeler explained, "that leads to where we be goin'."

"We should be continuing north," argued Aven. "We don't have time for this."

"And when we get back to the ship, where then?" Bert admonished. "We have no guide, and the Winter King can only be strengthened by the chaos of the Council. He'll still be looking for the *Geographica*—and us. Perhaps here we can find someone to translate the *Imaginarium Geographica*—and maybe restore some semblance of order to the lands before all is lost."

The others nodded in agreement, save for John, who hung his head in shame. He had never felt so useless, and would have said so, if it weren't for the fear that not one of his friends would dispute it.

As they walked, Bert explained that when the Silver Throne was created, alliances had yet to be formed. "There was a loose fealty to Arthur, but his children had a harder row to hoe," he said. "The Dwarves were first to form a pact with the king, then the Goblins. The Elves were next, in an alliance formed by marriage— and then, much later, the Trolls. During that time, Artigel found it useful to have a seat of power that could be defended and protected. This canyon was the ideal place.

"The consent of the Four Kingdoms, represented by the four major races—the Trolls, the Elves, the Goblins, and the Dwarves—to be ruled by Men was predicated on the continuity of rule," said Bert. "It's because of the Parliament that they have allowed an empty throne for so long. And even then, only because the Steward was governing at their behest."

"The Steward of Paralon," said John. "He seemed familiar somehow."

"After all of the assorted characters we've seen," said Jack, "any human would seem familiar."

"Not like that," said John. "I'm quite certain I've seen him somewhere before. I wish I'd gotten a closer look. . . ."

"Never mind," said Bert. "He fled before anyone else. It's all but certain that he had something to do with the deception of the Clockwork Parliament."

At this, Tummeler clicked his teeth nervously but kept his eyes on the path ahead.

"There," said Tummeler at last. "There she be."

He gestured ahead at the steep rock face of the canyon, where an enormous edifice seemed to have been carved into the stone itself, in much the same manner as Paralon. It was rougher, cruder, but bore the same unmistakable craftsmanship. A great framework of stone and iron was inset into the southern wall of the canyon, and two huge wooden doors within that. Above, wrapped protectively around the upper part of the doors, was a stone bas-relief of a dragon, surrounded by exotic golden lettering.

"Elvish," Tummeler stated, as Bert nodded in agreement.

"How do we get in?" Jack asked, examining the doors. "There doesn't seem to be a handle or keyhole."

"Perhaps the inscription is a magical instruction," said Charles. "Remember where we are, and how things work in this place."

"I don't suppose *you* can read that," Jack said to John, who scowled, face reddening.

"Jack," Charles admonished. "Mr. Tummeler brought us here— I'm sure he can facilitate our entry."

"Oh, drat and darn," said Tummeler. "I've forgotten the magic word again."

"What does the writing say?" John asked, not quite daring to touch the inscriptions, which were deeply engraved into the granite, yet were worn smooth with extreme age.

"It's Elvish," Tummeler repeated. "It says, basically, 'Declare allegiance, and be welcomed.'"

"Well, doesn't it perhaps mean that the magic word that opens the door is 'allegiance'?" said Jack. "In Elvish?"

"That's a stupid idea," said John. "Then anyone who spoke Elvish could get in."

"Pr'cisely," said Tummeler. "No, it be an actuated magic word. One of the oldest magic words there be. It was made so by one of th' great Elven Kings of old, called Eledin, he be."

"Eledin?" said Charles. "That's close to 'Aladdin,'" he said, waving his hand across the doors. "If only it was that easy—to simply say, 'Alakazam.'"

With a low groaning of wood and metal, the giant oaken doors cracked apart and slowly began to spread open.

"Y' know the sacred magic word," said Tummeler, eyes wide with respect. "Y' be a true scowler, master Charles."

"Good show, Charles," said Jack.

"Bravo," said Bert.

"That shouldn't have worked," said John. "It was supposed to be Ali Baba and 'Open Sesame.'"

"Oh, for heaven's sake," said Charles.

There were several skeletons strewn about the entryway, robed in various styles of clothing. A few of the remains were misshapen, the bones either too short or elongated and overly large. It was Jack who realized that not all of the remains were human.

"Does everyone still think this is a good idea?" Jack said. "It looks as if other adventurers weren't entirely successful at getting very far."

"Oh, don't mind the bones," said Tummeler. "The Archivist keeps 'em about to give th' place atmosphere."

"Scared, Jack?" Aven said with a mischievous grin.

He straightened his posture and stepped forward. "No."

With Jack leading the way, the companions moved down the corridor, which was as tall as the doors and lit by the supernatural glow of runes engraved in the walls some ten feet above their heads.

"More Elvish," said Bert.

The corridor opened into a broad cavern that was honeycombed with holes, each of which was filled with books, or artifacts, or in some cases, gold and jewels.

"Hello?" said Tummeler. "Is anyone there?"

"Welcome," rumbled a deep, smoky voice. "I hope you've come by for a cup of tea, because those are the only kind of visitors I permit here anymore.

"Otherwise," the voice continued, "I'm going to have to kill you all."

CHAPTER EIGHT
AN INVITATION TO TEA

EVEN THE LIGHT from the Elvish runes seemed to recede as an immense red dragon rose slowly to its feet and moved toward them from the shadowed recesses of the cavern.

"My name is Samaranth," said the great red beast, "and all those you see around you declined my invitation, opting instead to help themselves to the treasure. So, Sons of Adam, choose. Will you drink with me, or do you want to plunder, and die?"

"Are you serious?" said Jack. "Tea or death? Of course we'll take the tea." The others all nodded in enthusiastic agreement. "What kind of fool would choose death?"

"Bet they wuz Cambridge scowlers, eh, master Charles?" said Tummeler with a wink.

"Undoubtedly," said Charles.

The stone floor was covered with an assortment of Persian rugs of varying sizes. The largest lay squarely before them, where the dragon indicated they should sit.

"This is quite an honor," Bert whispered to John as they seated themselves in a semicircle at the feet of the dragon. "There are no other dragons left in the Archipelago. Haven't been since the old king died. But to share tea with Samaranth . . ."

"What's special about Samaranth?" John whispered back, keeping a wary eye on the dragon, "as opposed to, well, regular dragons?"

"He's the first," Bert replied. "The oldest. The original dragon of the Archipelago. In fact, he may be the oldest creature alive."

"Perhaps you are correct," Samaranth said, smiling. "I may indeed be the oldest. But time, as you well know, Son of Adam, is relative."

Bert reddened at this and folded his arms, bowing. "I meant no disrespect, Samaranth. I am indeed honored to meet you. And, ah, to partake of your hospitality."

The dragon bowed his head to Bert in acknowledgment, then to each of them in turn, pausing only at Bug, to whom he bowed a bit more deeply, and for a moment longer than the others. Bug, for his part, blushed visibly.

Samaranth straightened and gestured toward the badger, who was standing to one side, beaming. "And you, Child of the Earth—will you join us?"

"Certainly," said Tummeler. "Y' wouldn' happen t' have those crackers I fancy, would y'?"

Samaranth made a huffing noise not unlike a steam engine, which after a moment the companions realized was laughter.

"Yes," said Samaranth. "I have the Leprechaun crackers. One moment, and I'll get them."

"They ain't made from real Leprechauns," Tummeler confided to Charles. "I just calls 'em that."

The dragon returned with a silver tea service delicately balanced on one arm, and a small bundle of crackers on the other.

"Mistress," he said to Aven. "Will you do the pleasure of serving?"

Aven began to retort something about not being servile to

men, but the dragon's tone and manner was so respectful that she could not refuse. She took the tray from him, and Jack rose to his feet to help, taking the parcel of crackers.

"These are tea biscuits," he said, puzzled. "Just like we have at home."

"There are those who trade with your world," said Samaranth, "and they in turn trade with the animals, who in turn trade with me."

"Umm-hmm," Tummeler said happily through a mouthful of crackers.

"What do you trade?" Charles asked. "Jewels? Gold?"

Samaranth turned to him. "Is that all you see of worth here, O Son of Adam? The riches of the Earth?"

Charles shrank back. "Ah, just wondering."

"Knowledge," Bert interjected. "You trade in knowledge."

"Hurm," the dragon growled in satisfaction. "A Caretaker of the *Geographica* would understand this."

"That's the second thing you've said that indicates you know me," said Bert. "Pardon my asking, but have we met before? Because I'm certain I would not have forgotten, I assure you."

"No," said Samaranth, "but it is in my interests to keep abreast of what occurs in the Archipelago—and those who seek to influence its affairs. And to that end," the dragon continued, "tell me what it is that has brought you here to have tea with an old dragon."

It took them the better part of an hour to recount everything that had happened, from the murder of Professor Sigurdsson to the flight from London, to the prophecy of the Morgaine, the battle with the *Black Dragon*, and the Grand Council at Paralon. They also recounted, much to John's embarrassment, his failure to translate the differing languages of the *Imaginarium Geographica*, and the urgent need to do so, that they might find a way to defeat the Winter King.

The dragon said nothing but merely listened, pausing only to refill the teapot with fresh tea and to replenish the Leprechaun crackers for Tummeler, who had not stopped munching them the entire time.

When the companions finished their accounting, Samaranth said nothing, but sat, considering. When he finally spoke, it was about the past.

"Ages ago," Samaranth began, "the Archipelago of Dreams was guarded by thousands of dragons. The skies were filled with them. Then, not all that long ago, they began to disappear, until they were all gone, save for myself. And the only knowledge that remained of them was found in myth, and legend, and in books." This last was said with a rather pointed look at John.

"We guarded the boundary between the Archipelago and the world beyond, using flame and fear to turn back travelers that ventured too close. But I have not seen another dragon for almost twenty years, and men like the one you call the Winter King have risen to power—men who would learn the secrets of the lands not to rule justly, but to conquer cruelly."

"He has already placed many lands in Shadow," said Bert, "and for some reason, he believes that possession of the *Geographica* will aid him in his efforts."

"Why he wishes to possess the *Geographica*, I cannot say," mused Samaranth, "but there are already too many plans afoot in the lands, and were it to fall into his hands, it would not bode well for the Archipelago."

"Then what can we do?" said Bert. "There is no king, and not even a real Parliament to give counsel. Worse, there apparently hasn't been a real Parliament in some time—and the revealed deception ended the possibility of unity in the Archipelago."

"Yes, that is a problem," said Samaranth, turning to face Tummeler. "Would you care to tell us, little Child of the Earth, just what the animals were thinking?"

Tummeler froze, a half-eaten Leprechaun cracker hanging out of his mouth.

"The animals?" said Aven. "Do you mean to say that they built those imposters in the Parliament?"

"It makes sense," said Charles. "They are the only ones aside from Nemo who know how to build the vehicles, and the clock-work kings and queens were at least as complicated as that."

The companions turned to look at Tummeler, who was twisting the ends of his vest and twitching his whiskers mournfully.

"Aye, 'tis true, I be afeared to say," Tummeler began. "We—the animals, that is—built them several years back, to avoid just this sort o' calamity."

"But why did you build them?" Jack asked. "There are plenty of humans on Paralon who could have served."

"Not kings and queens," wailed Tummeler. "Th' Parliament must be kings and queens of the greater islands of the Archipelago, and none wuz left alive."

"*None* of them?" Bert said. "That's not possible."

"Both possible an' true," said Tummeler. "With no High King, no royal heirs, an' no real kings an' queens in Parliament, it were only a matter o' time before the other kingdoms would start to fight for th' Silver Throne.

"So it were decided that we—th' animals—should build replacement-likes, to keep a Parliament t'gether so's a new High King could be decided on."

"Who decided that you should build the replacements?" Bert asked.

Tummeler wiped a paw across his snout and shrugged. "I don't know. I never saw. Ol' Tummeler never did anyfing but drive supplies to and fro in the Curious Diversity."

"The Steward," said Charles. "Was he clockwork too?"

Tummeler shook his head. "I don't know."

"It stands to reason," said Charles. "If no one knew the other kings and queens were being murdered, as the High King's family had been, then they could be replaced with fakes."

"But why would anyone want to do that?" Jack asked.

"Consensus," said John. "Only the continuity of human rule kept the other races in check. And a consensus of Parliament and the delegates of the other kingdoms could put someone on the Silver Throne—someone like the Winter King, which is exactly what the Steward was trying to do."

"And Bert stopped him," said Charles. "Well done, Bert."

"Of course, now the capital city is on fire, and the entire Archipelago may be at war," said Jack. "But let's not dwell on the past."

"So what do we do now?" asked Aven. "Whatever is occurring among the races, the Winter King will still be pursuing the *Geographica*, and we can't let him find it."

"Agreed," Samaranth said. "As much as it pains me to suggest, the *Imaginarium Geographica* must be destroyed."

"We tried that," said Jack. "Nemo threw it on a brazier, but it wouldn't burn."

"No," said Samaranth. "Only he who created it can destroy what he has wrought. It must be taken," the dragon finished with a smoky exhalation, "to the Cartographer of Lost Places."

"That brings us full circle to our original problem," Aven said with a contemptuous glance at John. "We don't have any way to read all but the most basic maps and annotations in the *Geographica*—and with no way to translate the rest of the maps, we can never find our way to the Cartographer's island, even if he still really exists."

"Oh, he still exists," said Samaranth. "He created maps constantly for the Caretakers in years past, although he has since come to distance himself from contact with anyone from either world."

Bert nodded in agreement. "I never met him myself," he said, "but Stellan did on several occasions, very early on in our Stewardship of the *Geographica*. The last three maps were all added under our watch. Unfortunately," he added, "they are all for islands on the outer edges of the Archipelago, and will be of no use to us in finding the Cartographer."

"So," the dragon said, turning to John, "you were not properly trained as a Caretaker?"

"I was trained, but I never knew the import of my studies," said John. "I have a basic functional knowledge of several languages, but know almost nothing of the rest of them."

"Nothing?" snorted Samaranth. "Not even a single letter?"

"Single letters, sure," John said, "but not enough to translate from map to map."

"Nothing?" the dragon repeated. "Not even a single recurring phrase?"

"That's right," John said. "But wait, I forgot—there was one thing I *could* translate right away."

He took the oilskin-wrapped book from the pack on Bug's back, unwrapped it, and flipped to a map near the center of the book.

"There," he said, pointing to an engraving of a dragonlike creature and the annotation below it. "It's much like the caution on an old mariner's map I once saw: 'Here, There Be Dragons.'"

"Correct," said Samaranth. "With one difference."

The companions crowded around John and the *Geographica*, but none of them understood what point the dragon was making. Finally, the realization dawned on John.

"It's to the east of the lands depicted," John said. "On the mariner's map at the British Museum, the caution is on the western edge—the outermost edge of the world as it was known then; but all these," he continued, paging through the maps, "are on the eastern edge."

"Correct again," said Samaranth, leaning closer to John. "One more gives you the tournament."

John studied the maps, paging from one to another before he saw it. "It's on every one," he said.

Samaranth bowed his head. "That same phrase, in one variation or another, is on every map, and," he concluded, "in every language."

"A primer," Charles said. "John, you said you'd studied all of the languages, at least a little."

"Yes," said John. "I see where you're going. I can use the common phrase as a primer to work out grammar and syntax, based on the differences between versions."

"If you work from the back of the atlas forward," offered Bert, "you can also unravel the languages chronologically. Most recent languages first."

"What do you say, John?" Charles asked. "Do you think you can do it?"

John looked doubtful, but he was quickly becoming absorbed in the maps. "Old English to Teutonic, to Italian, and . . . mmm, Latin . . . ," he murmured, more to himself than anyone else.

Aven and Jack exchanged skeptical glances, but Bert smiled broadly, as did Bug. Charles offered a pencil from his vest pocket, and without another word, John sat on the rug and began to make notes, now fully absorbed in his task.

"Well," said Samaranth. "It seems as if you had your translator with you all along."

As John worked, Bug and Aven cleaned up the tea service while Bert, Charles, Jack, and Tummeler discussed their strategy with Samaranth.

"The seas will be treacherous," said Bert. "The trolls will be out en masse, if they are not already."

"Arawn," Samaranth said with a hiss, spitting embers across the rugs that Jack hurried to stamp out. "Spoiled brat of a troll. His father is a diplomat—but that one would burn a tree to cook an apple. And then he'd discard the apple, and beat his servants for not putting out the fire."

"If only something of the old Royal House of Paralon remained," sighed Bert, "then we could simply have a coronation and get back to business."

Samaranth laughed in that huffing way and arched an eyebrow at the little old man.

"If only it were that easy," the dragon said, "you'd already be done." Bert started to ask what he meant by this, but Samaranth continued speaking. "Quests are never easy—at least, any that are worth their while.

"You want a coronation?" Samaranth said, rooting around in one of the honeycomb caches in the walls. "Take this—maybe you can put it on anyone foolish enough to sit on a throne, who seeks to rule a kingdom."

With that, the dragon tossed a small object to Bert, who looked at it briefly before tossing it back, eyes wide.

"Hah!" Samaranth snorted. "So quick to turn away a kingdom, are you, little Traveler?"

"What is it?" Charles asked.

"A ring," said Bert. "The High King's ring."

"Indeed," said Samaranth. "It was I who made it, and I who gave it to each king in turn as they assumed the Silver Throne. And it was I who took it back, when the last king demonstrated through the choices he had made that he was no longer worthy to bear it."

"But it's just a ring, isn't it?" asked Jack.

"The High King's ring—called by some the Ring of Power— was the symbol of his office," said Bert, "and was said to be the source of his power in the Archipelago."

Samaranth seemed surprised by this. "You think so? There are many rings in the Archipelago. The Elves bear rings, as do the Dwarves. And Men. Is it the ring that makes the wearer, or the wearer that makes the ring? It makes no difference to me whether you take it," he finished, proffering the ring in his open claw.

"Although," the great dragon added, considering, "it may not be what you—or the Winter King—expect it to be."

"That's all right," Jack said, reaching to take the ring from the huge palm of the dragon. "Maybe we'll discover its power along the way."

"Power is a thing earned," Samaranth said, "not something that may be passed along with the possession of objects like thrones . . . or rings, for that matter.

"Power, true power, comes from the belief in true things, and the willingness to stand behind that belief, even if the universe itself conspires to thwart your plans. Chaos may settle; flames may die; worlds may rise and fall. But true things will remain so, and will never fail to guide you to your goals. Isn't that so, Master John?"

As they talked, John had come up behind his companions. There were graphite marks on the corners of his mouth, and oddly, on his forehead, but his eyes were shining, and there were a dozen strips of cloth with scribbled notations sticking out of various parts of the *Geographica*.

"John, dear fellow," said Charles. "What is it?"

"I've done it," John said, his voice trembling in triumph and excitement. "There's still a lot of footwork to do, but Samaranth gave me the key, and I've been able to make sense of most of the maps."

"Does that mean . . . ," Bert began.

"Yes," said John. "I've found the island. I know how to find the Cartographer of Lost Places."

The companions' farewells to Samaranth were considerably less strained than their introduction. The great dragon showed them how to reach a northern inlet where the *Indigo Dragon* would most likely be waiting, far removed from the fray at Paralon, and then saw their provisions for the ship restocked from his own stores.

Each of the companions thanked him in turn for his assistance and hospitality, save for Bug, who jumped when Samaranth winked at him, and John, who was too consumed with notetaking and translating to notice they were leaving until they were actually sitting in the Curious Diversity. A short ride later, and they were once more out of the canyon and approaching the inlet. Sure enough, the *Indigo Dragon* was there, gangplank at the ready.

In less than an hour, they had unloaded their supplies and were prepared to set sail for the Cartographer's island. Somewhat shyly, Tummeler tugged at Charles's coat.

"Master Scowlers?" said Tummeler. "I—I have somethin' I'd like t' be givin' y', if you don't mind."

Charles and John knelt down next to the small animal, as he offered them a largish book that smelled of crisp ink and freshly bound leather. "What is it, my good fellow?" said Charles.

"I wrote an' published it myself," Tummeler said, twisting the ends of his vest in his paws. "It's a cookbook."

The cover was embossed with the title: *Mr. B. Tummeler Esquire Presents Exotik Foods of the Lands and How They Is Cookt.*

"Very impressive," Charles said with genuine sincerity. "How's it doing for you?"

"Oh, y' know how it goes, bein' an Oxford scowler an' all," said Tummeler. "I published it durin' th' high season, and set up shop on Rivington Lane down at th' merchant district. I even had a sign what said 'Locale Author' on it, but, ah . . ."

"Haven't sold any?" said Jack.

"Not a one," admitted Tummeler. "But I've got *prospects*."

"Well, I think it's an admirable effort," said Charles. "Thank you, Tummeler."

"Y'know," the badger said, "bein' as I've not sold any, I'd have more than enough f'r you all t' have copies of y'r own. . . ."

"No, no, one will be fine," said John. "We already have one very important book to look after, remember? Having one more will be as much as we can handle."

Tummeler beamed so much at the compliment it seemed the buttons on his vest were about to pop off. "Very wise, Master Scowler. Be well on your journey."

The badger stood on a small rise, waving his farewells, as the *Indigo Dragon* pulled away from the inlet and headed for open waters, and he continued to wave long after the ship had disappeared from view.

PART THREE

THE CHILDREN
OF THE EARTH

CHAPTER NINE
INTO THE SHADOWS

JACK STOOD NEAR the prow of the ship, a bit put out at John's newfound confidence. Aven and her crew were taking direction from the Caretaker as if the fiascoes of the previous days had never occurred. It was bad enough that the potboy from Avalon acted as if John were a knight and not just a mediocre scholar from Oxford, but Jack couldn't understand why Aven seemed to forgive and forget so quickly. He didn't resent the fact that as captain, Aven had to consult with John about the navigation. He just couldn't understand why she had to keep *smiling* at him as they conferred.

The fauns seemed to have the ship's operations well in hand, so Jack excused himself from the group and went belowdecks to do whatever it was that could be done on a ship to look productive and kill time.

"There are a few gaps in the order," John was explaining as Jack elbowed his way past to the hatch, "due to the Shadowed Maps. I don't think the maps have disappeared entirely. If we knew what caused them to vanish, we might be able to reverse it—but it may be that the only one who does know that is the Winter King, and I'd rather avoid asking, if we can help it."

"When the Winter King conquers a land, its map disappears from the *Geographica?*" Bug asked.

"Yes," said John. "The outlines of the lands themselves remain, but they are covered in shadow." He thumbed through several pages until he came to one of the vanished maps. It was a yellow-tinged sheet of parchment, like many of the others, but taking the place of the illuminations and notations were several large, indistinct smudges, as if the drawings had been hastily rubbed out.

"What happens to the people?" said Bug. "The ones who live in the Shadowed Lands?"

"They become something called 'Shadow-Born,'" said Bert, "although I've rarely seen any myself."

"Is that like a Wendigo?" asked Charles.

"Worse, if you can imagine that," said Bert. "Wendigo, as bad as they are, are little more than mercenaries. Shadow-Born have long been rumored to be the darkest of the Winter King's servants. They are shells, living without true life—dark, cloaked figures, mute, who do his bidding without question. Or remorse," he added. "How it is done, I cannot tell—all I know is what the stories say: that the Winter King somehow steals and traps the shadows of his victims, and forever after compels them to serve *him.*"

"What do you mean, 'true life'?" said Charles.

"That's another rumor," said Bert. "It's said that the Shadow-Born cannot be killed. If it's true, then they would be worse than any Wendigo."

Aven looked at John. "How many maps in the *Geographica* are Shadowed?"

"Perhaps a quarter of them."

No one had anything to say after that.

◆ ◆ ◆

John estimated that the Cartographer's island was maybe a full day's sail away, give or take a few hours. Aven conferred with Bert, while Jack and Bug pretended to examine one of the ramshackle cannons near the cabin—where they could also keep an eye on Aven.

Aven glanced around and caught Bug staring at her. He blinked and immediately began examining knots in the rigging—which came loose, much to the dismay of the fauns.

"Sorry," said Bug, who moved quickly to the other end of the ship while the crew re-drew the rigging.

Aven smiled, then frowned and furrowed her brow.

"What is it?" asked Bert.

"There," she said, pointing behind them.

On the horizon, moving fast from out of the setting sun, was the shape of a ship. The *Black Dragon* had found them once again.

The crew quickly mobilized, and in moments there was no question: It was definitely the ship of the Winter King.

Aven continued watching through the spyglass, as if confirming something she hadn't expected to see.

"What is it?" asked John.

"Trouble," said Aven.

"Really?" John said. "I hadn't guessed."

Aven shot him a poisonous look and turned to her father, handing him the spyglass. "That's not what I meant. He has Shadow-Born on board the ship. Four of them."

"Four!" Bert exclaimed, peering at the pursuing ship. "I've never heard of more than two ever being together at any time. If he's brought four Shadow-Born, that bodes very badly for us."

"You can stop trying to cheer us up now, Bert," said Charles. "I think I'm about as happy as I'm going to get."

"Our only hope is to outrun him," Aven said, "and I don't think that's possible—not without Nemo to buy us time."

"I've been examining the weapons stores below," said Jack. "We don't have much, do we?"

Aven shook her head. "We're stripped for speed—and we were never really equipped for battle to begin with."

"I have an idea," said Jack. "Hey, potboy," he called to Bug. "Give me a hand belowdecks."

"What are you thinking, Jack?" said Aven.

"No time to explain," Jack shouted. "Just get the fauns to prepare a cannon on the aft deck."

"Aft?" Aven exclaimed.

"Just do it!" said Jack, as he disappeared below.

In moments Jack and Bug had brought up a massive cannonball and were loading it into the cannon.

"A few of those would show them what's what," said Charles.

"It's the only one we have," said Jack.

"Oh. Well then," said Charles. "Aim like an Oxford man, Jack."

"That's my plan," said Jack. "Turn us around," he called to Aven. "Quickly!"

"They'll be prepared for that," she yelled back, "since your stunt the last time."

"That's what I'm counting on," said Jack. "Turn us around! Quickly!"

The crew turned the ship and pointed it at the *Black Dragon*. As Jack had predicted, the bigger ship slowed down so as not to lose too much distance when the *Indigo Dragon* passed.

A hail of arrows and spears showered the deck as they sped past the *Black Dragon*, and Aven climbed onto the rigging to get a better look at their adversary.

"That's our advantage, used and gone," she called down to Jack. "They'll not let us get the distance to turn again, and they're too fast to evade."

"It won't matter if they're faster if they can't steer," said Jack as they passed the aft of the *Black Dragon*. "Fire! Now! Now!"

The fauns lit the fuse, and an instant later a booming cough erupted from the cannon, expelling with it their solitary cannonball.

The iron ball shot through the air and found its mark, exactly where Jack had intended it to hit. The *Black Dragon*'s rudder shattered in an explosion of splintered wood and iron.

The crew of the *Indigo Dragon* let out a cheer and hastened to raise the sails for speed. John, Charles, and Bert clapped Jack enthusiastically on the back, and, best of all, Aven climbed down from her perch and kissed him on the cheek. Only Bug was nonplussed.

"I don't want to be a wet blanket," he said, "but I don't think this is over yet."

He was right. Despite having lost their rudder, the crew aboard the *Black Dragon* were making no efforts to even respond to the loss. They were still milling about, cursing and waving weapons, and looking for all the world like they hadn't even completed the preamble to this nautical overture.

Suddenly, inexplicably, the *Black Dragon* turned sharply, and, picking up speed, began to come straight at the *Indigo Dragon*.

Jack was incredulous. "But—but his rudder is gone! How in heaven's name did they turn like that?"

"Only one answer," said Bert. "The *Black Dragon* is not such in name only, but a true Dragonship—although how he managed to get his hands on one I cannot imagine. Dragonships are alive and have wills of their own—and more powers available to them than ordinary vessels."

"So what do we do now?" said Jack.

In answer, Aven drew her sword. "We do whatever we can. Arm yourselves, and prepare to be boarded."

While the fauns worked to coax more speed out of the *Indigo Dragon*, Bert, Bug, Jack, and Charles divvied up the remaining weaponry, which was old and rather shopworn. John had disappeared.

"Sure," said Jack, "the only soldier among us, and he's hiding somewhere. It's no wonder he got sent home."

Charles looked disapprovingly at his younger friend but said nothing, instead turning his attention to the rapidly approaching ship.

With the ease born of a superior motive power, the *Black Dragon* glided alongside the *Indigo Dragon* and aimed a brace of cannons at her.

"Oh, dear," said Bert, as the cannons erupted in echoing thunder and masses of hot iron began screaming through the air above their heads.

"He's not aiming to sink us?" Charles shouted.

"He can't risk losing what he's after," Jack shouted back. "He still wants the *Geographica*. Where is John and that damned book, anyway?"

"I saw him go into the cabin," Charles yelled.

"It figures," said Jack, as the *Black Dragon*'s cannons continued their relentless fire.

Bert and Aven were arguing as to strategy (she advocating more offensive maneuvers, he advocating flight), and John had just reemerged to take up a sword and join the fray when a well-aimed cannonball shattered the mainsail mast and ended any debate. A second destroyed the rudder. And a third, to their horror, sheared the masthead itself—the soul of the Dragonship—cleanly from the prow. The *Indigo Dragon* was dead in the water.

It took only moments for the smaller ship to become completely overrun by Wendigo. Whatever bravado the companions' swords had birthed was swallowed up by common sense, and they dropped their weapons.

The Wendigo forced them to their knees, tying their hands behind their backs, and then lined them up along the far railing.

The Winter King's servants had begun to light torches, which cast fearful shadows across the deck; as against Aven's vehement protestations, the fauns were herded aboard the *Black Dragon*, casting back mournful glances as they went.

"I suppose they'll be put to service for the Winter King now?" Charles asked.

"Not quite," Aven said, looking at the ravenous stares the Wendigo were giving their new shipmates. "Less service to him than served to his crew."

"Dear God," breathed Charles.

"They may still have the better end of the licorice whip," said Bert. "Look—we have more company."

Two of the Shadow-Born had stepped onto the deck, bringing with their presence a chill to the atmosphere. Where they moved, the color seemed to drain out of the air itself. The robes they wore were featureless and black; hoods covered their faces. Only the hands, pale and ethereal, which extended below the draped sleeves, bore witness that the Shadow-Born had once been human. Even the Wendigo stepped aside as they passed.

"That's a Shadow-Born?" Jack whispered to Charles. "They don't look very terrifying to me. I don't know why Bert and Aven got so worked up about them."

Just then, one of the fauns broke free from its captors and ran squealing back across the gangplank to the *Indigo Dragon*. Moving with incredible speed, the first of the Shadow-Born stepped in front of the fleeing creature. The faun stopped in its tracks.

The Shadow-Born reached out and grasped the poor beast by its own shadow. The faun began to jerk about as if it were a puppet on a string, letting loose a shriek that was cut short as its shadow ripped free in the specter's grip.

The Shadow-Born clutched its prize to its chest, and as they watched, the shadow of the faun wavered and disappeared, and the substance of the Shadow-Born seemed to grow darker.

The faun dropped to the deck, glazed eyes rolling back in its head. The color had been drained from its flesh and fur along with its shadow, leaving it all but dead. Or worse. The limp body on the deck would normally have been too tempting for the Wendigo to resist, but they all stayed well clear of the motionless form.

None of the companions had anything to say about the Shadow-Born after that.

Then a third figure came aboard, and for the first time, the companions got to take a good look at their pursuer, their adversary, the man called the Winter King.

He was not tall; rather shorter than they might have expected. His countenance and dress was that of a Mongol, but of a high caste—more Genghis Khan than Attila the Hun. His skin was swarthy and gleamed with the sweat of the battle. He wore a slight mustache and wispy beard in keeping with the upper Asian bent of his appearance, but even his stride bespoke power. Even John had to admit reluctantly that the bearing and manner of the Winter King, enemy though he was, exuded a regal nobility that demanded attention, if not respect.

Also, disturbingly, the Winter King cast no shadow.

Still, the most distinguishing characteristic of his appearance was his right hand—or rather, his lack of it. Where his hand should have been was a gleaming steel brace that ended in a sharp, curved hook.

The Winter King stepped across to the deck of the *Indigo Dragon* and surveyed his captives. Aven spit at him, hitting him on the cheek.

He drew his left hand across his face, wiping off the spittle, then licked it, much to the disgust of the companions.

"Not the reception I'd hoped for—but not unexpected, either."

His voice was vaguely European, with an accent that was difficult to place. The inflections and tone seemed to be equal parts British and Roman, in the old sense of the term. Nevertheless, the Winter King spoke with a timbre of authority that would brook no opposition.

"You sailed with the Indian, didn't you?" he asked Aven, almost casually. "His first mate, as I recall. You should have stayed with him. Better for you that you had."

"He escaped you, didn't he?" said Aven.

An almost imperceptible sheen of anger flashed across the Winter King's features. "For the moment. But there will be a reckoning, I think, in the future. It was my mistake to engage the *Yellow Dragon* in combat—the delay it caused was just long enough that I missed returning to Paralon and the Council, else I would be your king now."

"Not bloody likely," said Bert. "You should have built a better Parliament."

The Winter King moved on to Bert, smiling in what was almost an expression of old camaraderie. "Ah, yes—my old friend the Far Traveler."

"We are not friends," said Bert.

"Too true," said the Winter King. "Thank you for pointing it out." He moved again to face John, Jack, and Charles. "And who might you three be? More Caretakers drafted from the Children of Adam and Eve?"

"I'm the Caretaker," John said quickly. "They're just friends of mine."

"So noble," said the Winter King, "to try to draw attention to yourself. Not that it will help them, mind you, but a noble effort, nonetheless. And you," he continued, turning to Bug. "What are you?"

"I'm his squire," Bug said, nodding at John.

The Winter King's eyes widened in surprise. "His squire?"

"Yes," said Bug. "But I plan to become a knight."

"Really? Have you any knightly training?"

"I thought I killed a dragon once," said Bug, "but I recently found out I was mistaken. So, no, not really. But I think I'd be good at it, and I'm getting much better with a sword, so you should let us go now, before Sir John and I have to get really upset and take you and your crew prisoner."

"Oh, ho, ho!" The Winter King laughed. "I think I like this one best. He has more mettle than the rest of you put together."

He turned back to John. "You are outnumbered, outgunned, and outmaneuvered. And I can kill you all with a word. But you know what I really want."

"Yes," John said.

"Oh, my boy . . . ," said Bert.

"It's all right, Bert," said John. "If we give him what he wants, he won't hurt any of us. Isn't that right?"

"I said no such thing," replied the Winter King. "But there's no question of what will happen if you fail to cooperate."

John nodded. "It's in the cabin, wrapped in oilcloth, inside a buckled leather bag."

Aven hissed something unintelligible and looked away. Charles and Bert visibly drooped, and Jack stared straight ahead, focused on the *Black Dragon*. Only Bug seemed to act as if John had done the right thing—and in truth, done the only thing he *could* do.

One of the Shadow-Born moved swiftly through the cabin door and emerged a moment later with the oilcloth-bound parcel, which it handed to the Winter King.

"The *Imaginarium Geographica*," the Winter King murmured with what was almost a purr as he stroked the oilcloth. "Magnificent. There are countless wonders to be found in this book, if you but know how to discern them—but you don't, do you? Otherwise, I would never have been able to catch up to you."

John's face burned with shame, but he remained silent.

"I think our business here is almost concluded," said the Winter King, "save for one or two loose threads."

He gestured with his hook, and a clutch of Wendigo brought

a whining, struggling figure across from the *Black Dragon*. They thrust him to the deck alongside the companions, and when he lifted his head, they all gasped with the shock of recognition.

It was the Steward of Paralon.

"Please!" the Steward begged. "You have to help me!"

"Is he asking us, or asking him?" Charles said to Bert. "Because I'm not feeling very charitably toward him right now."

The Steward overheard the whisper and threw himself to the deck, wailing.

"I don't have any further need of you, Magwich," the Winter King said to the prostrate man. "But another may come with me, if he wishes." He had moved down the line of companions and was now standing directly in front of Jack.

"What?" said Jack. "Me?"

"You," said the Winter King. "In our earlier encounter, I saw enough to realize that it was due to your ingenuity that the *Indigo Dragon* escaped. And in our battle just concluded, you again proved yourself to be resourceful, courageous, and a more than worthy adversary."

"Pfft," said Aven. "You can't be serious."

"I am," said the Winter King, who had not taken his eyes off Jack. "Not all of my servants are Shadow-Born. Some of them— the greatest of them—have chosen to seize greatness, to forge their own path. . . ."

"Their own path as your lackeys, you mean," said Bert.

"Keep a civil tongue, Far Traveler," the Winter King retorted. "As I recall, you have been less than successful with your own pro- tégés. They seem to either quit on you or come into the job with half a heart.

"Be honest with yourself—you define yourself as 'good,' and me as 'evil,' but it seems to be my followers and not your own who live by the courage of their convictions."

"Is that why you had to kill the kings and queens of the Parliament," Bert said, "and replace them with clockwork constructs?"

The Winter King shot a poisonous glance at the cowering Steward. "Those toys were not meant to engage in debate, much less function indefinitely," he said, "just to keep a semblance of order until I could assume my place on the Silver Throne. But you are mistaken about one thing—I didn't kill the kings and queens. They continue to serve—merely in a different capacity."

He gestured with his hook, and the two Shadow-Born removed their hoods. Both Aven and Bert gasped in recognition.

"The King of Hearts," Bert began.

"And the King of Spades," finished Aven.

On the *Black Dragon*, the other Shadow-Born also removed their hoods, and a nod from Bert confirmed that they were the other two kings, Clubs and Diamonds.

"They wouldn't join you, so you stole their spirits and compelled them to serve you," said Bert.

"The exceptions that prove the rule." The Winter King shrugged. "It makes the others who do that much more determined not to disappoint me.

"Still, they are merely servants, and as powerful as they are, not always as useful as the Wendigo, who have more . . ."

"Life?" said John.

"I was going to say, 'substance,'" said the Winter King, "but yes, life. Which is what I'm offering to young Jack: life eternal. The chance to never grow old. Willingly cast aside that which makes you human, and weak—set aside your spirit, and become truly Shadowless, and you will discover a power that makes you greater than any king."

He looked again at Jack. "So what's it to be? I know you are conflicted, but that's what life is—the choices you make, and the consequences they bring. Do you want to become a pirate king, and take a path of adventure with me? Or do you want to stay with this broken-down old vagabond and become one of his lost boys, spending your days entombed in stacks of dusty books?"

"I—I have to think about this," said Jack.

"Jack!" Charles hissed. "You can't possibly be considering . . . He—he murdered the professor!"

"Jack," said Aven, an uncommon sincerity in her voice, and oddly, a gentleness, too. "Please. Don't listen to him. You're better than he is—you know this."

Jack looked at the earnest, pleading faces of his companions, then drew himself up and looked at the Winter King. "Thanks anyway. But I can't go with you."

The Winter King looked at Jack and stroked his chin with the gleaming hook, considering. Suddenly he moved closer, and Jack puffed up his chest in what he hoped looked more like a gesture of defiance than fear.

Jack could feel the hot breath of their captor as the Winter King leaned in and began to whisper in his ear. He spoke too quietly for the others to hear, and Jack's face gave no hint as to the content of the words.

A moment later, the Winter King straightened, spun about on his heel, and crossed back to the deck of the *Black Dragon*.

One of the Shadow-Born gestured at the *Indigo Dragon* and their captives, indicating a question as to what to do with them.

The Winter King hefted the parcel in his hand and snorted, giving the order without even a cursory backward glance.

"Break it. Break it into pieces, and let them drown."

CHAPTER TEN
MAROONED

"WELL, THIS IS a fine how-do-you-do," said Charles. "Although I think I may welcome being drowned if I don't have to listen to this wailing."

The Steward of Paralon had taken up with a high-pitched keening, punctuated by frequent snorts and gasps. Charles kicked him, which only made the terrified man wail louder.

"Leave him be," said John. "He's useless anyway."

"It's your own fault," Bug said to the Steward. "You're not a Shadow-Born, or a Shadowless. You're not even a Wendigo. Didn't you think your master might someday just get rid of you?"

"That's pathetic," said Charles. "He's not even the Devil's right-hand man. He's just the lackey who runs to the corner to buy him tobacco."

The Steward took a handkerchief from his pocket and blew his nose. "I'm just a contract worker—I don't deserve to be treated this way."

"Bloody hell," said Charles. "Your hands are free, you fool! Untie the rest of us!"

"Don't want to," sniffed the Steward. "You'll hit me, or pummel me, or something equally nasty. And I think, all things considered, I'd rather just drown without taking a beating first."

"You idiot," said Aven. "Can't you swim?"

"No."

"If we're free, none of us will drown—including you!" The others all nodded enthusiastically, each of them keeping a watchful eye on the departing *Black Dragon*.

"Promise?" said the Steward, looking warily at Charles.

"I promise," said Charles. "Untie us, and there will be no pummeling until we're all safe on dry land."

"Okay," said the Steward. "Now, if I can just get that in writing . . ."

Charles screamed and kicked Magwich in the head. The Steward of Paralon dropped to the deck, out cold.

"Great," said Jack, as the other ship wheeled about and began speeding toward them. "He was our only chance."

"Sorry, sorry," said Charles. "But can you blame me?"

"Not really," Jack admitted.

"Brace yourselves," said Bert. "Here comes the *Black Dragon*."

The companions had hardly any time to react further before the great black ship had rammed the defenseless *Indigo Dragon*, cracking her in two.

They were thrown violently into the water as the aft section of the ship began to sink almost immediately. The fore was still buoyant, but sinking fast, and more torches were extinguished with each passing moment, plunging the companions into darkness.

The *Black Dragon* had already begun to move away. The Winter King was apparently confident that there would be no recovery for the helpless companions.

His mistake was one that any of them might have made

themselves—he'd underestimated Bug, whose hands were free instants after they hit the water.

Swimming swiftly among them, Bug freed first John, then Aven, who untied her father and Jack. Jack freed Charles, who then realized he'd have to take responsibility for the unconscious Steward, lest he drown.

"Drat," said Charles.

Jack and Aven swam away from the sinking pieces of the boat, while John swam toward it, disappearing into the cabin moments before it was completely submerged. He reappeared moments later. "Got my coat," he said, smiling broadly.

"You really need to readjust your priorities," said Charles.

"Look who's talking," Jack said, pointing at the hapless Steward, who was beginning to awaken.

"Point taken," said Charles.

Bert was faring the worst. He had more clothes on than the rest of them—clothes that had become immediately waterlogged.

"I've got you," said Bug, lending assistance to the older man.

"Thank you," said Bert. "How did you manage to free yourself, anyway?"

Bug grinned. "Easy. Swimming lessons on Avalon. The Morgaine used to tie my hands behind my back every morning and make the Green Knight row me to the middle of the pond, where I'd have to free myself and swim back."

"That's terrible," said Bert,

"Naw," said Bug. "The only really hard part was getting out of the burlap bag."

"Jack!" Aven shouted. "John needs your help!"

John was indeed in trouble. He was treading water, but he

had his arms wrapped around his coat, which he'd folded into a bundle that he was clutching tightly to his chest. This position made it all but impossible to keep his face above water.

With strong, sure strokes, Jack reached his companion in seconds and flipped him over into a dead man's carry. John refused to relinquish his coat and continued swallowing water for his trouble.

"I think he's gone into some kind of shock again," said Jack. "He's not going to be much help, and I can't carry us both for very long."

"I don't think you'll have to," said Bert, pointing into the moonlit night sky. "Look."

High above them, circling, observing, were several immense birds, each with a wingspan as broad as the deck of the *Indigo Dragon*.

"Are they birds?" said Charles. "I've never seen the like."

"Bloody big birds," said Jack.

"Steady on, lads," said Bert. "They're friends—I think," he added quickly.

Seven great crimson and silver cranes glided down at an angle crosscurrent to the breeze, and one by one picked up each of the companions in tapered claws that were enormously strong. The rescue complete, the great avians turned and flew swiftly toward the southern horizon, while below, the last remnants of what had been the *Indigo Dragon* sank beneath the waves.

The companions awoke one by one to find themselves on a beach, both cooled and drying from a gentle breeze that blew from the south. There was no sign of the giant birds that had rescued them from the water.

They were spread across some fifty yards of sand, well away

from the high-water mark. Their rescuers had obviously intended for them to be safely up out of harm's way, where they could sleep without fear of being pulled back in by the receding tide.

John was lying outstretched, drowsing, his head resting on his jacket and his face pointed toward the rising sun.

Bert was several yards to his right, snoring peacefully, and had even somehow managed to retain his hat.

A bit farther on to the left, and much to Jack's chagrin, Aven had fallen asleep with her head nestled in the crook of Bug's arm, while in between, he and Charles were clustered with the Steward of Paralon, who was watching them from half-closed eyes.

"All right, you git," said Charles, sitting upright and grabbing the Steward by the lapels. "Awake is awake and asleep is asleep, but I'll bash your head in with a coconut before I'll let you spy on us for that king of yours."

At this the Steward set up such a mournful howling that everyone was soon awake, and even feeling a bit sympathetic.

"You've put quite a scare into him, Charles," said John, yawning, "but can't you get him to shut up?"

"What was it the Winter King called him?" said Jack. "Maggot?"

"Magwich, if you please," sniffed the Steward. "It's Magwich. And I was his prisoner, just as you were."

Aven had awakened and blinked sleepily a few times before realizing what position she'd ended up in and with whom. Quickly she and Bug stood up and stretched, hoping the others wouldn't notice that they were both blushing.

"So, uh, how did you sleep?" asked Bug.

"I'm wet," said Aven. "I hate sleeping in wet clothes."

"You look good in wet clothes," Bug offered.

"Oh, shut up," said Aven, unable to hide the quick grin as she spoke. She walked over to the loose circle that was forming around the Steward. "What is this idiot yammering about?"

"He claims he was a prisoner of the Winter King," said Charles. "Which doesn't explain why he wasn't tied up like the rest of us. Nor does it explain the comment about having been 'useful.'"

"What are you all looking at me for?" said Magwich. "I was his hostage, not his collaborator!"

"Mmm-hmm," said John. "As if we're likely to believe *you*."

"He used me!" Magwich wailed. "I didn't want to do it, but he made me!"

"It is possible," John admitted. "After all, Tummeler and the animals were used in just that way too."

Bert nodded. "There's would be little point in hiding his allegiance to the Winter King now," he said. "Whatever has gone before, it's obvious he was intended to die along with the rest of us."

"Sure," said Aven, "because the Winter King no longer needed him. He said as much. I say we just kill him and spare ourselves the trouble of watching our backs."

"Seconded," said Charles.

"Kind of bloodthirsty, don't you think, Charles?" said John.

"I'm an editor," said Charles. "I have to make decisions like that all the time."

"You should be looking to that one, if you want to root out a traitor," the Steward said, pointing an accusing finger at Jack. "The Winter King obviously had something particular to say to *him*."

"I don't even understand what he whispered to me," Jack retorted. "And you saw the rest—he asked me to join him, and I told him no."

"But you thought about it," Magwich said.

"I didn't see you tied up," Jack retorted. "Your hands were free. If it was so bad aboard the *Black Dragon*, why didn't you just throw yourself overboard?"

"I hate the water," said Magwich. "Can't swim. Hate all this business with ships. If the Winter King hadn't needed me for that little deception at Paralon, he could just as well have left me in London—and believe me, I'd have been much better off."

"Speaking of Paralon, you seemed more like an advocate of his than a hostage," said Charles. "And . . . wait. Did you say you were in London?"

"I knew it!" John exclaimed, jostling Charles aside and coming nose-to-nose with Magwich. "I knew I'd seen you before."

He turned to his companions. "He *was* in London—and Staffordshire before that. He was on the train with me, and I saw him again at the docks, with the Wendigo."

Another puzzle piece fell into place. "You were the one who led the Wendigo to the club," John said to the cowering Magwich. "We had to flee for our lives, and it was all your fault!"

The terrified Steward stammered in protest. "Not to kill you! Just to find the book! That's all! All he ever wanted was the book!"

"Did you also lead him to the professor?" said Bert. "Did you help him murder my friend?"

"Oh, no," Magwich said with some relief. "I was only supposed to lead him to this one—John—but he didn't have the *Geographica* either. You all managed to escape from him anyway, so what's the problem?"

John turned to Charles. "I've changed my mind," he said. "Go ahead and kill him."

Magwich shrieked again and started to run until he realized John's suggestion wasn't intended to be taken seriously—mostly, anyway.

"None of this matters," said Aven, "because he got what he was looking for. The Winter King has the *Imaginarium Geographica.*"

"No, he doesn't," said John. He took his bundled jacket from underneath his head and began to unfold it.

"If you hadn't been so determined not to lose your coat," said Jack, "I wouldn't have had to save you, you know."

"Don't think I'm not grateful, but wasn't the coat I was trying to save," John retorted. "It was what I'd wrapped inside."

John pulled open the flaps to reveal a slightly damp but otherwise unharmed *Imaginarium Geographica.*

All of the companions crowded around him with exclamations of surprise and astonished whoops, save for Magwich, who stood a distance away, sniffing in disdain at the camaraderie of the others.

"My lad," Bert said, beaming, "today you have done the role of Caretaker proud."

"Bravo, John," said Charles.

"I'll admit, I'm impressed," said Aven. "But if you had the *Geographica,* what was wrapped in the oilcloth the Winter King stole?"

Jack realized it before the others, and convulsed with laughter. "Of course! It was the right shape, the right size . . ."

John grinned. "I thought it might buy us a few minutes, but I never really expected it to work.

"I gave him Tummeler's recipe book."

◆   ◆   ◆

"So for the moment," Charles said, "we appear to have regained the upper hand, at least with regard to what he wants and what we have. But the question still remains: Why does the Winter King want the *Geographica* so badly that he would destroy the Archipelago to get his hands on it?"

As one, the companions all turned to look at Magwich, who sighed in resignation.

"The Ring of Power," Magwich said sullenly. "He needs the *Geographica* to find the High King's ring."

The companions exchanged astonished looks, and Charles crouched down in front of the pouting Steward of Paralon. "What does he need with the High King's ring?" he asked. "What makes it so important?"

"The dragons," said Magwich. "It says as much inside your book there. The proper summoning, read by the High King while wielding the Ring of Power, calls the dragons."

"So *that* is the real power of the Silver Throne," said Bert. "The ability to control the dragons *would* be the ability to control the border between the worlds, if not the entirety of the Archipelago itself."

"Precisely." Magwich nodded. "The Winter King believes the location of the ring is hidden within the *Geographica*. Used together with the summoning, he thinks the dragons would return to the service of the new High King—himself."

"Well, he's out of luck twice then," said Jack, tossing a bauble from his vest pocket into the air and then catching it again, "because I have the High King's ring right here."

"What?" Magwich shrieked, abruptly standing up. "You mean you've had it all along?"

"Since that mess at Paralon," said Jack. "We were given it by—"

"By an ally of the old king," Bert interjected. "But remember—we were warned that it may not be what we think it is."

"I wonder if that's why the Winter King tried so hard to convince you to join him," Charles said to Jack. "Maybe he sensed that you had it."

"Not likely," said Aven. "He thought he was taking the *Geographica*. Why leave the ring behind when that was part of the reason he needed the *Geographica* to begin with?"

"I think I've found the summoning he's talking about," said John, who'd been leafing through the *Geographica*. "It does say something about a 'Ring of Power,' and calling on the dragons, but it's in some combination of Latin and Egyptian. It's going to take a while to work it out."

"What else is new?" said Aven. "At least you kept him from getting the atlas," she finished in what was practically a compliment. "You're not nearly as stupid as I thought you were."

"Thanks a lot," said John.

"Not to interrupt your discussion, Sir John," said Bug, who'd been observing the proceedings from a distance, "but a very, very large cat is watching us."

An immense golden creature, mane flowing to and fro with the breeze, was sitting just inside the treeline about thirty feet away. It watched them with a lazy, disinterested expression, as if it came across marooned travelers every other day.

"That's not a cat," Jack said, his voice as still as he could manage. "That's a lion."

"Oh!" Bug said. "The Green Knight told me about them. He said lions were called Kings of the Forest."

Before any of the companions could stop him, Bug strode quickly toward the great cat, hand outstretched. Instead of turning the boy into an opportune snack, as they half expected would happen, the lion allowed Bug to stroke its mane, then scratch behind its ears. A low rumbling sound began to emanate from the beast, and after a moment they realized it was purring.

"I hit my head," said Charles. "I hit my head in the wreck, and I'm seeing things again."

The companions' attention had been so drawn by the lion that they only just realized it was not alone. Throughout the woods, under trees and in them, were hundreds of cats, and they were all watching the arrivals on the beach.

"I can't tell if we're in trouble or not," said Charles, "but I'm glad Bug made friends with the big one first."

"Cats . . . ," Bert mused. "An island of cats . . . That sounds very familiar to me. John? May we consult the *Geographica?*"

"Sure."

They opened the book, and John handed it to Bert. "I know it's here somewhere," said Bert. "It'll be among the pages in the back, near the map to the Cartographer's island—if I'm right, this is one of the elder islands."

As they looked, the others tried not to notice the fact that the cats came in all shapes and sizes—including more than a few in the predator class, a fact that Jack mentioned to Charles.

"Aren't all cats predators, though?" Charles responded.

"Probably," said Jack. "But this is the first time I've ever wondered if I classified as *prey*."

After a few minutes, Bert thumped a triumphant fist on an open page. "There! I knew it!"

He summoned the others to where he and John were examining the *Geographica* and pointed to a map of a roughly oval-shaped island. "I think I know where we are," he began.

"You are on our home," a voice, amused but welcoming, said from the trees. "Uninvited, but welcome nonetheless."

The cats parted like clouds of dust in a monsoon, and an ancient man, gray-haired and white-bearded, moved through them to the beach. He was carrying a gnarled staff, which spouted a flame from its top. Seven other men, the youngest of whom seemed of an age with Bug and Jack, were also approaching from the treeline.

"I am Ordo Maas," said the ancient man. "Welcome to Byblos."

It was a tradition common throughout cultures of the world to revere the elders of a society, and since the days of Methuselah, it had simply been assumed that the older a person was, the more life experience they'd had: Therefore, they were probably wiser than anyone else.

By that measure, John surmised, Ordo Maas might have been wiser than every other living being on Earth. He emanated the aura of such advanced age that one could suppose he might have predated the great Mesopotamian cities of antiquity, the Chinese Empire, and several of the lesser mountain ranges like the Andes and the Alps (being merely a contemporary of the Himalayas). At the very least, he was probably wiser than anyone John had ever met, or was likely to meet, short of Adam himself.

If there had been any question as to whether or not Ordo Maas deserved a large measure of respect, it was obliterated by Bert's response to his appearance. He whipped off his hat and threw himself prostrate on the ground in front of the ancient man. Even Samaranth had not received this measure of outright worshipfulness.

Aven hesitated only an instant before dropping to a slightly more dignified kneeling position, which Jack, John, Charles, and Bug quickly emulated. Only Magwich remained standing, but he seemed to be frightened out of his wits and was hunched over, trembling (which Charles figured was just as good).

Ordo Maas frowned and covered his eyes. "This is why I gave up being a king," he said, shaking his head. "Everyone wants to waste time bowing, and scraping, and 'if-you-please'-ing, and at my age, that just won't do. Please," he finished, tapping Bert with the torch-topped staff he was holding, "do get up."

"My apologies," said Bert. "I didn't think it would hurt to start with the formalities, just in case."

"Formalities?" said John.

"This is the island of Byblos, my boy," Bert said. "I'd heard of it since the first day I became a Caretaker."

"Begging your pardon," said Charles, "but we've been to Paralon, and as impressive islands go, it's a pretty hard act to follow."

"Paralon?" said Ordo Maas. "Tell me, how is my good friend Mr. Tummeler? Is he still writing books?"

"You know Tummeler?" said Charles.

"Very well," said Ordo Maas. "I know all of the Children of the Earth."

"How is that?"

"Because," said the eldest of the seven men accompanying Ordo Maas, "all of the Children of the Earth—the animals—are descended from those he brought here, thousands of years ago."

"Yes," said Bert. "That's what I was trying to say. While there were wilder lands, occupied by creatures that were the precursors of the other races scattered throughout the islands, the true beginning of the Archipelago was here, on the island of Byblos. What Samaranth is to the dragons, Ordo Maas is to men."

"Well, now I really feel old," said Ordo Maas. "Raising the animals was easy—teaching them to speak was much harder."

"In that case," said Charles, "I'm very pleased to meet you indeed."

"The feeling is mutual," said Ordo Maas. "Please," he continued, gesturing with the staff toward the slight path in the woods from which they had come, "let us repair to my home, and you may rest, and sup. And as we walk, you can tell me about what my friend Tummeler has been up to."

CHAPTER ELEVEN
THE SHIPBUILDER

ORDO MAAS AND the seven men—all his sons—led the companions through the thickly forested trail to a small compound of pale-wooded cottages in the center of the island, trailed by cats all the while.

"Interesting homes," said John. "Were they made of wood from another part of the island? It doesn't look like any from the trees we passed."

"Our original ship was quite large," said Ordo Maas, "and we never expected to use it again, not in the same manner we originally did. So we used the timbers from its hull to build our homes, and one or two other useful things."

"That's an understatement," said Bert, "if the rest of the legend of Byblos is true."

"There are lots of legends," said Ordo Maas, "but yes. What you've heard is true."

"What are you talking about?" said John.

"He built the ships," said the youngest son. "All of them."

"Hap," Ordo Maas chided. "Do not be boastful."

"Ships?" said Charles. "You mean the Dragonships, don't you? Did you really build them?"

Ordo Maas nodded, a small smile playing at the corners of his mouth.

"I, and my children."

"Your sons?" said John.

"I have many children, but these seven are those who helped me, in the beginning, to build the first of what you call the Dragonships, yes."

The companions (plus Magwich) were shown to an expansive room in the largest cottage, where they sat on overstuffed cushions scattered across the floor. Jack noticed that the cushions smelled slightly of livestock—a thought that went with the fact that the broad double doors were large enough to admit a horse, or more likely, a lion.

The house was plain, but in a manner that was simple rather than drab. Ordo Maas's sons served them cups of hot tea and a platter of bread thick with pepper, which they needed little encouragement to devour. They noticed that dozens of saucers of tea—several of which were already being attended to by the cats that had followed them—had also been set along the walls.

The companions were curious as to what Ordo Maas would say about the Dragonships, but they held back from asking for details while their host was so graciously serving them. And to be honest, they were grateful for the respite and sustenance, stretching luxuriously on the cushions and drinking a large quantity of tea.

Once the companions had sated their hunger and thirst, the dishes had all been cleared away, and everyone was comfortably settled, Ordo Maas began his tale.

◆   ◆   ◆

"A very, very long time ago, when this world and your own were much younger, and not so different, the boundaries between them were as gossamer, and could be freely passed.

"I traveled to the lands herein often, most frequently to those islands now called the Drowned Lands, but then, we lived in *your* world—"

"Where father was a very wise king," interjected Hap.

"Where I was already very old," Ordo Maas continued, "and was relied on to remember things that others had forgotten. I discovered that the world would soon be engulfed in a cataclysm. It would be covered in water, in a great flood that would last for a year, and many of the empires that then existed would be destroyed.

"I was mocked by the other elders and forbidden to reveal my beliefs to any over whom we ruled, nor to take steps to protect myself and my beloved wife. So, under the cover of darkness, we fled to a vast desert, and it was there that she and I began our family. And together, my sons and I started to build a great ship. It took us many years, but finally, it was complete, and we started to gather into it all the things that would be needed to rebuild the world."

"This sounds very familiar," said Jack.

Charles nudged him. "Don't interrupt. Keep good form, Jack."

"It should sound familiar," said Ordo Maas. "The gods have been destroying mankind by flood since time began. It was necessary until the point that men had learned enough to begin destroying themselves all on their own.

"To begin on the paths of the gods, one must first perfect one's weaknesses.

"When the ship, which we called the ark, was complete, we

took into it the power of the gods, which had been stolen from them by my father, to be given to me, so that when we once more emerged into the world, we would begin with one of their strengths."

Ordo Maas gestured with his staff, and the flame danced with movement. "He brought it from the home of the gods with his own hands, and ever since, it has never left mine," he said. "And, when someday I must pass, as all things do, into the Summer Country, I shall give it on to my own sons."

"We also had with us one other object of power, the last great gift of our gods—given, we believed, to aid us in rebuilding the world. But it was a burden as much as a gift, and more than one man—or woman—could be expected to bear.

"As I was given Fire, so that we could make tools, so was my wife given a gift: a great kettle of iron, emblazoned with the symbols of Creation, lidded with the shield of Perseus, and sealed with wax.

"We were told that within the kettle were the Talents of Man—everything necessary for the world to be reborn when the great waters of the flood receded—and that it must never be opened until the world was prepared. But, believing ourselves to be the equals of the gods, we did not listen. She opened the seal, and the world paid a heavy price—for within were not only the Talents of Man, but all of the Vices as well. All the evils of the world, held captive in the kettle, and freed by a moment's hubris."

He sighed heavily, and one of his sons placed his hands on Ordo Maas's shoulders.

"She was cast from the Archipelago," the ancient man continued, "and the kettle was given into the safekeeping of another. Not," he added, "that we believed such a caution would be a permanent remedy—for it is the mandate of Men to seek after change. Even if that change is not for the better.

"But I digress—I was telling you about the ships," said Ordo Maas. "When the flood had passed, we found ourselves here, on the island we came to call Byblos. Much of the geography of the world had been changed—but the Archipelago had remained largely unaffected by the flood, and we came to realize that it was not truly a part of the world from which we had come. Connected, but not in full.

"The Frontier had protected the lands herein and had barred passage during the flood to all vessels but our own. It was the Flame, you see," he said, pointing to the staff. "It was a living manifestation of divinity, and it was what allowed passage through to the Archipelago.

"In time, as the world began to heal, our children began to cross back and forth, sometimes successfully, others, less so. That was how I realized what it was that had allowed the passages, and I determined that I would try to create another ship that might pass freely throughout any waters in which it was guided.

"In time I came across a shipwreck—a ship from your world, which nevertheless had that touch of divinity. And I rebuilt it, slowly, laboriously, and then made a gift of it to a distant descendant."

"The *Red Dragon*," Bert said. "That was the *Red Dragon*."

"Yes," Ordo Maas said, nodding. "The first of the Dragonships. There had been a masthead sculpted to its prow, which had been battered away in a storm. And so when I remade it, I fashioned it after the protectors of the Archipelago, the bearers of divinity in this world—the dragons.

"It seemed appropriate that those ships that followed after were not constructed wholly new, but were instead rebuilt from ships that had already seen much service—ships that had a soul, so to speak.

"Then, more than a thousand years later, when it seemed that the world was on the edge of destroying itself yet again, a great king came to the Archipelago—Arthur Pendragon.

"Arthur had the ability to command the dragons—the protectors of the Archipelago and guardians of the Frontier—and also had created a great empire in your world. It was an opportunity to reunite the two worlds under a protector who would rule with wisdom and strength. And so with him, and him alone, I shared the secret of the Dragonships that I had created."

"Begging your pardon," said Charles, "but after a buildup like that, I do hope you're going to share it with us, too."

"Their eyes," said Ordo Maas. "The Golden Eyes of the Dragons are what allow passage between the worlds.

"I tell you this now, because you are the Caretakers of the *Imaginarium Geographica*, and as such, would have use of one of the ships—the *Indigo Dragon*, I believe. So how is it that you came to be floundering without her, in the waters near my home?"

"That," said Bert, "is where our story begins."

And, with occasional contributions from the others, Bert told Ordo Maas all that had happened.

"The *Black Dragon*," mused Ordo Maas. "It isn't one of ours. I haven't built any new ships in more than four centuries—not since the *Indigo Dragon*, bless her heart. At present, I am simply a Cat-Herder."

"How can you be a Cat-Herder?" said Jack. "They never come when you call them one at a time, so I don't know how you can control an entire, ah, herd."

"Simple," replied Ordo Maas. "You just have to call them by their true names. Cats are very secretive and reveal their names to but a few—but those who do know may summon them at will. And cats always come when called by their true names."

"Oh, for heaven's sake," said Jack.

"Knowing the true name of a thing gives you power over that thing," said Ordo Maas. "Sometimes a small power, not a great one, but power nonetheless."

"Can you tell us the Winter King's true name?" asked Jack. "That's one fellow I wouldn't mind having a bit of power over."

Ordo Maas shook his head. "I cannot give you the true name of the Winter King. It is one of his greatest secrets."

Jack drooped. "It was worth asking."

"You didn't hesitate in telling us *your* name," said John.

"I have had many names," said Ordo Maas, "and hope to live long enough to add many more."

"It seems strange to have more than one name," said Charles, "much less a true name instead of a false one."

"There are those of your own fellowship who do not go by their true names," said Ordo Maas.

"It's a diminutive," Bert began.

"Not you."

"You see," said Jack, explaining, "I hated my given name, so my brother began calling me—"

"Or you," said Ordo Maas.

He was looking at Bug.

"But," the young man said, stammering, "I've always been called Bug. That's what the Morgaine named me. . . ."

"No," Ordo Maas corrected. "That's what the Morgaine *called* you. You were named before you came to them."

"How do you know that?"

"Because," said Ordo Maas, "this is not the first time you have taken shelter on my island."

"A number of years ago—almost twenty, in fact—my sons were fishing in the southerly waters and came across a small, badly battered boat. In it was a young woman, who was barely older than a child herself.

"Her name was unknown to me, but I knew she was the old King's youngest daughter, and the only one to escape the slaughter at Paralon. She had been at sea for many days and barely clung to life—and when we removed the blanket that was covering her, we discovered why.

"Nursing at her breast, given life by the last few drops of milk her thirst-ravaged body could provide, was a child—an infant boy. And as we lifted him from her arms, the last spark faded from her eyes and she died, having held on to the last, so her son would survive.

"We buried her here, atop the island, and then turned our attentions to the child. There was no family left to claim him, and all that remained to him of his heritage was the medallion he wore around his neck. It read 'Artus.'"

"What did you do with him?" Charles asked, looking around at Ordo Maas's sons.

"Oh, I couldn't care for him here," said Ordo Maas. "Perhaps in years past, when the mother of my children was still here . . . But alas, I am too old, and my sons have too much work to also add the duties of caring for and raising a small child to manhood.

"No, I decided the upbringing of the last heir to the Silver Throne required a more . . . maternal touch. So I took him to someone who could provide that for him. To three someones, to be exact.

"It was someone I knew from your world, who had a spiritual connection to both—called by some the Three Who Are One. I knew her—them—as the Pandora."

It was John who made the connection first. "The Morgaine. You took the child to the Morgaine."

Ordo Maas nodded. "Yes. I suggested that they call him Artus—after all, it was the child's true name. Two agreed with me, but the third wouldn't hear of it."

"Probably Cul," Charles said to Bert. "Very disagreeable, that one."

"She said the child was too small for a proper name like Artus," said Ordo Maas, "so she suggested they just call him Bug."

"Hey," said Bug. "That's *my* name."

The companions turned and looked at their stowaway in stunned silence.

"I don't believe it for a second," said Jack. "You're telling me that this potboy is the heir to the Throne of Paralon?"

"Jack," said Charles. "No need to be mean."

"I'm a squire now," said Bug, "not a potboy."

"Hah!" said Jack. "A squire to whom? To *him*? He's not even a real knight."

"Don't bring me into this," said John.

"Hang on," said Charles. "Bug—ah, Artus—can what he's saying be true?"

Artus shrugged. "I don't know. The Morgaine never said anything about it to me. But the Green Knight said once that I had a great destiny—I always thought he meant that I might someday be a knight."

"Greater than that, lad," said Bert. "You are descended from the blood of Arthur himself—making *you* the true king of the Archipelago."

With that, he bowed deeply, followed in turn by John and Charles. Aven hesitated slightly before bowing herself, but Jack and Magwich refused to do it at all and watched the scene with bewilderment.

"See?" Ordo Maas whispered to Artus. "Once they get started with this sort of thing, they want to just keep doing it."

"Get up, please," said Artus. "I don't think I like you bowing to me—even if I am the heir, I'm not a king. Not yet." He thought a moment, then turned to the old shipbuilder. "That means my grandfather was the king who killed my family. And he would have killed me, too, if he'd been able."

"Yes."

"That makes you very powerful," said Aven. "If an heir is alive to sit on the Silver Throne, then the Winter King is no longer a threat. We have the *Geographica*, a descendant of Arthur, and the Ring of Power. He's lost, plain and simple."

"That's right," said John. "I'd forgotten about the ring. Do you still have it, Jack?"

Reluctantly, Jack took the ring from his pocket and proffered it to a hesitant Artus, who finally took it and placed it on his finger.

"Hey," he said brightly. "It fits."

"There is one more thing to consider," said Ordo Maas. "Having a king, and the trappings of the office, may not be enough to over-come the Winter King. He still possesses a talisman that may yet turn the events in the Archipelago in his favor. And despite all you have done, it is a power you may be unable to defeat."

"What talisman?" said Bert. "He's searching for the *Geographica*, which we have, in order to find the ring, which we also have. How can he possibly be a threat now?"

"He murdered a king before," said Seti, the eldest of Ordo Maas's sons. "He can do so again."

"Yes," said another of the sons, called Amun. "And in the years since, he has amassed great power, conquering many lands with-out the ring or the *Imaginarium Geographica* to help him."

"That's right," John said, crestfallen. "I'd forgotten. He's taken over the Shadowed Lands without being able to control the dragons. At best, we haven't stopped him—we'll just be keeping him from making things worse."

"How has he done it?" said Jack. "Where does his power come from?"

"He has found a way to harness the evil within men," Ordo Maas said. "You have seen them with him on the *Black Dragon*. He calls them Shadow-Born."

"What do you know of the old king, Archibald?" asked Ordo Maas. "Of his rule, and his decline?"

"We know he turned evil," said John, "and murdered his family."

"Essentially," replied Ordo Maas, "but that is not the whole of the story.

"Archibald ruled over the Archipelago during a very tumul-
tuous time in your world. There had been several great conflicts
there, and that upset the balance here. For the first time in a
number of generations, there was unrest in the Archipelago, and
Archibald was bearing the brunt of it.

"He had the best of intentions, right before the fall—but intentions cannot pay the price for the actions that follow. Several times
he called upon his allies from the Four Races, and more than once
on the dragons themselves, to maintain peace. But Archibald
was always seeking after a way to make the peace *permanent*. He
wished for a more compelling force with which to rule his subjects.
And then finally, after many years of searching, he found one.

"He discovered a record of an ancient mythical object that
could draw out the spirits from living men, leaving them as stone,
trapped in a living death.

"Worse, their spirits—their Shadows—would then be compelled to his service. With enough of them, he could create a
deathless army that no force on Earth could defeat."

"I thought he was a good king," said Charles. "It sounds like he
was a villain all along."

"Archibald's intentions were good," said Ordo Maas. "Where
he erred was in believing that he could replace free will with his
own. But he was determined to achieve peace at any cost—and
this talisman was the object that he believed would help him to
do it."

"Something that dangerous would not be unknown," said
Bert. "One of the Caretakers would have known of it, surely? Or
Samaranth?"

"It's well known," said Ordo Maas, "in both this world and

your own. In fact, we have spoken of it here, today, in my house. But no one believed it existed, much less how to use it. It has had many names, but the one by which it is known best comes from those who had it when it was stolen: Pandora's Box."

"The kettle you brought aboard the ark," said John, "which held all the evils of mankind."

"Yes," said Ordo Maas. "It remained on Avalon for centuries until an agent of King Archibald found it and stole it.

"Archibald opened it again and discovered how to use it to create the Shadow-Born; and then he made his great mistake—he attempted to use it to steal the spirits of the dragons, to create the most powerful servants of all."

"I take it that didn't work," said John.

"Not at all," said Ordo Maas. "The dragons were of an age and power equal to that of the box and could not be trapped within it. But in that moment, they saw the king for what he was becoming.

"Samaranth took his ring and declared Archibald no longer worthy to summon the aid of the dragons. And that was when they began to leave the Archipelago.

"Soon after, the king went mad and slaughtered his whole family. None escaped, save for the youngest daughter—young Artus's mother—and Artus himself.

"This was when the Winter King began his rise in the Archipelago. He killed Archibald and took Pandora's Box—and in the years that followed, when one after another of the lands of the Archipelago fell under Shadow, I realized that Pandora's Box was still open, and that he was using it to create an army of Shadow-Born. And thus began his conquest of the Archipelago."

"The Morgaine—or as you called them, the Pandora—are not

easily tricked," said Charles, "and they were able to keep the box hidden and protected for a very long time. How did Archibald's lackey manage to make away with it?"

"An excellent question," said Ordo Maas. "Especially since you're keeping company with the thief."

"What?" said John. "The thief is here?"

In answer, Ordo Maas lifted his gnarled staff and pointed it at Magwich.

CHAPTER TWELVE
THE WHITE DRAGON

"THAT'S RIGHT, THAT'S right," Magwich wailed. "Blame everything bad in the world on the poor Steward."

Jack and Aven stood up and cornered the Steward, who seemed coiled to spring and flee. Resigned, he flopped back onto his cushion and nodded his head.

"Yes, yes," Magwich said. "I took it. I'm not proud of it, you know, being ordered around by someone like Archibald, who was weak—and then having to follow the Winter King, just so that he would spare my life."

"You just go from bad to worse," said Charles. "What kind of man are you?"

"I tell you," said Aven, "if we don't just kill him, sooner or later we're going to regret it."

"You can't kill me!" sputtered Magwich, grasping at Jack's trouser legs. "I'm one of you! A man from the real world! I came here, years ago, with another Caretaker who abandoned me! All I've done since is just try to survive!"

"Which Caretaker?" asked Bert.

"Does it matter?" said Magwich. "I went to a lecture he gave, and he talked me into coming here with him."

"You were an apprentice Caretaker?" said Bert. "I don't believe it!"

"You should," Magwich sniffed. "He even named a character in a book after me, so I couldn't have been as bad as you want to make me out to be."

It hit them all at once. "Dickens," said Bert. "Charles Dickens recruited you."

"Why did he abandon you, if he was training you and even brought you into the Archipelago?" said Jack.

Magwich waved his hands. "A total misunderstanding, I assure you."

"He probably stole something and got caught," said Charles.

"I was never indicted," said Magwich. "But he left me here anyway. I always knew it was a mistake to leave Cambridge."

John slapped his forehead.

Jack looked at Charles. "Don't say it."

"I won't," said Charles. "But I know you're all thinking it too."

"You're the one who told him," Bert said, rising to his feet and pointing at Magwich. "You told the Winter King about the *Geographica*—and the little training you did have from Dickens is how you were able to translate the passage about the Ring of Power and the summoning of the dragons."

"You'd have done the same," said Magwich, "if he was threatening to make you look into the kettle and take your shadow."

"Well, it's clear what we have to do now," said Aven. "We have to find him and close Pandora's Box—or this may never be over."

"Agreed," said John, "especially if the conflict here truly does affect the war in our own world."

"The Morgaine certainly had *you* pegged," said Charles. "So,

Maggot, tell us this, since you're the one who stole it: How do we close the box?"

"You can't," Magwich said. "No man can. Because you would have to look into its abyss, and when you do, you're lost. It cannot be closed."

"We'll cross that bridge when we come to it," said John. "We still have another task to finish first—to destroy the *Imaginarium Geographica.*"

"What?" Magwich and Bert screamed at the same time. "Destroy it?" Bert exclaimed. "But why, my boy?"

"Of course we're still going to destroy it," said John. "By now the Winter King will have realized that he doesn't have the *Geographica* after all—and how long do you think it will be before he has a hundred ships scouring the sea for us?"

"He has a point," said Jack. "The Winter King won't stop until he's found us, and it."

"Samaranth thought it was a good idea to destroy the *Geographica*, however regrettable," said John. "The only reason we have not to is Magwich's word that finding the ring was his sole purpose in searching for it."

"That does it for me," said Charles. "We must find the Cartographer's island and destroy that damned book. After that, we can decide what to do about Shadow-Born and boy kings."

"Before we go anywhere," said Artus, "may I ask a favor?"

"Certainly," said Ordo Maas.

"May I see my mother's grave?"

Together the companions felt a sudden mix of shame and sympathy—they had all been so immersed in talk of legends, and floods, and empires, and ships, that they had overlooked the fact that their friend Bug, young Artus, had just learned everything he'd never known about his family—including the story of the mother who loved him enough to die protecting him.

"Of course, lad," said Ordo Maas. "Please, follow me."

Hor, one of Ordo Maas's younger sons, led the way through a fern-shrouded path to a small clearing above the cottages. Great barkless trees towered above, curving up in odd angles high into the air.

Ordo Maas stopped, pointing into the clearing. "It's there, marked with the seal of Paralon," he said to Artus. "Do you want to go in alone?"

"I'd like Sir John to go with me, if it's okay," he added, casting a quick glance at John.

"Of course," John said. "Lead the way, Artus."

"I'll keep an eye on Maggot," said Charles.

"It's Magwich," said the Steward.

"Right—I keep forgetting," said Charles. "So tell us, how did you get the kettle away from the Morgaine, anyway?"

"It was simple," said Magwich. "American whiskey. Put them right out."

"You got them drunk?" Bert said.

Magwich shrugged. "It was efficient and nonconfrontational. One of them kept fighting it off, though, and I had to give her a backrub to get her to sleep."

"I hope for your sake it was Ceridwen," said Charles, "or Celedriel."

"No," Magwich said with a shudder. "It was Cul, all right. I couldn't get the smell off my hands for months."

◆   ◆   ◆

When Artus and John rejoined them, Bert raised the question of how they would get from Byblos to the Cartographer's island.

"I thought perhaps we might summon those cranes that rescued us," he said. "If they were to carry word to Paralon that we needed a ship, or to my friend Uruk Ko . . ."

"A good thought," said Ordo Maas, "but it would take too long. The Winter King may even now be returning to the waters around Byblos to seek you out. No, if you are to leave, it must be now, and with haste."

"But we need a Dragonship," said Bert. "Anything else would not be able to navigate as surely or as quickly, and there are only the seven Dragonships to be called on."

"No," said Ordo Maas. "There are only seven Dragonships to be called on that you *know* of."

Trailed by dozens of cats, Ordo Maas and his sons led the companions to the northern part of the island, where a great frigate was floating serenely in a small harbor.

"The *White Dragon*," said Ordo Maas with obvious pride. "The last legacy of the great ark."

"Did you anticipate another flood?" asked Charles.

"No," said Ordo Maas. "Then again, neither did any of my friends in the Empty Quarter—but there came a time when they wished they'd had one anyway."

"Hey," said Jack. "It has a rowboat, too."

"It occurred to us when the first great ark sprang a leak," said Ordo Maas. "It took a week to locate, and two days to mend, during which we took in a great deal of water. For a while, it seemed a very real possibility that we would sink—and, the animals notwithstanding, I suddenly wished I'd thought to build a rowboat, just in case of an emergency."

He turned to John and Artus, bowing. "To the Caretaker of the *Imaginarium Geographica*, and the High-King-in-waiting, I present my ship," he said. "Use it as you will, and go forth to seek your destiny."

"We will," said John. "Thank you."

"And remember," said Ordo Maas, "when the time comes, you shall not be alone. There are allegiances greater than any that bind the Winter King and his servants. Allegiances not bound by fear and pain, but by ancient promises of Spirit and Living Will.

"When the time comes, those allegiances will be called upon, and you will not fight alone."

With that he bowed deeply and stepped aside to allow the companions to board the *White Dragon*.

"Come look, lads," said Bert. "Come look, and see a sight such as you have never seen in your lives."

The companions moved to the railing as the *White Dragon* eased out into the channel and looked in the direction Bert was pointing.

High in the center of Byblos was a mountain with a crown. The skeletal remains of a great ark, come to rest atop the mountain thousands of years earlier, threw the spars of its frame high into the air on either side of the peak, framing it as if resting on the brow of a giant. End to end, the ship spanned half the diameter of the island itself and was fully as broad.

It was not hard to imagine that if they had wished it so, Ordo Maas and his family might have also taken with them everything they needed to begin anew after a deluge great enough to cover the Earth.

Everything they needed to restore the peoples of the Earth, and the flora, and the fauna.

A scattering of raindrops hit the deck of the *White Dragon*, a forerunner of the storms that loomed on the horizon—the very horizon toward which they were sailing.

And suddenly, the *White Dragon* felt very small. Very small indeed.

Ordo Maas and his sons watched the ship until it had disappeared in the distance.

"Father," said Amun. "There's one thing I don't understand. If you knew Magwich was their enemy, why did you speak so openly to them in front of him? Why give secrets to one who wished them harm, and may still?"

The ancient shipbuilder chuckled. "You are truly your mother's son. No one else thought to ask.

"Yes, it was a choice that had risks. But to try to talk to the Caretakers in secret might have warned him that I knew the depth of his treachery. And then he would truly have been the Serpent in the Garden, waiting to strike.

"No," he continued, "better that they know him as their enemy, and that *he* know that they know it. Secrecy is the weapon of those like the Winter King—they have power only so long as the secrets are kept."

His sons did not fully understand, but they nodded in agreement, for they believed their father to be wiser than themselves.

"My sons," said Ordo Maas, "I have a request of you.

"There will be a great conflict. Greater perhaps than any we have seen in this world. And those who go to fight against the evil Shadows do so with little hope of survival. They are brave, and their hearts are pure. But they cannot prevail without help, and there is no High King to draw together those who might come to their aid.

"There are those who may help turn the tide, but there is only one way to summon them in time, if at all."

The sons of Ordo Maas did not reply, for they knew what it was their father was asking of them, just as he knew they would not refuse.

"That will take longer than one night," said Sobek. "We will have to remain changed into the day to reach—"

"Yes," said Ordo Maas.

"But if we have not changed back by sunrise . . . ," Aki began.

"Is there no way?" asked Amun. "There was a way, once, to allow the change to be reversed."

"It is lost to us," Ordo Maas said. "It left the Archipelago with your mother, Pyrrha. Should you choose to do this—"

"We will not be able to change back," said Seti, the eldest, his posture resolute. "We will remain as we once were—but still honored to be sons of our true father, Deucalion. And honored to do this thing he asks."

Tears filled the ancient shipbuilder's eyes as he stood in the circle of his sons, all of whom knew what their answer would be, each bowing his head as he met their eyes.

As they nodded their assent, the transformation had already begun. Their necks grew long and tapered, as silver and scarlet feathers began to emerge all across their skin, shivering, shimmering.

One by one, the sons of Ordo Maas turned into cranes, beautiful and elegant, and took flight into the deepening night sky.

◆ ◆ ◆

The experience of sailing in the *White Dragon* was very similar to that of sailing in the *Indigo Dragon*, with a few exceptions. For one, it was a much, much bigger boat. And for another, it was faster.

"I loved the *Indigo Dragon*," Aven said, standing at the great wheel, "but a girl could get used to this kind of vessel. I wonder if Nemo's seen her?"

"We'll make good time, that's certain," said Bert. "What's the word, John? Where in the Archipelago are we?"

John, Charles, and Artus had spread the *Geographica* out on the deck and were charting the course between Byblos and their destination. Jack was busying himself with examining the riggings and sails. No one quite cared what Magwich was up to, and for his part, he didn't care that they didn't care, as long as he could stay as far away from Charles as was physically possible. His head still ached from the earlier kick.

John bit his lip and made another quick notation before replying to Bert's question. "More to the south than I'd hoped, but farther west than I'd expected. Can you keep us about six degrees north by northwest?" he called out to Aven. "That should do the trick."

"No problem."

John put his arm around Bert's shoulders and indicated the path he was plotting among a series of the maps. "The island where the Cartographer can be found is the largest in a chain of islands," he explained. "An archipelago within the Archipelago. They seem to be the remnants of a great volcanic crater that rose up from the ocean floor millennia ago. Eventually, it settled back into itself, or the waters rose, or both, leaving only pieces of the rim remaining as a rough circlet of islands."

"How many are there?" asked Artus.

John looked back down at the *Geographica*. "Almost a dozen," he said. "The one we're looking for is ahead of us in the center—like a pendant on a necklace."

Charles had helped himself to a bag of Tummeler's Leprechaun crackers that had been included with the supplies, and he peered over John's shoulder at the *Geographica* as he munched on them. "What's it called, John?"

"I can't see that the island itself has a name," John replied. "The entire grouping is indicated with a notation that is a mixed-up version of Latin and ancient Greek. It says *Chamenos Liber*."

"A strange name," said Charles. "Does it say why they're called that?"

John leafed through several pages before shaking his head, then looked up at Bert, who shrugged. "I can't say," said Bert. "Stellan may have known, but he never told me. And I can't recall ever reading or hearing about it.

"Remember," he continued, "this is one of the oldest places in the Archipelago, and the Cartographer is the one who created the *Geographica*. If it's not in here to be found out, it may be possible that even *he* does not know."

Having set their course, Aven left the *White Dragon* to her more than able self-corrections and went into the larder to assist Artus with preparing some dinner. Like their meal on Byblos, the foodstuffs were vegetarian in nature: lots of breads and grains, and various compotes and preserves. Still, they were a welcome change of pace from Tummeler's crackers and the stale cheeses favored by the crew of the *Indigo Dragon*.

John continued to examine the *Geographica*, working through the extensive annotations dealing with the Cartographer's island.

"According to this note—if my Italian is reliable enough," he said to himself as much as the others, "the place where we can find the Cartographer is an immense tower called the Keep of Time. Inside is a winding stairway lined with doors. The Cartographer must be behind one of them."

"But it doesn't say which one?" asked Charles.

"No. But there is a caution here not to open any of the doors. I can't quite follow why. . . ."

"I suppose we could just stand at the bottom and bellow his name until he answers," said Artus, appearing at the galley door holding a tray heavily laden with food. "At least, that's how I used to call the Green Knight when he left me at the bottom of the Wishing Well on Avalon."

"They really put you through it, didn't they?" said Charles.

"You have no idea," said Artus. "They claimed it was 'knightly training,' but I think it was mostly to keep me out of the way when they didn't need any work done."

"Why do you call it a Wishing Well?" asked John. "Was it magic of some sort?"

"No," said Artus. "I just call it that because I spent most of my time in it wishing I was someplace else."

John wrapped the *Geographica* in a fresh sheet of oilcloth he'd found in the ship's stores and stowed it securely in the rear cabin. Despite the constancy of the thunderheads on the horizon, the moon was again very bright, making the weather pleasant, and in other circumstances, their simple feast on the deck would have been considered an exceptionally fine midnight picnic.

Jack and Bert joined them for the meal, but other than whining about the lack of marmalade, Magwich showed little interest in eating, asking instead when Aven planned to serve drinks.

The bread knife she threw in response struck the mast next to the Steward's head with a loud *tung*, and Artus quickly jumped to his feet to show Magwich where the water was stored, before Aven started throwing larger, sharper things.

Charles shook his head in wonder. "How did Dickens ever think that someone like Magwich could be a Caretaker?"

Bert shrugged. "He never said anything to me about it. But then, when I met Charles Dickens, he'd already retired and turned the *Geographica* over to Jules, who in turn recruited me."

"It's possible then," said John, "that you were recruited as a Caretaker because Magwich didn't work out."

Bert thought on that a moment, chewing idly on a carroway seed and stroking his mustache. "I don't know if that would be a good thing or a bad thing."

"He's certainly been no end of trouble," said Jack, as Aven agreed with an enthusiastic nod. "When you think about it, he's been a pivotal point for every bad event that's happened: the theft of the kettle; the death of Archibald; the murder of the professor; the sham Council at Paralon. In fact, if it weren't for him, the Winter King wouldn't have been chasing us at all—because he wouldn't know about the *Geographica*."

Suddenly, the *White Dragon* jerked violently, as if struck. Then again. "What the hell?" said Aven. "That shouldn't be happening."

Rising, she bolted for the wheel, which was lurching back and forth as if the ship itself wanted to change course.

"What's wrong with it?" Jack yelled.

"I haven't the faintest idea," Aven shouted back as she wrestled with the wheel. "The ship is fighting our course, as if she wants us to turn around."

Jack ran to the foredeck and quickly scanned the sea with Aven's spyglass. "I can't see anything—no ships, no islands. Not even any debris in the water."

"Could we have lost something?" said Bert. "Maybe someone fell overboard."

John did a quick head count, and a terrible realization came over him.

"Jack," he said, his voice low, "where is Artus?"

The others understood immediately.

Charles rose, glowering. "Where is he?" he said, anger rising in his voice. "Where's Magwich?"

"Worse than that," Jack yelled from the port side. "Where's the rowboat?"

John found his squire in the galley, where Artus lay unconscious and bleeding on the floor.

"He knew," John said, gesturing at Charles. "He knew—and I refused to listen. Forgive me, Artus."

The boy king-in-waiting blinked and slowly sat up. "He hit me—I'm so sorry. . . ."

"Not your fault," said Aven. "It's ours. We should have killed him. I said as much."

"At least we're rid of him," said Charles. "Did he take anything?"

"Not much, as far as I can tell," said Aven. "The rowboat, a few food stores, some water."

"It was planned, then," said Bert. "He knew what he planned to do the minute we set foot on the *White Dragon*, and he saw that rowboat. He planned to escape all along."

"To what end?" said John. "Everyone in the Archipelago hates him."

"The ring!" Jack exclaimed, looking at Artus's hands. "The ring is gone!"

John closed his eyes, and his head dropped. "Oh. Oh, no."

He moved quickly out of the galley and returned a few minutes later, empty-handed. "It's gone," he said. "He took the *Imaginarium Geographica* as well."

"That's why the ship was fighting our course," said Aven. "She knew what he'd done and was trying to warn us."

A quick assessment of the nearby seas bore no trace of Magwich's passage. Whichever direction he had taken the boat, it was impossible to tell. There would be no pursuit.

"Now what?" said Charles. "Should we return to Paralon to consult with Samaranth?"

Aven shook her head. "He already told us all he could," she said. "He made that clear."

"But without the *Geographica*," said Jack, "is there any reason to seek the Cartographer?"

"No one knows more about it than he," said Charles. "Even without it in our possession, he may still be able to tell us something we can use to destroy it. If—when—we find it again."

"It seems," Bert said, "that we have no choice. We must continue forward."

PART FOUR

IN THE KEEP OF TIME

CHAPTER THIRTEEN
THE TOWER

THE COURSE HAD been determined well enough that no further corrections or navigation were necessary—but once again, John felt as if he'd failed them all utterly. Aven was furious and not speaking to anyone, and even Artus was keeping a protracted distance. Only Charles and Bert were conciliatory—to a degree.

"We couldn't have known," said Bert. "We had all the cards, and we thought the game was over—we didn't expect that the Steward was still playing."

"I can't believe I saved him," said Charles.

"What I don't understand," said John, "is why take the *Geographica*, too? He had the Ring of Power. If he planned to take it to the Winter King, or try to sell it, or even try using it himself, then what did he need the *Geographica* for?"

"The summoning," Jack said from the foredeck, keeping his back to them. "He needed it for the summoning of the dragons. The ring alone is not enough—the words must also be spoken. And now he has them both."

Dawn eventually came, passing into morning then afternoon as the companions slept, ate, and generally stayed out of one another's way.

Finally, the *White Dragon* approached a great circular chain of islands just as the sun had begun to set. The islands were gray granite and rose prominently out of the sea like sentinels—which in a fashion they were.

There were no slopes, no low rises to the islands of Chamenos Liber—it was as if columns of stone had dropped from the sky and impaled themselves upon the glassine surface of the ocean.

In the distance the largest of them could be seen faintly through the mists. Aven tipped her head at John, and he nodded. That would be their goal. She had started to turn the ship to steer between the columns when Jack grabbed the wheel and gave it a vicious turn. The *White Dragon* came about, narrowly missing an impact with the nearest island.

"What are you doing, you idiot?" Aven said, incredulous. "I'm doing the steering here."

"Sorry," said Jack. "There was no time to argue with you—but I think it's better that we skirt the smaller islands and approach the large one from the eastern side."

"It's faster and more direct to cut straight through."

"Probably," said Jack, "but I don't think that's mist out there— I think it's steam."

The companions went to the railing and looked out into the center of the circle of islands, and they realized that Jack was right. The mist that obscured their view of the Cartographer's island was contained within the granite pillars.

"I remembered what John had said about these islands once being part of a volcano," said Jack. "I thought it wiser to steer clear, even if we lose time."

"Well done, Jack," said Bert. "It seems as if you're the Caretaker of the *White Dragon*."

"Look," Artus said, pointing. "On the island. That tower . . ." He leaned back, toppling into Charles. "I can't see the top of it."

"The Keep," John said, his voice hushed in the night mists. "The Keep of Time."

The island was nearly a mile across and, unlike its smaller, harsher siblings, was covered with grasses that sloped gently up to the base of the tower. The tower itself was perhaps forty feet in circumference, and it was inset with windows at staggered intervals as it rose, one about every twenty feet. The frame was wood, but the walls were granite. The stone of the tower was very ancient, and of a somewhat lesser gray than that of the islands, as if it were slightly ethereal, or not in the same focus as the ground on which it stood.

Aven steered the *White Dragon* into the shallows where they could clamber off and walk to the pebbled beach that gave way to the grass. Standing on the shore, they looked at one another and realized they had no idea what they were going to do once they were inside. The entire purpose of their ordeals and long journey had been to bring the *Geographica* to the one person who could destroy it—and they had lost the book mere hours before they'd reached their goal.

Expectantly, they all looked to John to lead the way into the tower. He felt like an idiot.

The base of the tower was ringed with open arches that led inside, as if it stood on four massive feet one could walk between. The interior was more brightly lit than could be ascertained from without. A luminosity emanated from the floor, which faded farther up, to be replaced by the light from the windows.

In the center of the floor was a raised circular platform, like a dais. On either side of it were two sets of steps that rose into the tower before curving back into each other in a great braided pattern. At each point where the braid of steps crossed was a door set deep into the stone walls, but they bore no visible hinges or handles. They were simply there.

Jack stepped into the center of the tower. "I can't see the top of it," he said. "It seems endless."

"I couldn't see the top from outside, either," said Charles. "No doubt about it—unless the Cartographer is behind the first door we open, we're in for a bit of a climb."

"Knock on wood that he is, then," said Artus, reaching out his fist to rap on the bottommost door.

Before his hand touched the polished wood, the door swung open. Inside was *outside*—the door didn't open into a room within the tower, as they had every reason to expect, but onto the broad expanse of a mist-laden forest primeval.

"It's a swamp," said Artus.

"More than that," said Bert. "I think it's a doorway into the past—to the dawn of mankind itself."

"Is that an elephant over there?" said Charles.

"That's not an elephant," said Bert, "that's a mammoth."

"A woolly mammoth?" Charles said, incredulous. "You can't be serious."

"It couldn't be a mammoth," said Jack. "They lived in colder climates—on steppes, snowy plateaus, that sort of place. This is a swamp."

"Argue with your own eyes," said Bert. "Mine see a woolly mammoth in a swamp."

"It doesn't appear to be moving," said John. "Look—nothing in here is. It's as if everything were made of stone."

It was true: The leaves on the trees did not stir; the clouds in front of the immense moon did not drift. Even the insects in the air were frozen in place, as if trapped in colorless amber. Until, that is, Artus took a step forward, past the threshold.

The buzzing of the insects was immediate, as was the tang of rotting flesh and, they assumed, mammoth dung.

The flora were swaying gently alongside the great river that lay just past the entrance, as were the fauna. An extraordinarily large head rose from the water and continued to rise, until the neck atop which it rested had grown to more than forty feet in length.

"Is that a sea monster?" said Artus.

"My old teacher, Sir Richard, called them 'dinosaurs,'" said Bert. "Regardless, I think it's time we took our leave of this place—he looks hungry, and I can't run as fast as the rest of you."

Artus quickly stepped back, pulling the door behind him. "Agreed. I don't think the Cartographer's behind this one."

"Right," said John. "Onward and upward it is."

Charles pointed to the twin stairways. "Clockwise or counter-clockwise?"

"Widdershins is always the prudent choice," said Bert. "Counter-clockwise."

Thus agreed, the companions began to climb.

Every few levels, one of them would stop to open a door, each time revealing a different landscape from a different period of time. It was Charles who realized that the scenes were not random, but following a very distinct progression.

"We're moving upward in time," he explained. "Each doorway is opening into a different point in the past. At the bottom, the beginnings of civilization. And as we move up, so do we move forward in time."

"What's at the top, then?" said Aven.

"Good question," said Charles. "We may yet have a chance to find out—as far as I can tell, we haven't even hit the Bronze Age yet."

"One thing about the past," said Bert, "it smells awful. My clothes still reek of mammoth dung."

Jack took the next door, which also swung open at a mere gesture. Inside, a frozen diorama like the others depicted a brutal scene of combat between what Bert claimed were Mongols and ancient Icelandic warriors. There were missing limbs, and the ground was awash in blood.

"I think this one's a 'no' too," said Jack, "but I'd say we're firmly in the Bronze Age now, if we're to judge by those axes they're swinging."

"Uh, Jack?" said Charles.

"Yes?'

"Those huntsmen," Charles said. "They're coming this way."

Jack looked down and realized he'd inadvertently stepped over part of the threshold, unlocking the scenario from its frozen state. He quickly shuffled back—but the huntsmen, scenting fresh prey, and still maddened with bloodlust, were now coming at a full run.

"You can turn it on," said Jack, "but can you turn it off?"

"Shut the door!" the others yelled together, and Jack did, just as a gore-laden bardiche buried itself on the other side.

They held their breath, but heard no further impacts.

"Apparently," said Bert, "closing the door closes the portal."

"Thank God," said Jack.

Just then, a rumbling sound echoed throughout the tower, and the floor seemed to shift beneath their feet. As quickly as it had begun, it stopped.

"What was that?" said John.

"No clue," said Bert. "But it still smells awful in here."

"Yes," said Aven, "it does. But why? That smelly prehistoric doorway was at the bottom of the stairs, and we've been climbing for hours. We have to be several miles high by now—why do we still smell it?"

Jack was looking at the door the huntsmen had just attacked. "Artus? The door you opened below—you did close it, right?"

"I'm almost certain I did," said Artus. "Almost. Certain."

Before Jack could respond, a great mucous-colored maw with rows of sharp teeth rose up between the stairwells and chewed, swallowed, and regurgitated Artus's certainty.

The head and neck of the sea monster trailed downward to a great bulbous body, supported by four enormous flippers that were braced against both stairwells, using them like ladders.

"How did it get through that door?" Artus shouted, startled. "It's too large to fit!"

"Curse it," said Aven. "I left my sword on the ship!"

Jack was casting about for a means of defense. There was nothing to be found—the walls of the keep were bare. Suddenly, he snapped his fingers. "If it came in, it can go out again," said Jack. "John! Go over and below with Charles, and stand ready! Artus! Open a door behind me!"

"Which door?"

"Any! I don't care which! Just be ready!"

The monster had turned its head to focus on Charles, who was the closest. "Well, this is a fine how-do-you-do," said Charles. "I've finally found something big enough to eat Maggot, and he's nowhere around."

"Hey!" Jack yelled at the beast, waving his arms to get its attention. "Over here!"

The sea monster scooped the air with its neck, and came nose-to-nose with the young man. "Damnation," Jack exclaimed as he cocked his arm. "That worked too well."

Jack let fly with his fist and smacked the great beast square in the left eye.

With an enraged roar, the sea monster lunged forward at Jack, who threw himself into the air across the open stairwell. John and Charles caught him by the arms and lifted him safely onto the opposite stair.

The momentum of the sea monster's attack propelled its head and neck through the open doorway, where it caught—impossibly, the beast's body constricted until it fit through the doorway. When it had passed through entirely, Artus slammed the door shut.

"That was very close," he said. "I'm sure this one is closed. Sorry about the other one."

"Bravo, lads!" Bert exclaimed, clapping his hands. "Bravo! Well done!"

"Did you get a look inside the door when he opened it?" asked Charles.

"Yes," Jack said, breathing heavily. "There were Scotsmen—Scotsmen in kilts, maybe sixteenth century."

"Well," said Charles. "A sea monster loose in Scotland. That's going to have some interesting repercussions."

The companions sat on the stairs to catch their collective breath. All of them seemed overjoyed by their narrow escape except for John, who seemed on the verge of tears.

"What's the matter, John?" said Bert. "Chin up—we seem to have a knack for beating the odds."

"Jack has a knack, you mean," John muttered. "No matter what our dilemma, it seems he can always come up with some way to resolve it."

"It seems like I can, doesn't it?" said Jack.

"Bad form, Jack," said Charles. "We're each doing our part. I'm as much to blame as anyone for not keeping a firmer hand on Magwich."

"It's more than Magwich, though," said Jack. "It's a matter of taking action when action is called for. Of just seeing something that needs doing, and doing it. And it seems as if John never does."

John stared at his friends for a moment, then stood and began climbing the stairs. With anxious glances both upward and below, the others followed.

They climbed.

Conserving their breath for the exertion, they climbed in silence that was interrupted only by the strange rumbling that occurred every hour or so.

Charles had started counting levels when they began, lost count after the run-in with the sea monster, started again, and gave up sometime after counting to four hundred.

"I'm starting to see why he removed himself from the affairs of the Archipelago," said Charles. "It takes him a century just to go downstairs to greet the milkman."

"Is it me," said Artus, "or is it growing darker up above?"

Bert looked up and gave a joyful shout. "A ceiling! I see the ceiling! We're almost at the top!"

There were three more landings, and four more doors. The one at the top had no stairs. "The future," said Bert. "Unreachable. That means the next-to-last will be the Cartographer. I'm sure of it."

John, however, had paused at the nearest door below. He was looking at it curiously and sniffing the air.

"What is it, John?" said Aven. "Trouble?"

"No," said John. "Cinnamon."

CHAPTER FOURTEEN
NIGHT PASSAGE

THE CARETAKER OF the *Imaginarium Geographica* had been transported by a smell—and suddenly, he was no longer responsible for the fate of two worlds, or the resolution of a war, or the many failures he felt had become chains around his neck, grown heavier with each passing hour. He was once again merely a student/soldier, whose greatest responsibilities involved reading Old English manuscripts and making sure he didn't leave his rifle in a trench.

John reached out a tentative hand and stroked the air a whisper above the surface of the door.

"John!" Charles exclaimed. "After what just happened below, I can't believe you're going to risk opening another door!"

"Agreed," said Jack. "We should proceed to the last door and find out if the Cartographer really is here. We've wasted enough time on the past—uh, so to speak."

"This one is different," John said. "Can't you smell it?"

Aven moved next to John and sniffed at the air. "Yes, I can. It's a tobacco of some kind."

"A cinnamon tobacco," said John. "A special mix."

"How odd," said Bert, scratching his head. "The only person I ever knew who liked cinnamon tobacco was . . ." His voice trailed off and his eyes widened in surprise. "Open the door, John."

John reached out with a steady hand and pushed. The door swung open effortlessly on silent hinges, and a fresh wafting of cinnamon-scented tobacco smoke drifted across the companions.

Through the door was a tableaux more familiar to them than any other they'd seen in the keep—because most of them, save for Aven and Artus, had been there mere days before.

It was a study, unmistakably British in decor; a library filled with books and a very familiar figure who could not possibly be sitting in his chair, examining centuries-old incunabula with a magnifying glass and calmly puffing away on a large pipe.

Unlike the other tableaux, which required a crossing of the threshold to spur into motion, this setting was already active, as if it had been waiting for someone to open the door and enter the flow. The figure at the desk noticed them through the open door and spoke; the familiar timbre of his voice left no doubt as to who it was sitting at the broad oaken desk.

Professor Sigurdsson gestured to his young protégé to enter and sit. "John, my dear boy. Please, come inside. We have much to discuss, I think.

"Are there others with you, John?" continued the professor, peering through the smoke at the doorway. "It seems I saw someone else outside."

John looked back at Bert, who shook his head. Whatever import this had was meant for John, and John alone. He stepped forward into the study and closed the door behind him. "No, Professor," he said. "Just me."

The professor stood and took John's proffered hand in both of his own, pumping it frenetically. "So happy to see you, John," he said. "Wasn't expecting you for another day or so, given the state of transportation in these troubled times."

"Believe me, Professor," John said, taking a seat opposite his mentor, "I wasn't expecting to see you, either."

It was almost too much to take in. There had barely been enough time to accept the news of the professor's death, much less come to terms with it. The adventure to the Archipelago had begun almost immediately. And since, all his thoughts of the professor had been fleeting and commingled with regret, and sorrow, and an overwhelming sense of failure.

For an instant John considered whether this visit might be the universe's equivalent of sending him to the rector's office for a reprimand, notwithstanding the fact that the rector was dead.

"I do not know why we have been given this strange opportunity," said the professor, "but I am glad we have, for I fear I shall not live out the night."

John started. Was it possible the professor had had a premonition of his own murder?

"It's true," the professor continued, keeping his own counsel as to whether or not he'd answered John's unspoken question. "Strange elements are loose in the city these days, and they involve me far more than I hoped they would at this age. But I have responsibilities, and I must see them through, whatever the cost."

"I got your note, Professor," said John. "What did you need to tell me?"

"I know from your letters that you are filled with fear, young John. Not just because of the war, but fear for your future.

"I know you are conflicted—that you are at a crossroads and

are not sure which path to take. But know this: I chose you for a reason. You have gifts, John. Remarkable gifts. And if you develop them, as I hope I have helped you begin to do, then you may yet go forth to lead an exceptional, extraordinary life."

John was taken aback—whatever he had expected, it was not this. The professor had always been friendly toward him, in the way that a mentor might be, but such directness, especially with such passionate encouragement, was more than unusual.

"I have not been entirely honest with you, John," said the professor. "The studies I have given you—I've pushed you, I know. But it was all for a purpose. A purpose far greater than I have told you. I'm ready to do so now."

John considered what was happening. Had he indeed stepped backward in time, to the night the professor was killed? Or was he experiencing some other kind of spectral visitation, a phenomenon generated by the strange energies of the keep? And if so, what might be the effect of his revealing the future to the professor? Would it change the events of the past? Or merely complicate the present to a worse degree than he already had?

John made his decision.

"You have been training me," he said, "to become a Caretaker."

The professor relaxed. "You know, then. Wonderful, my boy. How did you come to realize it?"

"I've met Bert. And I've seen the *Imaginarium Geographica*. But—"

"Excellent," the professor said, cutting him off. "Then it doesn't matter what happens to me. Not now."

"Of course it matters!" said John. "How can it not?"

Professor Sigurdsson puffed away on his pipe, filling the room with the aromatic smoke.

"Because," he said at length, "we each have our role to play, and mine was to train you, to prepare you for the mantle you've claimed. No more, no less. And I can see that I did it well enough that I can take whatever is to come with a wink and a nod and a how-do-you-do."

"That's the problem," said John. "You did do your part—but I didn't do mine. I was a terrible student, Professor! And I think I've failed you in every way that one can fail."

Professor Sigurdsson started to laugh, then realized that the young man was serious.

"Boys will be boys, John, and the distractions of life are there to color your work, and vice versa. Besides, you were called away to war, and that's bound to have an effect on your studies."

"That's not what I'm talking about," said John. He couldn't quite bring himself to admit all that had gone wrong in the Archipelago: the inability to function as a translator, followed by the actual loss of the *Geographica* itself. "Bert told me what would be expected of me as Caretaker Principia of the *Geographica*, and I'm not sure I'll be able to do it. I'm just not ready."

"Bert had the same concerns, when last we discussed you," admitted the professor. "But I assured him that when called upon, you would rise to the challenge. And that was enough for him. He never questioned it again. Although in truth, he was a supporter of you before I was. I'm a good scholar—but Bert has the imagination. Not many like him. But in you, my boy, he found a kindred spirit.

"Listen to him, John. He'll advise you well, when I'm not able to, and in ways that I cannot. Heed the words of the Caretakers who preceded you, whose wisdom can be found in the *Geographica*, for they have learned lessons you will need to learn yourself. And make note of the things you observe, so that you can pass the knowledge on to those who will come after—for you have joined a grand tradition, my boy. And once you have accepted this, it will remain forever a part of your life.

"Believe in yourself," the professor said, grasping John's hands in his own. "You have all that you need within you. You are strong enough. You are intelligent enough. You have learned more than you need to complete the tasks that lie before you. Now you must overcome the fear that is preventing you from embracing your destiny."

"The fear that I am too weak?" asked John.

"No," said the professor. "The fear that you are too strong."

John was taken aback. "Too strong? How can I be too strong? I've failed at every task I've been given."

"Because of your fear," said the professor. "Not because you were incapable. Our weaknesses are always evident, both to ourselves and to others. But our strengths are hidden until we choose to reveal them—and that is when we are truly tested. When all that we have within is exposed, and we may no longer blame our inadequacies for our failure, but must instead depend upon our strengths to succeed . . . that is when the measure of a man is taken, my boy.

"Believe in yourself. Believe that you were not meant to spend your life in dusty libraries, nor in the battlefields of war, but in doing something greater.

"Believe in yourself, John, and that you have it within you to lead an extraordinary life.

"Just believe, my boy. My dear boy. Believe."

The wind rattled the windows of the study, the first indication that the weather was shifting.

"I think a storm is coming in," said the professor. "I've said what needed saying, and I think it's time for you to go."

As if punctuating his words, a tapping sound had begun down the street outside. The professor rose and clapped his student on the shoulders.

"You'll do fine, my boy," he said as he opened the door, "and remember, whatever happens—I have been, and always shall be, very proud of you."

With that, John stepped out of the study and closed the door.

Once more he found himself standing in the Keep of Time.

"Is something wrong?" asked Aven.

"What do you mean?"

"You just stepped inside," said Charles. "Just this moment. The door closed, then opened again. You weren't gone for but a second or two."

"Impossible," said John. "I've been talking with Professor Sigurdsson for the past half hour."

"The doorways," said Jack. "They manipulate one's perceptions of time. To John, it was half an hour. To us, out here in the keep, it was no time at all."

"What did he say to you, John?" Bert pressed.

John tilted his head, then smiled. "He said we have a job to do."

As he spoke, the familiar rumbling sound started again, and as the companions watched, the floor shifted beneath their feet, and the ceiling expanded, as if the keep were taking in a breath.

"I think the tower just grew," said Charles.

"That makes sense," said Bert. "This is nearly the last room—if all of the other doorways led to points in the past, then it stands to reason that the Cartographer's room, there near the top, is constantly moving into the future, and the one above is *in* the future."

The door they had determined to be the Cartographer's was the only one in the entire keep that had a keyhole. Jack squatted down on his haunches and peered through.

"Spare me your furtiveness," said a clipped, slightly irritated voice from behind the door. "It's very rude to peep through keyholes—either knock down the door or go away."

Jack stood upright. "Do you have a key?"

"I have a thousand keys," said Bert, "but none that would fit this lock."

Charles reached out a hand and pushed. The door didn't budge. "Solid," he said. "Not like any of the others. Maybe we're *meant* to try to knock it down?"

"Perhaps we could pick the lock," Artus said, as he reached out to examine the mechanism. At his touch there was a sharp click, and the door opened with a slight creaking.

"Hmm," said Artus. "Didn't expect *that* to happen."

He pushed it open the rest of the way, and together, the companions entered the room at the top of the stairs.

CHAPTER FIFTEEN

THE CARTOGRAPHER OF LOST PLACES

THE ROOM WAS expansive, but not overly so. The walls—what could be seen of them—were stone, but every available surface was covered with maps. Old ones, new ones, maps topographical, cultural, political, and agricultural. There were maps of the moon, as well as Antarctica, and even maps that were obviously of the Earth, but of a kind that seemed to have coalesced the continents into a single landmass.

There was a scattering of bookshelves, all laden with volumes of what they presumed were more maps. And save for the two pieces immediately in front of them, no other furniture. The rest of the room was filled with globes, surveying equipment, and rolls upon rolls of parchment, all of which served the purpose and namesake of the man they had come to find.

There, in the center of the room, sketching at a carved wooden desk, was the Cartographer of Lost Places. He was sitting on the edge of a high-backed chair with the emblem of a Sun King carved into the top, intensely focused on the task at hand. He would draw a few quick lines with a large quill, before dipping it into an inkwell on the desk while considering what to do next.

He would then make a few more lines, and repeat the entire process.

The Cartographer, for all the legendary dross of rumor and mystique that surrounded him, was rather unremarkable in appearance. He was shortish and stocky, and he wore spectacles that were perched on a bulbous nose. His hair, which was dark save for two streaks of white that grew above his temples, was swept back and flowed to his shoulders.

He wore the scarlet robes that a knight who might have served during the Crusades, or possibly the Inquisition, would have worn. His belt was Roman or Greek, bound tightly over a skirt fashioned from strips of studded leather; and underneath all the rest, he was wrapped in strips of cloth that covered his legs and feet and extended to his wrists.

"Yes?" he said, finally taking notice of his visitors. "If you're here about the annotations, you're early. It's the wrong damned Friday."

With that he resumed his work as if they were not even there.

The clock in the corner ticked away for a few minutes before John finally cleared his throat, loudly. Twice.

The Cartographer rubbed his pen on the blotter and looked up. "Aren't you from the Merchants' Guild? You are Lorenzo de Medici, are you not?"

"Uh, no," said John. "I'm the Caretaker of the *Imaginarium Geographica.*"

The Cartographer's eyes widened, and he dropped his pen. "The Caretaker? Really? How extraordinary."

He hopped out of his chair and gestured for them to enter. "Do come in, come in," the Cartographer said. "I hope you will understand and forgive. I've been under this terrible deadline to complete the maps of Florence Below for the Magnificent—"

"Excuse me," said Charles, "but Lorenzo de Medici died in 1492."

"Did he really?" said the Cartographer. "That would explain his failure to forward the additional reference material. I should have expected he would lose track of everything once he started getting distracted by this 'New World' nonsense."

"Do you mean the Americas?" Jack asked.

"It was called something like that, yes," the Cartographer said. "I'm not sure—I tend not to pay attention to these newish countries until they've had a chance to become better established."

"They've been settled for going on three centuries now," said John.

"Well then, they've got a decent start now, don't they?" said the Cartographer. "Another century or four and they might turn into a place worth taking note of."

"I beg your pardon," said Bert, "but we've come seeking your help."

The Cartographer lifted his spectacles and peered more closely at Bert. "I know you, don't I?" he said matter-of-factly. "You seem familiar to me. Not in a 'blood brothers' way, but more of a 'so-you've-come-to-date-my-daughter' sort of way."

"He was one of the most recent Caretakers," Charles said.

"That's not it," said the Cartographer. "I can't place the face, but the hat is memorable." He snapped his fingers. "That's it— we met in the future. I remember now. That nasty business with the Albinos. How is that dear girl Rose, anyway? Is she well?"

"How can you remember him from the future?" asked John.

"Because those who forget the past are doomed to repeat it," came the reply, "but those who remember the future can plan ahead for the weather."

"What good is it to know the future if you can't remember the past?" said Charles. "It seems impractical."

"You could stand with a little impracticality, I think. Your springs seem to be wound a little too tightly. Besides, the past is over, and if you think on it too closely, you either get lost in the misery of the things done poorly, or you get tangled up patting yourself on the back for the things you did well—which no longer matter, because they're in the past, anyway.

"The future, however, is still to come—and it's always fun to look forward to the good events, as well as have an opportunity to plan for the bad."

"If you know something bad is coming, can't you plan to avoid it or try to do something differently?" said Charles.

"Probably," said the Cartographer, "but then the good events would have no flavor. The joy you find in life is paid for by suffering that comes later, just as sometimes, the suffering is redeemed by a joy unexpected. That's the trade that makes a life worth living.

"Take this tower," he explained, gesturing at the room around them. "An extraordinary place to visit, but you wouldn't necessarily want to live here—especially if you could not leave."

"You're a prisoner here, you mean," said Charles.

"The circumstances that resulted in, shall we say, my compulsory residency here in the Keep of Time were of my own making. And while there are moments when I wish I could regain my freedom, given the opportunity, I would still make the same choices."

"How long have you been here?" asked Jack.

"What year did you say it was?"

"It's March of 1917," said Charles.

"About one thousand five hundred years, give or take," said the Cartographer. "But it's not as if I haven't had plenty to do. It is a large Archipelago, after all, and *someone* has to keep track of it."

"You haven't been outside of this room in over a millennium?" Charles said.

"Oh, it hasn't been easy," said the Cartographer. "It can be excruciating waiting for someone to come along with something interesting to do, or better yet, someone who brings gifts, like Paralon apples, or whiskey from Heather Blether. There are also times I think it would be interesting to have stayed in your world," he finished. "I would like to have seen what Hitler would make of someone like me."

"Who?" said Charles.

"Never mind," said the Cartographer. He turned to John. "As you were saying, you're the Caretaker—so you've either come to have me make additions to the *Geographica*, or you want me to destroy it, which I should state right now is just not an option. I'm not about to shred something I spent nearly two thousand years making. So, where is it?"

"I, ah, I seem to have lost it," John said.

The Cartographer rolled his eyes and sighed. "I should have guessed as much. The simple things can be done solo; catastrophes require an entourage."

He shook his head. "It's the Cervantes Dilemma all over again. But what's done is done, and it can't be helped."

The Cartographer walked briskly back to his desk, took a seat, and, whistling a little tune, began working on another map.

The companions looked at each other, bewildered. Finally, John cleared his throat again.

The Cartographer looked at them. "What, are you still here? Do you need validation?"

"Ah, no," John began, "that is, I mean—"

"Spit it out, boy. I'm a very busy man."

"Well, what are we supposed to do now?" said John.

The Cartographer turned to them and pushed his spectacles up onto his forehead. "I'm sorry if I was oblique. Let me try to summarize things in a more concise manner.

"You need the *Imaginarium Geographica* to avert whatever disaster is looming on the world at large. You are the Caretaker of the *Geographica*. You lost the *Geographica*. Ergo, you and everyone you know, love, care about, or exchange pleasantries with as you gather your mail are about to perish in darkness and misery. I hope that's cleared things up for you."

With that, the Cartographer turned back to his map and continued to draw.

John leaned close to Bert. "What do we do now?" he whispered.

"I haven't the faintest idea," Bert replied. "I've never been here. Maybe you should go back and ask Stellan."

John shook his head. "I don't think that's a good idea. The tower grew, remember? That door may not open into the same time or place."

"Drat," said Bert.

"Pardon me," said the Cartographer, "but just how did you people get in here, anyway?"

"You said to come in," said Jack.

"I said to knock down the door or go away," said the Cartographer, "and I expected you to go away, because that door is impossible to knock down. I know. I spent most of the seventh century trying to do it myself."

"Then how does anyone ever get in?" asked Charles.

"The Caretakers are always permitted to enter with the *Imaginarium Geographica*," said the Cartographer. "It's like a golden ticket that opens doors, or a magic word, like 'Open Sesame.'"

"Actually, that's two words," said Jack, "and the magic word was 'Alakazam.'"

"Don't correct your elders, boy," said the Cartographer. "So, out with it. How did you open the door? You said yourself that you'd lost the *Geographica*, and the only other way to get in is with the permission of the king—and pardon my assessment, but none of you look to be the kingly sort."

"You'd be wrong," said Aven, stepping forward and giving Artus a nudge. "*He* opened the door."

The Cartographer hopped off of his chair and shuffled over to Artus. "Ah," he muttered, looking at the young man, who was reddening under the scrutiny. "Ah, I see it now. That nose is unmistakable—a descendant of Arundel, of the House of Eligure, unless I miss my guess. What do they call you, boy?"

"Um, Bug—Artus, that is."

"Umbugartis—unusual name for a king, but there's no accounting for taste," said the Cartographer. "What may the Cartographer of Lost Places do for King Umbugartis?"

"*There* we go," whispered Charles. "We finally have his attention."

"It's just Artus," said Artus, "and it's my friend Sir John, the Caretaker, who needs your help."

The Cartographer looked warily at John over the top of his glasses. "You again. I thought we'd established that there was nothing to be done, since at the moment you don't seem to be the Caretaker of anything."

Charles and Bert started to come to John's defense, but he cut them off with a gesture and looked squarely at the Cartographer. "That's not true," John said. "I may have lost the Geographica, but that doesn't mean I'm not still the Caretaker."

The Cartographer held his gaze, then folded his arms and sighed. "Continue."

"When I was asked to be the Caretaker of the *Imaginarium Geographica*," said John, "I didn't *want* the job. I wasn't prepared. And I certainly didn't want the responsibility. But then I realized there was no one else who *could* do it—and that a lot of people were counting on me to see it through. And there is only one thing you can do in a situation like that—rise to the challenge and bear whatever must be borne to complete the task."

"Interesting," said the Cartographer, "but I'll point it out again: You don't *have* the *Geographica*. How can you fulfill any obligations as Caretaker?"

"It's about more than the book, isn't it?" said John. "It's about taking care of the lands within it too—and right now, that's all I'm trying to do. Having a book of maps won't do anyone any good if the Archipelago is consumed by war—but if we can find a way to prevent that happening, wouldn't that be more important than whether or not I've been able to safeguard the book?"

"That," said the Cartographer, as his eyes glittered and a smile began to spread across his face, "is the first time I've heard you speak like a *real* Caretaker."

He moved back to his chair and picked up his quill. "I'm sorry I don't have anything for you to sit on," said the Cartographer as he resumed working. "So you'll just have to make do with the seating apparatus the gods gave you. Pull up a piece of floor, and tell me what's been going on in the world."

It took the better part of three hours to recount all that had happened to the companions since they left London up to the point where they reached the tower. It was a silent consensus among them not to mention the incident with the sea monster; and the others left it to John to decide whether or not to mention his encounter with the professor, which he chose not to do.

"Ah, yes. Sigurdsson," said the Cartographer when they mentioned the murder. "Pleasant fellow. Came by to visit several times. Brought cookies. Do you have any cookies?"

"We did have a cookbook," said Charles. "But we gave it away."

"You lot seem to have an awful time holding on to books, don't you?" said the Cartographer. "How on earth did you get picked to be Caretakers?"

"It's a long story," said John. "So, can you help us?"

"I'm a little fuzzy on the details," said the Cartographer. "What exactly is it you think I can do?"

"To be honest, I'm a little unclear on that myself," said John. "We think that Magwich is taking the *Geographica* and the Ring of Power to the Winter King, so that he can summon the dragons—"

"Oh he *has* the Ring of Power, does he?" the Cartographer said, interrupting John. "Wears it around his neck, hey?"

"Uh, no—probably on his finger," said Jack.

"Oh ho—even better," said the Cartographer. "I'd like to see *that.* Hmf," he snorted. "That fellow is in for a surprise, I think.

"Well, if you're bound and determined to try to do something constructive, I suppose I should go ahead and help you. That way, if it all goes badly and the world starts to be consumed in death and fire, you can't go around saying, 'It's the Cartographer's fault. If only he'd helped us, we wouldn't be in this pickle.'"

"Fair enough," said John.

"You don't need the *Geographica*, because there is only one island in the Archipelago where he *might* summon the dragons," the Cartographer said. "That's where you'll find him with his 'ring,' trying to summon dragons, and stealing people's shadows, and whatever else it is evil conquerors do these days."

"We'll still need directions to the island," said John. "The *Geographica*—"

"Young man, I am the Cartographer. I *created* the *Geographica*. It is certainly within my powers to recreate a single, solitary map."

He drew a single tanned sheet of parchment from the stack next to his desk, dipped his pen in the crusted inkwell, and quickly began sketching in light, fluid strokes.

As his hand flew back and forth across the parchment, a picture of the island began to emerge.

"Amazing how he can keep his maps so clean when he makes such a mess of the work," Jack whispered to Charles. "He must have ink up to his elbows."

The Cartographer paused and looked up at John. "Navigational directions?"

John nodded. "Yes, please."

"No, no, no," said the Cartographer. "In what language would you like the navigational directions?"

John shrugged. "Whatever you like."

The Cartographer's head lifted almost imperceptibly. "Very good, young man."

He continued adding lines and notations to the sheet until it seemed complete enough to be fully useful. Finally, he set aside the pen and sat back in his chair, giving the freshly created map one last cursory glance and a nod of satisfaction.

The Cartographer sprinkled drying dust across the ink, rolled up the map, bound it with twine, and handed it to John.

"Remember," he said, taking them all in with his gaze, "there is a price to pay for the choices we make, and my permanent confinement in the Keep of Time is part of the price I've paid for choices of my own. Be wary that the choices you make in the coming days do not limit your own paths into the future. Remember it for what you want it to be, and then do that.

"You will find the one you call the Winter King on the Island at the Edge of the World."

CHAPTER SIXTEEN
FIRE AND FLIGHT

AS THE COMPANIONS descended the staircase, the tower grew three more times. "Walk faster," Bert admonished. "It's literally going to be a longer walk going down than it was coming up." Nevertheless, surprisingly, it took them a considerably shorter time going down.

"Just like sledding," Charles observed. "It's the long walk up that makes the slide down fun."

Unlike their ascent, which had been done in silence, the companions could not resist discussing the strangeness of the Cartographer as they descended.

"I think it was a great waste of time," said Aven, who had taken the lead along with Jack. "Even if we'd had the *Geographica*, it was clear he wouldn't have destroyed it."

"We might have just left it," John said thoughtfully. "For him to safeguard."

"Yes," added Bert. "I doubt the Winter King would have made the effort to go clear to the top."

"Not to mention that he wouldn't have gotten in," said Charles, giving a knowing smile at Artus. "Not without royal blood."

"Or the *Geographica*," Aven put in, "which he *does* have."

"At least we know he can't destroy it either," said John.

Aven stopped. "Isn't that what we wanted?"

"Not now," said John. "Not now that we know the real stakes."

"Meaning what?"

"Meaning that he intends to use both the Ring of Power and the summoning in the *Geographica* to try to call on the dragons," said John, "and I don't think that's all there is to it. Look at what happened above—Artus opened the locked door with a touch, because he is the true heir. Don't you think the same conditions might hold for summoning the dragons as well?"

"That's an excellent deduction, John," said Charles.

"Agreed," said Bert.

"No pressure," Jack said to Artus.

At the bottom of the staircase (where Artus surreptitiously closed a certain door), the companions laughed with relief and gratitude—happy sounds that ceased the moment they stepped free of the keep.

There, silhouetted by the rising sun, they saw a ship equally as large as their own moored next to the *White Dragon*. It was the *Black Dragon*—the Winter King had been searching for them after all.

Aven cursed and cast a venomous look at John. All of his notes in the *Geographica* had been in unaffected modern English—a child could have located the island.

Leading the Winter King and several dozen Shadow-Born–bearing longboats onto the shore was Magwich. The Steward was clutching the *Imaginarium Geographica* closely to his chest. And even at that distance, they could see that the Winter King was wearing the ring.

"He has what he wanted," said Jack. "There's no reason to come looking for us here."

"Unless he came to the same conclusion we did," said Charles. "Magwich heard the same story from Ordo Maas that we did, remember? The Winter King now knows exactly who Artus is."

"Do we run?" said John. "He's cut off any chance of retreat to the *White Dragon*."

"Quickly," Charles said to the others, "come back onto the stairs."

"Are you stupid?" said Aven. "We'll be trapped."

"No," said Charles. "I don't think we will." Without another word, he started racing back up the steps.

Jack and John exchanged looks of confusion.

"It took us half the night to reach the top," said Jack. "I'm already exhausted. We can't repeat that again, even if we're being chased."

Aven grabbed them both and propelled them toward the stairs, where Bert and Artus were already following closely behind Charles. "No time to argue," she said. "It's the only option we have."

Strangely, the Winter King's henchmen didn't seem to be pursuing them, instead remaining at the bottom.

They were several flights up when Jack stopped, sniffing at the air, then peering down the stairwell.

"Smoke," he cried. "They've set fire to the keep! We have to go back!"

Charles stopped and looked at Jack. The younger man was breathing hard, more from fear than exertion.

"Jack," Charles said, "throughout this entire adventure, you have jumped willingly into every fray. You have accepted every fantastic marvel and irregularity we have encountered as if nothing were amiss. And all the while, I've done very little but question the reality of what we have seen."

"That's why I don't understand what you're doing now," said Jack. "It doesn't make any sense. It's not logical to climb higher into a tower that's just been set on fire."

"Precisely my point," Charles said as he continued to climb. "It *isn't* logical. But then, nothing about this tower is. But I just saw my friend John go into a room and talk to someone we know to be dead, and emerge a changed man for having done it. And I believe that it happened. So if I'm going to take one thing on faith, I think I can take another—so shut up and follow me!"

"Are you going back to the Cartographer?" Jack said, panting. "He's more trapped here than we are, remember?"

"Not that high," Charles said over his shoulder. "Not quite."

Bert grinned. "I think I know what he has in mind. Quickly now—do as he says."

The companions continued their flight up the stairway as the minions of the Winter King began to fill the openings at the base of the tower, while the smoke rose up behind them, as if it were a predator in pursuit of its prey.

Charles's assessment that the tower did not play fairly with the laws of space and time appeared to be correct: In a fraction of the time taken for their original ascent, they had reached the upper levels of the keep. The smoke from the fire below, while still evident, was no longer the air-constricting cloud it had been earlier, and the sounds of their pursuit had faded.

"Why wouldn't they follow us?" Jack said.

"I think they are," said Bert. "The Shadow-Born wouldn't fear the fire—but perhaps the tower is growing for them while it's been shrinking for us."

"It's the same kettle," said Charles. "To them, it's not yet begun to boil—while to us, it's boiling already, even though it's been the same amount of time."

"We're nearly at the top," John said. "We've passed the door that led into London, so we won't be going to last week. And the Cartographer can't help us. So where *are* we going, Charles?"

"There was one more door before the Cartographer's, remember?" said Charles. "If the one below was the recent past, and the one above is the present, then the one in-between might be just what we need."

"And what if it opens onto Outer Mongolia?" said Jack.

"It won't," said Charles.

"How do you know?"

"I don't," Charles said, grinning. "But I believe."

"That's not very logical," said Bert, trying to suppress a grin.

"No, it isn't," said Charles as they reached the next-to-last landing, "but it wasn't logical for John's door to open into a study in London, either. It was just what he needed it to be."

"And what do you need it to be?" Bert asked as Charles extended his hand to touch the door.

"The base of the keep, right after we entered," said Charles.

The door swung open onto the grassy knoll that sloped down to where the *White Dragon* was anchored. The moon was still directly overhead; not morning, but midnight. And there was no sign of the *Black Dragon* or the Winter King.

"Hang on," said Jack. "If we just came out of the keep right after we entered it, then aren't we still inside somewhere? And won't we—they—still be trapped when the Winter King *does* arrive?"

"I don't think so," said Charles. "I think they'll do as we've just done, and escape unscathed as we're about to do."

"What if they choose a different course?" asked Jack. "What if the 'us' in the keep now don't listen to you?"

"It doesn't work that way," Bert assured them. "Trust me—I've done research.

"That's the thing about time travel—you're always moving forward, even when you go back."

Safely aboard the *White Dragon*, they cast off from the shore and circled around to the other side of the island before they unrolled the Cartographer's map.

"It's a simpler course than it would seem," said John. "We have to go a bit farther north, but then, it's all due west. West, to the very edge of the world."

"Best watch we don't sail right off, eh, Aven?" Charles joked.

"Agreed," she said, folding her arms. "Good thinking, Charles."

"Oh, ah, thanks," Charles stammered. "I wasn't serious, you know."

"You should be," said Aven. "I've heard of this place—Nemo said the other sailors all talk of it in hushed whispers when they've had too much ale. It really is the end of the world, and if we're not careful, it's entirely possible that we'll sail right over the edge. But don't worry," she added with mock sweetness. "I understand that there's no ending to the void beyond, so we'd never hit bottom."

"Well, that's good, isn't it?" said Artus.

"No," said Bert. "It means we'd just keep falling, and falling, and falling, for all eternity."

"Oh," said Artus.

"If we set out right away," said John, "we'll have the entire night to gain an advantage over the Winter King. Remember—he's going to be coming here, looking for us."

"I still don't understand why he won't find 'us,'" said Jack. "This time stuff makes my head hurt."

"Trust me," Bert said again. "We're ahead of him, in more ways than one."

"What happens when we do reach the island?" said Aven.

"We have the advantage of surprise," said John. "Whatever is to take place there, we'll be able to prepare for, long before he reaches us. We have the *White Dragon*—it should get us there with exceptional speed."

"She, not it," said Aven. "Let's do it."

Jack and Charles set about preparing the sails for travel northward—although the ship was already prodding itself in that direction. Not all of the motive power would come from the winds.

Aven took the wheel, and Artus, trying to make himself useful, climbed up to the crow's nest.

Bert and John stood at the prow, enjoying the respite they'd found, however limited it might be.

"Tell me, lad," said Bert. "What did the professor say to you in the tower?"

John smiled. "He said to listen to you, and that he had all the confidence in the world that we would defeat the Winter King."

Bert gave John an odd look. "Did he really say that?"

"Close enough," said John. "But then, the Cartographer said as much, didn't he? We went in with nothing, and came out with little more. What did he tell us that we didn't already know, except that our victory or defeat may come down to a matter of will?"

The old man nodded. "I'm glad you got that chance," he said, "to see him—Stellan—one more time. I would have liked to myself. Ah, well—plenty of time to do that in the future, eh, my boy?"

Bert walked away to speak to Aven before John had a chance to ask him what he meant.

The *White Dragon* left the islands of Chamenos Liber in relative silence, and calm seas. Only one pair of eyes watched it pass. High above them in the clear night sky, the great silver and crimson crane watched a few minutes longer, then wheeled about and began to fly south with increasing speed.

PART FIVE

THE ISLAND AT THE EDGE OF THE WORLD

CHAPTER SEVENTEEN
HOPE AND DESPAIR

THE JOURNEY FROM the Cartographer's island to the Island at the Edge of the World was the most peaceful and least eventful passage they had experienced since the original voyage from London into the Archipelago. The night air was clear, and the stars above stunning in their brilliance.

Artus was pointing out constellations to his companions; constellations, not all of which existed in the world beyond.

"Do you see that pattern of stars in the east?" he was saying to John. "The jagged grouping, there?"

"Yes, I see them."

"That's Athamas and Themisto. They're pursuing that cluster there, to the north—we call that one Salmoneus. He was a merchant who stole forty pieces of silver from Athamas, and they are chasing him across the sky, to make him give back the silver."

"What's that one, there?" asked Charles, pointing. "The line that looks like Orion's Belt?"

"It's Orion's Belt," said Artus.

"Ah," said Charles.

"What is that one?" asked John, pointing to the west. "The bright grouping, shaped rather like a tree?"

"Astraeus," Aven called out. "God of the four winds and friend to sailors. Say a little prayer when you look at him, so he will give us what we need to keep our course."

"A little prayer?" said Jack. "To a constellation?"

"To what it represents," said Aven.

"But I don't believe in what it represents," said Jack.

"Prayers aren't for the deity," said Aven. "They're for you, to recommit yourself to what you believe."

"Can't you do that without praying to a dead Greek god?"

"Sure," said Aven. "But how often would anyone do that, if not in prayer?"

The companions slept in shifts throughout the remainder of the night: John, Artus, and Bert first, then Aven, Jack, and Charles, with Bert assuming control of the wheel.

Aven awoke just as the sun was cresting into view, a wheel shooting great spokes of radiance across the sky. The light was brilliant, and the sky at the horizon a startling robin's egg blue, which paled farther up into the sky along the sun's eventual arc.

But to the west, directly in their path, was the darkness they'd earlier assumed to be a line of storms; a sister Frontier to the one that guarded the boundary at Avalon. But they weren't storms at all—it was simply, purely, darkness. Darkness . . .

. . . or Shadow.

They heard the sound first, before the island came into view, and John was very grateful for the Cartographer's precise navigational instructions, for if they had approached the island at an angle just a few degrees less or more, the *White Dragon* would not have been able to resist the pull.

The sound was a roar as big as the world; it was the sound of a waterfall as wide as an ocean, falling into an endless void as deep as Hades itself.

The Island at the Edge of the World was larger than Avalon and Byblos together. It was a flat, rocky plain, which rose to a scattering of hills in the center, then sloped up westward to a peak that extended beyond the edge, over the waterfall.

John shuddered with the realization of what must lay beyond. There were no stars, and the light from the rising sun seemed to be swallowed up by the darkness. The island truly was an Ending of Endings, and somehow he knew that the confrontation with the Winter King would end here.

One way or the other, it would end.

Aven guided the *White Dragon* through a wicked-looking reef to a spot on the southern shore where she could be safely anchored. They could see the entire shoreline in both directions—to the east, from which they'd just arrived, and west to the edge. There were no other vessels in sight, and most importantly, no sign of the *Black Dragon*.

The companions disembarked so they could begin to explore the island, and they quickly determined that it was a singularly unremarkable place.

"Well, except for that waterfall," said Charles. "It's sort of like that place in America, where that big canyon is—somewhere you wouldn't really go to, except to see a great big hole that will be your death if you fall in."

There were no structures of any kind, save for the occasional standing stones that were set pell-mell across the fields and at the top of the bluff on the western side.

"So what do we do now?" said Jack. "Do we just camp out and wait for the Winter King to arrive, or what?"

"We should finish scouting the rest of the island," said Aven. "We have a good lead on him—we should endeavor to make the most of it."

"Sensible," said Bert.

With Aven leading, they crossed the first low valley and headed for the hills in the center. It was, except for the bluff and peak itself, the highest point on the island, and would be an excellent vantage point from which to organize their efforts.

The darkness beyond gave the landscape an unearthly glow, with the sunlight highlighting the muted colors of the rocks and grasses. Everything stood out in high relief—which made the sight beyond the hills more unreal than they could have imagined.

They'd been correct about the view: From the center, they could see the entire expanse of the island, including the north side that had been hidden from sight on their seaward approach.

All along the northern edge of the island were encampments; glowing fires, and the bustle and clatter of warriors preparing for combat. They could see trolls by the thousand, and more Wendigo than they could have imagined existed. And all throughout the encampment rose the black banner of the Winter King.

Even John, who had seen combat, and the most terrible battlefields of war, was struck speechless by the implied violence and destructive force spread before them.

"No wonder we could never find him," Aven whispered. "In all these years, he always evaded his pursuers, and simply moved from land to land, conquering them, then returning to a place we could never discover. He found the best hiding place in existence—the actual ends of the Earth."

"He didn't need to beat us here," Bert said. "The Winter King's army has been here all along."

"I think we're in trouble," said Charles.

"That's the understatement of the year," said Jack. "We're in for a difficult battle, that's for certain."

Aven stared ahead at the hundreds of glowing fires. "There must be thousands of them," she said. "This is not going to be a battle—it's going to be a slaughter. *Our* slaughter."

"I don't think I want to be king anymore," said Artus. "I nominate Jack."

"Aw, don't give up hope," said Tummeler. "This is the part in stories where they gets real good—valiant friends in a struggle 'gainst impossible odds."

The companions heard what the badger said, but it took a few seconds to process that he was standing on the rise next to them, since they had left Tummeler on Paralon.

"Tummeler?" Charles said, incredulous. "Is it really you?"

"Su'prise," said Tummeler. "I brung . . . brang . . . bringed . . . I'm with th' cavalry. We've come t' save th' day."

After a round of excited hugs and greetings, Tummeler explained to the companions what else was transpiring in the Archipelago, and for the first time, they felt a glimmering of hope.

"It were ol' Ordo Maas," said Tummeler. "He said y' would be needin' some help, an' he sent out his sons to all the corners of the Archipelago. One of them watched the *White Dragon*, t' see where y' be going, and the others went t' alert all your friends—and you have more than y' be knowing y' do."

"His sons?" Jack said in surprise. "How could they go to find allies? We took the only ship on Byblos."

In answer, Tummeler pointed to the sky. Circling above the *White Dragon* was a scarlet and silver crane, which dipped its wings in greeting.

"I was with Mister Samaranth when the crane come in, an' I hitched a ride back on one o' th' ships. And I came ready to fight," said Tummeler, proudly showing off his battered knapsack and an equally battered shield that was larger than he was, and that he could lift only with considerable effort. "After all," he finished, "I don't want to be missin' any o' th' fun."

"Is Samaranth coming?" asked Bert. "Will he be joining the battle?"

Tummeler shrugged. "Can't say if he will. I know he left Paralon when we did, an' said he was going to find some others t' help, but what that means I can't say."

"How did you get here, then?" said Charles, "if not with Samaranth?"

"I brought him," said a voice of command, "and while he's skilled with maintenance of the ship, it's his culinary skills I find most valuable. We've never eaten better."

It was Nemo.

In the distance behind him, out in the shallows of the expansive inlet and to the rear of the *White Dragon*, lay the gleaming form of the *Nautilus*.

"Ho, Aven," Nemo said in greeting, laying his fist across his chest.

"Ho, Nemo," Aven responded, offering the gesture in return. "Well met."

Nemo turned to say hello to Bert, but before he could voice a greeting, the little man rushed over and embraced the surprised captain in a bear hug.

"Oh, my stars and garters!" Bert exclaimed. "I've never been so happy to see . . . well, almost anyone!"

"Is that so?" Nemo said with a wink at the others. "That's too bad," he finished, gesturing over his shoulder with his thumb, "because they'll be disappointed if they get less of a reception, just because I beat them here."

"What is it?" said Jack. "Who's coming?"

"It's the other ships," Bert said, eyes glittering with barely contained excitement. "The Dragonships have come together once more."

The companions, together with Nemo and Tummeler, raced back to the beach where the ships were anchored, as the first of the other Dragonships began to arrive.

"The *Orange Dragon*," said Bert. "The Dwarves, I think, run that one these days."

It was a Viking longship, broad and flat across the middle, from which extended three steeply pointed prows and a tall mast with the largest sail John, Jack, and Charles had ever seen. It was also, Bert explained, the only one of the Dragonships with three dragonheads, one on each prow.

"I suppose the Vikings thought that where one was good, three might be better. Although," he added, "given their successful track record for looting and pillaging, I can't say that they were incorrect."

The captain of the *Orange Dragon*, who Aven explained was also the king of the Dwarves, splashed through the shallows carrying a massive ax and a stern expression. He shook hands with Nemo and gave a curt nod to Bert and the others.

"A little grim, isn't he?" said Charles.

"Grim?" said Bert in surprise. "You don't know dwarves. For him, that greeting was positively giddy."

"That, I'm assuming," said Charles, pointing seaward, "is the *Blue Dragon*, unless I miss my guess."

It was. The Elves had arrived with the greatest of the Dragonships, an immense vessel that towered over the other ships as if they were toys. It was fully five stories tall, and almost three times as long and as broad as the *White Dragon*. The sails were barely visible, but it obviously had other means of propulsion, much like the *Nautilus*.

The Elders of the Elves disembarked through a hatch that appeared just above the waterline and came over to greet the companions. They were several of the same elves who'd been present at the Council on Paralon, and they greeted John, Jack, and Charles as if they were visiting dignitaries.

"Ho, Caretaker," the Elf King, Eledir, said in greeting to Bert. "The Ancient of Days told us that you could use our assistance."

Bert bowed his head. "And we are grateful for it," he said with sincerity. "How many have you brought?"

Eledir pointed at the *Blue Dragon* in answer, as dozens of elves, armored and equipped for battle, flowed out onto the beach.

"Six hundred," said the Elf King. "More ships will follow, but this number was the best we could arrange and still arrive in time."

"Every one is a help," said Bert. "We won't complain."

The next ship to arrive was the *Green Dragon*—which seemed to be under the stewardship of the mythological creatures of the Archipelago.

It was not unlike the *White Dragon* in appearance, except for the fact that it seemed the timbers from which it was made had never lost their ambition to be trees, and had kept on growing accordingly. There were branches and tufts of leaves everywhere. And the sails were so overgrown as to nearly collapse with the weight. The occupants were not merely on the deck, but also clambered up and around the branches and spars as easily as walking on the ground.

From their vantage point on the beach, the companions were able to make out fauns and satyrs ("Great," Aven grumbled. "As if they'll be a lot of help."), more than a few animals (including several badgers, wolverines, and at least one creature Jack identified as a Tasmanian devil), and the core of their force, a herd of centaurs.

The captain of the *Green Dragon* was a centaur whom Nemo greeted as Charys. He was massive, standing eight feet tall at the shoulder, and kicked up a curtain of sand as he trotted over to the companions.

"Greetings, Sons of Adam," said Charys. "Which one of you is the Caretaker Principia?"

"That would be me," John said.

"Nemo told me of you when he came to Praxis to enlist our aid," said Charys. "I like your style. 'Let's go thataway,'" he said with a deep horsey laugh. "Oh ho ho! Now that's the way we navigated in the olden days!" He laughed again and trotted off to greet the dwarves.

"I think he was poking fun at me," said John.

"He was," Charles agreed, "but I don't think it's advisable to make an issue of it."

Bert was pacing the shoreline, watching the water for more arrivals. By their count, there were two more Dragonships that might still come.

"One, actually," said Aven. "The *Violet Dragon*—the ship of the Goblin King."

"I don't know," said Bert. "I feel we may yet see the other as well."

"Is it possible?" said Aven.

Bert scanned the horizon, then shook his head. "No, I don't think so. It was too much to hope for, I know, but still . . ."

"What are you looking for?" John asked.

"The first Dragonship," said Aven. "The *Red Dragon*. It hasn't been seen since shortly after Ordo Maas created it.

"As Ordo Maas said, all of the ships—even our own *Indigo Dragon*, bless her spars—were made from existing hulls. They were not new-built, but created from ships that knew surf and storm and had proven themselves able to cross into waters of a new world. And the *Red Dragon* was the greatest of them all."

"What was the *Red Dragon*?" asked Charles. "Anything we might know?"

"Yes," said Bert. "In fact, it was the original ship that showed Ordo Maas the secret of passage between the worlds and led him to the idea of living mastheads—for it had one of its own.

"Before it was remade as the *Red Dragon*, it was a ship known as the *Argo*."

◆　◆　◆

The kings and captains of the ships sat together in a council of war, while the others helped to organize their troops and make themselves ready for whatever was to come.

Jack immediately positioned himself alongside Nemo and Eledir as a representative of Man, although Bert had already explained Artus's true identity and put him forth as the heir to the Silver Throne.

Nemo seemed to accept this news with aplomb, but Eledir and Falladay Finn, the Dwarf King, were more reserved.

"We've been through one round of false kings and queens, presented by the humans," Eledir said, referring to the Council. "The Archipelago cannot continue to be supportive of a race that is unable to even police its own."

Falladay Finn nodded in agreement. "If what you say is true, you will have the support of the dwarves. But," he added, looking at Artus, "the first duty of a king is to rule for the benefit of his subjects, and not for himself. Your grandfather forgot that. If you survive this day, see to it that you do not."

He placed his hand over Artus's own in a gesture of support, followed quickly by Charys and more grudgingly by Eledir. Despite the official endorsement, their faces still showed the doubt and fear they felt.

"Cheer up, boy," Charys said, bellowing with laughter at Artus's crestfallen expression. "The way things are looking, none of us is going to survive anyway, so you won't have to worry about it."

Farther south on the beach, Charles was struggling with a leather-and-mail vest that one of the dwarves had offered him—which was three sizes too small. As he tried unsuccessfully to fasten the buckles, his little friend from Paralon plopped down on the sand next to him.

"Ready when you are, Master Scowler," said Tummeler. He still had the heavy knapsack, which he was dragging around inside the old bronze shield he'd arrived with, and he had fashioned a helmet from an apple pail. It kept slipping down onto his nose.

"Tummeler!" Charles exclaimed. "No offense, but I don't think badgers are suited for battle!"

"Really, think as such, do ye, Master Scowler?" replied Tummeler. "We badgers be gentle creatures, true—but I be thinkin' ye've ne'er seed a badger with his fur all adander."

"Now, now," Charles began, keeping a nervous eye on the all-too-close soon-to-be battlefield over the rise.

"I know what ye be thinkin'," said Tummeler. "My smallish happearance an' happy-go-nancy nature bein' what they is, ol' Tummeler can't possibly be a warrior.

"Well," he continued, "I's hopin' that th' enemy thinks as such—then I c'n take 'em out with my secret weapons."

"Secret weapons?" said Charles.

"Yup," nodded Tummeler. "Gots 'em right here."

The small mammal opened his heavy carryall and showed its contents to Charles and John, who had been eavesdropping as he strapped on armor of his own.

"Muffins?" Charles and John exclaimed together. "Your secret weapons are muffins?"

"Not just any muffins," said Tummeler. "Blueberry."

"I'm sorry," Charles began.

Tummeler ignored him and instead removed a fist-size (badger-fist-size) muffin from the bag, took careful aim, and lobbed it considerably farther than either of the men expected was possible. It soared into the air and landed with a thunk onto the helmet of a satyr who had been slinking around the *Orange Dragon* at the landing fifty yards away. The satyr dropped to the ground, knocked out cold.

"Bloody hell," said John.

"Amazing," said Charles.

"Hard as rocks," said Tummeler. "Whipped them up after I saw y' off from Paralon, just in case."

"Amazing," Charles said again. "You made a blueberry muffin into a weapon."

"Atchly, any kind of muffin will do," said Tummeler, "but I found out that y' needs t' use blueberries if y' wants t' get it *just so*. It's my own secret contribution," he added.

"Won't breathe a word of it," said Charles.

Jack came running over to his friends, breathing hard.

"What is it?" said Charles. "What's happened?"

"It's the Goblins," Jack panted. "The *Violet Dragon* has arrived at last."

The last of the Dragonships resembled an elaborate Chinese junk, which was in line with the elegant mannerisms of the Goblin King and his entourage. It was smaller than the rest, more of a size with the *Indigo Dragon*, but tall, and it had a beautiful mainsail that shimmered in the light.

"I am very happy to see you," said Bert, offering his hand in greeting. "My friend, Uruk Ko."

The Goblin King hesitated, then took the old man's hand, giving it a single dignified shake. "I greet you also, my friend the Far Traveler."

"How many have you brought with you?" asked Nemo, looking with a barely disguised disdain at the *Violet Dragon*, which seemed manned by only a few officious types, none of whom were outfitted for war. "Are they coming by other means?"

"Yes," said Uruk Ko. "Other ships of the kingdom bore my warriors here—more than a thousand, to be exact."

Bert and Aven exchanged relieved glances. This battle would be more evenly matched than they'd first feared. "Do you realize," Bert said, "that your goblins represent more than half of our defensive force?"

"Yes, I do," Uruk Ko said. "I am pleased you also realize that. It will make what must happen easier to bear."

"Whatever do you mean?" said Bert, scanning the horizon for a sign of the Goblin army's ships. "When are they expected to arrive?"

"You misunderstand me," said Uruk Ko. "They are already here."

"Really?" Bert said, squinting. "How did I miss them?"

"Because," said the Goblin King, "you are looking in the wrong direction."

"What?" Bert breathed.

As one, the other captains and kings turned, then made their way up to the first of the hills, where they could look out over the enemy's encampments. There they saw the black standards of the Winter King, as well as the flags of Arawn—but also, to the north, they saw with rising dread the unmistakable silken banners of the Goblin King.

"It was because of our friendship that I felt honor-bound to tell you myself, and in person," said Uruk Ko, "and now I have done so. Please—as one who has stood with you as an ally, choose wisely, and leave the battlefield before we must come face-to-face as enemies."

The expressions of the other kings darkened, and a menacing growl came from deep inside Charys's massive chest, as he moved defensively in front of Artus.

Aven spit, cursed, and began to lunge forward, drawing her sword. "What kind of man . . . ," she began, just as Bert stopped her advance.

"Not a man," said Uruk Ko, as he turned to make his way back to the *Violet Dragon*. "A goblin, and a Child of the True Archipelago, who wishes only to drive out the usurpers that have ruled for far too long.

"Leave, my friends. A new age is dawning, and it will be birthed in fire. A new age; an age of Goblin, Troll, and Shadow.

"The age of Man is over."

CHAPTER EIGHTEEN
THE FINAL BATTLE

AT NOON THE *Black Dragon* arrived.

It eased along the eastern edge of the island, safely in the lee of the pull of the falls, where the Winter King could take stock of the allies before making his way to where his army was massing.

"They will attack within the hour," Charys said to the assembled war council, which was still reeling from the defection of the Goblin King.

"How can you be sure?" said Bert.

The centaur indicated the motion of the sun across the sky, moving westward, and the council saw what Charys had surmised. The terminus of the void, the edge to the darkness beyond, was only a few degrees away from the sun's position and would soon engulf it.

"That's why they have the fires and torches lit in broad daylight," said Jack. "The Winter King is used to being here and knows it's going to be dark soon."

Charys nodded. "We will be in absolute darkness, and it will be difficult to separate friend from foe, much less counter the attacks of the Shadow-Born."

Aven volunteered to start gathering torches, or anything that could be assembled into torches, from the ships, taking with her a company of fauns.

"Despite the stated intentions of Uruk Ko," said Bert, "we must remember that the Winter King has another agenda. He plans to attempt to summon the dragons back to the Archipelago."

Eledir gave what amounted to a restrained snort of derision. "Impossible. Only the High King has ever known how to do this. Even my own ancestors, who were confidants of the great Samaranth, did not know the secret."

"Yes," said Falladay Finn. "When Archibald offended them, the dragons left the Archipelago forever. We need to deal with the army that has been assembled here and now, and not the imaginary one we worry may come."

"With respect, I disagree," said John. "The secret of the summoning is in the *Imaginarium Geographica*, which was stolen and is now in the possession of the Winter King. He also has Archibald's Ring of Power, which the *Geographica* says will allow the summoning to take place."

"Even I have a Ring of Power," snorted Falladay Finn, extending his hand, which bore a ring identical to the one Magwich had stolen.

"As do I," said Eledir, "as do my lieutenants. Rings of Power, as you call them, are symbols of office and fealty, nothing more. My ancestor Eledin received his at the same time as the High King Arthur, and he never saw a difference in the two."

"It doesn't matter if we believe it," said John. "The Winter King does. And if he's right, then we'll be lost. But if he's wrong, then maybe we can divert his attentions away from the battle long enough to gain an advantage."

The kings and captains exchanged knowing glances, and John realized that there would be no advantages to be gained by a distraction. Once joined in battle, the opposing force would be irresistible and would flow over the assembled forces of the allies like a wave.

"We still do not know the real scope of his army," said Falladay Finn. "As yet, we have not seen any of the Shadow-Born among the assembly."

"That's a concern," Eledir said. "Perhaps greater than the Trolls and Goblins, who can still be killed."

"May I say something?"

The council turned to look at the speaker—Artus, who had not ventured an opinion since they'd begun, instead allowing John, Jack, or Bert to speak for Men and Paralon.

Charys nodded. "You are the heir to the Silver Throne," he said. "Speak, and we will listen."

"Well," Artus began, "I've been thinking—Ordo Maas told us that the Shadow-Born were created by that magic kettle, right?"

"Pandora's Box," Eledir said. "A myth. Nothing more."

"Ordo Maas didn't think so," said Artus. "And besides, the Shadow-Born came from somewhere, didn't they? Do you have a better explanation?"

Eledir remained silent and indicated with a nod for Artus to continue.

"If my grandfather—King Archibald—started creating the Shadow-Born by opening the box, and the Winter King created more of them and began taking over the Archipelago by keeping it open, then why don't we just do what Aven suggested, and find it, and close it?"

This suggestion was met with a resounding silence, which was then shattered by Charys's booming laugh.

"By my body and bones, that's either the most kingly thing I've ever heard, or it's the single stupidest plan on Earth," he said, laughing and stomping his hind legs.

"If that is the source of his ability to create Shadow-Born," Artus continued, "then by closing it, we can prevent him from creating more."

"That's a good plan," said Nemo. "I wonder what effect closing the box would have on the existing Shadow-Born?"

"Also," said Artus, growing bolder with each comment of support, "it's probably here, on the island. The Winter King wouldn't have risked losing it to combat or weather by keeping it on board the *Black Dragon*, so if this is really his base, it's probably somewhere around here."

Bert, Nemo, Eledir, and Falladay Finn exchanged glances of unabashed admiration over the boy king's conclusions.

"If he does possess such a weapon," mused the Dwarf King, "he *would* keep it here. There may be something to this strategy after all."

"Right," said Artus. "So all we have to do now is go into his camp, sneak past all the goblins, trolls, Shadow-Born, and Wendigo, find Pandora's Box, and close it. It's simple, really."

Charys slapped his forehead. "Ah, boy," he said, resigned. "You had it going so well, up until the end."

"But he's right," said Charles, who'd been listening in from the perimeter of the council. "That's *exactly* what needs to be done.

"Look," he said, gesturing at the island beyond. "It's a natural battlefield—everyone is expecting that both sides will meet in the middle, and the Winter King's side is expecting the cover of darkness to be to their advantage. So no one would be looking if someone went behind their camp to snoop around while all their attention is focused on us in the center."

"That sounds like a plan," said Charys. "Good luck."

"What?" Charles said, his face suddenly gone pale. "I—I wasn't really volunteering. I'm not a soldier."

"Not many here are, lad," Nemo said. "But we're going to do what we can, all of us, nevertheless."

"We'll do it!" came an excited voice from somewhere nearer the ground. "Master Charles an' his faithful squire, Tummeler, vanquishing foes and, uh, closin' boxes!"

Charles blinked, then grinned. "I guess we're the stealth force," he said, looking down at the exuberant badger. "God help us all."

"The torches are ready," said Aven, approaching the council with several in hand.

"And just in time," said Nemo, shading his eyes and looking up at the sky. The sun was half-covered in Shadow. In minutes the island would be plunged into darkness.

It was determined that Eledir would command the primary force of the allies' army—appropriate, given that it was comprised mostly of elves from the *Blue Dragon*. The elves were primarily armed as archers, although they all bore wicked long swords for one-to-one battle.

Falladay Finn and his dwarves were the most heavily armed, as they'd been at the Council at Paralon, with each of them bearing heavy axes, braces of short knives, and archery equipment of their own. Finn, along with Nemo, served as Eledir's primary lieutenants, with Charys and the assembled creatures bringing up the rear.

Jack, despite cautions from both Charys and the Elf King, had chosen to join in the battle alongside Nemo. Aven and Bert tried to dissuade him, but Jack would brook none of their concerns. His eyes were shining from the fire that blazed in his belly to see real combat. He didn't understand that skirmishes aboard a ship, which were all he'd really experienced, were not the same as war, and further justified his choice by pointing out that he was at least as physically able as John, who'd been a soldier, and was more willing to boot.

"I'll be fine," said Jack. "No one's gotten killed so far, have they? And you know it yourself—I've proven myself to be braver and more resourceful than you thought I'd be. So don't worry. I'm going to do things on this battlefield you'll remember for the rest of your life."

Aven flashed a concerned look at Nemo, who indicated with a brief nod that he would try not to be separated from Jack during the battle.

As she walked back to the beach for more torches, Aven wondered if of the two, she was actually concerned for the right one. Like a drowning man can drag down his rescuer, she hoped that Jack's inexperience in combat would not similarly impair Nemo. She though of going back and saying something more, but she had other matters to attend to and soon forgot about her concerns.

"We're going to find the Winter King."

John said it matter-of-factly, but it sounded more ludicrous out loud than it had inside his head.

He and Bert had reasoned that the Winter King would not engage in the actual battle—not if his goal was still to summon the dragons. John surmised that to make the attempt, the Winter King would move as far away from the battlefield as he could get— and that meant the rocky bluff to the west, which sharpened to a peak high above the roaring falls.

"That's where he'll be, I'm sure of it," said John. "And Artus and I will have to be there too."

"Why me?" asked Artus. "Shouldn't I be on the field, with all the rest?"

Bert took the young man by the shoulders and peered at him over the top of his glasses. "You should not," he said with equal parts sternness and affection. "If John is right, then you may be the only one of us who is able to summon the dragons, and that means you are too valuable to risk putting in open combat. Go with John, and see what you discover. We'll buy you as much time as we can."

The old Caretaker embraced the boy king in a brief hug, then turned and walked to the top of the hill, where Aven was waving a torch.

The sun vanished, and a cry and hue rose up from the other side of the island.

The battle was beginning.

The enemy force was moving south with a slow, deliberate pace, but Eledir directed the elves to rush forward and establish a center line to hold as far into the shallow valley as possible. Against the greater force, they would eventually, inevitably lose ground and be driven back to their ships. Eledir wanted to make sure they had as much ground to lose as possible.

Falladay Finn and the dwarves could not quite keep pace with the elves, so he instructed them to sheath their axes and pull out their bows and arrows. They would fire behind the enemy lines, then pick up their axes again to push forward when the elves were pressed to their first retreat.

Charys and the centaurs had one mandate: to flank the rest, and make sure that none of their enemies were trying to outflank *them*. It was bound to happen at some point, as battles frequently spill past their prescribed boundaries, but with John and Artus heading to the west, and Charles and Tummeler heading east, it would be better to keep as much of the action corralled in the valley as possible.

Nemo, for his part, was firing a weapon of his own manufacture, an air-propelled gun of some kind, which had greater range than anything in use by the other races, and he was augmenting his assistance to Eledir by taking out the Troll and Goblin commanders long-distance.

From the hills behind, Bert watched and worried, too old to join in himself. It was not the battle ensuing that worried him, but the one still to come. The trolls and goblins had engaged them, but the hundreds of Wendigo, who were better fighters than the trolls, and more fearsome than the goblins, were still inexplicably clustered around the tents. He had also been scanning the encampment with Aven's spyglass since the battle began, but still . . .

. . . there was no sign of the Shadow-Born.

Charles's plan was for himself and Tummeler to skirt around the eastern shore of the island and come around behind the Winter King's encampment, there to look for the kettle. They were dressed in dark leathers and would carry no torches, planning on Tummeler's animal senses to guide them through the darkness.

They were preparing to move down to the beach, when something in the torchlight caught Charles's attention. He stopped and looked more closely, then his eyes widened in shock, and he dropped his supplies to go find Aven.

"Master scowler?" said Tummeler.

"Stay there," said Charles. "I'll be right back."

"Aven!" Charles said, finding her gathering more flammable materials from the *Green Dragon*. "Listen to me. Something is wrong! Something is wrong with Jack!"

Aven started a curt retort, but bit it back. Something in Charles's tone told her that this was not an unconsidered assessment. "What is it? What's wrong with him?"

Charles took her arm and pulled her closer. "I couldn't put my finger on it until just now. For the last few days, he's grown more and more brash, reckless even. I thought . . ."

He blushed. "I thought he was just trying overhard to impress you."

"Since the moment we met," said Aven. "What of it? He's grown confident. He's become a man—maybe even a warrior, although I'd cut out my own tongue before I let him hear me say that."

"I thought the same, but—"

"But what, Charles?"

Charles pointed to the rise twenty yards off where Jack was organizing several of the fauns and satyrs into a staggered line of archers. Aven was right: He *was* more confident. He *did* direct them with an authority that belied his youth, and he had proven himself in every battle they had joined. But Charles's suspicions had manifested themselves in a form visible yet subtle, and Aven's breath caught in her throat when she saw it.

Jack had no shadow.

The first engagement had gone badly.

The elves, impressive as they were in battle, were not a match for the trolls, the smallest of which outweighed the largest, stockiest elf. It was only the quality of their elf-forged armor that saved them from being completely overrun, and they retreated to switch to bows and arrows.

Unexpectedly, the dwarves fared better at hand-to-hand combat against the trolls, and they added to the attack a benefit for the Elven archers to the rear. The dwarves' short stature meant that the huge trolls had to stoop to strike a blow, exposing the backs of their heads and shoulders to the arrows, while the dwarves whaled away at their legs and midriffs with the massive battle-axes. Still, the overwhelming might of the trolls was something to be held, and held only, not beaten back.

As they'd feared, the goblins had attempted a flanking action, only to be forced back into line with the others by the centaurs. The goblin archers' aim was deadly, but the centaurs shrugged off the arrows as if they were wasps.

The other archers and pikemen gleaned from the mythbeasts and animals, led by Jack, came in behind the centaurs, and in moments the goblins were in full retreat. The trolls made another great push forward, then, amazingly, began to pull back as well.

"They're retreating," Charys said in amazement, blood streaming from his wounds, running freely down his flanks. "The goblins, and the trolls—they're retreating!"

As unlikely as it seemed, the centaur was right.

With a cheer, the elves drew their swords and pressed ahead—then, suddenly, Eledir gave the command to stop, and the dwarves and centaurs also wheeled about.

Nemo signaled desperately to Bert, then gestured to the Winter King's encampment, calling out something Bert couldn't discern over the din of battle and roar of the falls.

He put the spyglass to his eye and looked in the direction Nemo had indicated. As if on cue, the Wendigo opened the tents all along the shore, which they'd assumed to belong to trolls and goblins who'd come from their homelands to fight.

They were mistaken. The Shadow-Born had been there all along—they had merely waited until the light and heat of the noonday sun had been enveloped in Shadow, when their power would be at its strongest, and they would be able to move almost invisibly in the dark.

"Dear God in Heaven," said Bert. "This may truly be the end for us all."

Aven spun around and suppressed a shudder, then, worse, began to silently weep.

John and Artus, who had not yet gone west, exchanged worried looks, then clambered up the rise to see what had shaken Bert and Aven so badly. A moment's glance and an instant of comprehension was all that they needed.

They had expected, even planned for, the army of Wendigo; the trolls, guided by the traitorous Prince Arawn, had also come as no great surprise. Even a few of the lesser races from the edges of the Archipelago could have added to the bulk of the opposing army without rattling a veteran such as Aven. But what they saw not a mile away chilled the marrow in their bones and clenched their spirits in fear and growing horror.

At the edge of the vast plain of the battlefield, the great host of the Winter King had begun its approach. Marching toward them, from horizon to horizon, were the howling, snarling forms of Wendigo, and with them, mute and relentless, came the hooded specters of thousands and thousands of Shadow-Born.

CHAPTER NINETEEN
THE CIRCLE OF STONES

THERE WAS AN unusual kind of quietude on the stony peak that rose above the waterfall at the edge of the world. An almost white noise, created by the commingling of the sounds of battle from the valley to the east and the never-ending combustion engine of the falls to the remaining west.

The Winter King made his way along the bluff line, taking care not to slip on the rocks that were dampened and slick from the eternal spray. It was slow going, for he had only the hook to reach out with to steady himself. In his good hand he was clutching the *Imaginarium Geographica*. He didn't trust his translator to carry it—if Magwich were to drop it over the edge, accidentally or otherwise, he'd have to kill him, and as it was, he was merely planning on forcing the hapless Steward to look into Pandora's Box and become a Shadow-Born.

He'd have done it long before, were it not for the fact that Shadow-Born were mute—and annoying as it was, he still needed Magwich to retain the ability to speak.

For a little longer, anyway.

"How much farther?" whined Magwich, who trailed his master by several yards.

The Winter King spun about. "What? You're the one who said this was where we had to be to speak the summoning!"

"Well," said Magwich, "I told you it said in the *Geographica* that you could use the Ring of Power only at the place in the Archipelago farthest to the west, which, technically, is here on the bluff. I don't really know if the exact spot where you do it is important."

The Winter King glowered. "Don't waste my time, Steward. Are we there or not?"

In reply, Magwich motioned for the *Geographica*. The Winter King passed it over, then watched impatiently as the Steward thumbed through several pages, leafing back and forth between them, making little humming noises as he did so.

"Well?"

The Steward shook his head. "I don't think it matters. I'm pretty sure we have all you need, and we're in the best place to do it."

"Pretty sure?" said the Winter King. "I thought you had been trained to read that atlas."

Magwich shrugged. "I never actually finished training, remember? A few of the languages here are just beyond me—but I can still get the gist of it, so what does it matter if we miss a few details?"

"Never mind," the Winter King snapped, snatching the book back. "Let's just get this done, and then after I've assumed control of the entire Archipelago, I'll make sure you get the reward you've earned."

Magwich licked his lips and bowed deeply. "Thank you, my Lord."

"Idiot," said the Winter King.

"Whatever you say, my Lord."

"Just shut up, will you?"

"As you command, my Lord."

The Winter King clenched his jaw. "If you say one more word, I'm going to put my hook through both of your eyes and pull your brain out through the sockets."

"Sorry, my Lord."

The Winter King sighed heavily and opened the *Geographica*. "Just show me where the summoning is, and tell me what to say."

A hundred yards into their mission, Charles already regretted having agreed to it. He was soaked from head to toe in seawater, and he smelled faintly of brine. Worse, Tummeler was also soaked, and the odor of wet badger fur emanated from him in waves.

They had decided to keep to the edge of the shoreline, the better to steer clear of any stragglers from the Troll or Goblin armies. But unlike the beaches on the south, which were smooth and sand-covered, the eastern side had been subject to the unending tidal forces created by the pull of the falls—and as a result, the beach was rocky and uneven. Every few steps, one or the other of them had taken a tumble into the surf, only to reemerge splashing and sputtering.

They were noisy, dragging a trail throughout the visible sand, and were projecting a smell that could be followed by a blind Wendigo with a head cold.

They were, Charles decided, the worst stealth force ever to be sent on a mission during wartime.

"Don't mind my sayin' so," said Tummeler, "but you're starting t' smell funny."

"I was about to say the same thing," said Charles.

Tummeler stopped, and looked visibly hurt by the remark. "What d' you mean?"

"Nothing—forget it," said Charles, realizing the badger had meant *his* remark as a compliment.

He was outfitted in light armor the elves had given him to replace the ill-fitting Dwarven tunic, but otherwise carried only a short sword and small hatchet, as he thought appropriate for a stealth mission. Tummeler, however, not only had a large knife, but also was still dragging his supply of rock-hard muffins inside the battered bronze shield.

"Listen, Tummeler," Charles began, "do you really think it's justified to take along all this, this, *stuff*? After all, we're supposed to be sneaking in to search for Pandora's Box—not engaging in a conflict."

Tummeler puffed up his chest in a gesture of badgerly defiance. "Better t' make th' effort t' bring it, then t' find ourselves in a situation where we wants t' have it, and finds it's not there."

Charles thought about that a moment. "Now that you've put it that way," he said, "it is a bit comforting to have more weapons along. But do you really need the shield? It's leaving quite a track."

"Mister Samaranth gave it t' me," said Tummeler, "and told me t' bring it here. He said we'd need it, sooner or later, so bring it I done."

"Fair enough," said Charles, "but what say I carry it, so we make better time?"

"Okee-dokee," said Tummeler, hefting the knapsack over his shoulders and passing the shield to Charles.

"Heavy," Charles muttered as he slipped the shield over his back.

"Y'r not kidding," said Tummeler. "Onward."

❖ ❖ ❖

With the retreat of the trolls and goblins, the strategy of the Winter King was now obvious. The first onslaught by the denizens of the Archipelago was meant merely to test the resistance of the allies at best, and to cut down as many of the opposing forces as they could at worst. For their part, the trolls and goblins were merely cannon fodder—if they survived the initial attack, and damaged the allies in the process, then all was good. But if they faltered, and many lost their lives—just as good. Because the main force of the Winter King's army were the Wendigo and the Shadow-Born, and there would be no testing or trials, no retreat and withdrawal—just brutal, bloody combat to the end.

The nearest wave of Shadow-Born had reached the advance line of elves and dwarves, and the method of battle they intended to use to defeat the allies became blindingly clear.

The Shadow-Born brushed off arrows like toothpicks, and while a direct blow from an ax or a pike might slow them it wouldn't stop or damage them. And then they were close enough to grasp the shadows of the warriors and rip them free.

The dwarves and elves who lost their shadows screamed, then dropped to the ground, drained of their will and resistance. Then, as the Shadow-Born moved on to other victims, the Wendigo fell on the helpless soldiers to slaughter them in a rending of claws and teeth.

"Douse your torches!" Charys called out. "Put them out!"

Eledir and Falladay Finn exchanged startled glances. It would reduce the threat of the Shadow-Born, true—but then they would be facing the Wendigo in the dark.

"There's no choice!" Charys yelled again. "Douse your torches and pull back, or we are already lost!"

At the rear of the field, Aven and Bert rushed forward to confer with Jack and Nemo.

"What are they doing?" Aven cried. "How can we fight in the dark?"

"Charys is right," said Nemo. "But it won't be completely dark. The Wendigo carry their own torches—but the light from those will cast our shadows backward, not ahead. That will give us a chance to fight, at least, before—"

He stopped and looked down at the ground where they were standing, where his own shadow overlapped with Bert's and Aven's—but not Jack's.

Bert saw it too, and looked at Jack with an expression both sorrowful and fearful.

Jack looked at the ground, then back at the others with a defiant set to his jaw. "I know. I saw it vanish some time ago. But I don't think it means anything—I'm on your side, remember?"

"Doesn't mean anything!" Bert exclaimed. "Jack—you've become a Shadowless! That's worse than a Shadow-Born!"

"How?" Jack said stubbornly.

"It means you have the capacity for darkness," said Nemo. "You may be choosing to stand with us in the light, but your heart is choosing to be in Shadow."

Jack made a cutting motion with his hand. "I don't believe you. Judge me on what I'm actually doing, not on what you think I believe."

"Remember what the Cartographer said about choices and consequences, Jack," said Bert. "Think about what happened to him, over choices he made!"

"The Winter King said the same thing on the *Black Dragon*, remember?" said Jack. "Which one do I believe? The one who's imprisoned and couldn't help us, or the one who's able to conquer?"

"The one who's trying to kill us, you mean," said Nemo.

"Can't I have both?" said Jack. "The conviction of the Cartographer and the strength of the Winter King?"

"You can't have one foot in and the other out," said Bert. "It doesn't work that way."

Nemo looked grimly at Aven. "We don't have time for this. If he's going to become one of the Lost Boys, it'll be his own cross to bear—but I have a battle to fight."

"Wait," Aven said, grabbing Nemo by the arm. "He is good, I know it. Take him, fight with him! If you can't trust him, then trust me!"

Nemo looked at Aven for a long second, then motioned to Jack. "Come on, then," he said. "If nothing else, you'll be the one fighter we have that the Shadow-Born can't touch."

The Steward of Paralon, previously a Caretaker-in-training, went over the summoning of the dragons for the third time before he was certain (to a degree) of the exact wording. It had been sandwiched in with the notations on the map for the Island at the Edge of the World and the actual location where the ritual was to be performed.

He was a bit relieved that the Winter King didn't question him (too) extensively as to the accuracy of the translation—if his master really knew how much supposition and guesswork was involved, he'd have already cut the Steward's throat.

But then, Magwich justified, if the Caretakers of the *Geographica* weren't meant to exercise a little creative license, then why were they given credit for having a good imagination?

"Well?" said the Winter King.

"I have it," replied Magwich. "Stand here, at the edge of the peak, hold forth the Ring of Power, and repeat what I say."

As Magwich began to read, the Winter King smiled and felt a shiver of anticipation run through him. Repeating the phrases given to him by the Steward, the Winter King raised his hand. The ring shimmered in the cloying air above the falls, at the edge of the void. And, suddenly . . .

Nothing happened.

Standing, hand upraised, the Winter King's eyes narrowed, and he looked sideways at Magwich.

"Perhaps you have to read it more than once," the Steward said.

The Winter King dropped his hand and looked closely at the ring. It was not a question of whether he'd been given a fake— the ring was embossed with the seal of the king: a scarlet letter *A*. It was the High King's ring.

Still, nothing. It wasn't working.

"So be it," the Winter King hissed. "If I must take the Archipelago with sharpened steel and smoke and blood and death, so be it."

He tossed the *Imaginarium Geographica* to Magwich and drew his sword. "Let us finish this."

With that, the Winter King turned and began to stalk back down the embankment.

"Wh-where are you going?" sputtered Magwich.

"I'm going to go to the battlefield and oversee my victory," the Winter King said without bothering to stop or turn around. "I could care less what you do."

"B-but what do you want me to do with the *Geographica?*"

The Winter King stopped and stiffened, then turned and spoke, his voice icy with hatred.

"Burn it."

It had taken very little time for John and Artus to make their way around the southern tip of the island, then scale the sloping rise of rock that led to the flat bluff and the peak beyond. They actually wasted more time than they'd spent climbing arguing about whether or not their place was alongside their friends on the battlefield.

John's logic won out over a still-reluctant Artus; a choice proven wise when they saw, off in the distance, the shapes of the Winter King and the Steward, arguing.

"Let's go!" whispered Artus. "He has the *Geographica*, and I'll bet my ring, too! Come on—we can take them!"

John knew Artus was more than a match for the Steward, but he was less confident about his ability to take on the Winter King mano a mano. But more than that, he was held back by a nagging in his subconscious; a sixth sense that was saying things to him in a still, small voice: *Wait. Wait. They do not have the power they believe they have. Wait.*

He shook his head and pulled Artus behind one of the scattered standing stones. "Not yet."

Artus arched an eyebrow. "But why? What if he's able to summon the dragons?"

"I've been thinking about that," said John. "Summoning and commanding are two different things."

"What do you mean?"

"Remember what Samaranth was like?"

"Sure."

"He said he took the ring from your grandfather when he proved himself no longer worthy to use it. Does it seem to you like the Winter King is any more worthy?"

"Not bloody likely," said Artus.

"Right. Now, if the Winter King *could* summon the dragons, can you imagine Samaranth doing anything he ordered him to do?"

"No."

"Exactly. So we wait. And watch."

Magwich cursed and stomped his foot on the ground in frustration. He'd used up all the matches he'd had in his wallet, and tried using his sleeves (which burned quite nicely) as tinder, but he couldn't so much as singe the cover of the *Imaginarium Geographica*.

He'd tried tearing out pages, to use them as starters, but they were tougher than leather and wouldn't even wrinkle. He had just about decided to chuck the thing over the edge and report in that he'd burned it to ashes, when he heard the footfalls behind him.

"Master, I was just about to . . . ," he said, turning. He didn't finish. John smashed him across the face with a left cross, and the Steward of Paralon dropped to the earth like a puppet whose strings had been cut.

"Excellent!" Artus exclaimed. "Charles will be so disappointed that he didn't get to do it."

In the distance they could see the descending form of the Winter King, who was moving to join the fray. Suddenly, as they watched, all the torches on the allies' side of the battle went out, as if they'd been snuffed.

Artus and John looked at each other and swallowed hard.

John picked up the *Geographica* and turned to the pages with the summoning. "All of the information is here," he said. "Either they got it right, and the ring didn't work, or the ring could work, and they got the summoning wrong."

"Or," Artus said as John read, "the ring doesn't work and the summoning doesn't work. In any regard, we don't have the ring."

"I don't think we need it," said John, an undisguised excitement rising in his voice.

"Why not?"

John read, then reread, then re-reread the passages. "It's not a piece of jewelry," he said, astonished at the realization. "It's a *place*. The Ring of Power is a *place*."

He started pacing around in a broad circle, looking for all the world to Artus as if he'd gone insane.

"There," said John, pointing eastward, nearer the base of the peak. "Farther back, on the ridge."

Artus looked to where John was pointing, but there was nothing there except for more of the queer standing stones, which they'd seen a dozen of on their hike.

"That's the place," said John, his confidence rising with a flush in his cheeks and a quickening of his pulse. "I'm certain of it."

"How can you be sure?"

"We have a circle of standing stones just like it back home," said John. "We call it Stonehenge."

CHAPTER TWENTY
THE RETURN OF THE DRAGONS

THE WINTER KING stepped onto the battlefield just as all of the torches began to go out, and he smiled broadly in response. His enemies would be doubly handicapped now. Fighting in the dark, against warriors who could not be killed. If they were wise, they'd drop their weapons and run for their ships, which would give them a temporary respite at best. As long as he had the ability to create more Shadow-Born, it would only be a matter of time before he eventually got around to conquering all the lands in the Archipelago.

Both the battle and the conquest, not to mention his inevitable expansion into the larger world beyond, would have been faster had he been able to summon the dragons. But there was no use complaining about what might have been when all he needed now was patience.

He'd waited for things before. He could wait again. Raising his sword, he shouted a battle cry and ran to join the Shadow-Born.

In minutes the elves had lost almost a quarter of their soldiers, and the dwarves, scarcely less.

Dousing the torches had helped, but it was only a remedy, not a cure. The Shadow-Born could push through archers like stones through water, and only heavy weapons gave them any pause at all.

Eledir ordered his troops to pull back, but Falladay Finn had fallen, his shadow torn away by a Shadow-Born. Only the swift actions of the dwarves, and the self-sacrifice of several of them, allowed his limp, pallid form to be taken to safety.

Charys, leading the centaurs, took over the front lines. They had the greatest reach, and using pikes and long bardiches, could hold the line of Shadow-Born from advancing too quickly. Under their flanks, the Dwarven, faun, and animal archers held back the Wendigo in a similar fashion with a never-ending hail of arrows.

They were defending with darkness; Jack decided they needed to create an offense of light.

Jack had taken a few moments to examine Nemo's weaponry aboard the *Nautilus*, and he'd found among the various hydraulic and steam-powered weaponry a few devices of a more conventional nature, which he could adapt to better use. Including, namely, the ingredients for gunpowder.

Nemo had been running back and forth, guiding the efforts of the mythbeasts and animals, taking shots at the Wendigo when he could. Jack yelled at him and they dropped behind a hillock to examine Jack's contraption.

"It's called a grenade," Jack said.

Nemo was incredulous. "There are reasons I don't use explosives in warfare, young Jack," he said. "They're too unpredictable."

"In your world, maybe," said Jack, "but not in mine. This is my kind of weapon, from the real world. If Shadow-Born can be pushed back, they can be blown up."

Nemo looked unconvinced. "Do you have any experience making this sort of device?"

"I've read a lot about them," said Jack, "and I used the cannon on the *Indigo Dragon* pretty effectively."

Nemo started to rise in protest, but Jack cut him off.

"This is the place where imagination counts for as much as everything else, right?" said Jack. "So I improvised a little. It'll still work. I've been improvising since I came here—and I always seem to come through."

Nemo bowed his head, considering, then met Jack's eyes. "All right. What do we need to do?"

"Sound a retreat from the valley," said Jack. "Get our troops coming up the hill, then light the fuse and fling it into the center of the enemy force, at the lowest point. If it works, I can fashion several more from what you have aboard the *Nautilus*."

Nemo seemed impressed, then took a closer look.

"I don't think there's a long enough fuse," he said, examining Jack's handiwork. "What if—"

"Are you questioning me?" Jack shot back. "Just do as I tell you, and everything will be fine."

Nemo gave him a long, considered look, then nodded. "Aven trusts you, and so I cannot do less. Get more of them ready. We're going to need them."

Nemo conferred with Charys and Eledir, and the retreat was sounded. The allies turned and ran up and out of the small valley, away from the carnage that was taking place among their fallen comrades.

The enemy wasted no time in surging forward, only now they were under the direct command of the Winter King, who led the charge.

Jack was running down the hill past the retreating centaurs with the second grenade as Nemo lit the first device and threw it directly at the Winter King.

The charge exploded prematurely, almost as soon as it was thrown, showering the phalanx of Wendigo and Shadow-Born in dirt, but nothing more. The effect on the captain of the *Nautilus* was a different matter.

The right half of Nemo's torso, including his arm and shoulder, was completely gone, blown away by the charge. His face was burned and blistered, and the corneas of his eyes had been utterly scorched. He was blind, and dying in agony.

All because he had trusted Jack.

Jack ran to his fallen comrade and dropped to his knees. With the retreat, he and Nemo were alone on the battlefield with several thousand of the enemy approaching fast. Jack fumbled with the second grenade, but before he could light it, the Shadow-Born were on him.

Without a pause, the Shadow-Born rushed past and continued up the hillside.

Jack looked around wildly, confused, as thousands of the cold, black forms flowed around him. Even the Wendigo did little more than pause to sniff at Nemo before moving on. Then the Winter King was there, looking down at him.

In answer to Jack's silent plea, the Winter King spoke, a cruel light glittering in his eyes.

"They left you, Jack, because Shadow-Born do not consume their own."

With a cold smile and a wink, the Winter King ran past.

As he stared on in horror, Jack's shadow flickered back into view, then solidified. But it was too late—the damage had been done. Nemo was dead.

Jack knelt in the blood-soaked earth and began to scream.

Charles and Tummeler had to twice submerge themselves in the surf to avoid random groups of Wendigo that had caught their scent and come looking. Being completely under water hid their smell, but did little for their spirits.

Nevertheless, they had managed to make their way around the entirety of the east side and had drawn up alongside the *Black Dragon* itself. Charles's biggest concern had been identifying the tent of the Winter King, but that proved not to be a problem. It was not only the largest tent in the encampment, but also the only one with posted guards—two nasty-looking Wendigo.

"That'll be what we're looking for, no doubt about it," Charles whispered. "I'm sure Pandora's Box is inside. Why else bother posting guards on a tent behind an army the size of the one he's got?"

"Agreed, Master Scowler," said Tummeler. "So—when we gets inside, what's y'r plan? Do we try t' steal th' kettle, or just cap it here?"

"Steal it, if we can," said Charles. "I haven't the faintest idea how we'd go about closing it. There's bound to be some sort of magic involved, so I doubt it'll be as simple as nailing a board to the top and adding a 'Do Not Touch' sign."

"Okay," said Tummeler. "I know you'll do for th' best."

"We should have brought Jack," Charles lamented. "He's got a knack for improvising in difficult situations."

As they whispered back and forth, they moved stealthily out of the water, using the bulk of the *Black Dragon* as a blind. On the sand, Tummeler shook the water out of his fur and plopped down on his haunches, and Charles squatted down next to him, dropping the heavy shield to rest.

"There be just somethin' I been wond'ring," said Tummeler. "If it's a big ol' cooking pot, why does everyone call it 'Aunt Dora's Box'?"

"Pandora's Box," Charles corrected, "and it's just the nature of things to change. That's the nature of storytelling—a kettle becomes a cauldron becomes a crochan becomes a box, all depending on who's telling the story. And since Pandora had it last, that's the story—and name—everyone knows.

"Take your shield, for example," he continued, turning over the shield and dusting off the sand. "It was probably used by a Roman soldier, or a legionnaire, or someone like that, and it was called 'Polemicus's Shield,' or something like that—but I'll always know it as 'Mr. Tummeler's . . .'"

He stopped, mouth gaping.

"Master Charles?" said Tummeler. "What is it?"

Charles was looking at the surface of the shield. The pattern forged on it was a bit tarnished, but still gleamed with visible detail. It was a stylized depiction of the Medusa, from Greek myth.

"Tell me again what Samaranth said when he gave this to you, Tummeler."

"Samaranth said it belonged to a famous hero in your world," said Tummeler. "Pericles, or Theseus, or . . . or . . ."

"Perseus," said Charles, as a connection clicked in his mind. "The shield belonged to Perseus."

"That's it!" Tummeler said excitedly. "Samaranth said that even th' smallest o' us c'n be a hero, if they have th' chance—and he said this shield would give me th' chance."

"Did he now?" said Charles as a smile began to cheshire over his face. "I think he's right—and I think we're about to deal a nasty blow to the Winter King."

"It only makes sense," John said as he and Artus climbed the low rise of the ridge. "Arthur created the Silver Throne to rule in both worlds—our world *and* the Archipelago. If part of his power was the ability to summon the dragons, he would want to be able to do it no matter which realm he was in."

Artus nodded, mute. It was beginning to be evident to him that John really believed he could make something useful happen—and Artus didn't believe that himself. In the last few days, he'd seen a sharp line drawn between his boyhood fantasies about being a knight and the realities of living in a world where actions had real consequences.

It took only a minute for them to ascend to the rough circle of stones. As they stepped inside, a chill wind began to rise, concentrated within the circle itself.

"I think this was maybe a bad idea . . . ," Artus began.

John gripped him by the shoulders and spun him around. Artus expected a lecture, but John just smiled at him, as the wind grew in speed and intensity. "Think of it this way—if it works, it works. If it doesn't, we tried. If knights only went on quests they were sure of, they'd never go at all."

"Good point."

The wind swirled about them as if it intended to rip them from the very Earth and fling them into the abyss. The roar of the falls echoed against the stone of the bluff, and the spray plastered their hair to their faces. The elements seemed to be conspiring to drive them back as John opened the *Geographica* and turned it to the page Artus needed.

"John," Artus called out, "are you certain of this?"

"As certain as I can be of anything," John called back over the violent storm.

"How can I do this, John?" Artus yelled. "I can't! I'm not ready for this!"

John thrust the *Geographica* into Artus's hands.

"You wished all your life to be a knight," he said, his voice firm and his eyes clear. "Now claim your destiny, and become a king."

Artus drew a deep breath and began to calm down. His eyes darted back and forth from the desperately earnest face of his friend to the near-holy book in his hands—a book that could create a king, that *would* create a king, if only he so chose.

Reading a few lines from a book to claim his heritage, his throne, and his destiny. As simple an action as drawing a sword from an anvil.

Artus looked over the lines a final time, then closed the book and began to recite:

> *By right and rule*
> *For need of might*
> *I call on thee*
> *I call on thee*
>
> *By blood bound*
> *By honor given*
> *I call on thee*
> *I call on thee*

For life and light your protection given
From within this ring by the power of Heaven
I call on thee
I call on thee

With the last word, the tempest around them suddenly began to fade.

Finished, Artus looked at the darkness, then at the book, then again out into the void. "Did I do it right?"

"You did just fine," said John. "You certainly did *something*."

"How long is it supposed to take?"

"It doesn't say."

They waited for five heartbeats, then ten.

Then twenty. Then twenty more.

Nothing happened.

Too much ground had been given in the effort to use Jack's offensive. Charys and Eledir had trusted Nemo and Nemo had trusted Jack, and the line had been irrevocably moved. The allies had lost more than half of their soldiers to the Shadow-Born, and although the Wendigo had at worst killed only a small number of the fallen, it was going to happen to the rest sooner or later.

What remained of the elves, dwarves, animals, and mythbeasts had come together in a hollow just opposite the beach, where they were ringed in by Charys and the centaurs, who stood as the last line of defense.

The Shadow-Born had swarmed past, and for a few moments Aven and Bert thought that some miracle had occurred—but it was no miracle, just more strategy. The dark specters had cut off the path of retreat to the ships. There would be no escape.

At the command of the Winter King, a Wendigo sounded a hunting horn and summoned the Troll and Goblin armies back to the field.

The battle was over.

Artus and John had not seen the events of the battlefield. They had fixed their attention outward, toward the void.

Artus drew in a sharp breath, then glanced quickly at John, who held his gaze steady.

"Something's wrong, John."

"Have patience, Artus. I believe in you."

Artus seemed to shrink inward. "I don't know if I do."

"That's all right," John said, gripping the younger man's shoulder. "I believe enough for both of us."

Then the world shifted. Something changed. The air was stilled, and even the eternal roar of the falls became muted, as if the world had begun to hold its breath.

The eye of the storm had opened up around the small, noble ring of standing stones, and it extended its pull into the distant reaches of eternity—and there, something entered the open doorway of the eye.

"Look!" said John. "Look to the void—there, in the darkness! Do you see it?"

Far above their heads, deep to the west, a single point of light had appeared, small, but sharp and bright.

A star.

"I see it," said Artus. "But what does it—"

"Another one!" said John, pointing. "And there! Another!"

As they watched, the sky beyond began to fill with stars that flickered and flared into bright life. Then, unexpectedly, some of the stars grew brighter. And brighter. And then they began to move.

"John," said Artus breathlessly, "those aren't stars . . .

". . . those are *dragons*."

At last—at long last, the dragons had returned to the Archipelago.

PART SIX

THE SUMMER COUNTRY

CHAPTER TWENTY-ONE
THE HIGH KING

THE AIR ABOVE the Island at the Edge of the World echoed with the sound of a hundred thunderclaps as the great beasts dropped out of the sky.

Three dragons, elders by appearance and manner, came swiftly to rest in front of the stone circle, where they bowed in deference before Artus.

"I think they want instructions," John whispered.

Artus looked at the magnificent creatures before him, then turned and pointed at the battlefield.

"Help them. Help my friends."

It was apparently instruction enough. The dragons bowed their heads a second time, then stroked their wings and rose into the air.

Directly to the east, the Troll and Goblin armies had just marched back onto the battlefield at the center of the small valley and were expecting to participate in the wholesale slaughter accorded to overwhelmingly victorious armies. Thus, they were surprised to suddenly be themselves overwhelmed by a larger, stronger army of dragons.

Uruk Ko, whether through wisdom or cowardice, immediately

signaled for his troops to lower their weapons and their banners. As many kings retained their thrones through diplomacy as through conquest, and it made more sense to acquiesce than to go through what would be a pointless loss of soldiers in the name of pride.

The commanders of the trolls did not engage in a similar burst of reasoning, and instead opted to fight the incoming dragons.

The conflict lasted all of three minutes, and that was only because the dragons kept having to move out of one another's way as they proceeded to incinerate, chew up, or step on the soldiers of the Troll army.

The Shadow-Born would not fall so quickly, or easily.

Tummeler was very disappointed.

"Cheer up, old sock," Charles said as they entered the tent of the Winter King. "I couldn't have done it with a dozen cannon-balls, let alone three blueberry muffins."

"It would've been just th' two," Tummeler complained, "if that first Wendigo hadn't turned 'is head just as I conked 'im."

"Still," said Charles, "when you got him with the third muffin, he was at a dead run—and that made for a much more impressive display of sportsmanship."

"Really?" Tummeler said, brightening. "Thanks, Master Charles."

Inside the tent, Charles lit the torchieres on either side of the door, and what their light revealed was unmistakable.

It was in the center of the tent, on a simple wooden platform that had leather handles for easier transport. As they'd expected, it was an iron kettle about three feet high and slightly less in circumference, giving it a somewhat elongated appearance. The exterior was decorated with bronze platings of cuneiform writings and stylized images of ravens.

They had found Pandora's Box.

There was no cover or lid, just the remnants of wax around the edges.

"So," said Tummeler, "what's y'r grand idea?"

"We can't look into it," said Charles, "so transport is going to be a problem. So we have to go with our original plan and close it—and I think that Samaranth knew more than he was telling us. That's why he gave you the shield."

"Let me do it," said Tummeler. "I can't see into it at all—it's an insufficiency of height, as my friend Falladay Finn would say."

"Go ahead," said Charles, handing him the shield.

With considerable effort, Tummeler hefted the heavy piece of bronze above his head and approached the open kettle. In one fluid motion, he slid the shield off his head and onto the top of the iron container—where it clicked into the raised lip, fitting perfectly.

Before Tummeler could move or speak, the kettle they called Pandora's Box began to glow with an unearthly light.

"That's either really good, or really bad," said Charles. "But I expect we're going to be finding out which sooner than we realize."

When the dragons arrived, the Winter King had been facing the leaders of the bruised and battered allies, appraising them. Charys and Eledir were prepared to fight to the death—but Aven and Bert had all but given up hope. The death of Nemo had been a great blow, and the apparent loss of Jack an even greater one. Thus, the Winter King was expecting a complete submission when, in a few moments, his world turned upside down.

At first he attributed the dragons' sudden appearance to his summoning, figuring the delay was due to the rotation of the Earth, or dragon inefficiency, or something he could get angry about, being that he now commanded them. It wasn't until they started squashing trolls that he realized they weren't there in service to *him*.

A shout of triumph rose from the ragged allies, which brought a snarl to his lips.

The Winter King spun about. "Cheer all you like," he said bitterly. "You won't be alive long enough to savor your victory—not while I still command the Shadow-Born!"

The timing could not have been better to render the Winter King utterly speechless—for as he spoke, the thousand-strong Shadow-Born wavered, and vanished.

"Well," said Charys, stamping his hind legs and shifting his grip on the massive pike he held, "I would like to announce that the school of 'Beating the Tar out of Wendigo' is once more in session."

Once more, the battlefield was a frenzy of activity, lit brightly by the flames of the dragons. The elves, dwarves, and centaurs formed a blockade around the Dragonships and their injured comrades and kept the Wendigo in a thick cluster with a flurry of arrows.

Staying together in a pack made sense when in combat against fauns; against dragons, not so much.

In the chaos of the fighting, the Winter King slipped away. Aven was making her way back into the valley to look for Jack, when she saw the Winter King scaling the embankment to the west. She paused for a second, uncertain of what to do, then turned and began to follow him.

◆   ◆   ◆

The rest of the fray lasted only minutes, as the dragons were pretty much impossible to defend against, much less attack with any success. With the battlefield clear of combatants, the allies were free to return and tend to their fallen comrades, where they made a startling discovery.

All the soldiers who'd been struck down were still *alive*.

The opposing army had lost many of their soldiers. But it was the plan of the Winter King to harvest the stolen shadows of the fallen warriors to create still more Shadow-Born. So while there was damage, and blood loss, and the occasional missing limb, the bodies of the elves, dwarves, and mythbeasts were otherwise unharmed.

It was not a total victory: Most of the fallen had lost their shadows to the now-vanished Shadow-Born and were little more than rag dolls. But they still lived. And where there was life, there was hope.

"Extraordinary," said Eledir. "The Winter King's own greed gave us more than a victory—we'd have lost more if he'd simply planned for slaughter, rather than angling to use our fallen as his servants." He shook his head in wonder. "When I saw the dragons arrive, I was hopeful of a victory, but to have *no casualties* . . ."

"You're wrong," Bert said sadly. "There *were* casualties—one dead, and one that may wish he had died."

Charys had returned to the campfires with two bodies slung across his massive back. One, the fallen captain of the former *Yellow Dragon*, who had been the most valiant of them all; the other, the young man who wanted more than anything to go to war, to be in battle, and show the world his worth and mettle. The eyes of both were closed—but only one would ever open them again.

*   *   *

In the circle of stones, John and Artus watched with amazement as the dragons utterly transformed the shape, scope, and outcome of the battle that had been raging below.

"It's no wonder that everyone swore oaths of fealty to Arthur," said Artus, "if this was what happened when someone ticked him off."

"I doubt he called on the dragons for every little dispute," said John, "but the possibility would certainly have been an effective deterrent."

"It was," said a cold voice, approaching from below. "Why else would the other races have been held in check on merely the possibility of a human king who could summon them?"

It was the Winter King. He stepped inside the circle of stones, sword drawn and at the ready.

"That was very impressive, the way you switched the books," he said. "I'd been torturing my chief navigator for nearly an hour before I realized why all of his incomprehensible coordinates involved mentions of blueberries."

"Thanks," said John. "I didn't expect it to work myself."

"Of course, you should have kept a better eye on it later," said the Winter King, noticing the just-stirring Steward of Paralon lying some distance away, "or else that imbecile wouldn't have been able to take it away from you."

"True," John admitted. "Still it seems to have worked out for the best—for everyone but you, anyway."

The Winter King's eyes blazed. "You think so? You've lost more than you know, boy—and I still intend to have my victory here and now."

"Artus summoned the dragons when you could not," said John. "If you'd had a better translator than that fool Steward, you might have too. But what victory can you have now? The ring you wear is meaningless, and even the *Geographica* won't do you any good now."

Hearing them talking about him, Magwich came fully awake. "Master!" he screamed. "Master, help me! That one, there—he hit me! On the head!"

The Winter King barely bothered to glance back at his hapless servant. "I told Magwich to burn it," he said, giving the Steward a withering glare, "but it seems he's unable to do even the simplest of tasks. But I don't need the book or the ring to become the High King."

"They will fight you," said John. "All the races of the Archipelago will fight you. They'll never let you take the Silver Throne—not while a true heir still lives."

A wicked smile spread across the Winter King's face, and John realized with horror that that was precisely what he had in mind.

Protectively, he moved in front of Artus, placing himself between the two kings.

"You can try to kill him," John said, "but that still will not make you king—not of a throne that has been passed along the only bloodline to have the mandate of the Parliament."

"But I *do* have the mandate," said the Winter King. "The blood that flows through his veins flows though my own."

"You're a member of the royal line?" John said in astonishment. "I don't believe you! It's a lie!"

The Winter King chuckled. "No, it isn't." He paced slowly in front of John and Artus, taking great pleasure in the effects of his revelations. "Do you think the Parliament would spend decades locked in debate, or even entertain the notion of a usurper taking the throne, if I didn't have a legitimate claim?

"No," he continued, "they have been unable to choose a new High King precisely *because* there was one of royal blood who could block all comers—myself—but whom they in their foolishness could not bear to appoint."

"How could you be an heir?" asked Artus. "All of the king's family—my family—were killed."

The Winter King laughed. "Boy, I am much older than you give me credit for—in fact, I am almost as old as that fool shipbuilder Thoth, or Deucalion, or whatever it is he calls himself now.

"I am even older than the Silver Throne itself," he continued, "and I swore to your grandfather's grandfather's grandfather's grandfather that his heirs would one day kneel before me. And here you are."

Suddenly, the Winter King struck out with his sword, creating a deep, brutal gash across John's chest. The Caretaker screamed and dropped to his knees, trying futilely to draw his own sword. The Winter King kicked it away, then gestured for the approaching Magwich to take it up and hold the sword over John.

Artus managed to get his own short sword free of the sheath, but he was no match for the Winter King's prowess. In seconds the heir to the Silver Throne was weaponless and helpless before his attacker.

"It's ironic," said the Winter King, "that I should be holding a blade to your throat twenty years after I held it at the throat of your grandfather, and your father before him."

Artus looked up. "*You* killed my family?"

The Winter King nodded. "That's what I find ironic—the entire Archipelago believed your grandfather to be an evil man, when he was actually one of the greatest kings ever to rule here. His only mistake was in placing too high a value on protecting his family."

"What do you mean?" said John, who was still breathing hard, although the bleeding from his wound had slowed. "Archibald killed his family."

"So the story goes," said the Winter King. "But in truth, all he ever did wrong was overstep his bounds, when he asked that idiot to steal Pandora's Box. That was a forbidden magic—and its use brought with it a mandatory expulsion from the Archipelago."

"Then why did he risk using it?" said Artus. "What was so terrible that he would risk losing even the support of the dragons?"

The Winter King grinned. "That would be me. I had been in exile myself for many years in his world," he said, flicking his hook at John, "and had only recently returned after discovering the secret of passage to the Archipelago. I built the *Black Dragon* and went to Paralon to demand that Archibald relinquish the throne.

"He equivocated and stalled long enough to find a greater magic with which he could defeat me—Pandora's Box. And when he opened it, he lost the mandate of the dragons, and that fool Samaranth took his ring, when he should have taken the box instead."

"Why didn't Samaranth just let him use the box?" said Artus.

"Because," John cut in, spitting flecks of blood as he spoke, "even the king has to abide by the rules—and using evil to fight evil was not the way of the Silver Throne."

"Well put, if misguided," said the Winter King. "Archibald had lost the ability to summon the dragons—but would not name me his successor. So I killed his family, one by one, and then the king himself. I thought I'd gotten them all," he said to Artus, "but it seems I was mistaken.

"And now I will offer you one small, final mercy. The same one I offered your grandfather, which he refused."

He sheathed his sword and stepped closer to Artus, extending his hand, palm down. "Kneel before me, boy. Swear fealty to me. Make me the rightful heir. And I will give you a quick and painless death. Refuse, and your agonies shall be unending.

"Kneel and swear fealty to your ancestor. . . .

"Kneel, and swear by my true name—Mordred."

"Mordred!" John said, eyes blazing. "I don't believe it!"

"It doesn't matter what you believe," said Mordred. "All I need is his oath—and then I shall be king of *your* world, too."

"I don't think that's going to happen."

Aven stood just outside the circle of stones. She was holding two swords—one pointed at Magwich, and one pointed at Mordred.

"Ah—the Pirate Queen," Mordred said, redrawing his sword. "If you don't mind, we're dealing with men's business here, and we'd like our privacy."

"Not going to happen," Aven said again. "Everyone in the Archipelago will know what you've done, and there's no way in hell you'll ever sit on the Silver Throne."

"There are two of us, and one of you," Mordred said.

"Two of us, and one of you," Magwich repeated with shaky bravado.

"How can you get to me before I cut the young king's throat?"

"You won't cut his throat," said Aven, "because you need him to swear the oath to you—and he won't."

"He will," said Mordred, "if I order Magwich to kill his friend the Caretaker."

Aven looked at Magwich. "Listen to me, Steward. Whatever else happens here, I will kill you. Whether or not John dies, or Artus dies, or I die—I will kill you with the last of my strength, no matter what."

Magwich screamed and dropped John's sword, then ran down the hill, shrieking and madly waving his arms.

"Well?" said Aven, turning back to Mordred, as John scrambled to his feet and retrieved his sword. "Two against one, in our favor this time."

"But my sword is at the boy king's throat," said Mordred, "so it seems we have a stalemate."

"Actually," a deep voice rumbled from above, "this is what's called a 'checkmate.'"

Samaranth dropped out of the sky, and with one swift motion disarmed Mordred and carried him back into the air, clutching the Winter King in a great gnarled claw. He stroked the air with ancient wings, and they hovered almost motionless high over the edge of the waterfall.

"You were a terrible student," said Samaranth, shaking his head. "I understand your ambition, and your desire for greatness, but you've handled things so poorly these last twenty years since your return, that I think it's time for you to step offstage, so to speak, and let others direct the course of affairs in the Archipelago."

"You don't have the right to command who rules in the Archipelago," said Mordred.

"Neither do you—but Archibald deserved better than to die. And you'll die yourself long before you ever have a chance to sit on the Silver Throne."

"I'll live to suck the marrow from your bones, you old fool," Mordred spat. With a sudden motion, he drew a wicked-looking dagger from one of his boots and stabbed it into the great dragon's claw. The dagger broke off at the hilt.

Samaranth sighed.

"It's not that I dislike you, Mordred," the dragon said, "because I do like you, a great deal. But at heart, you really are a stupid little man."

Samaranth opened his claw.

Mordred—the Winter King—fell soundlessly into the void and disappeared into the darkness.

CHAPTER TWENTY-TWO
ALL THEIR ROADS BEFORE THEM

THE REMAINDER OF the night was spent in caring for the wounded and obtaining oaths of fealty from the Goblin King and Troll commanders, and all of the things that must be attended to at the conclusion of a war—which, all things considered, was far preferable to going through the same motions from the losing side. However, despite the return of the dragons and the victory over the Winter King, the struggle for control of the Archipelago was not yet over.

Arawn, the Troll Prince, had claimed the Silver Throne for himself and had overrun Paralon with his own armies, while sending the rest to fight with the Winter King. It would take planning and the support of the other races to regain command of Paralon— but given the ease with which the dragons had dispatched the trolls the night before, it was less a matter of "if" than "when."

The Wendigo, the worst and most fearsome of the enemy force, had been cornered against the base of the western bluff by Charys and his centaurs—and thus had an unobstructed view of the fate of the Winter King. Their response was unexpected. They turned from the centaurs, howling, teeth gnashing, and began to flee in the only direction available to them.

As they went over the edge, they continued to howl and screech in rage, but the roaring of the waterfall quickly overwhelmed the sound, and no one heard them as they fell.

That left only one question to be resolved: What exactly had happened to the Shadow-Born?

"I think they may be able to tell us," said Bert, pointing down the shoreline.

Approaching along the sand from the east was a very unusual sight: Charles, walking slowly, was pulling on straps of leather attached to a makeshift wooden sled. In the center of the sled was the unmistakable shape of Pandora's Box—a great black kettle, lidded with a gleaming bronze shield. Tummeler was perched on top, munching away on a stale muffin.

"Hello, Master Scowlers!" Tummeler said. "We brung . . . brang . . . bringed . . . We got Aunt Dora's Box!"

Bert, Aven, Artus, and John ran over and joyfully embraced their two friends. "You did it!" Artus exclaimed. "You closed the box!"

"Well, that was the plan, wasn't it?" said Charles. "It would have looked bad for us if you'd asked us to do this one thing and we let you down."

"Right," said Tummeler. "Not that there was ever a question— after all, Master Charles be an Oxford scowler, an' he has a reputation t' maintain."

"Indeed," said Charles. "And I have to say, it's been a very difficult night, all told. So," he added, stretching his back and looking around. "How did everything go on this end?"

All the allies wanted to know what had happened in the enemy camp, and Charles and Tummeler told the story in a rush, there on the beach, pausing now and then to compliment one another on their stealth and prowess.

The elves removed Pandora's Box from the sled and, after some debate, secured it in the hold of the *White Dragon*. It wasn't until Charles and Tummeler had changed into fresh clothes and had something to eat, that their companions recounted all the events of the night—with one exception.

"Mordred, you say?" said Charles. "Astonishing. Absolutely astonishing. But tell me, where's Jack? I expected he'd have dispatched them all single-handedly, and you'd all have been carrying him around on a platform by now, giving him medals and whatnot."

No one answered, but the expressions on their faces said that something was terribly wrong.

"John?" Charles began. "He's not . . . Jack isn't dead, is he?"

"No," said John. "Not him—someone else."

"John wasn't there," said Bert. "Let me tell you what else has happened."

They talked for a long while, and wept, and mourned—not just for the loss of one friend, but for the burden the other would carry, which none of them knew how to lift.

Late in the morning, the landscape of the island had changed yet again. When they first arrived, it had been an unblemished plain, motionless in the serene anticipation of what was to come. Then, an overrun battlefield of warriors and churning movement, and later, a charnel field of suffering and loss. Now it was much as it had begun. The enemies had either become uneasy friends or been dispatched entirely. And those who'd come to their aid had been taken onto the ships to mend or were surveying the land, watchful, not quite certain that it was indeed over.

The dragons, having done what they were summoned to do, had largely left the island, appearing only in brief glimpses in the clouds above.

Only Samaranth remained, and he and the companions gathered together near the circle of stones to say their farewells.

"We have but a few moments to talk, here, in this sacred place," Samaranth said to them. "So speak. Ask of me what you will, and I shall do my best to answer."

Artus, John, Aven, Bert, and Charles were sitting on a flat patch of grass a short distance away from the standing stones, where Samaranth landed and sat, folding his wings deferentially.

"What do I do now?" said Artus.

Samaranth laughed, with a great huffing noise. "Do? Whatever you choose to. You are the High King now."

"That's what makes me nervous," said Artus. "I don't know anything about being a king."

"Your friends did not know anything about being Caretakers, and yet somehow they managed," said Samaranth. "Although they seem to be missing one of their number."

"Jack," said Aven. "He hasn't spoken to anyone all morning. He's locked himself in the cabin of the *White Dragon* and refuses to come out."

"Yes," said Samaranth, nodding. "Tummeler has explained to me what happened. Regrettable."

"Regrettable?" said John. "Captain Nemo is dead! And it was Jack's fault!"

"Perhaps," said Samaranth, "but Nemo was not a child. He

was not coerced. And he knew the stakes and the risks. Jack should learn from this and become stronger for the experience."

"Become stronger?" said John. "How?"

"An interesting question coming from you, little Caretaker," said the dragon, "for as I recall, much of this journey was set in motion because of another death."

John hesitated. "You mean the professor."

"Indeed."

"But that wasn't my fault," said John. "Not directly. There was no way I could have prevented it."

"Perhaps," said Samaranth. "But when he was offered the chance, did he not say that he was willing to die, because his work was done?"

"How could you know that?" said John.

Samaranth shrugged. "Ask yourself this, young Caretaker—do you feel you have achieved your purpose?"

John thought a moment. "Yes."

"Would the professor?"

"Yes."

"Then your redemption did not come through his resurrection, but through your belief in a greater purpose. Something Jack would benefit to remember."

"You know," said Charles. "I think you knew all along that you had the means to close Pandora's Box, and you could have given it to us on Paralon."

"Yes," said Samaranth. "I had Perseus's shield. When Archibald opened the box, Mordred stole it, but left behind the shield, never having foreseen needing it. I kept it, and Archibald's ring, for a time when both would be needed."

"But why didn't you just tell us that was how we could overcome the Shadow-Born?" said Charles.

"You didn't ask me that," said Samaranth. "You asked me how to deal with the pursuit of the *Geographica*."

"Couldn't you have just told us?" asked John. "It might have saved us a lot of time and trouble."

"The dragons do not exist to solve your problems for you," said Samaranth, "but to help you learn to help yourselves, and you have.

"You and your friends," he said to John, "needed to solve the riddles of the *Imaginarium Geographica* and the mysteries of the Archipelago, and you did. There was a price to pay, and each of you has paid it in your own way.

"You have managed to establish a new rule in the Archipelago, and that can only reflect well in your own world. And those who have paid a dearer price know this, and would not see you suffer for doing what you had to. Tell that to Jack, when you see him. And that should he ever need them, he has many, many friends in the Archipelago to call upon."

"I have one question," said Charles. "In all the hullabaloo, I lost track of that snake Magwich. What will we do with *him?*"

"Already dispatched," said the dragon. "He was taken up by one of my kin, who asked the same question, and after conferring with the king"—he finished, winking at Artus—"we realized that the Archipelago already had a means in place for dealing with his kind. We can only hope he redeems himself as well as did the last Guardian of Avalon."

Charles looked at his friends and shrugged. "Fair enough. I just wished I'd gotten to smack him across the head one more time."

Samaranth stood and stretched his wings to take flight.

"Wait!" said Artus. "Have the dragons really returned? They're back for good?"

Samaranth looked at the young king and smiled. "Yes," he said at last. "The dragons have returned, true—but whether or not we stay is up to you. Rule wisely. Rule well. And should the need arise, call on us."

He leaned over, covering the young man in shadow, and offered his claw. Artus held out his hand, and into it dropped the ring of the High King of Paralon.

"I took it from one king who was not worthy to wear it," the dragon said, "and did so again last night. I hope that you will never give me cause to do the same.

"Fare thee well, King Artus of the Silver Throne."

The companions gathered for one final council with the kings of the races and captains of the Dragonships to confer before going on to Paralon, and then their own homes. Command of the *Yellow Dragon* was given to Aven, until such time as the *Indigo Dragon* could be salvaged and repaired. Then she could choose which of the ships to command. In consultation with the cranes, which had remained at the island throughout the night, Bert had agreed to continue using the *White Dragon*, so that he could return Pandora's Box to Avalon, and John, Jack, and Charles to London.

Artus had decided that for the time being, the island would serve as an auxiliary to the Silver Throne on Paralon, reasoning that the seat of power was wherever the king wished it to be. "I've given the island a name," said Artus. "Not that what it was called before wasn't a name, but it's rather unwieldy to keep calling it 'The Island at the Edge of the World,' don't you think?"

"Probably," said John. Tell me what you call it, and I'll make the appropriate changes in the *Geographica*."

"Terminus," said Artus. "The name of the island is Terminus."

Aside from continuing to care for those affected by the Shadow-Born, the effort of which was being guided by Charys and the centaurs, preparing the ships for departure from Terminus was the last item on the allies' agenda.

"I think the High King may be angling for a queen," John murmured to Bert, tipping his head in the direction of Artus and Aven, who were examining the repairs to the hull of the *White Dragon*.

Aven was as sharp-tongued as ever, but when Artus spoke, she now looked at him differently, considering his words with gravity and respect—and something more. Not quite affection, but the whisper of it. And there was no mistaking the way that he looked at her, nor the familiar way he placed—and she allowed him to place—his hand around her waist as he guided her around the ship.

"Yes," Bert sighed. "I could see it coming several days ago. Still," he said, "there are worse fellows she could have chosen, you know?"

A bag dropped behind them, and they turned to see Jack striding away.

"Oh, dear," said Bert. "Do you think he overheard me? I certainly didn't mean . . ."

"I know you didn't," said John. "But I think of all of us, he's had the worst of it."

Aven also noticed Jack's abrupt departure. She gave Artus an affectionate squeeze on the shoulder and walked across the sand to find Jack.

Among the supplies being loaded onto each of the ships were multiple copies of Tummeler's cookbook, which he had managed to convince Nemo to bring from Paralon "just in case."

"Tummeler!" said Charles. "I'm quite impressed with your fortitude. I have no doubt your book will eventually become very successful."

"I've got a plan," said Tummeler, proudly showing some designs he'd been scribbling on a sheet of parchment. "Th' next one will be even better. Take a look."

"I don't understand," said Charles, peering closely at the parchment. "You're going to publish the *Imaginarium Geographica?*"

"Yup," Tummeler nodded. "I discussed it with th' High King. We decided that part o' the problems caused by th' Winter King were because of all th' secrets. Secret lands, secret places, secret secrets. But if all the captains have their own *Geographica*, then no more secrets. And maybe, we can all just start getting' along."

"Sensible thinking," said Charles. "It certainly would have helped us out every time we lost ours if we could have popped around to the local shop for a replacement."

"It'll look good next to the cookbook, too," said Tummeler.

"I still don't understand the significance of the blueberries," said Charles.

"Simple," Tummeler replied. "Blueberries is one of the great forces o' good in the world."

"How do you figure that?" said Charles.

"Well," said Tummeler, "have you ever seen a troll, or a Wendigo, or," he shuddered, "a Shadow-Borned ever eating a blueberry pie?"

"No," Charles admitted.

"There y' go," said Tummeler. "It's cause they can't stand the *goodness* in it."

"Can't argue with you there," said Charles.

"Foods is good and evil, just like people, or badgers, or even scowlers."

"Evil food?" said Charles.

"Parsnips," said Tummeler. "Them's as evil as they come."

"Hang on a minute," Charles said, thumbing through Tummeler's recipe book, "you've got a recipe for Parsnip Pudding right here on page forty-three. If parsnips are evil, how do you explain that?"

Tummeler looked at him thoughtfully for a moment. "Two reasons. One, because th' Harpy sisters invented it, and they always come t' market days in Paralon, and they found out about my book, and one thing led t' another, and before I knew it, they wuz insistin' that I put their recipe in my book. And believe you me, y' don't ever want t' upset th' Harpy sisters.

"And second, just because parsnips is evil doesn't mean that they won't someday become good—or at th' least, be part of a good recipe.

"Mind you, I don't think ol' Tummeler will be th' one t' do it, but somehow it didn't seem fair to pretend there's nothin' but good foods in th' world. There has to be balance, y' know? Do y' understand, scowler Charles?"

"Yes," said Charles, "I do."

◆   ◆   ◆

Aven found Jack at a window high in the cabin of the *White Dragon*, where he could watch the loading of the other ships. He didn't acknowledge her as she entered, but the pattern of his breathing changed, and she knew he was aware of her presence.

"Jack," said Aven. "Will you be all right?"

"I don't know," he replied at length. "Truthfully, I feel like I may never be all right, not truly, ever again."

"There was much at risk," Aven said. "No one who fought in that battle was there without knowing the risks involved, or the stakes."

"Not true," said Jack. "I didn't know the stakes—or at least, chose not to believe them. And Nemo died because of me. Because he trusted that I knew what I was doing, and I didn't, and I failed him, and he died."

"Jack," Aven began again, "you hadn't been in a situation like that before. Everyone knows you were doing you best."

"Don't treat me like a child," Jack shot back. "Don't you think I knew what was happening? Don't you think a man notices when he begins to lose his own shadow? And it didn't happen last night—it wasn't even because of the Winter King. I started giving it up on my own."

Aven was taken aback. "You mean on the *Indigo Dragon?*"

"Of course," said Jack. "And he saw it there, too. Th-the Winter King. Mor-Mordred. He knew."

"He knew you had the potential, Jack. That's all he saw in you. And when it came time to make a choice, you chose to be with us, and that was what mattered."

"My choices killed Nemo," said Jack. "You say what was in my heart was different than what I chose to do, but I think you're wrong. I think what is within affects what we do. Sooner or later, we have to face that."

"And you did," said Aven, looking at his shadow on the floor.

"Yes," he replied, looking at the shadow. "I just did it too late."

Aven's face showed the conflict she felt in deciding what to say next. Finally, one side of the struggle bested the other.

"Jack," she said. "You . . . you could stay here, in the Archipelago."

He shot her a glance, and briefly, there was a light in his eyes and countenance that said he'd considered doing just that. But the light sparked and died, and he slowly shook his head.

"I can't. I—I don't think it would help. I let my emotions, my passions, get the better of me," he said, again looking fleetingly at her, "and that's exactly what he knew would happen. And someone suffered and died."

He shook his head again and chuckled, a bitter, mirthless sound. "I won't make that mistake again."

Jack turned back to the window and watched as Bert continued to guide the loading of supplies onto the *White Dragon*. Aven remained standing behind him, silent.

After a time, she extended her hand to touch him, to say something to change his mind, to reassure him that what he was going through, while bitter, and a harsh lesson to learn, was nevertheless just a part of growing up. But somehow, none of the words seemed adequate to express what she felt, and they died in her throat.

Aven held her hand near his shoulder a moment more, then dropped her hand and walked out of the room.

◆   ◆   ◆

Aboard the *Blue Dragon*, which had been converted into a make-shift hospital, Charys shook his head in defeat. "I don't think there's anything I can do."

The centaur was tending to the pallid forms of those who had fallen to the Shadow-Born, including Falladay Finn. The centaurs had long been valued for their knowledge of medicine and the healing arts, but what had been done to his friends and comrades was beyond his ken.

"I don't know," he said again, with uncharacteristic reserve. "They live, but have no will, no fire. Their spirits are gone, and I have no idea how to restore them."

"It stands to reason," Charles suggested, "that they are trapped inside Pandora's Box, doesn't it? If the Shadow-Born are created by forcing someone to look inside, and they are capable of ripping away and . . . and . . . *absorbing* the shadows of others, then where else could they have gone?"

"That's true," said Aven. "They all disappeared at the moment you and Tummeler closed the box."

"I think the best thing we can do is to take it back to the Morgaine on Avalon," said Bert. "They've had it longer than anyone. They might be able to help us."

"Or Ordo Maas," said Charles. "He has experience with it as well, although considering that it involved his wife, and her expulsion from the Archipelago, I can imagine that he won't be too happy to see it again."

"There must be some way to do it," said John. "I can't believe that the process is irreversible. The problem is, the only way to let anything out is to open it," he continued, "and then you're back to the problem of not being able to look inside without being trapped yourself."

"There's obviously some trick to it," said Charles, "or else Mordred wouldn't have been able to use it either."

"I know how the Winter King did it," said a voice from the doorway.

It was Jack.

"I know how the Winter King did it," Jack said again. "And I can do it too.

"I can free the Shadow-Born."

CHAPTER TWENTY-THREE
INTO THE SHADOWED LANDS

JACK CAME INTO the room and stood facing his friends, arms folded in a gesture that, John thought, seemed very much like one the old Jack would have made: defiant, confident, sure.

"Now, Jack," Bert began, "I know you want to help, but . . ."

Jack ignored him. "I've been thinking about this a lot," he said, pacing across the room, "and there is only one reason that the Winter King could use the box without being trapped in it himself—he had no shadow."

John and Charles looked at each other, startled. That was one point they hadn't considered.

"So," Jack continued, "it stands to reason that only someone with a similar condition could reopen, and use, Pandora's Box to free the shadows trapped within."

"That's a huge leap of logic," said Bert. "None of us knows enough about it, or even the process he used to steal shadows, to risk using the box."

"I can," Jack said for the third time. "Do you remember, on the *Indigo Dragon*, when the Winter King asked me to join him, and I refused?"

"Yes," said John. "He whispered something to you—something you claimed you couldn't even understand."

"I didn't understand it until now," said Jack. "It didn't make any sense to me then, but after Aven and I talked a little while ago, I remembered something similar the Cartographer said. And that's when I realized what I could do."

"What did Mordred say to you, Jack?"

"He said, 'Shadows cannot exist without the light. But without the shadows, the light has no meaning.'"

"A wise statement," said Charys, "even considering the source. But why would that make you think you could look into the vessel without losing your shadow?"

"Because," said Jack, "I'm the only one here who knows what it is to give up one's shadow—and then to choose to take it back."

"There remains one problem," said Eledir. "The box is known to be a forbidden magic. Samaranth has made this clear. It was not to be used by Archibald, and we know what happened when Mordred used it. If you were to try, would that not incur the wrath of the dragons yet again?"

"Not to make it worse," Charles put in, "but we also need to consider something else. When Tummeler and I closed the Box, the Shadow-Born disappeared. What if we open it again, and they all reappear? We could suddenly find ourselves up to our necks in Shadow-Born."

"No, I don't think they would, and I don't think we will," said Artus.

"Archibald and Mordred both used it to subvert another's will," he continued, "to control. Jack would not be using it to conquer, but to restore. And I don't think even the dragons would have an argument with that. And I think bringing forth Shadow-Born is a matter of intent. Sometimes Mordred needed a dozen, and sometimes a thousand. He just withdrew the number he needed. But it was always an act of will, not just happenstance. The same rules apply."

"The High King has spoken," said Charys. "I will not oppose it if Jack wishes to try."

"Agreed," said Eledir.

"All right," Artus said to Jack. "Do what you will."

The rest of the group moved to the far side of the room, so as not to inadvertantly look into the cauldron. Jack sat in a wooden chair between it and the bed where they'd lain Falladay Finn, facing away from the others. He looked back at his friends and gave a little smile. Then, with no preamble, he reached up and removed the shield from the top of Pandora's Box and looked directly inside the opening.

He sat motionless for a few seconds, and then his shoulders started to shake.

The companions exchanged worried glances, unsure if he was in trouble, or if they should risk stepping forward to help him. They could not see his face, so they were not sure if what was happening was affecting him for better or worse. Then Jack turned and looked at them, and they realized he'd been weeping.

"It's beautiful," he said. "It's full of light."

Whatever he was seeing was for his eyes alone; from their vantage point, nothing exceptional was happening.

Jack turned back and reached one hand into Pandora's Box, and it was quickly absorbed into the darkness visible. Without hesitating, he reached out with the other hand and placed it on Falladay Finn's chest.

As they watched, a tendril of darkness wound its way out of the cauldron and along Jack's arm, then across his chest, and down his other arm, finally bleeding out across Falladay Finn's limp body until it formed a complete, whole, natural shadow on the far side of the light.

Jack withdrew his arm from the cauldron and placed his hand on Finn's forehead, bowing his head as he did so—whether in prayer or concentration, they couldn't tell.

A minute passed, then another. Then Finn's eyelids fluttered, and opened.

He looked around at the group clustered around him. "Drat and damnation," he growled. "Is it over? Did I miss the entire fight? Will someone please tell me what's going on?"

The king of the Dwarves had his shadow back, and with it, his spirit, and his life.

And Jack still retained his own.

"All right," Jack said, rolling up his sleeves, the old fire shining in his eyes once more, "who's next?"

It took the rest of the day and well into the night for Jack to restore the shadows to the warriors who had had them torn away during the battle. It was a great relief to the kings and captains to see their warriors, who had become soulless, half-living shades, restored once more to their old selves. And it was a greater relief to the companions to see how the praise for the task only he could do was restoring Jack's own spirit.

As Jack worked with Charys and the centaurs on the restorations, John pulled Bert aside to talk.

"Those who fell on the battlefield are not really Shadow-Born, are they?" he asked. "Not like the ones who were forced into service by Mordred."

"Not exactly," said Bert, "although I don't really know all the specifics myself. I know that a Shadow-Born can tear away and then absorb a shadow, and we know that Mordred was keeping the victims here alive because he planned to make Shadow-Born out of the captured shadows and increase his army.

"Shadow-Born become more substantial with age. As they steal the shadows of others, they gain in substance themselves. That's why we could recognize the features of the kings of Parliament—they must have been among the first taken.

"Shadows just taken, but not yet pressed into service—I suppose these are like Shadow-Born-in-waiting. Why do you ask?"

"I've been looking through the *Geographica*," said John. "And while the Shadow-Born disappeared when the box was closed, the maps of the Shadowed Lands are still in shadow. Why would that be?"

"No one knows," said Bert. "Any expeditions to the Shadowed Lands never returned. Even Nemo could only get so close before turning back. He said they were guarded by Shadow-Born."

"That's what I thought," said John. "What were the Shadow-Born guarding?"

"I don't see what you're getting at."

"It's simple," said John. "If the bodies that provided the shadows for Mordred's invincible army had to be kept alive, then it stands to reason that all of the people in the lands he conquered are still there, with no Shadow-Born to keep us out."

Bert's eyes widened. "Oh, my dear boy . . ."

"Exactly," John said. "Jack may be able to free everyone conquered by the Winter King.

"He can free the entire Archipelago."

✦   ✦   ✦

When Jack had finished his labors with the restorations, and was able to rest and have some tea, John and Bert explained their theory to him. He accepted without pause. "I think you're right," said Jack. "I can feel all of them in there, and I know that there has to be a way to free them all."

"You realize, Jack," said Charles, "that those you've freed here numbered in the hundreds—but the Winter King had been claiming shadows for two decades. There could be thousands upon thousands of spirits in there to be restored."

"I know," Jack said, eyes shining. "I think I'm the luckiest man in the world."

The companions went to say their good-byes to all of their new-found friends as, one by one, the Dragonships began to leave Terminus. Tummeler had elected to go with Aven and Artus aboard the *Yellow Dragon*, and he embraced them all with tears and promises to visit.

To his surprise, Charles was reluctant to part with the small mammal.

"Chin up, Tummeler," said Charles. "I'll be back—and I'm sure you'll have an occasion or two to visit Oxford, eh?"

Tummeler's whiskers twitched. "Oxford? Really? Oh, Master Charles, that would be the greatest day, just th' greatest day!"

He gave Charles one more hug, then scampered aboard the *Yellow Dragon*.

"That's it, then," said Bert. "I think we must be on our way—there's no telling how long our expedition's going to take, so we'd best get started right away."

"Wait," said Jack. "There's one more thing that needs to be done, and with everyone's permission, I'd like to do it here."

"What's that, my boy?"

In answer, he turned to Aven. "Where . . . where is he?"

She started, then answered. "In his cabin, wrapped in one of the High King's banners. We thought to bury him on Paralon."

Jack turned to Artus. "You declared Terminus to be an extension of your throne, so this would be as good. And besides," he added, "no one paid a higher price for the victory won here. I think he'd like it."

"I agree," said Artus.

"Do you need a hand, Jack?" said John.

"No," said Jack. "I think I'd rather do this on my own, if you don't mind."

"Of course, old boy," said Charles, "of course."

"Jack," Aven began.

"You can come too," said Jack. "I know you were close to him. It's only right."

The two of them had started to walk up the hillside, when Jack stopped and walked back.

"Artus," said Jack, extending his hand. "Will you help us?"

"Of course, my friend," said Artus, taking Jack's hand. "You didn't even have to ask."

They buried Nemo just west of the circle of stones. Samaranth had called it a sacred place, and they reasoned that there could not be a better resting place for the captain of the *Nautilus* than at the far reaches of the world, where his spirit could look out over the limits of existence.

"Technically speaking," said Charles when they'd returned, "that's the same place Samaranth left the Winter King."

"One difference," said Bert. "Nemo is at rest—but Mordred will never stop falling. He's going to spend the rest of eternity dreading the inevitable impact that will never come."

It took less than a day to reach the first of the Shadowed Lands, and according to Bert, it was the greatest loss of the Archipelago.

"It's called Prydain," Bert said, showing them the blank parchment in the *Geographica* where the map had been. "A number of the kings and queens of Parliament were from this place, and most of the great warlords who served directly under Arthur himself.

"It was also the source of much of the music and literature of the entire Archipelago," he said, "with libraries second only to those at Paralon. Its loss was profoundly felt."

The shadows that obscured the islands were in fact clouds, thick and black, that had settled down onto the land itself. The clouds not only cut off the land from view, but also the light of the sun. A dead gray light was all that penetrated through the clotted air, leaving a soft, chalky, shadowless light that resembled nothing so much as the mythical land of the dead.

The *White Dragon* approached slowly and cautiously, but no signal heralded their arrival. It was as if no one noticed they were there.

A small harbor was found, where they could moor the ship and get a closer look at the shore. And what they saw was both horrifying and heartbreaking in its enormity.

The island was thickly wooded, with trees similar to those on both Byblos and Paralon. All along the shore were willow trees that had wildly overgrown, as if they'd not been tended to in many years. Among the trees was a throng of people—hooded, gray as death, and all but motionless.

As they looked, they could see thousands upon thousands more silhouetted in the dim light. This was indeed the source of Mordred's army, for these half-living beings looked just like the fallen warriors on Terminus.

"Oh my," Bert said softly. "This may take a very long time."

"No," said Jack. "Maybe not. It's not just the people—the spirit of the land is sick too. Can't you feel it?"

"What do you want to do, Jack?" said John.

"Help me carry the cauldron to the shore," said Jack. "Then I'll do what I've always done, and make it up as I go along."

On a rocky outcropping of the shoreline of Prydain, Jack once again opened Pandora's Box—but instead of placing his hand over the heart of one of Mordred's human victims, he placed one hand inside the box and put the other deep into the loamy soil of the land.

In moments there was a flash from the cauldron. Then a river of shadow and light twined together and ran across Jack's shoulders and into the earth.

As they watched, the light and shadow streaked across the landscape, touching every tree, rock, house, and hovel as it raced along unopposed by anything in its path.

All of the people touched by shadow wavered and fell, then began to stir, and finally rose to their feet, shaking their heads as if waking from a bad dream.

And, in a manner, they were.

"How is this possible?" John said to Bert. "How can he be doing this, all from a talisman that caused so much evil and misery?"

"He can do this," said Bert, "because he reached into it more deeply than the Winter King wanted to, or ever would.

"Remember the legend of Pandora's Box? When it was opened for the first time, and all the evils of man escaped out into the world, there was still one thing left inside, which was the redemption of all the rest.

"Hope."

In minutes the entire land had been completely transformed. Every person in sight bore a shadow, now clearly visible as the clouds burned away and let the unaffected sunlight stream through.

Jack turned to his friends, panting from exertion but smiling broadly. "How's that?"

John and Bert cheered, and Charles pumped his fist in the air. "That's the way, Jack! That's how an Oxford man gets things done!"

All the lands that had been shadowed were along the southern edge of the Archipelago. So the *White Dragon* simply traveled in a slow curve along the lands, guided to where they needed to be by the telltale smudge of darkness the shadow created on the horizon.

As Jack transformed each land, the map would reappear in the *Imaginarium Geographica*, as if it had always been there and always would.

"We'll have to let Tummeler know," said Charles. "Or he'll be stuck publishing an abridged edition."

They visited land after land; lands they had never heard of, and others they knew well from story and myth. Hy-Breasil. Lilliput. Charos and Styx. Hel. Asmund. And on and on and on.

And finally, at the end of more days than they would have liked, but far, far fewer than they had first expected, they realized that there were no more blank pages in the *Geographica*, and no more dark clouds below the horizon.

They could, at last, go home.

Bert turned the great wheel and pointed the *White Dragon* in the direction of the Frontier.

"Bert," John began, as he, Jack, and Charles approached the little man one evening. "We've been looking through the *Imaginarium Geographica*, and we think there's a land missing."

"Really?" said Bert. "But I thought we'd taken care of all the shadowed lands. How could we have overlooked one?"

"Not one of the vanished maps," said Charles. "A map that's never been in it to begin with."

"Ah, I see," said Bert. "Which land were you thinking we've misplaced?"

"We've only heard about it here and there," said Jack. "But Ordo Maas mentioned it first. He called it the Summer Country."

"Ah," said Bert, smiling. "The Summer Country. One of the greatest of the lands, and spoken about with reverence for many, many years. It's interesting that you should mention it, for the Summer Country was one of the lands that Mordred—the Winter King—wished to find more than anywhere else."

"The way Ordo Maas spoke of it," said Jack, "made it seem as if it might be another place altogether—as if that's where he would go when he died."

"Heaven?" said Bert. "It's entirely possible. It all depends on your point of view."

"How can the existence of a place depend on one's point of view?" asked Charles.

"Very easily," said Bert, "or have you already forgotten the Keep of Time? There were real, physical places behind those doors—but you can argue that they didn't exist until the door was opened. When John opened a door and found the professor, that place existed for him, based on his belief that it was there. As did the door that provided our escape. It was what Charles needed it to be. In a manner of speaking, he believed it into existence. So is it with the Summer Country."

"So the Summer Country is whatever people want it to be?" said Jack.

"It is the way most people speak of it," said Bert, "but you are correct—the legend is based on a place that actually exists.

"The Summer Country is a land greater than any in the Archipelago of Dreams, because it has within it everything to be found in the Archipelago, and more. But where someone like Ordo Maas could find it anywhere, the Winter King would never find it at all. Because to him, it is always just out of his reach—when, in truth, he had it in reach all along."

"It sounds," John said, "as if you're talking about *our* world."

"Yes," said Bert. "Your world *is* the Summer Country."

CHAPTER TWENTY-FOUR
THE RETURN TO LONDON

MUCH OF THE remaining voyage back was spent reexamining the *Geographica* and making notations on the maps that had reappeared since the defeat of the Winter King and the reawakening of the Shadowed Lands. Until just a few days before, the companions would have given—would have done—anything, for immediate passage home. Now it seemed as if England were in the dream world to which they might travel, if only they believed in it enough. And while they still believed in England, and London, and Oxford, and all the rest in the world of men, they had come to know that there was another world that was just as real. And they were no longer certain they wanted to leave.

"We've got a limited crew this time through," said Charles. "Namely, us. Will the *White Dragon* have any trouble navigating the storm line?"

"It's meant to keep people out, not in," said Bert. "You'll find it's a much easier passage going east than west."

John didn't say what he was thinking—that he was already anticipating having to push through the storms again, going in the opposite direction. That he wanted to return to the Archipelago, and soon.

"Here's something I never expected I'd be saying out loud," said Jack, "but does anyone else find it comforting that there are at least three dragons shadowing us from above?"

High in the atmosphere, a greenish dragon and two smaller amber ones were diving and soaring in and among the clouds of the storm line, dipping their wings in greeting as they noticed that the companions were watching.

"The mariners had it wrong," said Charles. "'Here, There Be Dragons' wasn't a caution. It was a reassurance."

"I think that would depend on your relationship with the dragons," said John. "Remember—when we met, Samaranth's other option was to eat us."

As the *White Dragon* passed through the storm line and into more traditional waters, the dragons wheeled away and vanished into the ether.

In the distance, they could just make out the silhouette of Avalon, soft and verdant in the light of dusk.

"What do you say, lads?" asked Bert. "Want to stop off and pay your respects to the Morgaine?"

"Depends on the day, doesn't it?" said Jack. "Tuesday we can manage, but I'd rather not catch Cul in a fouler mood."

"Good call, Jack," said Bert. "Next time, then."

The sunlight faded quickly with the sudden smothering of clouds that marked the crossing of the last boundary. Soon, the familiar English fog had begun to coalesce around the ship, and then, twinkling in friendly greeting, the lights of London began to appear.

"Now I know we're home!" exclaimed Charles. "Look at that water! It's absolutely filthy! God bless the Thames!"

The companions' happy laughter was cut short when the shrill-ness of an air-raid siren split the night air, shattering the stillness into pieces that fell with John's smile. He looked to each of his friends, and then to Bert.

"We're still at war," John said, crestfallen. "We defeated the Winter King, but our world is still at war."

"Well, of course it is," Bert said, chiding. "The conflict in the Archipelago is not over either, for that matter."

John furrowed his brow. "But we won. Artus is the new High King. We restored order in the Archipelago, and Jack freed the Shadow-Born."

"Did we now?" said Bert. "Yes, we found the heir and reestab-lished the continuity of rule in the Archipelago. But just because a man sits on a throne doesn't mean automatic fealty."

"He has a point," Charles put in. "There's still the Troll Prince, Arawn, to deal with—and the Four Kingdoms have to come to grips with having a new king on the Silver Throne. Artus has quite a row to hoe."

"Does that mean we're going to remain at war until Artus has things in hand in the Archipelago?" said John.

"You misunderstand," said Bert. "It isn't like pulling a lever—as the conflict in one world is mirrored in the other, so is the peace and harmony we helped to set in motion in the Archipelago going to be reflected in this world. But the events that have occurred here must still take their course. There is the matter of free will to consider. We have removed the catalyst, true—but the world of men must still work to repair the damage that has been done, and then, ultimately, must choose peace."

"I think I understand," said John. "I suppose that somehow I was hoping for a more magical instant solution. Like 'drink me' and 'eat me' in *Alice's Adventures in Wonderland.*"

"Now, John," Bert chided. "That's just a story. We should stay focused on the real world, don't you think?"

The journey ended exactly where it began, at the dock in London where they had fled from the pursuing Wendigo. It had only been days, but it already seemed a lifetime ago—and in a sense, it had been.

"I have to let my wife know I'm all right, then I'm back to Staffordshire, I expect," said John. "And then probably back to France, as I'm still enlisted for the duration. I just hope my absence hasn't been long enough for them to notice and declare me missing—I'll never be able to explain where I've been!"

"I'm overdue myself," said Charles, "although I expect that the Oxford dons might be more forgiving than the military."

"I still think I'll be joining up before I start my term at Oxford," said Jack. "After all, the war should be over soon anyway, right?"

"We can hope, young Jack," said Bert. He turned to John. "I'll check in now and again, to see how you're coming along. I must admit, it's a nice thought to realize that I can actually retire, knowing that the *Geographica* will be in good hands. Now I must go—I have to return the *White Dragon* to Ordo Maas, and then attend to the repair of the *Indigo Dragon*, bless her timbers."

He bowed his head, chewing his lower lip, before continuing to speak. "There is one last detail to which we must attend," Bert said, his voice trembling with emotion. "It has been tradition, these many centuries, for the Caretakers to add their names to those who came before. I would be honored if the three of you would do so now."

"The three of us?" said Jack. "But John is the Caretaker."

"The Caretaker Principia," Bert corrected, "but there have always been three. The purpose of the other two Caretakers is to help the Caretaker Principia fulfill his responsibilities—and I daresay that's what the both of you have been doing these long days."

"Not to seem ungrateful," said Charles, "but with Tummeler about to start a publishing empire based on the twin pillars of cookbooks and atlases—namely, the *Geographica*—what is the point of having Caretakers? Why take care of a book that everyone in the Archipelago will now have access to?"

"Remember what John told the Cartographer?" said Bert. "It's about more than safeguarding a mere book—it's a far greater responsibility than that. You are the Caretakers of the lands within it. The Caretakers of the Imagination of the World. And you've proven yourselves more than worthy, and more than able."

Jack and Charles looked at each other, then at John, who tilted his head and smiled. "Why not? Who else can we tell about all these adventures we've had, if not each other?"

"Sounds good to me," said Jack. "I for one intend to write it all down before I forget what happened. Not that there's much chance of that," he added quickly.

"I don't suppose it's coincidence that we're all Oxford men, is it?" Charles joked.

"No, it's not," said Bert. "It isn't a rule that the Caretakers be from Oxford, or even English; but for some reason it seems to better the odds. Both times we had a Cambridge man—John Dee, and then Lord Byron—it was an absolute disaster. I even heard rumors that Dee had something to do with Atlantis sinking, although how that might have occurred I have no clue."

"Sorry I asked," said Charles.

"Where do you want us to sign?" said John. "Do we choose a favorite map, or what?"

"Do you mean to tell me that in all this time, you never took a look at the endpapers inside the cover?" Bert said with astonishment. "Blow me down and call me Shirley."

"It wasn't a map," said John. "Forgive me for being goal-oriented. I was under a lot of stress, you know."

Bert smiled and shook his head in mock dismay as he opened the front cover of the *Geographica* and turned it around for them to read.

"Amazing," said Charles. "If we hadn't just been through what we have, I don't quite think I'd believe this was real."

"Amen," said Jack.

John said nothing, but began tracing his finger underneath the names inscribed on the two pages; names that contained within them much of the cultural and scientific history of the entire human race.

Edmund Spenser. Johannes Kepler. William Shakespeare. Chaucer was there, as were Roger Bacon, Alexandre Dumas, Cervantes, Nathaniel Hawthorne, and Jonathan Swift. Tycho Brahe. Jacob (but not Wilhelm) Grimm. Hans Christian Andersen, and Washington Irving.

Coleridge was there, and both Shelleys: Percy Bysshe and Mary Wollstonecraft. Arthur Conan Doyle, whom they expected, and Harry Houdini, whom they did not. Goethe. Dante. Edgar Allan Poe. And on and on and on.

"Poe?" Jack said in surprise. "And Mark Twain?"

"Jules Verne, as well," said Bert. "He's the one who passed it on to me."

"Extraordinary," said Charles.

"The earliest of the Mapmakers' names are not there, of course," said Bert. "It was almost a thousand years after the Cartographer began to compile it that the first Caretaker took over."

"Who was that?" said John.

"Geoffrey of Monmouth," said Bert.

"These aren't copies," said John, touching the pages with reverence. "These signatures are all originals."

"Here," said Bert. "You can sign underneath our names."

There at the lower part of the right-hand page was the elegant script of Professor Sigurdsson's name, followed by a signature that had been crossed out.

"That's the rebel Caretaker's name, isn't it?" asked Charles.

"Yes," nodded Bert. "Stellan never forgave Jamie for turning his back on us."

"What was his full name?" asked John, peering at the list.

"You may have heard of him," said Bert. "He's just been knighted recently—Sir James Barrie."

John stood up abruptly and looked at Charles and Jack in astonishment. Jack leaned forward and furrowed his brow. "Where's your name, Bert?" he asked. "Shouldn't it be under the other two?"

"Not under," said Bert, "above. I was given it first, remember? I then recruited Stellan, who in turn recruited Jamie."

As one, the three men looked to the name above the professor's—and as one, all three jaws dropped open in surprise.

The signature read "Herbert George Wells."

"I never really liked Herbert," said Bert, "and couldn't see myself as a George either, for that matter."

"It's an honor to . . . ah . . . ," John began, raising his hand for a shake. He looked at his proffered hand, then sheepishly withdrew it. After all they had been through together, Bert was no longer a stranger to them, but family—whatever his true name.

"Hang on a minute," said Charles. "There's a problem with that. You see, I've actually met H. G. Wells, and—no offense, Bert—but he's a lot younger than you are."

"Oh, you've misunderstood me," said Bert. "I'm not that H. G. Wells. I mean, I am him, but not the him from now—I'm the him from then, in the future."

"The future?" said John.

"Eight hundred thousand years," Bert said, checking his watch, "next Thursday."

"That's fantastic," said John. "You *are* the Time Traveler you wrote about in your book."

"Guilty, I'm afraid," said Bert. "Nemo and I built the device based on designs conceived by Leonardo Da Vinci, and my first journey 'out' was when I met Aven's mother, Weena. I wrote down an account of the whole adventure and wished desperately to share it with the world at large—but I realized that it would never be taken seriously as a nonfictional, biographical accounting. So I revised it—considerably, I might add—and published it in the version you all know."

"That's not a bad idea," said Jack. "To disguise the true story as fiction or allegory. I might take a stab at that myself."

"It seems a shame, though," said John, "not to be able to tell anyone what really happened. But then again," he added, "I don't think I could talk about what's gone on in the Archipelago with anyone but you three. No one else would believe it."

"So, Bert, when I met him, uh, you . . . ," Charles began.

"You met a much younger version of me," said Bert, "and I remember the meeting well. That's when I first pegged you as a potential Caretaker."

"You were scouting me?" said Charles.

"Sure," said Bert. "Who do you think it was who recommended you for the editorial position at the Oxford University Press?"

"Were you watching me, too?" said Jack.

"No," said Bert. "You hadn't written enough yet to draw my attention."

"Oh," said Jack, a bit crestfallen.

"Awfully glad you came along, though, Jack," said John. "Couldn't imagine having gotten through it all without you."

"Thanks," said Jack.

"When you came to the club," Charles said, "you didn't act as if you knew me."

"Because I didn't," said Bert. "I knew your work, and that's it, and that's all. There were about a dozen of you whose writing bore the marks of a potential Caretaker—imagination, innovation, conviction, and clarity—and I left it to Stellan to choose who to train further. He chose John."

"But if there were potential Caretakers available to be trained," said Charles, "couldn't we have been recruited sooner, after the other Caretaker left his post, so that the crisis with the Winter King could have been averted?"

"Mordred's plot was already well under way before Jamie came along," said Bert, "or even myself and Stellan, for that matter. Nothing could have been done to prevent the events from proceeding as they did up until the point where he came out in the open. And by then it was too late."

"You don't think James Barrie could have prevented the war if he'd stayed on with the professor?" said John.

Bert shook his head and walked past them, clasping his hands behind his back. "I've wondered that myself," he admitted, "but I doubt it. Jamie just wasn't suited to it, and it all but broke Stellan's heart when he walked away. I do know this," he added. "Whatever the difficulty was in seeing through your obligations, I know that Stellan saw your acceptance as a redemption of sorts."

"A redemption of himself? Or of me?" said John.

"Does it matter?"

"Maybe. Maybe it does."

"Then take this as your answer: When the time came, you did all that the professor and I hoped you would be able to do. And while the struggle was not pleasant to endure, I think it made your victory all the sweeter. And wherever he is now, I think the professor is glad of the faith he placed in you, and I know he's proud of you, John."

"I have a pen," said Charles. "Who's to go first?"

"Go ahead," said John.

Smiling, and with a trembling hand, Charles inscribed his name in long, looping letters:

Charles Williams

He handed the book and pen to Jack. "Thanks," said Jack. "Can you steady the book for me?"

"Certainly."

Jack thought a moment, then signed, and passed the book over to John, who looked quizzically at the signature:

C. S. Lewis.

"I always hated the name Clive," said Jack. "My brother Warnie called me Jack, and it stuck."

"Fair enough," said Bert. "And now you, John."

John took the pen in hand and paused to look at his friends, who had become his allies, and confidants, and his family in the short time they had known each other. He considered how they had come together, and the price each of them had paid to do what needed to be done—but even then, it had been a grand adventure, and, he suspected, only the first they would have together. It was, after all, a very big world.

"Here's to remembering the future," said John.

"To the future," said Jack and Charles.

"Well said, my boy," said Bert.

John signed his name with clear, tight strokes:

JRR Tolkien.

And closed the book.

EPILOGUE

HIGH ON A *bluff on the Island at the Edge of the World, the High King sat, idly chewing on one of the long grasses that had begun to grow again on the fields decimated by the battle.*

Nearby was a ring of standing stones that brought him comfort by their very presence, and the newly blessed grave of a dear friend, which, strangely, had the same comforting effect.

He sat, chewing, and looking into the darkness beyond the great waterfall, and wondered.

In just a few short days, the world—two worlds, in fact—had been irrevocably altered, and as High King of the Silver Throne of Paralon, it was now his duty to see that the changes benefitted the peoples of a hundred lands, even those peoples who did not claim him as king, or support his rule. Such was the burden of a kingdom.

He wondered about the woman with whom he'd been traveling, and working beside, and sharing his dreams with, and whether she would stay with him, and help him rule his kingdom, if he asked.

Artus wondered if it had really been his summoning that drew the dragons, or if it had been the intervention and call of Samaranth.

He wondered what might have happened had the dragons not come at that precise moment he appeared to summon them, or worse, not come at all.

He wondered what might happen if he should ever need to call on them again. In the days since the conflict, dragons soaring high in the skies above were not an uncommon sight—but neither were they seen in the numbers that had appeared at that crucial moment during the battle.

He wondered what was really out in the void; and what lay below. He wondered if, when someone went over the waterfall, if there was eventually an ending to it, or if you would just keep on falling for eternity.

And sometimes . . .

Sometimes, he just wondered.

Author's Note

History is comprised less of certainty than of supposition. Go back far enough, and fact begins to merge with fiction—or at least with traditional tales, which bear a truth all their own.

To me, the most interesting stories are those that have one foot firmly planted in fantasy, and the other in the real world; and the best way to create a marriage of the two is to find those gaps in history where there is no certainty, and create a supposition.

Suppose the worlds of make-believe had a basis in reality. Suppose that we could, in the right circumstances, visit them. And suppose that the proof of their substance was strewn throughout both history and fiction, if only we knew where to look. . . .

At first glance, it seems that Ordo Maas's story is that of Noah; but in fact, the origin is deeper and older. Ordo Maas says he has many names; and later on, Mordred refers to him as "Deucalion." In Greek myth, Deucalion was the son of Prometheus (who gave him the fire at the end of his staff) and was married to Pyrrha— who was Pandora's daughter. When the gods punished mankind by flooding the Earth, they were saved when Prometheus gave them fire, and told them to build an ark. After the flood, they repopulated the Earth. As Deucalion's father gave *him* a gift, so did Pyrrha's mother give *her* one: Pandora's Box. My supposition here was that Pyrrha, not her mother, was the one who opened the box, after the flood.

The Egyptian equivalent of Deucalion was Thoth—whose daughter, Bast, was the goddess of Cats.

Tying the Pandora myth to the Fates (The Three Who Are One) and calling them the Morgaine ties together Greek myth with Welsh and Celtic lore—as does Ordo Maas's claim that the first Dragonship was the rebuilt *Argo*, which the Greek hero Jason used to find the Golden Fleece.

The Green Knight ties the Arthurian myth to contemporary fiction via Dickens's *Tale of Two Cities*, as, of course, does Magwich.

The Cartographer of Lost Places is entirely my own invention—but as with the rest, his origins lie in a supposition, and the clues to his true identity are there for careful enough readers.

And finally, I wanted to start off the adventure in a place that had a mysterious resonance of its own. The address of the club Charles leads John and Jack to—221B Baker Street—is well known to any Sherlock Holmes reader as the detective's home. A perfect place to begin a "dark and stormy night" story.

James A. Owen
Silvertown, USA

THE SEARCH FOR
THE RED DRAGON

PROLOGUE

IT WAS NOT *the soothing notes of a lullaby that lured the children from their beds, but it was a song nonetheless. Their parents never heard it, for the tune had not been intended for them.*

It was a song played for children; and when they heard it, the children came.

Half-asleep and barefoot, still in their nightshirts, the children climbed from their beds and through windows that had been opened, unknowingly, to let in the cool breezes of evening.

They walked, entranced, down winding lanes that converged into a single path that none of them had ever seen before, but that had always been there.

It had many names, for it was only ever walked by children, and children have a fondness for naming things. But each child, as they passed, knew it for what it truly was—the Road to Paradise. They knew this, because the song they heard told them so.

The notes of the music seemed to emanate from all around them, played everywhere and nowhere all at once, and the music maker, when they glimpsed him in the twilight air, seemed to change shape in time with the music.

His flickering, ghostlike form was sometimes a grown-up, and other times a child like themselves. And sometimes he seemed not to be human at all. The music told them his name: the King of Crickets. And none of them could resist the song he played.

None, save for one.

She had been cautioned that one day the King of Crickets would come, and that unless she was prepared, she would not be able to resist his song. No children could, unless they were crippled, and could not follow, or were unable to hear the tune and fall under its spell.

The beeswax she put into her ears, as the dream had told her to do, kept out enough of the music for her to resist its lure—but not so completely that she couldn't feel the desire, nor hold back the tears that streamed onto her pillow as she finally slept, still dreaming of Paradise.

For some children, the path ended at a great mountain face that split open to embrace them, and closed as they passed through. For others, it ended at a great precipice, which they stepped over, willingly, because the song told them they could fly. But for most, it led them to the Men of Iron, and the great ships that departed with the dawn.

In the light of morning, the path would again vanish, but it would have a new name: the Sorrow Road.

As they awoke to find the beds of their sons and daughters empty, the mothers and fathers in the towns and villages would feel bewilderment, then fear, and then terror. And they would name the path with their cries.

But it was too late. Much, much too late.

The children were already gone.

PART ONE

NINE YEARS IN THE
SUMMER COUNTRY

CHAPTER ONE
THE ANGEL IN THE GARDEN

JOHN RARELY DREAMED, and it was even more seldom that he could recall what he dreamed about. But as of late, he had had dreams every night, and he remembered them all—because when he dreamed, he dreamed of Giants.

Massive continents of bone and sinew, creating their own topographies as they strode across the landscapes, giving little notice to the awed creatures watching from below. The Giants were so great it seemed they had both gravity and weightlessness; as if the next thundering step would suddenly launch them into space, to join with the gods and Titans among the constellations.

Standing with the populace of his dream world (all of whom, strangely, seemed to be children), John watched in mute wonder as the Giants strode past with geological slowness. Then, as in each of the dreams, one of the Giants turned and looked down, directly at John. Shifting its weight, it bent and reached for him with a hand the size of a barn as the children around him began shrieking. . . .

The train whistle was shrill in the afternoon air, startling John out of his troubled reverie. He stood and quickly scanned the crowd departing the train that had just come in from London.

The station at Oxford was not large, but the afternoon schedules were always full of both comings and goings, and he didn't want to miss the person for whom he was waiting.

He realized with a rising thrill that he was far more excited to see his old friend than he'd expected to be. They had, in point of fact, spent only a few weeks together a number of years before—but the events of those days were enough to make them closer than mere colleagues. And so when the thin, nervous-looking man with the high forehead and round spectacles finally emerged from the train onto the platform, John rushed forward and greeted him like a brother.

"Charles!" he exclaimed joyfully. "I say, it's terribly good to see you!"

"I'm very pleased to see you, too, John," said Charles, clapping his friend on the back. "It's odd—as I got closer and closer to Oxford, I kept feeling as if I was coming home. But it wasn't because of the place—rather because I knew I was going to be seeing you and Jack. Does that sound strange to you?"

"Yes," replied John, chuckling, "but in all the right ways. Come on—let me help you with your bags."

As they loaded Charles's belongings into John's vehicle, Charles looked around nervously and leaned closer to his friend. "I wanted to ask," he said in a conspiratorial whisper, "do you, ah, do you, you know, have, ah, 'it' with you?"

"Of course," said John, pointing to a bundle of books and papers on the rear seat. "It's there in the middle somewhere."

Charles's eyes widened in shock. "Here? Out in the open?" he exclaimed. "Not locked away or anything? John, are you out of your mind? That's, that's . . ." He lowered his voice again. "That's the *Imaginarium Geographica*. The single most valuable book on Earth. Don't you think it's a bit, ah, risky?"

"Not at all," John said with a trace of smugness. "Take a look at the lecture on top of the pile."

Charles adjusted his spectacles and peered more closely at the document. "It says, 'A proposal for syllabus reform as regards the study of Ancient Icelandic.' And the rest appear to be notes on courses in Comparative Philologies."

He climbed into the seat next to John and gave his friend a puzzled look. "Don't take this the wrong way, but how many people, even at Oxford, would care about such things?"

"Precisely my thinking," said John as he started up the car. "I have a hard enough time getting the undergraduates to pay any attention to Anglo-Saxon, much less Old Icelandic. What better protection for the *Geographica* than to bury it amongst manuscripts that no one else will care about?"

It had been nine years to the day since John and Charles had met each other in London. Nine years since they and the companion they were going to see had gone on the most extraordinary expedition of their lives.

Exceptional circumstances had brought the three young men together at the scene of a murder. The dead man, John's mentor, Professor Sigurdsson, had been one of the Caretakers of the *Imaginarium Geographica*.

The *Geographica* was an atlas of maps of a place called the Archipelago of Dreams—a great chain of islands that had been coexisting with our own world since time began and had influenced many of the great men and women of history.

But not all of those influenced by the Archipelago were influenced for the better.

A man called the Winter King tried to use the *Geographica* and the knowledge found within to conquer the Archipelago. Another Caretaker, Bert, enlisted John and his two friends to travel into the Archipelago to try to stop the Winter King. And somehow, despite terrible odds, they managed to do it.

The Winter King lost, and fell to his death over the edge of an endless waterfall. A new order was established in the Archipelago, under a new king and queen. And the *Geographica* now had three new Caretakers: John, Charles, and the youngest of the three friends, Jack.

But there had been prices paid for their victory. Allies were lost. Mistakes were made. And although there had been a measure of redemption, there were some events that would never be far from their thoughts.

Events in the Archipelago resonate with those in our world— which was then still in the midst of World War I. John resumed his service in the military just as Jack began his. Only Charles was spared, due to his general nervous nature and age. And when finally, the war ended, they all resumed their lives as if the war, and their adventure in the Archipelago, had been imaginary aberrations, or dreams.

And perhaps John could have convinced himself that it all *had* been a dream, if it were not for the great leatherbound book that he still possessed. He had not had so much as a message from Bert since the old tatterdemalion had returned them to London aboard the *White Dragon*—one of the great living Dragonships that were able to cross the boundary between our world and the Archipelago.

At least, John mused, there hadn't been any more murders. Or another war. He didn't think the planet could survive a second war on the scale of the one they'd come through. But then again, much of the responsibility for those events could be attributed to the Winter King—and he had been dealt with.

John had been working in his study at Oxford when the messenger boy arrived with the note from Jack's brother Warren that requested he come to see Jack immediately. As he was reading it, the telephone rang. John picked it up and was happily surprised to find Charles on the other end, having just received a telegram of his own. In short order, arrangements were made for Charles to travel to Oxford, where he and John could meet and then go together to see Jack.

When they had parted ways in London years earlier, they had made a pact to never contact one another except in the event of a situation arising that involved the care of the *Geographica*, or the Archipelago, or in case of another extreme emergency. It was, they decided, the only way to protect the secrets they had been entrusted with.

It was likely, if not inevitable, that their academic pursuits would sooner or later bring them into contact with one another; but otherwise, it might foster too many questions for the three to be in one another's company. And in nine years, no occasion had arisen for any of them to cross paths—so for Jack to deliberately break their pact and contact each of them directly was, John suspected, probably more for a bad reason than a good one. Unlikely as it was, he hoped it was the latter.

The small cottage where Jack was staying was near a cozy little village at the edge of Oxford city. They parked the car on a patch of gravel just off the road, and after checking on the *Geographica*, went to the front door and knocked.

The door was opened immediately by a thickset, tanned fellow in military dress, who bore more than a passing resemblance to the young man they both remembered. John and Charles both hesitated, before remembering that it was Jack's brother who had summoned them there in the first place.

John immediately stiffened into the formal posture he affected when addressing a fellow officer. "You are a captain, I believe?" he asked before the other waved off the question.

"Please, we're all informal here," the man said, shaking John's proffered hand. "I'm heading swiftly for retirement in a few more years and plan to soon be devoting my time to assembling the family papers and as much reading as I can manage."

"I'm John, and this is Charles. We came as quickly as we could."

"A pleasure," said Charles, stepping forward to shake the man's hand. "You're Warren?"

"Call me Warnie—Jack does. I'm very grateful to both of you for coming. Although I must admit, it is a bit odd that he should ask for you."

"Why is that?" said Charles.

"As I understand it," Warnie explained, "you've not actually become officially acquainted since he began teaching at Magdalen. In fact, before yesterday, Jack never so much as mentioned either of you at all."

It was a testament to the swiftness of their self-control that neither John nor Charles exchanged a glance at this.

"It's just that Jack is an intensely private person," Warnie continued, "and while he's an excellent tutor, and is very affable with our circle of friends, it's unlike him to be so open about personal matters with, er, ah, strangers, so to speak. And especially so to invite them here to his private study. No offense."

"None taken," said Charles, trying to keep the mood light. "If I'd come here for a bit of solitude, I wouldn't want to be disturbed either. This is a lovely accommodation. It's called the Kilns, isn't it?"

"Yes, it is," said Warnie, nodding, "after the brick buildings down the way.

"We've taken it for a few months so that Jack could get some work done," he went on. "It's a very pleasant place, actually, and very convenient to Oxford, as you've seen. The gardens are quite large—almost a park—and extremely overgrown. But I wouldn't mind settling here for good, if we had the coin to afford the price."

He regarded Charles appraisingly. "You called it the Kilns— you know Headington Quarry, then?"

"I've had my opportunities for walking expeditions from the city," replied Charles. "Not so much now that I'm based in London, but I do like returning here to Oxford now and again."

"I haven't been out this direction yet," John said, "but now that I've been given the new position at the university, I expect I'll have plenty of opportunities."

"New professor of Anglo-Saxon, Jack said?" asked Warnie.

John nodded. "Yes. The professors and college tutors don't have too many occasions to socialize, but I imagine we'll be coming together sooner or later."

"How is it that you know Jack, if you don't mind my asking?"

"We, ah, we met during the war," said John. "The three of us, that is. It was a very unusual circumstance. . . ."

Warnie made a dismissive gesture but smiled knowingly. "Say no more. It's all clear to me now. The war created brothers in an instant, and made allies of enemies and vice versa. I was wary that he's asked me to summon colleagues he's never mentioned to me— but if you served together in the war . . . I didn't mean to pry, but brothers should look out for one another, you understand?"

"We do," said Charles. "That's why we didn't hesitate to answer your summons."

Warnie smiled again. "Good show, good show. Let me take you back to Jack's study—he's waiting for you there."

"You said it was personal matters he wanted to discuss," John said. "But it wasn't clear in the telegram you sent what exactly Jack wanted to see us about."

"He's stopped writing in his journal—stopped writing altogether, now I think on it," said Warnie. "Then he stopped reading. That's when I really began to worry."

"Why?" asked John.

"He lost a very close friend in the war. And although he was nowhere near at the time, Jack feels he is somehow responsible for the fellow's death."

Charles and John each drew a sharp breath. That had to be a factor in why Jack had asked for them. In the battle with the Winter King, he had been responsible for the death of an ally, and it had affected him greatly. But Jack seemed to have reconciled himself to it well before their return to London—or so they had assumed. Apparently they were mistaken.

"How is he sleeping?" John asked.

"He isn't. Night terrors, I'm afraid," Warnie said somberly. "They've been going on for several days now, and there's been little

I could do to help. The worst was two nights ago. Lots of screaming and thrashing about, and calling out a word over and over—
'Aven.' I have no idea what it means, and Jack wouldn't speak of it.
It was that next morning he told me to seek out the two of you and
ask you to come here."

He paused at a sturdy door and hesitated before knocking.
"I'll leave the three of you to catch up. I'll be puttering about in the
garden if you need anything."

As Warnie moved back down the hall, John and Charles
opened the door and entered the book-crammed study. Jack—
taller, broader, more manlike than the boy they'd known—stood
at the window with his back to the door.

"Jack?" Charles ventured. "Jack, we've come. It's Charles and
John."

Jack tilted his head slightly, acknowledging their presence, but
he did not turn around. Instead he asked a question.

"Was it real? Did it all really happen, after all?"

It took a moment for them to realize what he was asking.

"Yes," said John. "If you're asking what I think you are."

"So . . . the Archipelago of Dreams . . . the *Imaginarium
Geographica* . . ."

"Yes," John repeated. "It's all real."

Jack turned to look at them, his face inscrutable. "Do you have
the atlas with you? Can—can I see it?"

"It's, ah, it's in the backseat of the car," John admitted sheepishly.

"In a lockbox, or a leather bag, I'd assume?"

"No," said Charles. "It's protected by a thick layer of lectures
on Ancient Icelandic."

Jack blinked and then snorted. "And they call you the Caretaker

Principia. Did you at least mix in a few papers on old Anglo-Saxon? Or are you giving your professorship short shrift too?"

John and Charles stared at their friend for a moment before the somber expressions on their faces were broken by broad, transcendent smiles.

"Of course it happened, my good fellow," said Charles, clasping Jack by the shoulders. "Our adventure in the Archipelago of Dreams has become the stuff of legend. And you are one of the heroes."

Jack embraced each of his friends, then stepped back to look at them. "Charles," he said with a hint of teasing, "you've gotten *old*."

"Editors don't grow *old*," Charles retorted. "They just become more *distinguished*."

"And you," he said to John, "how are you finding teaching at your old stomping grounds?"

"I like it as much as I expected," said John. "Although I think I'd prefer to be left alone to write if I have another crop of students like the current bunch. Hardly an inquisitive or creative mind among them."

"It could be worse," said Charles. "You could be teaching at Cambridge."

At the mention of their old joke, the three friends doubled over in laughter. But soon enough a more serious mood settled upon them again, and the haunted look Jack had worn when they entered returned to his face.

"Why have you called us, Jack?" John asked. "What's happened?"

"It's hard to say," Jack replied. "I came up here with Warnie to work on some of my poems—and perhaps a book or three—but several weeks ago I began to have nightmares, and in the last few days, they've gotten worse."

"Warnie said you called out Aven's name," said Charles.

"Yes," admitted Jack, wincing visibly. "I've tried not to think much about her since our return to England—but I've been dreaming about her. I—I think she's in terrible trouble of some kind. But I can't say what."

"Hmm," John mused. "What else has been in these dreams?"

"Well, dreamstuff, naturally," said Jack. "Things that come bubbling up from one's subconscious. Indians, and crows, and strangely . . . children."

"Do tell," John said, considering his own recent dreams. "If there were children, I'm assuming there were also . . ."

". . . Giants," finished Charles. "If there were children, then there were also Giants. I've been having the same dream."

"As have I," said John. *About the Giants, but not about Aven*, he said silently to himself.

Before any of them could elaborate further, they were interrupted by a knock at the study door.

"I'm dreadfully sorry to interrupt," said Warnie, "but it seems we've, ah . . ." He paused and bit his lip, as a curious and puzzled expression came over his face.

"Warn?" said Jack. "What is it? What's happened?"

"Oh, nothing bad—I think," Warnie replied. "But it appears we have an angel in the garden."

There was indeed, as Warnie had surmised, an angel in the cottage's garden; or at least, something that was as close to a description of an angel as one might give if one was unaccustomed to finding such things in one's garden.

Sitting in a disarray of just-blooming bluebells, mud, and

free-floating feathers was a small girl. A small girl with *wings*.

Her face was smudged with dirt, and her clothing, a simple brown tunic, belted at the waist and across the shoulders, was tattered and torn. Her wings were spread out behind her in a manner that was more awkward than graceful, and they were bare in patches where the feathers had detached themselves in an apparently difficult landing.

"More of a cherub, really, don't you think, John?" said Charles.

"And you would know this how?" asked John. "When have you ever seen a cherub?"

"Look," said Charles, "when he said 'angel,' I was expecting something a little more grown-up. This cherub can't be more than five years old."

"I'm eight, I'll have you know," the girl piped up. "Next Thursday, anyway. And I'm not a cherub or an angel, whatever those are. I'm Laura Glue, and Laura Glue is me."

"Your name is Glue?" asked Charles.

"Laura Glue," the girl protested. "There is a difference, you know."

She stood up and dusted off her clothes, all the while keeping a wary eye on her accidental hosts.

"How did you get here?" Warnie asked, looking around. "Are you with your parents, or on a school outing, perhaps? This is a private garden, not a picnic spot."

Laura Glue looked at him like he was speaking Swahili. "I flew here, I'll have you know. What d'you think the wings are for, anyways?"

Jack began examining Laura Glue's wings, and quickly discovered they were not naturally hers, but were in fact artificial.

Delicately made, of extraordinarily inventive design, but constructs nevertheless.

"Hey!" Laura Glue cried, stepping back defensively. "You should ask permission b'fore poking someone's wings, y'know."

"My apologies," said Jack with a deferential bow.

"'S okay," Laura Glue said. "Longbeards *never* ask."

"I would not have been able to tell," said Charles. "From a distance they looked like they were quite real."

"Uncle Daedalus makes 'em for all the Lost Boys," the girl said proudly, "but ol' Laura Glue's the only one what can fly with 'em. This far, anyways."

"Uncle Daedalus?" John exclaimed. "You don't mean to tell me these wings were made by the Greek Daedalus of myth? The one who lost his son Icarus when the boy flew too close to the sun?"

"What, are you daft?" said Laura Glue. "He'd have to be a thousand years old."

"Exactly," Charles agreed.

"You're thinkin' of Daedalus the Elder," explained Laura Glue. "The one what built my wings is Daedalus the Younger."

"A descendant?" John asked, teasing. "Or Icarus's brother, perhaps?"

"Pr'cisely," said Laura Glue. "An' the reason he don't use wax anymore when he makes the wings."

"All right," stated John. "So where were you flying to? Or do you mean to tell us that you planned to crash in Jack's garden?"

"Planned to crash, no," said the girl, "but this is where I'm supposed to be. I'm looking for the Caretaker. I got an important message from th' Archipelago."

John, Jack, and Charles exchanged terse looks with one another at the mention of the title. It could apply to any or all of them, but it most likely meant John. Warnie, of course, had no idea what she meant.

"I told you," he repeated, "this is a private garden. There is no caretaker."

"I'm not looking for a *gardener*," the girl retorted. "I'm looking for the Caretaker of the *Imaginarium Geographica*."

She rummaged around in her tunic and drew out a delicate flower that seemed to be made of parchment, on which three symbols had been carefully rendered. The flower also seemed to be glowing faintly.

John recognized the first symbol as the seal of the Cartographer of Lost Places—the man who had created the *Imaginarium Geographica*. The second was the seal of the High King of the Archipelago. "What's this third mark?" he asked.

"That's what makes it work," replied Laura Glue. "This is a Compass Rose. The seal of the king gets it through the frontier, the seal of the Cartographer tells it where everything is, and the third mark is what lets you find what you're looking for. In this case, the Caretaker. The closer I gets, the more it glows. And when I flew over your cottage, it went so bright it blinded me, and I crashed in your bluebells.

"So," she continued, marching around them with a determined look on her face, "where are you hiding him, anyway?"

"Look here, Jack," Warnie began.

"Perhaps you should go in and put a pot on to boil," Jack suggested. "She's obviously a troubled young girl, but I think we can sort it out."

Warnie nodded and headed for the cottage at a trot without looking back.

John knelt before the girl and noticed that the Rose was still glowing but got no brighter because of his proximity.

"I'm the Caretaker Principia, Laura Glue," he said gently. "Now can you tell us what this is all about?"

Her reaction wasn't what John expected. The girl's eyes grew wide with surprise, then narrowed in suspicion.

"You're not the Caretaker!" she exclaimed. "Where is he and what have you done with him? Tell me now, or I shall be very, very cross."

"But your Compass Rose is glowing," said John. "And I have the *Geographica* nearby. I *am* the Caretaker. Why would you think I'm not?"

"Because," answered Laura Glue, who had taken a defensive, defiant stance, "he called you John, and I know the *real* Caretaker's name is Jamie."

"Jamie?" Charles exclaimed, turning to the others. "It's no wonder she doesn't know any of us. She's looking for the *last* Caretaker—the one John replaced.

"She's looking for Sir James Barrie."

CHAPTER TWO
THE RELUCTANT CARETAKER

INSIDE THE COTTAGE, it became evident to Warnie that there was something happening among Jack, John, and Charles that didn't include him. So once he had served them all tea, he made the excuses a gentleman makes and cloistered himself in his own study, shutting the door behind him.

Jack saw the hurt expression in his brother's eyes and regretted it deeply, but there was simply no way he could begin to explain everything Warnie would want to know, and still have time to deal with the matter at hand: namely, Laura Glue. Never mind the fact that she'd mistakenly found them when she believed she was searching for one of the most famous playwrights of the time.

The girl sniffed at the tea Jack offered her, then wrinkled her nose in distaste. She allowed Jack to pour her a cupful of cream, which she sipped at dutifully, but she was more interested in the tea biscuits.

"You don't have any little ones, do you?" she asked.

"What, smaller biscuits?" asked Jack.

"Yup," said Laura Glue. "They're called Leprechaun crackers, although I'm pretty sure there ain't any real leprechauns in 'em."

"Really?" asked Charles with a knowing smirk. "And how can you be sure?"

"Because," the girl retorted, "usually you have to smoosh 'em up separate and spread 'em on top."

"Ew," said Charles.

"That's not part of the official recipe in the book, mind you," she continued, "but I added it in myself."

"Laura," Jack began.

"Laura *Glue*," she reiterated. "Just calling me 'Laura' is just as bad as calling me 'Glue.' My name is my name."

"Very well, Laura Glue. Tell us about the Caretaker you came to find. Tell us about Jamie."

"That's about all I knows," the girl admitted. "I've only ever seen him twice myself, and that was before I went to the Well. The first time, anyway."

Charles leaned close to John. "Not possible," he whispered. "She wasn't even born yet when we went to the Archipelago—and that was long after Barrie had given up being Caretaker."

"I knows what I knows," said Laura Glue, "and my ears hear like a fox."

"Well, er, ah," Charles stammered, "it's just that you *can't* have met him—"

"Can too!" Laura Glue exclaimed, standing and stomping her foot. "He said I was sweet, and he gave me a kiss. Look," she continued, as she fumbled around inside her tunic, "I still have it."

She held out her hand and showed them her "kiss"—a small, tarnished silver thimble.

"All right, Laura Glue," said John with a placating look at his friends, "we believe you. But you must also believe us. James Barrie isn't the Caretaker anymore. The *Imaginarium Geographica* was given to us, and we are the Caretakers now. So tell us what you need, and we shall do all that is within our power to help you."

Hearing this, Laura Glue slumped back in her chair and deflated like a spent balloon. It was not the reaction they had expected.

"Then I've come too late," she said mournfully. "I've failed. Grandfather will be so unhappy."

"Your grandfather," said Jack. "It was he who sent you?"

She nodded. "Yup. And he was sure that Jamie was still the Caretaker. So he sent me to find him, to help. Because he is who he is."

"He is what, Laura Glue?" asked Charles.

"Grandfather's enemy," the girl replied. "There is something happening in the Archipelago. Something terrible. And Grandfather said that sometimes something is so important that the only ones who can help are your enemies. And he gave me the Compass Rose and said to fly to the Summer Country and find his enemy, the Caretaker Jamie, and he would come and help us."

"And what was it that Jamie was supposed to do?" John asked.

The girl shrugged and sipped her cream. "I don't know. Grandfather said that the message would tell him everything he needed to know. He is, um, was, the Caretaker, after all."

"What message, my dear?" Charles asked.

"Oh!" the girl exclaimed. "I forgot." She stood at attention, as if preparing to recite a composition in school. "'The Crusade has begun.'"

"And?" promted John. "Is there more?"

"That's it and that's all," said Laura Glue. "May I have some more of the big crackers?"

◆   ◆   ◆

The three friends left Laura Glue munching on biscuits and moved into the hallway, where they could discuss the situation with some privacy.

"It's an incredible story," said Jack. "But there's too much credibility in it to disregard her."

"I agree," John said. "But I'm at a loss as to what we should do. Obviously someone there meant for us to do something. But I have no idea what."

"She does have that rose," mused Charles. "It bears the marks of both the High King and the Cartographer. I can't imagine they'd allow just anyone to use them."

"I concur," said John. "So how should we proceed?"

"Obviously," Charles said, "we should take her to see Barrie. He's in London, and colleagues of mine have often pointed out his residence to me. We can deliver her straight to his front door. And then perhaps we'll find out what this is all about."

"That sounds like a plan," said Jack. "It's time I was out and about for a bit anyway."

"Excellent," agreed John. "This sort of adventure I can handle. A little mystery, a little drama, and it's all wrapped up and done with a quick excursion into London."

It was decided that they would have to take John's car into the city. To take the train, especially from the Oxford station, would risk the three of them being seen on nonuniversity business and would engender too many questions that they'd have to make up answers for. And that was before any queries about their keeping company with a small winged girl with a penchant for yammering on about something called the Archipelago.

John went to make some adjustments to the engine, followed by a very inquisitive Laura Glue, while Jack and Charles made apologies to Warnie about having to leave. Warnie himself had already decided that this was a business he'd rather have no part in—and so nodded in agreement when they presented their plan to go into the city to locate the girl's family.

"I call navigation," said Jack as they walked out to the car.

"What does that mean?" asked Charles.

"It means I get the front passenger seat," said Jack, "and you have to sit in the back with Laura Glue."

"What?" sputtered Charles. "That's not fair. I came in with John. I get the passenger seat."

"What are you two arguing about?" John said, wiping his hands on an oilcloth. "The car's ready to load, if you haven't something more pressing to settle."

"We're arguing about the seating arrangement," Charles told him. "I wanted to sit in front—"

"But I called navigation," said Jack.

"Well, there you have it," stated John. "Can't be helped if he called navigation. Sorry, Charles."

"Drat," muttered Charles.

It was fortunate that Laura Glue's wings were artificial, because they would not have fit in the small cab of the car and still allowed room for any other passengers. It was difficult enough to get them into the boot, and then only with some amount of judicious folding and positioning.

Laura Glue was twisting her hair into knots with nervous concern for her wings, until John pointed out that he was putting the *Geographica* in the boot as well, so she could be assured it was a safe place for them to be.

Wings and atlas secured, Charles and Laura Glue bundled into the cramped backseat, and John and Jack climbed into the front.

"Okay," said Laura Glue, pointing at the threadbare seat covers. "There's an invisible line down the middle. This side is for girls, and that side is for boys. And you aren't allowed to cross the line."

"It's a little close in here for boundaries," Charles noted. "What happens if I cross the line?"

Laura Glue scowled. "I'll have to cut out your heart and feed it to the fairies."

Charles stared, wide-eyed and speechless, before the girl's face split into a broad grin to indicate that she was teasing him.

"You're not exactly a normal little girl, are you?" asked Charles.

"You have a funny-looking mouth," said Laura Glue.

"This is going to be a very long ride," said Charles.

It was actually a shorter ride than they expected, as the weather was good and there were few other vehicles on the road. Traffic became more congested once they arrived in London proper, but Charles's familiarity with the city streets aided with their navigation considerably.

"Ironic, isn't it?" remarked Jack.

"Oh, shut up," Charles said crossly. "Turn left up here, John, then park as close as you can to the house. The shorter the distance we have to walk in public with Laura Glue, the better."

"Hey," the girl said. "Why don't you want to walk with me?"

"Because," Charles told her with a teasing smile, "we've decided we like you, and we don't want some shady fellow swooping in when we aren't looking to carry you off."

Instead of the laugh or sarcastic retort he was expecting, Laura Glue's eyes grew wide with fear and she seemed to shrink back into the recesses of the seat.

"Don't," she whispered in a fragile, frightened voice. "Don't ever tease. Not about that."

Charles hesitated, but Jack saw the look on the girl's face and reached out a hand to her. "Don't worry," he said reassuringly. "You're with all three Caretakers. And do you know we're not just Caretakers of a musty old atlas? We're also Caretakers of everything else there is in the entire Archipelago of Dreams. Even little girls named Laura Glue. And as long as you're with us, no one will ever harm you."

Laura Glue blinked back a tear, then took Jack's hand and smiled. "Okay," she said. "But I still want to find Jamie, just the same."

It was the twilight hour when they finally trooped up the steps and rang the bell at the place Charles directed them to. The stately, well-situated town house was brightly lit within, but there was no answer to the bell, or to their repeated knocks on the stout mahogany door.

"Now what?" John wondered. "He must be out for the evening. Do we wait for him? Or is there another place to look?"

"There may be," said Charles. "Kensington Gardens is just down the way. Perhaps he's inclined to take evening walks there."

"It's certainly worth a stroll," Jack said. "Now that we've come this far, I'm just happy to have had reason to leave the Kilns."

Both John and Charles had noted the drastic change in Jack's countenance since the unusual apparition had crash-landed in his garden. He looked fully engaged once more, as if the girl were a fulcrum that had levered him out of his melancholy. And as such, neither one of them was inclined to mention their shared dreams again, until it seemed necessary to do so. The mystery at hand was more than enough to consume the evening anyway.

The gardens were indeed just a short distance away, and the lights of the city were just beginning to twinkle in the fading cobalt light of dusk when they arrived.

"It's a good-size park," said John. "Where should we begin looking?"

"Where else?" Charles replied. "The statue."

"Of course," said Jack, slapping his forehead. "The statue. It was erected for May Morning, was it not? I could be drummed out of Magdalen for forgetting that."

"Or worse," said Charles. "They'd make you take up residence at Cambridge."

Set just along one of the walking paths, the tall bronze statue of Sir James Barrie's most famous creation towered over passersby, who strolled along at a leisurely pace, hardly pausing to glance at the sculpture. Except for one.

The small, slight man was barely five feet tall, with a mustache and fringes of white hair that stuck out around the edges of his top hat. He stood holding a cane in one hand and a leash attached to an enormous Saint Bernard in the other. He looked at the statue with an expression that might have been construed as fondness, or longing—if it were not also for the immense sadness that seemed to lie underneath.

Charles, deciding that this was no time for furtiveness, called out to the man from some twenty yards away. "I say, are you James Barrie? Might we have a word?"

The man's eyes widened in surprise as he saw a cluster of people eagerly rushing toward him, and he quickly pulled down his hat, turned up his collar, and began walking briskly in the opposite direction, dragging the reluctant dog behind him.

"Didn't he hear me?" Charles said, puzzled.

"Oh, he heard you," Jack said wryly. "You have all the stealth of a wet badger."

"In some places that's a compliment," retorted Charles.

"Do shut up, you two," John scolded. He quickened his pace after the swiftly receding forms of Barrie and the Saint Bernard.

"Wait!" John shouted after him. "We only want to speak with you!"

"It's no use," said Charles. "We've frightened him off."

Laura Glue planted both her feet and flung out her arms. "Jamie!" she shouted. "Jamie, please don't go!"

And abruptly, the man stopped in his tracks.

Slowly he turned around and looked at them. Then, just as slowly, he walked back toward the four companions, his cane tapping gently on the cobblestones and the dog trailing obediently behind.

Several feet away, he stopped and considered them one by one, before finally looking down at Laura Glue.

"It's been a very, very long time since anyone has called me Jamie," he said slowly, "and it's not something I allow many people to do. So you must tell me, if you can, who you are and why you call me by that name."

The little girl's eyes began to well up. "Don't you remember me? The last time we met, you gave me a kiss." She showed him the thimble, and he knelt down in front of her.

"My dear, I am an old man, and in all my years, many, many children have seen that play, and they know that a thimble is a kiss, and a kiss a thimble. And please forgive my aged memory, but I can't have been the one who gave this to you, because I haven't done that sort of thing since long before you were born."

"But, but," she stammered, confused, "you *must* be Jamie. Otherwise it wouldn't have worked."

"What wouldn't have worked, my dear?"

"This," said Laura Glue, pulling the Compass Rose out of her tunic. In the presence of four Caretakers, it shone as brightly as a beacon.

The expression on Jamie's face changed rapidly from surprise, to disbelief, to, strangely, gratitude. "Put that away," he said gently. "And let me see your kiss again."

Laura Glue tucked the parchment flower back in a pocket and handed him the thimble.

"Hurm," he rumbled as he examined the kiss, "I see it now. I'm sorry I didn't recognize it before. I wasn't expecting anyone like you in Kensington Gardens. Not again, anyway."

He put his arm around the girl and drew her close. "Do you know, this kiss is one of the only items ever removed from the treasure trove of the great dragon Samaranth?"

"For really and truly?" said Laura Glue.

"Yes," Barrie replied, winking at John as he spoke. "It was acquired in an adventure of great peril, and my best friend and I barely escaped with our lives."

"Whatever else has gone on," John whispered to Charles, "it's obvious why he was chosen as a Caretaker."

"Yes," said Charles, nodding.

Laura Glue clapped her hands. "I know that story! I know it! That was before you got old again, and became his enemy."

A pained expression flashed over Jamie's face before he smiled and kissed Laura Glue on the forehead. "It was the best of my failures, my dear girl. Now, who's for some Leprechaun crackers in front of a fire? The sun has set, and it's obvious the fairies are going to be about in Kensington Gardens tonight."

CHAPTER THREE
THE LOST BOYS

TRUE TO HIS WORD, back at Jamie's home he had an ample supply of Leprechaun crackers, as well as an assortment of other biscuits, teas, jams, jellies, and chocolate.

"I find it useful to be prepared," Jamie said as he settled into an overstuffed chair with a cup of tea, "for even the most unexpected of visitors. Particularly the youthful ones."

"Thif if wuderful," mumbled Laura Glue through a mouthful of crackers and chocolate. "Fank hu."

"You're quite welcome, my dear," he said as he placed a saucer of cream and crackers on the floor for the great Saint Bernard, who was lounging comfortably before the fire.

"Aramis likes treats as well, but that's more often than not just an excuse to indulge in a nibble myself. And now," Jamie continued, turning to the three men, "can you tell me what's brought three gentlemen and a child of the Archipelago to Kensington Gardens, just to have tea with an old playwright?"

When they had finished eating to everyone's satisfaction, Laura Glue repeated the message she had been sent to deliver, and, her mission accomplished, promptly busied herself with grooming the dog while the Caretakers talked. It took more than an hour for John, Jack, and Charles to recount the events that had brought them together years earlier as the new Caretakers, during which time Laura Glue fell fast asleep on the cushions in one of the town house's deep bay windows. They continued with a brief accounting of the war with the Winter King, concluding with the afternoon's events and the sudden appearance of the girl with wings.

When they had finished, Jamie stared into the fire, considering, for several minutes.

"I was terribly sorry about Stellan," he finally said. "I read about his death in the papers, of course. But it never crossed my mind that it had been the work of the Winter King. In the next couple of years, as the war wound down, I suspected that Bert and Jules had taken some sort of action with regard to the Archipelago, but I tried to put it out of my mind. When I left, I vowed to be done with it—and for better or worse, I've kept that vow. Until tonight, that is."

"You were Arthur Conan Doyle's replacement, weren't you?" Charles asked.

"In a manner of speaking," said Jamie. "There have always been three Caretakers, more or less, although once called to the task, those who previously served as Caretakers never seem to be completely removed from the responsibilities it entails, as you may have noticed," he said, smiling broadly.

"Before Jules Verne, I believe it was three Americans who answered the Call. Then Jules, then Bert, who was to become the new Caretaker Principia. Harry Houdini and Doyle were recruited at the same time by Jules," he said. "But they both had the same problem—neither of them wished to keep the secrets of the Archipelago. Houdini, in fact, wished to expose them to the world, and did his best to do so."

"Whoo." Charles whistled. "That can't have gone over well with Bert."

"Bert was the least of their worries," said Jamie. "At one point, it had gotten so bad that Samaranth *himself* had come to England looking for both Houdini and Doyle—and it wasn't just to take back the *Geographica*. He'd heard about that business with the photographs and the fairies—which had been brought over on the *Green Dragon*, incidentally—and he planned to end their tenure definitively."

A shudder passed through John as he recalled watching Samaranth do that very thing in the final battle with the Winter King. When Samaranth was holding him in a claw high above the waterfall at the Edge of the World, and after every chance for redemption was given, the evil man *still* struck out at the great dragon, who subsequently dropped him. John couldn't imagine what it must have taken for Samaranth to go *looking* for vengeance.

"It's never been confirmed for me by Jules or Bert," Jamie continued, "and Arthur certainly wouldn't speak of it, but some mishap between Doyle and Houdini is what resulted in the Winter King's knowledge of the *Geographica*."

"You've got to be joking," exclaimed Charles. "How irresponsible can one be?"

"Up until that time, there were objects other than the *Geographica* that had been entrusted to the Caretakers," said Jamie. "And whatever those items were, the Winter King took them and used them to facilitate the construction of a new Dragonship."

"The *Black Dragon*," Jack said with a shudder. "I know it better than I'd have liked to."

"And that was the reason Doyle and Houdini were removed as Caretakers?"

"Mostly. One reason among many, I'm afraid. Bert was the Caretaker Principia at the time, so the responsibility was his. He took the brunt of it but managed to keep Samaranth from killing Houdini and Doyle. Jules returned briefly as the Caretaker Principia before Bert resumed the post. This was just prior to finding Stellan Sigurdsson, and then, after a succession of briefly tenured, well-intentioned replacements, I was finally enlisted as the new third Caretaker."

"And then you quit," declared Jack.

"I prefer to say I 'resigned,'" Jamie said mildly. "And I do hope that you'll take a more civil tone, Jack."

"Resigned, quit—whatever you call it, you abandoned your duties," Jack shot back.

"Duties I never asked for!" Jamie protested. "I didn't want any of that! I wasn't prepared! Arthur wanted it, and had it—and then they took it from him and made me take his place. And it terrified me to have that kind of responsibility suddenly thrust upon me. Do you have any idea what that was like?"

"I have every idea of what that was like," said John coolly. "That's precisely what happened to me after you gave it up. But because of what had happened with you, Professor Sigurdsson never told me what I was being trained for, or even mentioned the *Geographica*, until events were in motion. I only got to speak to him that much by stepping into the past, through a door in the Keep of Time—because by then, he'd already been murdered."

"Are you saying that's my fault?" said Jamie. "My fault he died? Bad form, John."

"Maybe," answered John. "Maybe things would have progressed differently if the professor and Bert felt they could be more open and honest with the new Caretaker. And maybe he wouldn't have died protecting the *Geographica*—because it would already have been passed to me."

"But wouldn't the Winter King have simply pursued *you* then, John?" Charles asked reasonably. "Instead of the professor?"

"There's no way to know what 'might' have happened," said Jack. "All we know is what did happen. And we know that when the time came to stand up like a man, Sir James Barrie turned and ran."

Jamie's face reddened, and his fist trembled as he rose from his seat.

"Take back that remark, sir. Or I shall be obliged on my honor as a gentleman to call you out."

Jack also stood and stepped close. "I'm right here. Say what you have to say. If you want to take a swing at me, feel free to do so."

"Now, now," Charles said placatingly as he rose and smoothly edged between the two men. "This isn't resolving anything. And you two are not going to help Aven by engaging in fisticuffs."

The mention of that name stunned both men into dropping their fists and retaking their seats.

"Aven," Jamie said, his voice low. "What does any of this have to do with Aven? Is she all right?"

"I can't say for certain," said Charles, looking askance at Jack. "There are a number of pieces I'm trying to put together, and I don't think any of them are before us by happenstance."

Beginning with Charles's account, and with frequent interruptions from John and Jack, they told Jamie about Aven's role in their great adventure—and about her closeness to both Jack and the young man they called Bug, who eventually became the new High King, Artus.

"So she's become queen of Paralon then, eh?" Jamie said with a wan smile. "This Artus must be quite a fellow to have wooed her away from the sea. I imagine Nemo had quite a bit to say about *that*."

At the mention of the former captain of the *Yellow Dragon*, Jack shifted uncomfortably in his chair, and John quickly leaned in. "Where Aven enters into this is the reason we've come together. It seems we've all been dreaming of the Archipelago—about strange creatures and events—and Jack summoned us together to discuss their import."

"Dreams are curious things," said Jamie, "but Jack did well to take heed of his. There is always meaning behind them, and it cannot be coincidence that you've had the same dreams. Laura Glue's appearance confirms this."

"Agreed," Charles said. "Laura Glue's claim that the Archipelago is in trouble and Jack's feeling that Aven may be in peril could be one and the same occurrence."

"And what of the message?" asked John. "What does it mean?"

"'The Crusade has begun,'" said Jamie. "It really doesn't say much at all, does it? I must confess I have no idea what it means. But . . ." He paused, then stood and moved to the fire, stoking the embers.

"There's an old myth in the Archipelago," he went on softly, shaking his head. "A legend, really . . . I recall it mentioned a Crusade, but those events happened seven centuries ago. We always thought it was only a *story*. . . ."

"I don't think this is going to be as easily resolved as anyone hoped," Jack said.

"Just so," agreed Jamie, sitting down again. "I think the best thing to do is find out what's happening in the Archipelago. Have you contacted them yet?"

"Ah, how exactly do we go about doing that?" asked John. "It's never really come up before."

"You don't say?" said Jamie with an expression both amused and incredulous. "You brought the means with you."

He moved to the sleeping child and delicately removed the still-glowing parchment flower from her tunic. The others huddled around him as he pointed out what the symbols on the Compass Rose meant.

"Everyone thinks the seal of the High King is *A* for Arthur, the first king of Paralon," said Jamie, "but it's really the Greek letter *A* for *alpha*—'the beginning.'"

"And that, there," said Charles, pointing at a symbol that resembled an inverted *u* with a tail. "The mark of the Cartographer. What is it?"

"*Mu,*" said John. "The equivalent to our *m,* although I have no idea what it means in relation to the Cartographer. Jamie?"

"Don't look at me. I've wondered about that myself," Jamie replied. "The Cartographer is a strange creature who keeps his own counsel.

"Now, this third symbol is how the child located you—ah, us," he continued. "*Pi.* It is the symbol of the Caretaker Principia. As I understand it, only one of the Caretakers, as its intended recipients, should be able to erase this mark and replace it with another. That should do the trick."

"Doesn't that still leave us with a problem?" wondered Charles. "The way Laura Glue explained how the Compass Rose works, it glows as you come into proximity of the person being sought. How will that help us?"

"It works that way if you want it to," Jamie explained, "but Bert explained it to me once. In principle, it functions like these 'radios' everyone is using nowadays. It can be tuned to receive, as it was used in locating us—or it can be adjusted to broadcast, as it will do once we've added a new symbol. Then we'll just have to wait and see if someone comes."

"But what if no one is listening?" asked Jack. "What if no one comes?"

"Then your job becomes a lot easier, doesn't it?" Jamie retorted. "But don't worry—someone is *always* listening . . .

". . . and someone always comes."

"So," said Jamie. "Who wants to do it?"

"I should," John replied gravely. "I'm the Caretaker Principia. It's my responsibility."

"Oh, for heaven's sake," Charles said, grabbing the Rose. He ran his thumb back and forth over the symbol, and in a trice, it had been completely erased. "Sometimes you shouldn't stand on ceremony. You should just do what needs doing and move on."

"Um, yes," said John. "Well done, Charles. So," he continued, turning again to Jamie, "whom should we summon?"

"In a crisis? The only man I'd want at my side would be Nemo," Jamie stated. "His mark is Persian, but I've seen it used, and I'm certain it will work . . . What? What is it?"

At the mention—again—of Nemo's name, all three of the companions started visibly, then seemed unwilling to meet Jamie's eyes.

"Regarding Nemo," John began.

"No," said Jack. "It's for me to say."

He folded his arms and drew a sharp breath. "Nemo won't be coming," he said at length. "Nemo is dead. He was killed in battle."

Jamie couldn't conceal his dismay. "But . . . but that can't be! Nemo is unbeatable in a conflict, whether on land or at sea! Not only is he one of the best strategists who ever lived, but he's charmed. He's the seventh son of the seventh son of Sinbad himself. No," he concluded, shaking his head. "You must be mistaken."

"I'm not," Jack insisted, his voice shaking with emotion. "I saw him die. And what's more, it was my fault. So please, say no more of it, but trust my word—if summoned, Nemo will not come."

Jamie regarded Jack, his expression inscrutable. "That's very interesting, Jack. Very interesting indeed. I can see the event had quite an effect on you."

"The 'event,' as you call it, was one of the worst experiences of my life," said Jack. "How do you think it makes me feel to know that choices I made led to someone's death?"

"Were they good choices or bad choices?" asked Jamie.

"What kind of question is that?" countered Jack. "How can they have been anything but bad choices? Paddy trusted me, and he died."

"Paddy?" John said. "You mean Nemo, don't you?"

"Well, yes," said Jack. "I meant to say Nemo."

"Warnie mentioned that you'd had a friend die in the war," put in Charles, "but he told us you were nowhere near the battle and had nothing to do with it."

"That doesn't matter," Jack said. "I promised Paddy's mother that I'd look after him, and I let him get killed, just as I did Nemo."

"It isn't the same," argued John.

"Sure it is," said Jack. "They both died because of choices I made. If I had done things differently before that conflict at the Western Front . . . gone a day earlier, or a day later . . . anything. If I had done anything differently, Paddy would still be alive. And I've had to see his mother's face every day since the war—loving me for trying, loving me for taking his place in caring for her, but always, always knowing that I failed, and let him die."

"Everyone makes choices," said Jamie, "and we have to live with those choices. Did Aven ever tell you what went on between us?"

"No," said Charles. "But we inferred a great deal from the number of opportunities she took to curse you."

"Heh." Jamie chuckled sadly. "I can't say I blame her. At one time, not really all that long ago, we were very much in love, she and I."

"Ah, not to give offense," said John, "but aren't you considerably older than Aven?"

Jamie squinted at him. "There are more mysteries in the Archipelago than you yet know, young John," he responded. "Aven is not as young as she appears to be—and at that time, I did not appear anywhere near as old as I was. But suffice it to say, she was the principal reason I agreed to become a Caretaker."

"I understand that," Jack said.

"I think you do," said Jamie. "But she was not the reason I left."

"The widow," offered Charles. "The woman here in London, with the children . . . Aven mentioned her, and not much more favorably than she did you, I'm afraid."

Jamie shook his head. "She never understood. There were responsibilities in the Archipelago for which I was not prepared.

And there were opportunities for responsibility here that I hoped to embrace. And so I did."

"And you've been happy ever since, I suppose?" asked Charles.

"Would that it were so," said Jamie. "All I wanted to do was be a father, a mentor, a brother to those five boys. To protect them from the evils of the world. And I didn't think I could do that from an archipelago of islands at the edges of existence. I thought I could do it if I were right here, with them. But I was wrong."

He lowered his head and closed his eyes. "You lost your friend Paddy in the war?" he asked Jack, looking up.

"Yes."

"And you, too, lost someone?" he said to John, who nodded. "And you?" to Charles, who also indicated a loss.

"You see?" Jamie said with a tremor in his voice. "I also lost someone in that war. One of my boys. And I lost another *after* the war, to a drowning that may have even been by his own hand. So what good has it done, that I chose to leave my role as Caretaker, if I could not protect those whom I loved, even from themselves?"

He banged a fist against the mantel, startling the dog. "At least you three jumped headlong into it and took the battle to one of the prime causes—the Winter King himself. Perhaps if I had done that, if I had stayed, the war might have ended sooner, and I might still have my George. So who am I to judge good choices from bad?

"But," he finished, turning again to Jack, "I know that you should not carry the guilt that you do for Nemo's death. Events on that day transpired exactly as they needed to."

"How can you say that?" said Jack, incredulous.

"Because I know Nemo was very close to Jules Verne," answered

Jamie, "and Jules knew many things that he never shared with any of us. But I know one thing he passed on to Nemo, that I am happy to share with you.

"Nemo knew the exact hour and means of his death. And, knowing this, he had the ability to change events if he so chose. He didn't. And thus the responsibility for his death was not yours, young Jack. Indeed, it never was."

Several stiff drinks were poured, and the four men sat in silence as they absorbed what had been said. Laura Glue stirred, and Jamie rose to cover her with a blanket.

"So," John said finally. "The Compass Rose."

"Yes," said Jack. "I'd nearly forgotten."

John looked at Jamie. "What symbol should we use, since Nemo's is not likely to do us any good?"

In response, Jamie took a book from one of his shelves and thumbed through to a Greek alphabet. He quickly scanned the letters, then pointed to one. "This one," he declared, tapping his finger. "It's the only one I can really be certain of."

"*Omega*," noted John. "'The ending.'"

"Yes," Jamie said without turning around. "That's Bert's little joke."

"This will summon Bert?" John said in surprise. "That would be delightful. I'd love to see him again."

"As would I," said Jamie. "He was always a bit more well-disposed toward my choices than his daughter was. But then, as a parent, I think he would be. Do any of you have children, if you don't mind my asking?"

Jack looked a little uncomfortable at the question, but he didn't want to seem rude—not after the personal information Jamie had shared, and especially after the remark about Nemo. "Not thus far," he admitted. "But the future is long."

"I have one," said Charles. "A son, Michael."

"Three for me," said John. "My eldest, John, is nine. Michael is second, and then young Christopher."

Jamie stared at them with a forced smile, then choked back a sob and turned away. "Michael was the name of my boy who drowned," he said in a small voice. "So—let's get this job done, and see to it that no more Michaels become Lost Boys, eh?"

Charles handed the Rose to John, who quickly inscribed the mark Jamie had indicated on the parchment. "Now what?"

"Now," said Jamie, wiping at his eyes with a handkerchief, "we wait and see."

CHAPTER FOUR

A DRAGON RESTORED

AS THE EVENING deepened into night, the four men busied themselves with small talk and took the opportunity to get to know one another a bit more. They were, after all, members of a very exclusive club. And John, Jack, and Charles found it very liberating to have someone else with whom to discuss the Archipelago. With most others, most recently Jack's brother Warnie, they had to guard their words carefully. But with Jamie, they were able to broach practically any topic.

For his part, Jamie was mostly interested in their academic careers. He had spent enough of his life as a novelist and playwright that academia was fascinating to him.

"You really worked on the *Oxford English Dictionary?*" Jamie remarked to John. "Extraordinary."

"I was only there for about a year," John admitted. "The problem was, having been trained to read the *Geographica*, I had a better than average knack for going right to the root definitions of words, and they started to get suspicious."

"Oh, that's rich," Charles said, chortling. "You were actually too qualified for the job. If they'd kept you on, they might be finished by now."

"Craigie's close enough, I think," said John. "But messing about in the Scriptorium with all those little notes crammed into cubbyholes . . . Not for me, I'm afraid."

"One of the researchers on the *OED* was briefly considered as a Caretaker back before Bert's time," said Jamie. "Murray. His impediment was that while he was a stellar researcher, he lacked imagination. Just didn't have the spark. Affable enough, but just not cut out for the job."

"Lucky bastard," murmured Charles.

"What was that?" John said.

"Who's for a bite?" said Charles. "I'm getting a bit peckish."

"As am I," Jamie agreed. "Charles, why don't you give me a hand, and we'll see if we can assemble some sandwiches to keep up our vigor."

As the two went down the hallway to the kitchen, Laura Glue stretched and yawned. "Hey," she exclaimed, patting herself. "Where's my flower?"

"Over here on the desk," said Jack.

"You changed it," she said appraisingly. "But I like it. It looks like a circle with feet."

"Indeed it does," concurred Jack, noting that since they'd erased the *pi* symbol and added the *omega*, the glowing had ceased. "But I don't know if it made it prettier to look at."

Jamie and Charles returned with a silver tray laden with ham, cheese, and thick cuts of dark rye bread.

"Sorry there's no milder bread in the house," said Jamie. "You can take the boy out of Scotland, but you can't make him give up his rye."

"Not a problem, I assure you," John said as he started slathering a piece of bread with a grainy mustard. "In fact, I think I prefer—"

He stopped speaking when he realized that none of the others were listening. Instead, they were all looking at Laura Glue, who was still holding the Compass Rose.

It was faint, and indistinct—but the parchment flower had begun to glow.

"Well," Jamie said wryly, rubbing his dog's head, "I think we may be in for more company."

"Do we need to be down by the river?" asked Charles. "If Bert is coming, won't he be piloting the *White Dragon?*"

"Or one of the other ships," Jack agreed. "Perhaps we should be waiting for him there."

"It's a pleasant night out," said John. "There's no storm, there's been no murder, no one is chasing us, we have a comfortable study to relax in, a delicious pile of food in front of us, and for company, James Barrie—with whom we can also talk about the *Geographica* and the Archipelago. And you seriously want me to consider leaving all this to go tromping alongside the Thames in the middle of the night, just in case it'll be easier for Bert to find us? I don't think so."

And with that, he plopped down on one of the chairs and began to happily devour a huge ham sandwich.

"See?" Charles said to Jamie. "That's why *he's* the Caretaker Principia."

After having consumed three sandwiches of her own, Laura Glue declared herself to be the Caretaker of the Compass Rose. Carefully monitoring it for any change, she nestled back into the haunches of the huge, still sleeping Saint Bernard, Aramis.

"His predecessors were Porthos and Athos," said Jamie. "If I myself make it to a D'Artagnan, I'll be very contented."

"There's something I've been meaning to ask you," said Jack as he licked mustard off his fingers. "When we found Laura Glue, she told us that she'd been sent to find you, specifically, not just because you were the Caretaker, but also because you were her grandfather's greatest enemy. And then, in the park, you said something about an adventure with your best friend—"

"Whom she said later became my enemy. And you've surmised they were the same person. Well done, Jack.

"Oddly enough, the reasons we became enemies have a lot to do with Aven as well. Although I must point out a very important distinction between myself and the girl's grandfather. Just because he no longer regards himself as my friend does not necessarily mean I am no longer his."

Before Jamie could elaborate, a newspaper struck the shutters, which clattered loudly against the windows of the library. "Hmm," said Jamie. "The wind has shifted. I wonder what that means?"

"Why?" asked John.

"It's March," Charles explained. "The wind never blows in from the west this time of year."

Wordlessly the four men looked at one another, each of them thinking the same thing.

"Look," a voice said, soft with wonder. It was Laura Glue, who on speaking woke the dog and was being given an involuntary bath by Aramis's massive tongue. "Look at my flower."

There on the desk the Compass Rose had begun to shine as if it were on fire, the symbols marked upon it swirling with an eldritch glow.

Suddenly a shadow passed over the windows, momentarily blocking the light from the waxing moon above.

Puzzled, Jamie jumped to his feet, as did John.

"Was that a dragon, perhaps?" asked Charles.

"Too slow," said Jamie. "Maybe it—"

A loud knocking from one of the upper floors interrupted him.

"I think you have a visitor, Jamie," said Laura Glue sleepily.

In an instant, all four Caretakers were running to the hall and up the stairs. Jamie led the way to the fourth-floor rooms, all of which had been tastefully appointed as bedrooms, save for the last.

"I don't suppose this is the nursery?" Jack asked with a grin.

"Ha," Jamie said over his shoulder. "Funny scholar you are. No, this is just a storage room. All I keep in here is an old, ah, wardrobe full of my mother's furs."

He flung the door wide, and together they entered the room. It was reasonably bare, save for the aforementioned wardrobe to the left, and an old pram on the right. Directly across from the door stood a double bay window, deep and uncurtained—so they could clearly see the silhouette of the figure, hanging from a rope ladder, who was rapping on the sill.

The strange visitor was short, stoutish, and most tellingly, had a tattered, tall, pointy hat perched precariously on his head.

He knocked again, then called to them through the glass. "Will someone please let me in? I've flown here all the way from the Archipelago, and my arms are very tired."

Charles raised an eyebrow and grinned as they all rushed to the window. "No question now. That's our man Bert right enough."

"Someone give me a hand inside, will you?" Bert cried as he clutched at the window with one hand and clung to the ladder with the other. "Else I'll end up a handsome stain on the cobble-stones."

"Bert, I'm so pleased to see you!" said John as he reached out to grasp his mentor's hands. "But what the devil are you flying? Is it an airplane of some sort?"

"Better!" Bert said with a gleam in his eye. "It's an old friend, all dressed up to go a-visiting."

The friends all leaned out the open windows and looked up at a sight both amazing and familiar. It was an airship: part blimp and part airplane. There was an air-filled balloon above an elaborate carriage that had been fitted with propellers. But what was most startling was the carriage itself, which bore a carved masthead.

It was the *Indigo Dragon*.

Jack let out a whoop, and Charles started clapping Bert on the back so vigorously he nearly lost his hat.

Once they had him safely inside and had anchored the ladder securely around the heavy wardrobe, each of the companions embraced Bert joyfully, and even Jamie gave him a warm, two-handed handshake.

"Old sock, good on you, good on you, I say!" Charles exclaimed happily. "When you said you were hoping to repair her, I never expected anything as grand as this! Well done, Bert!"

"In truth, it was more the craftsmen back on Paralon who did it," said Bert. "Ordo Maas was able to salvage the dragon itself, but the ship was a loss. Jules had had plans for an airship that Nemo had always wanted to . . . ah . . ." He paused, looking hesitantly at Jamie.

"It's all right, old chap," Jamie said. "They told me everything.

In fact, we've had quite the opportunity to get acquainted, your young Caretakers and I."

"But how did you get here so quickly?" John asked. "It hasn't been more than a couple of hours since we summoned you."

"Quickly?" exclaimed Bert. "I'm only sorry it took so long. I was already on the edge of the Frontier, on my way to Oxford to consult with John about a crisis in the Archipelago, when the sextant aboard the *Indigo Dragon* began to point toward London. That's when I realized someone had used a Compass Rose. But I scarcely expected to find you at Jamie's house."

"That's a story in and of itself," said John. "Let's go downstairs. There's someone you ought to meet."

Laura Glue was rolling around on the floor with Aramis when the group came downstairs. Introductions were made, and when she shook hands with Bert, her eyes became the size of saucers.

"The Far Traveler? For really and truly?" she exclaimed. "No one will believe I actually met you."

"Really?" said Bert, flattered. "And why is that, my dear?"

"Because—whenever you've been mentioned, my grandfather shakes his head an' says your wick isn't lit. But you don't look anything like a candle at all."

John and Jamie let out a burst of laughter, and even Jack chuckled. Charles just smiled grimly and patted Bert on the back. "Look at it this way—at least you didn't have to share the backseat of a car with her all day."

"All day?" said John. "It only took us a few hours to get to London."

"That's what it seemed like to *you*, maybe," Charles shot back.

"She'd come from the Archipelago seeking *me*," said Jamie. "Her grandfather sent her, apparently."

They quickly told Bert what had taken place during the day, including Laura Glue's mysterious message, and his features grew very dark. "That's troubling news indeed," Bert mused. "I'm as clueless as Jamie about the message—although it was clearly meant for a Caretaker to interpret, and obviously something greater than we know is going on in the Archipelago."

"The children," came a small voice. "Someone's taking all the children."

It was Laura Glue.

Bert knelt down in front of her. "What do you mean, darling girl? Is that why your grandfather sent you here?"

She nodded, and a single tear fell down her cheek. "Grandfather knew. He knew. He saw them coming in the big boats and knew what was going to happen, so he made me put on Uncle Daedalus's wings, gave me the flower, and sent me to find Jamie. He said he would know what to do."

"Who was coming, Laura Glue?" asked John. "Who was your grandfather protecting you from?"

"The men with the clocks in their bellies," replied Laura Glue, beginning to sob openly.

"Shh, shh, there, there," Bert told her gently. "It will be all right, my girl. But tell me, these men—how did you know they had clocks in their bellies?"

"Cuz you could hear it," she said. "When they was coming to get us, you could hear the sound—tick-tock, tick-tock—over and over and over. And they makes noises when they moves, like a principle."

"Like a car, you mean?" asked Charles.

"I don't know what that is," said Laura Glue. "But Grandfather called them the clock men, so . . ."

"Clockwork men," said Bert. "This grows worse and worse. They've been outlawed in the Archipelago for nearly a decade."

"You mentioned that you were already headed to see me because of a crisis in the Archipelago," said John. "That's not mere coincidence, is it?"

"No, I'm afraid it isn't," Bert said somberly. "A great catastrophe has befallen the Archipelago."

"Is Aven all right?" Jack asked quickly, recalling his recent dreams. "Has she—uh, the queen—been hurt?"

"You're three steps ahead of me, young Jack," answered Bert. "She's fine, mostly—but she's smack in the center of the crisis. Crises. One of the crises, anyway."

"Just how many, um, crises are we dealing with, Bert?" Charles asked.

"All in one and one in all, it seems," said Bert, "and what the child has just told me only confirms my worst fears—that the crisis that began it all, and happened slowly enough that no one knew it was happening until it was over, may not be over after all."

"What crisis, Bert?" asked John.

"Someone has stolen all the Dragonships," said Bert. "They're all gone, and no one knows where."

"Gone?" exclaimed John. "How can someone have simply taken them? After all, they have wills of their own—I don't think a Dragonship would go anywhere it didn't want to go. Not easily, anyway."

"That's part of the mystery," said Bert with a sigh. "There are no signs of struggle, or damage, or even cut anchor lines. The ships have simply disappeared. We think the *Green Dragon* went first, then the *Violet* . . . but there's no way to really be sure. It didn't take much longer to confirm the others—the *Orange, Yellow,* and *Blue* dragons—were also gone. Even the *White Dragon* is missing."

"And the *Black Dragon?*" queried Charles. "What of it?"

"Ordo Maas dismantled that beast long ago," Bert said with a shudder. "And good riddance, I say."

"Why was the *Indigo Dragon* spared?" asked Jack.

"She'd been completely rebuilt as an airship," Bert replied. "I think she was either just overlooked, or she no longer suited the thief's purposes."

"You haven't said how Aven is involved," noted Jack.

"That's how we began to discover the missing children," said Bert. "The prince—Aven's son—was aboard the *Yellow Dragon* when it disappeared. In fact, every place a Dragonship has vanished, many of the local children have disappeared as well."

"Aven has a son?" said Jack, casting a glance at Jamie. "I . . . I didn't know."

"A strapping lad, almost nine years old now," said Bert. "I was already preparing to come and seek you out regarding the missing Dragonships when she and Artus contacted me and told me about the prince."

He turned and took John by the shoulders. "I know this is very sudden, John—but we need the Caretaker's help. I don't think we can discover the answers we need to find here. We must go back to the Archipelago."

"I . . . I . . . of course I'll help," said John. "Of course."

"I'm coming too," put in Jack. "Charles? Are you with us?"

"My poor wife will never understand," Charles answered, "but I am loath to let the two of you go traipsing off to the Archipelago without any adult supervision at all."

"I beg your pardon," Bert huffed.

"No offense, Bert," Charles reassured him.

"I can send messages to your families," offered Jamie. "I'll give them an excuse about emergency business for the university."

"Thereby ensuring that we return to find ourselves in hotter water than when we left," said John. "Best make it attending to a friend in need. That's closer to the truth, anyway."

"Excellent," said Bert. "We have a plan. Let us now put it into action."

John and Charles quickly wrote out messages to their wives and children for Jamie to pass along, and Jack wrote a brief note to Warnie and one to his friend Paddy's mother, a Mrs. Moore. It was also decided that given the unusual circumstances in the Archipelago, Laura Glue would be safer remaining in London under Jamie's care. In fact, once the decision was made, she immediately set about building herself a nest—in the storage room upstairs, inside the great wardrobe.

Being able to close the doors made her feel safe, she explained, as if no one would be able to reach her there.

"And safe you will be," Jack said gently, tucking her in amidst the furs and the blankets Jamie had provided. He also had a small electric torch, which he gave her in case she should become frightened during the night.

"Now," he told her, "I want you to listen to me. This isn't just an ordinary wardrobe. It's a *magic* wardrobe."

Laura Glue's eyes widened and she gave him a lopsided grin. "For really and truly?"

"For really and truly." Jack nodded.

She looked at Jamie, who also nodded. "More than anyone knows, my dear girl."

"And if you need it to be," added Jack, "it can become another world altogether. It can take you wherever you want to go, for as long as you want, and in an instant, it can bring you back, as if no time had passed at all."

"Wowww . . . ," said the girl with a yawn. "How do I make it work, Jack?"

"That's easy," Jack told her. "Just close your eyes, and dream where you want to go, and suddenly, you're there."

"But I do that anyway," Laura Glue said, leaning back and closing her eyes.

"Yes," Jack replied as he closed the door, all but a crack, on the drowsing girl. "But here, you'll always come home. And here, someone will be watching over you. Always."

"All ready, Jack?" said John.

"Ready. Are we all loaded?"

"Just done," called Charles from the window. "Jamie's given us a few stores from his larder, and Bert is anxious to get back to start looking into this. Although," he added, "I think he's greatly relieved that we're coming with."

"Was there any doubt?" said John. "Even under these circumstances, now that the opportunity's here, I find I can't wait to get back."

"Same here," agreed Jack.

Bert's face, upside down, appeared in the window. "All aboard, lads. It's time to go."

Farewells were said to Jamie, and each of them looked in quietly on the angel sleeping soundly in the wardrobe. Of them all, only Jack had noticed that before she fell asleep, Laura Glue had carefully sealed her ears with plugs of beeswax she had had tucked in her tunic.

With Jamie steadying the rope ladder from below, the companions ascended it and climbed into the carriage of the reborn *Indigo Dragon*.

"It sounds like she's purring," Charles exclaimed.

"That's the engine driving the props," said John, looking around in awe. "I do kind of miss the old masts and sails, though."

"Magic lets you skip a lot of steps," Bert said, "but that doesn't mean one can completely disregard principles of engineering.

"Ladder up? Good, good," he continued. "Let's be off, then."

"Remember," Jamie called from the window below, "to get there, just look for the second star on the right. . . ."

"That's not funny," Bert replied. "Farewell, James."

"And you, Bert," Jamie called back, waving. "Tell your daughter I hope she will not think too ill of me in the future."

With a final wave, Bert spun the wheel, and the *Indigo Dragon* whirled about and began to rise into the night air.

Below them the lights of London spread out like glittering pebbles in a dark pool. Everything was edged in a cool light from the rich moon hanging above. And in the distance, clouds had begun to gather. In moments they would be passing into another world. Somehow it seemed less eventful to be doing it in the air, instead of on the more physical surface of the water below.

"That last joke Jamie made," John said to Bert. "He was quoting his book, wasn't he?"

"Book?" said Bert, puzzled. "Was that in the book? No." He shook his head. "It's an old game he played with Laura Glue's grandfather, when they were young and could still bear each other's company.

"In the Archipelago, navigating by the second star to the right— the North Star—makes you sail in a circle. You never get anywhere except where you already are."

"Who is Laura Glue's grandfather, anyway?" asked Charles.

Bert looked at them all in surprise, as the clouds began to close about the ship. "Didn't Jamie tell you? He probably figured that as Caretakers, you already knew."

"I think I do," said John, "but it seems impossible to believe."

"We're into the rarified air of the Archipelago now," Bert informed the others, gesturing to the waters below—and back to the now vanished lights of London. "It's required to believe sixteen impossible things before breakfast."

"Who are we talking about, John?" asked Jack.

Charles pieced it together first. "There's a statue of him in Kensington Gardens," he said quietly. "Am I right, John?"

John nodded and leaned over the railing, face to the wind. "Laura Glue's grandfather," he explained, "Sir James Barrie's best friend, who became his greatest enemy, was the boy who never grew up.

"We've been summoned to the Archipelago by Peter Pan."

PART TWO

A HISTORY UNDONE

CHAPTER FIVE
THE ERRANT KNIGHT

THE CROSSING INTO the Archipelago was as smooth and uneventful as they'd remembered. One moment they were above the waters of the world, and the next moment they were not. And in the transition, the English night gave way to a crisp morning light.

The crew were many of the same cloven-hoofed fauns that had operated the ship when it sailed on water, although this time the companions were far less hesitant to interact with them.

"Excellent ship you've got here," Charles said to a passing crewman. "Uh, lovely decks."

"Humph," replied the faun, shoving past.

"Nice chatting with you," said Charles.

"I returned the *White Dragon* to Ordo Maas, then set about salvaging the wreckage of the old girl," Bert said, patting the hull. "It took us a long time to decide how to proceed, but fortunately we had lots of support and funding from Paralon. Artus and Aven have ruled very well, if, ah, unconventionally, and are widely loved."

"That's good to hear," John said, noting how quickly Jack moved away at the mention of Aven's name. "I'm going to have a hard time calling the High King 'Artus,' though."

"Oh, he insists that his personal friends still call him 'Bug,'" said Bert. "Says it helps him keep 'the common touch,' although between you and me, I think he just misses the adventures we had, before all this running-a-kingdom business got dropped on him."

"What was Samaranth's opinion on all of this?" John asked. "I assume he was consulted?"

"First among the royal advisers," said Bert. "Even more so than I. Since the war with the Winter King, the dragons have never been far from the Archipelago. At times they have intervened in certain affairs, but nothing that ever dictated a formal summoning from the Ring on Terminus."

The companions looked at one another with somber expressions. A formal summoning could only be done by the High King, using the Ring of Power—the great circle of stones they had discovered in the conflict with the Winter King. It was an action Artus would take in only the gravest circumstances.

"Until now?" John guessed.

Bert nodded. "At Samaranth's suggestion. Every dragon alive has scoured the islands but has found no sign of the missing ships or children. As far as we can determine, they are nowhere in the Archipelago."

"Could they be in our world?"

"Not likely. They would stand out more, not less. Look at the complications you had with just one little girl."

"Jamie told us that he remembered an old Archipelago legend about a Crusade," said John. "Do you know of such a story?"

"It does sound familiar, I'll admit," said Bert, "but I can't put my finger on it. I'm hoping we may be able to ask the Morgaine what it refers to, and get right to the heart of it."

"You could do that without us," John pointed out, "and with all these things happening in the Archipelago, I must admit I don't see how we can help. We came because you asked us to come. But what good are the Caretakers going to be in finding missing ships and kidnapped children?"

"Maybe more than you know, John. You are here because you are supposed to be here, and you *are* the Caretakers, after all. You well know that the responsibility is far greater than just looking after a book. Even if you were not the Caretakers, you are still friends of the king and queen—and it is in times of peril that one must call on one's friends, wherever and whoever they may be."

"Even if they are enemies, according to Laura Glue."

"Yes," Bert said. "Even if they are enemies."

"I can see the smoke coming out of your ears," Charles said, sitting on the deck next to Jack. "What are you considering so mightily?"

"Something I've been thinking about for nine years," replied Jack. "When we were trying to keep the Winter King from getting his hands on the *Geographica* . . ."

"Yes?" said John, coming to sit opposite Charles.

"The first plan was to try destroying it, right?"

"Correct."

"But we couldn't, because only the Cartographer could destroy the book."

"Right again," said John. "What are you driving at, Jack?"

"Stay with me here," urged Jack. "Part of the Caretaker's job is to annotate maps, add new maps, and also to improve the translations attached to existing maps, right?"

"Yes," John said, "although I haven't yet had the opportunity to add any maps, only make corrections and notations to the existing ones. What of it?"

"I'm afraid I don't see it either," said Charles.

"What he's asking," Bert said without turning from the wheel, "is why you didn't simply vandalize the atlas, or scumble in false notations, or simply pour ink all over the pages, effectively destroying its usefulness, if not the book itself."

"Well, yes," said Jack. "That's exactly what I was wondering."

Bert turned his head and squinted at them. "Don't you think that hadn't occurred to me, or Jules, or Stellan long before you were ever recruited as Caretakers?"

"Then why didn't you do it?" asked John.

"Would *you* have been able to?" Bert shot back.

"We tried," said Jack. "We threw it on the brazier."

"No," said Bert, "*Nemo* threw it on the brazier. And when he'd proven it wouldn't burn, that was the end of any thoughts you had of destroying, or even damaging, the book."

"He's right," Charles said. "We never even considered it after that."

"Clever," noted John. "We'd eliminated the idea in principle, so we overlooked other specific aspects of it that may have solved the problem."

"*Would* have solved the problem," Jack corrected. "We could have solved a major problem with a relatively minor sacrifice."

"Jules and I had a similar discussion once," said Bert. "He offered me a hypothetical situation. What if a young man, say, a painter from Austria, seemingly normal, absolutely unremarkable, was destined to one day become a terrible ruler, responsible for the death of millions?

"If, knowing this future, and knowing what might be averted if this single, then innocent artist were to be killed, would you do it?"

"There's no way to know a man's future," observed John. "Not for certain. So it would be murder."

"Jamie told me Nemo was foretold of his death," said Jack. "And he did nothing to change that event. So is that a reverse-murder? Or a self-murder?"

"That decision was Nemo's to make for himself," said Bert. "It wasn't someone deciding his future for him. But answer the question: Would you kill the painter who had done no evil, to save the millions from the evil that he might one day become?"

"No," John and Jack answered together.

"I don't know," Charles admitted. "Maybe if it were real and not hypothetical, I could make that choice."

"Well, in a way, that was the choice you were making with the *Geographica*," said Bert. "A little murder, with pen and ink as the instruments of the death, and you could prevent the book from being used in greater evil. But that wasn't the choice you *wanted* to make, so you didn't."

"That's all well and good," Jack said, "but it still irritates me to no end that the option didn't at least occur to us. Maybe all we needed to alter were a few key maps, or the summoning. . . .

"Say," he said, tapping John's foot. "Why don't we give it a try, just for the sake of scientific experimentation? We can pick a minor map and ink in a 'No Trespassing' sign or a unicorn or some such. What do you say, John?"

Bert groaned and slapped his forehead. "Spinning in his grave. I'm certain Stellan is just spinning in his grave. I'd have been better off leaving the book with Harry and Arthur."

However irritated he tried to sound, Bert also produced a quill and a bottle of ink, which he proffered to Charles with a barely disguised grin.

"Okay, John," said Charles. "Let's have it. Time to deface a little history."

"Now, I'm not going to just . . . ," John began, before a strange expression came over his face. "Um."

Jack looked from Charles to John and back again, shrugging.

"Where did you put it when you brought it aboard?" Bert asked over his shoulder. "In the cabin, perhaps?"

"You did bring it aboard, didn't you, John?" said Jack.

"Oh dear," murmured Charles. "Oh dear, oh dear, oh dear."

"The *Imaginarium Geographica*," John said with rising horror. "It's . . . it's . . ."

"Don't tell me you've lost it," said Bert.

"Nothing of the sort," John stated. "I know precisely where it is."

Jack and Charles looked at each other in disbelief as the meaning of John's words sank in.

The *Imaginarium Geographica* was exactly where they had left it when they arrived in London—next to Laura Glue's wings, safely covered with academic papers in the boot of John's car.

John spent the remainder of the short voyage to Avalon pacing the foredeck and cursing to himself in Anglo-Saxon. The crew of fauns exchanged glances of "different dance, same song" and kept working to keep the ship in order. Bert, Jack, and Charles huddled around the wheel to discuss this awkward turn of events.

"Can we go back for it?" asked Jack. "We'll have lost only a few hours. . . ."

"Hours I'm afraid we cannot spare," said Bert. "Remember—the *Indigo Dragon* is, for the time being, the only Dragonship available to the Silver Throne, and the only ship left that is able to cross the Frontier.

"Inconvenient as it may be, we will have to do without the original *Geographica*, and hope that no circumstance arises in which it is needed."

"Original *Geographica*?" Charles exclaimed. "I don't understand."

Bert grinned. "Do you recall your little friend Tummeler? He was as good as his word—he published a facsimile edition of the *Imaginarium Geographica*, and practically everyone in the Archipelago has a copy now.

"It's nowhere near as complete as the original, of course," he continued, "but it's annotated in English, and shows all the major islands. It would do in a pinch."

"Good Old Tummeler," said Charles. "I've often thought of him—usually during breakfast. Never looked at a muffin in the same way since, I can tell you."

John finally quit pacing and approached the others. "There was a lot going on, you'll remember," he said apologetically. "In all the confusion and commotion . . ."

"Five ham sandwiches," stated Jack. "That's all I'm going to say about confusion and commotion and no time to retrieve the *Geographica*. The Caretaker Bloody Principia."

"All right, Jack," Charles said quickly. "No need for language."

"Avalon, ho," said Bert, pointing. "We're at the boundary. Let's get off here and collect ourselves, and then we'll decide what to do next."

◆   ◆   ◆

Once the ship had been anchored to a spot on the sloping hill above the beach, the companions climbed down and took deep breaths of the sea air.

"Very nice," said Charles. "Makes me feel like I was young again. Not that I feel particularly old, mind you, but this adventuring business is much more a young man's game."

"You called?" Jack said, grinning.

"You're a college tutor," Charles told him. "That means you age exponentially with each semester."

"How about him, then?" Jack said, hooking a thumb at John. "He's a full professor."

"Dog years," said Bert. "Professors age in dog years."

"And how about you, old hat?" asked Charles.

"Oh, I took the easy way out," said Bert. "I figured out that if I age all the way to the end, I just start over. So, practically speaking, I'm the youngest one here."

The first order of business was to announce themselves to the Guardian of Avalon—the Green Knight.

"I shouldn't mind seeing the dutiful old fellow again," Charles said jovially. "He was very affable—after he quit trying to behead us, that is."

"There's something you really ought to know," Bert began, when they crested the hill and stood in front of the entrance to the ruins of Avalon.

There, slumped against one of the fallen pilasters, arms akimbo, the Green Knight turned his head and regarded them with a resigned expression. He seemed younger than before but was still a mishmash of rusty armor, wooden limbs, and twigs that seemingly stuck out of every joint and crevice. But, oddly, he also affected a tattered top hat and trench coat over his armor.

It occurred to John that this apparition might be what would result if the Tin Woodsman and Scarecrow from Frank Baum's Oz were squeezed together.

The armored scarecrow was chewing something, his mossy beard swaying with the motion. Then he swallowed hard and spoke.

"I hope you're not expecting me to stand on ceremony. I may have to stand guard over this junk pile, and help you when asked, and all the other shabby things they make me do here, but if you're hoping for some sort of formal welcome, you can forget it."

Charles groaned and rubbed his temples.

"What?" said Jack. "Wasn't he Charles Darnay before?"

"Before, but not now," said Charles, and with the sound of his voice, the Green Knight recognized him.

"Hey," he exclaimed, standing straighter now, "you're not going to let him hit me, are you?"

John sighed. Now he knew who this was. "That's what Bert was trying to tell us," he said to the others. "This Green Knight isn't the one we met before."

It was Magwich.

"I thought the dragons had eaten you, or at the very least, dismembered you, Maggot," said Charles.

"I'm a knight now," Magwich sniffed, "so you have to treat me with more respect."

"If you're a knight, I'm Geoffrey Chaucer," retorted Charles. He turned to Bert, sputtering in anger and amazement. "Magwich? The Green Knight? How did this happen, Bert?"

"I wanted to explain," Bert said sheepishly. "This is law, part of the old code established by King Arthur centuries ago. The dragons saw it as a fitting punishment for a traitor like Magwich."

"Punishment?" Jack exclaimed. "He looks as if he's on holiday."

"I know, I know," said Bert. "It isn't supposed to be an *honor*—it's supposed to be a *penance*. But Magwich is the only knight in more than two dozen generations of them who actually *rose* in station because of it."

"Well, I'm not about to trust anything he says," Charles stated.

"See, now you've gone and hurt my feelings," said Magwich. "Just because I'm a murdering, thieving, cowardly, traitorous sort doesn't mean I can't do my job properly."

"Oh, for heaven's sake," said Charles. "Fine. Whatever you say. Just keep him away from me."

With a gesture, the Green Knight motioned for them to follow. John walked beside him, with Jack, Charles, and Bert trailing along a short distance behind.

"So," said John, "what's it like to be made of wood?"

"Not as bad as you'd think," replied Magwich. "Although you wouldn't believe the places termites can get to."

"Sorry I asked," said John.

The familiar path wound around the edge of the island, the grasses and craggy rocks standing out in sharp relief against the dark, roiling clouds of the Frontier beyond—the true boundary of the Archipelago. At the path's end they would find the Morgaine—the witches known as the Three Who Are One. Sometimes they were able to prophesy the future. Other times they were unwilling to try. Still, Bert explained, it was worth asking, as the Morgaine were likely to be the only entities who could shed any light on the events taking place.

Jack suppressed a shudder. "I'm really not looking forward to seeing them again," he confided to Charles.

"I know what you mean," Charles replied. "Those strange old women . . . especially the one—what was her name again?"

"Cul," Magwich said over his shoulder. "And I can sympathize. I don't come see them unless I'm compelled, which isn't often."

"Didn't she make you rub her feet once?" recalled Jack, suppressing a wicked smile.

Magwich groaned. "Why else do you think I stay on the far side of the island?"

They came into the small clearing, but there was no one to be seen. The great black cauldron that sat over a usually crackling fire was nestled among cold embers, and there were other cooking implements scattered here and there amidst the sharp grass.

At the far side were three tumbledown cottages in a state of extreme disrepair, around which were piled a number of artifacts of all shapes and sizes. Both John and Charles noticed, but said nothing about, the large iron kettle with the bronze adornments, leather handles, and Greek shield for a lid.

"Hey, ho, looks like no one's home," said Magwich, spinning around on his heel. "Time to go."

"Not so fast, Maggot." Charles caught Magwich by the collar of his breastplate. "You're the Green Knight now. You botch your job, I guarantee you I'll give a full report, omitting nothing, to Samaranth himself."

"Bloody hell," muttered Magwich. "A fellow just can't catch a break with you people."

He pointed down the slope. "You'll probably find them in the cave. That's where they spend most of their time these days."

"Excellent," Charles said, giving the reluctant knight a shove. "Lead the way, Sir Maggot."

CHAPTER SIX
THE WEAVING

THE CAVE WAS deeper than the opening would indicate, and although they all (with the exception of Bert, who simply removed his hat) had to stoop to enter, once inside they were able to stand erect without bumping their heads.

Rather than growing darker, the cave grew lighter the deeper they went. There, at the back, they saw three figures—but it took a moment for them to realize that these were not the figures they had expected to see.

Instead of the weathered old women draped in layers of dresses and beads and various charms, waiting to welcome the companions were three youthful, graceful women of astonishing beauty.

The nearest of them wore a dress of shimmering blue and had long, golden hair, pulled back into a bun at her neck. She sat at a large spinning wheel, which was idle. A pile of unspun wool was behind her, the topmost fibers of which were pulled together in the threads hanging from the wheel.

The second woman had hair like flame, tied in looping ringlets that fell onto a cream-colored dress with elaborate patterns embroidered across the chest. Her arms rested on an enormous loom, which seemed to be as unused as the spinning wheel, wrapped as it was in cobwebs. Hundreds and hundreds of threads grew together in a tangle underneath a giant comb, but she made no effort to unbind them.

And the third, near the back of the cave, was raven-haired and wore a blue dress of extraordinary richness. Of the three, only she seemed to be engaged in active work: She was slowly and methodically unraveling the threads of a great tapestry that hung across the entire rear wall of the cave.

John couldn't be sure, but it seemed as if the images depicted in the great weaving were in motion. It was too indistinct for his eyes to focus on any portion of it for more than an instant, however.

The companions and the three women regarded each other silently, until the quiet was broken by a loud wail—which was coming from the Green Knight.

"Nine years," whimpered Magwich. "All that time I've been dealing with those three hags outside, and I never knew these beauties were waiting in the cave."

"Quiet, you nit," said Charles. "I think these three are the old . . . ah, that is, I think they're the same women."

"Just so," concurred the fair-haired woman, bowing her head.

"Are you here for the spindle?" the dark-haired woman asked, without looking at them or pausing in her labors. "Because if you are, you're too late. We already gave it to that princess . . . what was her name again? Dawn?"

"Aurora," said the red-haired woman. "And you're forgetting the order of things. These young men aren't here for the spindle. They've come to ask us questions, haven't you?"

John looked askance at Bert, who nodded almost imperceptibly. "Yes," said John. "We have."

"One each, then," said the first woman. "Three questions asked, three answered. A question for Ceridwen, to set the stage. A question for Celedriel, to begin the play. And a question for Cul, to draw the curtain."

"I'll be drawn and quartered," Magwich moaned. "They are the same women. And I've been avoiding them all this time!"

He threw up his hands and wailed, "Why is life so unfair?"

"That is your first question, which I shall answer," said Ceridwen.

"That's done it!" Charles shouted at the former steward. "Out! Out!" He grabbed Magwich by the shoulders and all but threw him to the front of the cave.

"I'll keep him occupied," he called back to his friends. "Do what you can with the other two questions."

Ceridwen was already beginning to answer the first question—which, John thought to himself, was not really a terrible question to have asked. It just didn't have much to do with their current situation.

"Life is so unfair," Ceridwen was saying, "because it is you whose vision is too small. Mistakes may become opportunities; accidents may become a chance for redemption. What seems unbalanced in a moment may become level over time, if only the canvas upon which your lives are painted is large enough."

John and Jack looked at each other in puzzlement. It was certainly the answer of a prophetess.

"My question is next," said Celedriel. "Ask of me what you will, and I shall answer."

John nodded at Jack, indicating that it was his turn. And as uncomfortable as that made him, Jack was somewhat relieved that he wouldn't have to talk to Cul—no matter how beautiful her present form was.

He considered his options. His first impulse was to ask about his dreams, and Aven's son—but that would be too limited a use of the question. It stood to reason that there were only two questions that needed to be asked: the location of the missing Dragonships, and the location of the missing children. Jack chose the former, expecting—silently hoping—that John mirrored his train of thought and would ask the latter.

"The ships you seek," Celedriel began in response, "are not in the Archipelago, nor are they in the world of men. They have been taken into the Underneath. The Chamenos Liber are what guard them. Find them, and find the Dragonships you seek."

"Short and sweet," John muttered under his breath. "I hope Bert understood what that meant."

"I suppose I have to answer you now," said Cul, "so go ahead and ask your question, Son of Adam."

John thought for a moment, biting his lip in concentration. What to choose? What to ask? Then, suddenly, it came to him.

"What are you doing?" he asked.

Jack stared at John in amazement. That was not what he had expected his friend to ask. And judging by the expression on Bert's face, he didn't expect it either.

The reaction of the Morgaine was different. They looked at one another and nodded, as if confirming something they had suspected but not known until that moment. Even Cul's features softened as she began to answer, although she never stopped unraveling the tapestry.

"Well asked, young Caretaker John," she said, her voice a soft purr. "You understand that all that happens is not mere cause and effect, but that there are causes underlying causes, and it is those that truly shape the events of history.

"The world is unraveling. Someone has changed Time itself, and a new event has taken place that was not in the Tapestry before. Thus, we must unweave all that has happened since, for a new weaving must be created. You may ask another question."

"Do you have to unweave the entire Tapestry?"

Again came the nods, as if this question also met with their approval. "No," said Cul. "We must unravel it only to the moment of the change—seven centuries past. You may ask another question."

"What caused the change?" asked John.

"Caretakers of the *Imaginarium Geographica*," Cul replied, turning fully to stare at them. "*You* did."

Jack snorted. "Of course," he said flippantly. "We just went backward in time seven hundred years and accidentally killed Genghis Khan, or stepped on a butterfly, or something equally catastrophic."

"That can't be," Bert protested, with no hint of irony or mockery. "If that had happened, we would have a historical record of some sort. . . ."

"That's why you're unraveling the tapestry now—because the event that changed things didn't happen seven centuries ago, did it?" John asked the Morgaine.

"No," said Ceridwen, "it happened *nine years ago*."

"We have answered all the questions agreed upon," said Celedriel, "and more, because you have shown yourself to be wise."

"And because of the wisdom of your questions, we will offer you one further answer to do with as you will," Cul intoned. "The unraveling began when history was changed, but the thread was first loosened when two brothers made a *choice*.

"Both of them believed his choice may have been wrong. One

of them was. When you determine which, and in what way, you may yet have a chance to save the children of this world, and your own."

As a group, the companions exited the cave, shielding their eyes from the glare of daylight. They went across the clearing and sat to discuss what the Morgaine had said.

Over near the cottages, Charles had cornered Magwich by brandishing a pair of hedge shears and making suggestive threats about what might get pruned if he didn't keep his distance and stay quiet.

Jack waved for Charles to come over and join them. He left the Green Knight muttering to himself and kicking stones, and trotted over to the others, where Jack quickly filled him in on what had transpired in the cave.

"John's a deeper thinker than I've given him credit for," said Charles. "I react too much in the moment, I'm afraid. I wouldn't have had the sense to ask what he did."

"Nor did I," said Jack. "What made you think of it, John?"

He shrugged. "I don't know. It just seemed to me, in that moment, that if these women were as important and powerful as Bert has always claimed they are, then perhaps what they were doing had a larger purpose. I simply got lucky that it did."

"Not luck," said Bert. "Intuition. The best skill of a Caretaker, and you have it in spades. By the way—what do you make of their answer to Jack?"

"That the Dragonships are guarded by the Chamenos Liber?" John asked. "I'm not sure. It sounds familiar. *Liber* is Latin. It means 'book.' *Chamenos* I'm not entirely certain of—it sounds Greek, maybe."

"So we'll find the missing ships in a book?" said Charles. "I'm not sure that helps, as clues go."

"I'm afraid the rest of what they've told us only makes things worse," observed Bert.

"Not sure how it can get worse," said Charles.

"The story they told," Bert said, "about Time itself being broken—I can't think of anything more dangerous."

"We haven't noticed so far," reasoned Charles. "So I don't know why it would bother you so."

"Two reasons," Bert said, his face darkening. "One—you're correct. We wouldn't notice if history had been changed, because everything that follows will change accordingly, including our own memories. But the second reason is worse."

"Why?" asked John.

"Because," Bert explained, lifting his head, "if the change was indeed our fault, caused by something that happened nine years ago, then it's possible our memories of that event have also been altered."

John slapped his forehead. "Meaning there might be no way to know what caused the damage to begin with."

"Exactly," said Bert. "We must battle the effect, even though we may never know the cause—because in our 'Time,' it may never have happened at all."

It took less than a half hour for the companions to make their way back to where the *Indigo Dragon* was anchored, and there was no further discussion of what had transpired in the cave. This was in part because each of them was turning the revelations over and over in his head, thinking; and in part because the Green Knight never stopped complaining.

"But why?" Magwich whined. "Just tell me what they said. It was my question, after all."

"Oh, for heaven's sake," Charles said, rolling his eyes. He turned and took the shabby knight by the shoulders. "Do you want to know why life is so unfair? Well, I'll tell you. It's because you are a bitter, twisted, heartless villain with a lump of coal for a heart, who has never done a damned thing except for the most selfish reasons, no matter the suffering it has caused those around you.

"What's more, you never learn from your mistakes. You just keep doing the same stupid things over and over and over, and will probably end up spending the rest of eternity all alone on this island, until you finally crumble away to dust, having perished alone, unmourned, and unloved."

Magwich stared at Charles, who was breathing hard from his extended rant, before he finally blinked, then blinked again. Then, without warning, Magwich burst into tears and collapsed against Charles, sobbing.

"Oh, good job, Charles," declared Jack. "You've completely destroyed the poor fellow."

"Arrgghh," said Charles, as he dragged the whimpering, slobbering knight over to a rock, where he sat him down.

"Here," he said to Magwich, offering a handkerchief. "Do wipe the, er, sap off of your face. That's a good fellow."

"But, but, you're absolutely *right*!" wailed Magwich. "I'm a terrible person, and I deserve everything that's happened to me. Why, if there were any justice in the world, you'd just chip me up for firewood right now. And even then, the embers from my fire would probably burn a hole in your coat."

He threw up his arms and started such a pitiful keening that even Bert had to cover his ears.

"Kindling! That's all I'm good for! I'll never do anyone any good!"

"Now, that's not true," said Charles. "I'm, ah, I'm sure you're not completely devoid of redeeming qualities."

"Really?" Magwich said, sniffing. "Like what?"

"Don't look at us," John said to Charles. "You opened the door."

"Well, er," Charles stammered, rubbing his temples. "Give me a minute—I'm sure I can come up with something."

"You have to think about it?" sobbed Magwich. "I'm irredeemable, aren't I?"

"No one is completely irredeemable," said Charles. "But I must say . . ." His face went slack and his eyes widened as an idea occurred to him.

"You know, Magwich," he suggested, "perhaps we're looking at this the wrong way."

"How so?" sniffed the knight.

"Every story has a villain or two," Charles replied matter-of-factly, "and while you are more of a minor villain, I have to say you're far more irritating than the Winter King ever was. In fact, being despicable may just be your great talent in life."

"You really think so?" said Magwich. "I don't understand."

"Look," Charles explained. "You know I despise you, right?"

"You've made it very clear, yes," said Magwich.

"Well," Charles continued, "whenever we've met, you've demonstrated all the qualities I don't want to have. And I try to better myself so I don't become like you. So in a way . . ."

"My bad example is making you a better person?" finished Magwich.

"Something like that," said Charles. "If it wasn't for people like you, I don't think I would try so hard. And honestly, you're the worst I've ever encountered."

"Oh, you're just saying that," said Magwich.

"No, I really mean it," said Charles.

"I think I'm going to be sick," Jack declared. "Charles, it's time to go."

Charles stood and clapped the Green Knight on the back. "All right, then?" he asked. "Good. Don't ever change, Magwich."

"Oh, I won't," said the knight, glancing backward across the island. "So, ah—d'you think the three ladies in the cave would like some company?"

Charles frowned. "Ah, I can't say, Magwich. Wouldn't hurt to ask," he said, climbing up the ladder. "I think."

"Farewell, Caretakers," Magwich called over his shoulder as he clanked his way up the hill.

"What do you think will happen to him?" asked John.

"They'll probably turn him into a toad," said Charles. "But I don't think he'll notice."

"We must get to Paralon immediately," Bert said as the *Indigo Dragon* moved away from Avalon and toward the dark, roiling clouds that formed the Frontier. "Artus must be told all of this. The Morgaine do not often offer information so freely. The situation must be very dire for them to have said as much as they did."

Jack had moved to the rear of the deck, away from the others, thinking about the prince.

The High King's son.

Aven's son.

A son who, in other circumstances, might have been his own.

Whatever course John, or Bert, or Charles might decide, Jack's direction was clear. The others could pursue the missing Dragon-ships and find the children—but Jack would not let another night pass without doing everything in his power to find the missing son of his one great love. . . .

Or perish in the attempt.

CHAPTER SEVEN
THE GREAT WHATSIT

THE JOURNEY TO Paralon was uneventful—too much so, in Bert's estimation. He kept scuttling back and forth from port to starboard, peering over the edge, and making worried clucking sounds with his tongue.

"It's like the calm before the storm," he confided to John.

"The weather is beautiful," John said, looking around at the nearly cloudless sky.

"It's not the weather I'm concerned with," replied Bert. "It's the fact that we're almost to Paralon, and we've yet to see a single ship on the water below."

"That's right," put in Charles. "There ought to be trade ships full of apples going to and fro—or at the least, several fishing vessels."

"And yet not even a dinghy," Bert said. "This bodes very ill, I'm afraid."

The extent of Bert's worries was confirmed as they approached the island kingdom itself. Smoke ringed the harbor ahead of them, and a haze in the distance indicated that other fires had been set elsewhere on Paralon.

"You know," said Charles, "I'd really like to visit this place when someone hasn't set it on fire. Just once, mind you."

Below, it was starkly obvious: There were no ships of any kind in the harbor or at the docks. There had been a few—but those were the source of the smoke. They'd been set ablaze. Far beneath them, they could see crews of workers and sailors trying vainly to staunch the flames on vessels that were already lost.

"What the devil?" exclaimed Bert. "I haven't been gone a day. What can have happened in a day?"

"A lot," Jack said darkly, "if the day in question happened seven hundred years ago."

Bert piloted the airship past the smoke and headed into the city proper, which was built around and against the great tower of rock upon which the great castle of the Silver Throne stood.

He found a broad cobblestone plaza that was nearly devoid of people, and slowly set the *Indigo Dragon* down. The carriage settled heavily onto the street, and the propellers gradually came to a stop.

"The palace is just up the boulevard," Bert said, "but I wanted to stop and pick up a spare *Geographica*, and say hello to an old friend while we're at it."

Across the plaza, amidst shops selling pieces of the North Wind (fifty centimes a bag), and bezoars, and enchanted violins, was a small shopfront that was apparently dedicated to the sale of a single item: the *Imaginarium Geographica*. Piles of the books were the only things on display within and without the store.

A small figure burst through the door to a jangling of bells. "Bless my soul," he said, voice quivering with emotion. "Be it the scowlers, my friends, returned to us at long last?"

"Tummeler!" Charles shouted, as he raced forward and embraced the little badger. "Tummeler, it's grand to see you again!"

"I be filled with joyful thoughts myself, Scowler Charles," Tummeler said, wiping at his tear-filled eyes with a paw. "An' Scowler Jack an' Scowler John, too! This be a day of days, it be."

Jack and John both greeted their furry friend warmly, while Charles stepped inside the shop.

"I say, Tummeler," Charles began. "You have quite an enterprise going here."

He handed copies of the oversize book to both Jack and John, and all three made noises of praise and astonishment.

The book was roughly the shape of the real *Geographica*, and had a tooled leather cover, but it also bore an illustrated jacket and was annotated entirely in English.

"Th' language of Oxford scowlers, you know," explained Tummeler proudly.

"Tummeler, I'm greatly impressed," said Charles.

"I'm speechless," said John, flipping through the pages. "Most of the major islands are here—and with better notes than I remember."

"And look," Jack pointed out, "it's got an introduction by the king."

"It was a favor," Tummeler admitted. "But it helped get the word out."

"How did you do this, Tum?" John asked. "You even have Terminus in here."

The badger held up his paws and shrugged. "Badgers has good mem'ries," he explained. "I just wrote what I remembered when I came back to Paralon, and Bert helped me with copies o' th' maps."

"I'm terribly impressed," Charles said again, patting his small friend on the back.

"T'anks muchly," said Tummeler, beaming. "I does what I can."

"Don't let the humility fool you," said Bert. "He's sold through four printings of the concise edition of the *Imaginarium Geographica* to date."

"Five," Tummeler corrected. "We've only just delivered th' last of th' inventory to the libraries at Prydain . . . at least, I hope they arrived, what with all th' troubles."

"What's happened to the ships, Tummeler?" asked Bert.

"No one knows," replied the badger. "But peoples think it's a curse what began after th' Dragonships disappeared."

"What's cursed?" Jack asked.

"The rest of the ships in the Archipelago," said Tummeler. "They're *all* cursed. In a single night, we found all of 'em sunk, or put to th' torch. And worse, any new ships bein' built seem to sink the minute they're put to sea. Just fall apart before y'r eyes. And as a result . . ."

"Everything in the Archipelago has been disconnected," concluded John somberly. "All the unity that was achieved by the creation of the *Geographica* and the rule of the High King . . ."

"Utterly in a shambles," finished Bert. "At least we still have Tummeler's copies of the *Geographica*. By now they're on every land in the Archipelago."

"So everyone knows where everything is," said Jack, "but no one can get anywhere."

"That's been th' problem," agreed Tummeler. "Th' king an' queen have been using the Great Cranes of Byblos to take messages back an' forth, but that only works f'r th' nearby islands. The rest . . ."

"Are completely cut off," Charles finished.

"We'd better get to the palace," said Bert. "We must speak to Artus."

He turned to Tummeler. "We find ourselves in need of a *Geographica*, Master Tummeler. We've ah, neglected to bring along our own. May we purchase a copy from you?"

"Purchase? Y' mean buy a copy? Of *my* book?" Tummeler said, as his eyes grew wide. "Of course not! There be no charge for Oxford scowlers t' have a *Geographica*!"

With that the little badger scurried around them, pulling two clean, undamaged copies from the bottom of the pile and handing them to Jack and Charles. Then he raced to a small office at the back of the shop and returned a minute later with another copy for John that seemed slightly different from the others.

With extreme sincerity and gravity, Tummeler presented the book to John.

"F'r th' Master Caretaker," Tummeler said soberly. "This be my own original book, copied from yours. I wants y' t' have it, Scowler John."

"Tummeler, I can't accept this," John protested, holding up his hands. "You made it yourself."

"That's why I wants it t' be yours," insisted Tummeler. "It's not as clean as th' ones what we printed, but it's got character."

John finally acquiesced and took the gift as graciously as he could manage. "Thank you, Tummeler. I'm sure it will come in very handy."

"I say, Tummeler," said Charles. "Would you mind signing mine? Just for old times' sake?"

"Sign? Y' mean, like a *autograph*? Oh, Master Scowlers,"

Tummler said, nearly swooning. "This be th' proudest day in ol' Tummeler's life."

The little badger removed a quill from one of his pockets and carefully inscribed his name in all three books.

"One last favor to ask, if I may," Bert began.

"No need t' ask," Tummeler said, beaming. "When I saw y' landin' th' *Indigo Dragon*, I already started up th' Curious Diversity out back. I figured you'd be needin' a lift t' th' archive."

Charles thumped him on the back again and grinned. "Good old Tummeler."

"We're not going to the palace?" asked Charles as Tummeler guided the steam-belching vehicle onto one of the broad streets that led to the northern part of the island. "Don't we need to consult with Artus, ah, that is, the High King?"

"That's where I be taking y', Scowler Charles," the badger said without taking his eyes from the road ahead. "T' th' king."

As they traveled, Bert explained just how drastically things had changed in the Archipelago, particularly in regard to the Palace of Paralon, where the High King and Queen sat on the Silver Throne. On the outside, it looked much the same as it had when they had last been there. It was still a mighty and impressive edifice, and a number of ministers and officials circulated around an axis somewhere in the center—represented by King Artus. But it was no longer the true seat of authority in the Archipelago.

Rather than embrace and revel in the trappings of authority, wealth, and power, as would almost anyone who found themselves heir to a throne, Artus had apparently eschewed ceremony and was conducting the affairs of the kingdom in the ruins of the Old City, the first built by his ancestor Artigel, son of Arthur.

Artus reportedly liked to conduct affairs of state while sprawled on his stomach behind a makeshift throne in a vast hall with only half a ceiling. On the floor, he examined maps and parchments and a pile of various reports that was constantly being added to by the continuous stream of officials who made the trek from the palace.

"He wasn't in Paralon for a year," Bert said, "before he moved everything here, lock, stock, and powder horn. It turns out he had a passion for the old archives, and I daresay it's made him a better ruler for it."

"What do you know?" said Jack. "The potboy turned out to be a scholar after all."

Tummeler guided the Curious Diversity along the bottom of the canyon, which had been recently paved. They glided smoothly past the great doors that led to Samaranth's treasure hoard without so much as a swerve in its direction.

"Shouldn't we be consulting Samaranth as well?" asked John. "After all, he's probably the oldest creature in the Archipelago."

"Considered," said Bert, "but he's gone with the rest of his kind, searching for the Dragonships. And he may be old, but his knowledge is broad, not deep. Other than the royal family and the Caretakers, he hasn't paid as much attention to mankind as you'd think."

"'At's cause y'r still a young race," Tummeler commented over his shoulder. "Give it time, an' y' might yet turn out t' be an interestin' people."

"I can't imagine that Aven agreed to come here," Jack said,

glancing around at the steep stone walls to either side of the road. "It would take more persuasion than I'm capable of to get her to move this far from the sea."

Tummeler began to reply, but a raised eyebrow and slight shake of the head from Bert silenced him. Swallowing hard, the little animal increased his speed, and in short order they arrived at their destination.

"Well, Master Scowlers," Tummeler announced, beaming as if he'd built the place himself. "Here we be. Th' Great Whatsit."

Before them, carved deep into the granite walls of a junction in the canyon, were several towers of stone, accented and buttressed by wooden beams and golden embellishments. The structures were carved along the strata of the rock, and so the entire edifice resembled nothing so much as a great, glittering mica pipe organ.

"Great Whatsit?" Jack asked.

"Oh, that's just th' nickname we animals give it," said Tummeler. "On account of th' king can never decide what it is. Is it a library? Or an archive? Or a city? Or just a pile of rock? Or all o' that at once? So we just began t' call it th' Great Whatsit, an' th' name stuck.

"But don't tell th' king I told y' that," Tummeler said to Charles. "Decorum, an' all."

"Won't breathe a word of it," Charles assured him, as the companions said their farewells to the little mammal, thanking him again for the copies of the *Geographica*.

"It's nothing," he said, doing the badger equivalent of a blush and shuffle. "I wuz happy t' do it. And glad t' give y' a ride—but I needs t' attend my shop. Commerce never sleeps, y' know!"

"We do," said Jack. "Where to now, Bert?"

"This way." Bert gestured. "We just need to follow the smell of decaying parchment, and we'll find the High King."

Unlike the palace at Paralon, which was structurally ordered with geometric precision, the old city of Artigel was built according to geologic rules. As flowed the stone, so flowed the rooms. John had the fleeting thought that it resembled a labyrinth, and for a moment had a chill of premonition. But the thought vanished when they entered a spacious chamber distinguished both by its lack of decoration, save for the immense mess of documents scattered throughout, and its primary occupant.

Sprawled on the floor, Artus was deep in concentration, pausing only to scribble a note on a sheet of parchment or mutter an irritated "Yes, yes," when asked a direct question by one of his advisers hovering nearby.

And so it was that they were nearly standing on top of him before he even noticed the companions' presence.

"What is it, what is it?" said Artus without glancing up. "I am issuing edicts as fast as I am able, as you can plainly see."

"Take your time," replied John. "We've only come from the Summer Country, but I suppose we can wait for the king."

At the sound of John's voice, Artus jumped to his feet, scattering parchment everywhere. "What is this? What is this?" he exclaimed excitedly. "My dear friends! You've come at last!"

Whatever else they may have been expecting, this reaction—from the king, no less—took the companions completely off guard.

The slightly gawky youth they had known as Bug had grown into a barrel-chested man, who was taller and broader than any of them; and his reception of them was so unabashedly giddy that they couldn't help but respond in kind. Each of them in turn gave Artus a hug, and he slapped them on the back so repeatedly that they thought their teeth might fall out.

The deference the officials and ministers gave to Artus underscored the fact that he was indeed king—but underneath, he was the same friend they remembered.

"So happy to see you," Artus said. "You made great time—we dispatched Bert only yesterday."

"We had an advance warning," said John. "There's a lot we need to tell you, ah, Bug."

"Better make it 'Artus' or 'Your Majesty' inside the, ah, archive—library," Artus said with a furtive glance around at some of his underlings. "I prefer 'Bug' myself, but it's harder to motivate people when they have to take orders from a 'King Bug.'"

"Let's stick to Artus, then," declared Charles. "I'm not sure I can fit 'Bug' and 'Your Majesty' together in my brain at the same time."

It took a long while for the companions to explain everything that had transpired, during which Artus ordered several trays of food brought in—which the servants spread around them on the floor.

"I hope you don't mind," Artus said apologetically. "I'm just so much more comfortable working here on the floor. A throwback to my early days on Avalon, I suppose. The old witches didn't let me have any furniture, so I had to learn to make do.

"I can't quite get used to the fancy thrones and banquet halls and whatnot. Sure," he continued, "every so often, for an official function, we have to put on the robes and do all that kingly stuff. But mostly I like to spend time working among the people in the shops and on the docks. When they're not on fire, that is," he added.

"It's fine," John assured him. "What do you know about the ships? Who's setting them ablaze?"

"We don't know," said the king. "But everything you've told me has sparked an idea. Come with me." Artus jumped to his feet. "I want to show you something."

Artus led them through several cavernous rooms piled with loose papers that seemed newly made, fresh. They were certainly not typical archive materials. Past those rooms they came before a great set of doors, guarded by two powerful-looking elves.

"I've noticed a number of elves around the, uh, archive," Jack remarked.

"Yes," said Artus. "When the *Blue Dragon* was taken, King Eledir sent several other ships here to shore up any defense we might need—and those were the first ships to burn. So we've put the elves to work in places that need greater security.

"It's fitting that they're here in the Old City," he continued. "It was Elven craftsmen who built many of the structures here, and especially the doors, but these are special."

He pointed up at the intricately carved figures that ringed the arch at the top of each door. "These were built by a legendary craftsman who was rumored to be half elf and half troll. Made him crazy as a bedbug, but the work he did was second to none."

As he spoke, Artus removed his ring, the symbol of his office, and pressed it into a nearly imperceptible depression in the metal frame. There was an audible click from inside the doors, and only then did the guards relax their stance to allow the visitors to pass.

"I read somewhere that the rings and the locking mechanism

were both carved from a 'lodestone,'" said Artus, "but I haven't the faintest idea what that is."

He opened the massive doors. Inside they saw a honeycomb of shelves upon shelves filled with bound books, sheets of parchment, and rolls of papyrus, all in an incredible state of disarray.

"Please forgive the mess," Artus said mildly. "The main body of the library has been moved now and again, and we keep adding new materials before we've had a chance to fully catalogue what we already have."

"So this is the Great Whatsit," Charles said, unable to disguise the admiration in his voice. "I wonder what old Craigie at the *OED* would think about this, eh, John?"

"Ah," said Artus. "I see Tummeler's been talking. No, it's okay," he added when Charles began to stammer an apology. "I know that's what the animals began calling it. So does just about everyone else. It's not a bad name, Great Whatsit. It's better than what Aven called it, which, um, I can't really repeat—lots of sailor words and the like, you know."

It was the first time Artus had mentioned Aven in any context at all, and he did so in such a matter-of-fact way that none of the companions could discern anything from the remark.

Artus turned away from his friends, cupped his hands to his mouth, and bellowed, "Solomon! Solomon Kaw!"

In response to his call, an enormous black crow dropped down from the dark recesses of the ceiling above and perched on the desk next to Artus.

The bird wore glasses on the end of a giant, dusk-gray beak, and a tight-fitting cleric's vest. Charles half expected to see spats on its feet as well.

"Ho, Solomon," Artus said. "How goes the work?"

"It go-go-goes as it go-go-goes," the crow replied in a voice that sounded like a willow branch being swished through a pile of dry leaves. "We fi-fi-files the books, and no-no-note the files, as we have b-b-been doing these muh-muh-many centuries, oh King."

"Well done, my good, ah, bird," said Artus. "I need to ask: Have you a catalogue of myths, dating back . . . ah . . . ?" He turned to Bert.

"Seven centuries," said Bert. "Give or take."

Without a word, the crow dipped its head, spread its wings, and disappeared into the stacks.

"Can't beat crows for organizing a library," said Artus. "We used to also have a staff of very efficient hedgehogs, but when the crows arrived, there was an unfortunate misunderstanding at the commissary, and it's been just crows ever since."

"A few of these look singed," John observed, examining a stack of papyrus rolls. "Did someone get a little careless and leave them too close to a lamp?"

Artus peered over John's shoulder at the rolls. "Oh, those. They're from the old collection, in your world," he said. "There was indeed a fire—but fortunately, a number of scholars with ties to the Archipelago were able to rescue them before too much damage was done.

"Actually," he continued, "it was from these old documents that Arthur took the original seal of the High King."

"The *alpha?*" said Charles. "So these are Greek?"

"Yes, on both counts," Artus replied, "although I think they also used it to indicate the library these came from. A place called Alexandria, in the country of, um . . ."

"Egypt," said John, dumbfounded. "Alexandria is in Egypt."

"Right!" said Artus. "That's what they originally called this mess before it was the Great Whatsit, or the Royal Library, or the Archive of Paralon . . .

"It was called the Library of Alexandria."

CHAPTER EIGHT
THE FRIAR'S TALE

SOLOMON KAW RETURNED with a thick, hide-bound book clutched in his talons. Wings stroking mightily, he lowered the book gently to the nearby tabletop, then ducked his head in deference to the king and flew away.

"Allow me," said Artus. "It is my librar—uh, archive, after all." He opened the old tome and began scanning the pages intently, running his fingers along the faded writing and murmuring softly to himself.

"Ah, Artus?" John began.

"A moment, please," the king replied. "I'm just getting oriented. Even after years of studying them, I'm still finding my way around these old languages, you know."

"But—," said John.

"Tch," interrupted Artus. "I realize you have specialized training, but so do I. There's nothing you can do to make the translation process go any faster."

"Fine," John said, shrugging. "Read on."

After a minute or so of examining one page, then another, and another, it became obvious to all of them that the High King was stumped.

"May I make a suggestion?" offered John.

"All right," Artus said, finally resigned. "But I doubt you'll have an easier time of it. . . ."

His voice trailed off as John stepped forward and turned the old book upside down. "There," said John. "Give that a go."

"It's Latin," Artus said, crestfallen. "Now."

"Ah, why don't we all have a look together?" Charles suggested. "More eyes to the work, and all that."

The king put the book in the middle of the table, and the others leaned in closely to read.

"This is one of the Histories," said Bert in astonishment. "One of the official records written by the Caretakers."

"I thought the Caretakers just annotated the maps in the *Geographica*," said John. "We're meant to write Histories, too?"

"It's not an obligation," Bert explained, "but Caretakers have witnessed many happenings in the history of the Earth and felt compelled to record them. Originally, as with this volume and the many others like it, the accounts were simple and straightforward. It was only centuries later that we realized such documents could be dangerous in the wrong hands, and began fictionalizing our writings."

"As you did with *The Time Machine*," said Jack.

"Yes," said Bert, "and others. Jules did it too. And Cervantes, Shakespeare . . . A lot of real history, biography, and geography can be found in the fiction of the world.

"At least," he added with a wink, "those fictions written by Caretakers."

"This one was written by Geoffrey of Monmouth's immediate successor," said Bert. "Robert Wace. He also had a lot to say about the Arthurian histories."

"I remember," said John. "He wrote a French version of Geoffrey's Arthurian compilations and dedicated it to Eleanor of Aquitaine. He's also the source of the story about Arthur's legendary Round Table."

"It isn't actually round," Artus confided to Charles. "It's more oblong, but it still served the same purpose, I think."

"What does it say about the message?" asked Jack. "Does it say anything about a Crusade?"

"The actual Crusades in your world had already begun nearly a century earlier," said Bert. "But I don't think the message had anything to do with those. We have two clues to go on. First, Jamie mentioned a memory of a Crusade myth; then, the Morgaine said that something had changed Time—and they both alluded to it as an event that happened seven centuries ago.

"Seven hundred years ago the Caretaker was Master Wace. And he spent a great deal of time in the Archipelago, working on Histories of his own. If there is a myth about a Crusade dating to that time, I can't imagine he wouldn't have known about it—and written it down."

"I agree," said John. "The warning came from the Archipelago. It won't be an event that took place back in our world that we're looking for."

"Well, it's not that long a history," Charles said, tracing across the book's thickness with his thumb. "Between us, we should be able to skim through it in an hour or two."

Just then, Solomon Kaw dropped back down from the gloom at the top of the room, with a second identical book in his talons—followed closely by a flock of other crows, all carrying books that they lowered into an ever-increasing pile on and around the desk.

"I told you," Bert said. "Master Wace spent a lot of time here, and he loved to write."

"Just how many history books did he write?" asked John.

"For-for-forty-three," replied Solomon Kaw.

"I'll order some more food and drink," said Artus. "This is going to take a while."

As an academic exercise, poring over nearly four dozen incunabula would have been considered a fine weekend activity by John, Jack, and Charles. Artus, aided by Bert, had a slightly slower time of it but demonstrated a facility for quickly summarizing complex material that none of them would have guessed he had.

An as exercise of discovery, however, it was an absolute failure. Nothing in any of the books referred to a Crusade taking place in the Archipelago for a two-hundred-year span. There were events of import, and skirmishes, and minor wars—John had found a ten-page account of something called "The Chyckenne War of Gryffynne Baye"—but nothing that hinted at any solutions to their growing list of problems.

"Well," Artus said jovially, "still not a bad way to pass an afternoon, all things considered."

"Not a bad way to—," Jack began, rising to his feet. "Damn your eyes, Artus! We've been in here for hours now! We've been thumbing through old books, and eating, and generally having a leisurely afternoon of it, when we should be out there, looking for your son!"

Neither Artus nor the others said anything, but merely waited so Jack could finish saying what he needed to say. John and Charles had also wondered why their friend was not more concerned with his missing son, but they didn't feel it was their place to address it.

Jack's motivations, however, ran deeper.

"I'm sorry, Artus," he said. "But it must be said. How can you be expected to solve the problems of an entire kingdom if you can't even spare a moment's concern for your own son?"

Artus uncrossed his legs and stood up. Without a word, he strode from the room, only to return moments later with an armful of the papers that had been piled in the rooms they'd passed through earlier. He brusquely shoved Master Wace's Histories off the tabletop and dropped the papers on it. The pile was so large that many papers slid to the floor.

"It hasn't been two days since the ships started to vanish," Artus began, his back to them and his voice soft. "We can't really determine how long ago the children began disappearing. But their abductor knew we'd take quicker notice of the Dragonships being gone than if we couldn't find a few misbehaving children.

"We took even more notice yesterday when the *Yellow Dragon*—the *Nautilus*—vanished with my boy aboard. We—I—Aven and I—thought it would be the safest . . ."

Artus stood straighter. "When the reports of the missing children began to come in, we thought he'd be safer there, aboard a living ship. One that could take action on its own, if the situation demanded it. Then the elves arrived and anchored their ships alongside, and I don't think I could have arranged a better, more secure place if you'd asked. I even considered taking him to Terminus, except it would have been too long a journey.

"Then the *Yellow Dragon* vanished altogether, and the Elven ships were set ablaze. The guards were killed, their throats cut.

And there was no way to follow the missing ship, because no one had seen it go. It had simply vanished. That's when I summoned Bert and instructed him to seek you out."

"Then why, Artus?" said Jack. "If you knew more help was coming, why didn't you set out then to go find your son?"

In answer, Artus pointed to the pile of papers on the table. John stepped forward and looked at one of the topmost papers, then another.

"They're letters," he told the others.

"Correct," said Artus. "They began coming in three days ago, but my steward only brought them to my attention yesterday, just before the *Yellow Dragon* vanished.

"At last count, we have six thousand, eight hundred letters, and more were coming in before the ships were put to the torch. And every one of them is from a mother or father who lost a child in the night. Every one."

He turned to look at them, a quiet resolve on his face. This was no longer their old friend, the potboy of Avalon, talking. This was a man who had realized what it truly meant to be given a kingdom.

"What I've been doing," Artus said, looking directly at Jack, "is directing the affairs of Paralon, and the associated island-states and city-states who have representatives here, to try to control an uncontrollable crisis. You were here, with me, the last time a crisis arose and there was no one man, one leader, to whom the Archipelago could turn for guidance.

"I don't know if I'm able—but like it or not, I'm the High King. The people here trust that I will make the choices that will help us all, not just those that benefit me. So how could I possibly have left this to my steward, and the other officials, just to go look for my own son, when there is no one else in authority here to look out for the thousands of others who are lost?"

Jack couldn't speak, but simply extended his hand in response. Artus took it with no hesitation, then clapped his friend on the shoulder.

"Besides," he said, "if there were anyone on Earth who would see the value of saving the world through library maintenance, it'd be the three 'scowlers' from Oxford."

Charles snapped his fingers. "Oxford men! I say, Artus, that may be the key."

He turned to Bert. "Whom did you say was the Caretaker after Wace?"

"Easy to find out," Artus interjected. "Just check the list in the endpapers of the *Geographica*."

Quickly Charles opened the book Tummeler had given him to the list of names in the front.

"I wrote the introduction for that, you know," Artus said to Jack. "On market day, I've even been asked for my autograph."

"You don't say," Jack replied.

"Here it is," said Charles. "Roger Bacon had it after Wace. And didn't he spend a lot of time here?"

"Much," said Bert, "but he didn't assume the role until the Crusades were over—or nearly so, at any rate."

"It couldn't be a better perspective for a historian," stated John. "To be able to document events not too distant to not have credible accounts, but with enough years past that there's some objectivity."

"Maybe," Charles said, "but that's not why I'm asking. Remember what Laura Glue said? She said that the ones coming for the children were Clockworks."

"Impossible," Artus said flatly. "After the disaster with the Parliament nine years ago, we outlawed the construction of Clockworks. The animals had the best of intentions, but they were too easily manipulated by Magwich."

"The Clockworks? Or the animals?" asked John.

"Both," said Artus. "It took eighteen months just to round up and destroy the false Parliament. The Queen of Spades was one of the harder ones to find. She managed to disguise herself as a cow. We might never have found her if she'd just kept out of the milking rotation."

"Ouch," said John.

"Oh, she was fine," the king said. "But she beheaded three farmers before we caught her out."

"So you did destroy them all?" asked Bert.

"For all intents and purposes," said Artus. "The King of Hearts was the last—and we only found pieces of him."

"My point," said Charles, "is that Laura Glue did say she saw, and heard, the Clockwork Men coming. And I for one believe her."

"What does that have to do with Roger Bacon?" said Jack.

"He's the one who taught the secrets of building Clockworks to the animals," said Bert. "Them, and Nemo, and no others. And he did it just about seven centuries ago."

It took only a half hour for Solomon Kaw to locate the Histories of Roger Bacon, and there were many. Fortunately, they were also among the better-indexed books in the library, and so the companions were able to set aside all but a handful as unnecessary.

The remaining books were mostly thick vellum, lettered by hand in a crisp and pointed script. The books dating to the time in question included compilations of magic and mysteries from across the continents of the world: *The Picatrix*, from Arabia; the complete writings of Aristotle, from Greece; and many more.

Most interesting to the companions was a heavy book titled *The Key of Solomon*, which contained spells and formulas Bacon claimed had been created by the great Hebrew king himself. In the latter portion of the book were sketches and diagrams of machines, and annotations on how to build them. There were vehicles like Tummeler's principle, the Curious Diversity; directions for building mechanical men and women, like the false kings and queens of the Parliament; and even rudimentary drawings of aircraft.

"These must be fakes," said John. "Those are obviously sketches from Leonardo Da Vinci's notebooks."

Bert shook his head. "Leo swiped all of that from Bacon, who got much of it from King Solomon. The difference is, Bacon gave due credit to Solomon. Leo just preened about pretending to be a genius."

"I'm astonished," said Charles. "Leonardo Da Vinci?"

"He had a lot of potential," said Bert, sighing. "Then Michaelangelo came along, and all bets were off. After that, it was all about trying to show up the newcomer."

"Salieri and Mozart," said John.

"Precisely," agreed Bert. "Except Salieri didn't have someone better to steal from. Leo had Roger Bacon."

"At least we know the *Mona Lisa* was authentically his, anyway," said Charles.

In response, Bert laid a finger along his nose and looked over the books they'd set aside. In a moment he'd found the one he wanted and opened it to a center-spread engraving, which he showed to Charles.

"My God," Charles exclaimed. "Then who was she, really?"

"A kitchen maid from the court of King Edward," said Bert. "I imagine she was smiling because Bacon was doing something profane while he sketched her."

"Well, that's one mystery solved," said Charles.

"I think I've found something," said Artus, who'd been reading as the others talked. "It's in a Latin grammar, which he seems to have been developing as a primer for some of the languages in the Archipelago."

Artus sat with the book, and the others crowded behind him for a look. He pointed at a passage written in the margins. "Here. It looks as if he wanted to record a happening and had no other materials to write on. See?" he said, thumbing through the sheets of vellum. "It goes on for several pages."

"What makes you think it's important, Artus?" asked John.

"This," said the king, indicating at the second page. "He refers to the 'construction' of two mechanical men, but calls them by name before the task has been completed—so perhaps they weren't entirely mechanical after all."

"Half man and half machine?" said Jack. "That's quite a concept, especially for the thirteenth century."

"He calls them Hugh the Iron and William the Pig," continued Artus, reading. "They may have been . . . John? Can you read this?"

John leaned closer and examined the text. "Brothers? Or . . . comrades, maybe. It's unclear. But it does indicate that they may have represented his first experiment with constructing Clockworks—even if they began as men."

"It says there was a shipwreck of some kind, and they were nearly killed. Bacon may have saved their lives. They were both mortally wounded, and . . . how strange," said John. "Bacon also says that he thought they were deaf, but that it turned out their ears had been sealed with beeswax."

"That's all interesting enough," put in Jack, "but what makes you think it's relevant to what's occurring now?"

"The last paragraph," said Artus excitedly. "I think this is the myth the Caretaker in London was referring to. Can you translate, John? You're faster than I."

Artus stood and let the Caretaker take his seat. Clearing his throat, John began to translate the sharp writing.

"It says that when he had made 'new' men of them, Hugh the Iron and William the Pig repaid him by turning on him and beating him nearly to death. Only the presence of several animals—including, strangely, chickens—and a friendly griffin saved him.

"Bacon writes that the brothers seemed to be entranced, or enchanted. But the whole time they were beating him, they did not speak.

"Suddenly the sky grew dark and seemed to split into shards, which fell to the horizon. A great shape, absent of form, rose and covered the sky, and Bacon swears that all the while, he could hear the faint notes of a children's rhyme being whistled, or played, perhaps on a pipe.

"Then, from the shattered sky, a great ship appeared and beached itself in front of them. Hugh moved to one side of it, and William to the other, and each of them placed a hand upon the prow, then together began to recite a verse:

By right and rule
For need of might
We two bind thee
We two bind thee

By blood bound
By honor given
We two bind thee
We two bind thee

For strength and speed and heaven's power
By ancient claim in this dark hour
We two bind thee
We two bind thee

John's voice had dropped to a whisper. "That's uncomfortably close to another verse I once heard read."

Artus nodded slowly in understanding. "The Summoning. For the Dragons, in the Ring on Terminus. But as I interpreted it, that could only have been spoken—effectively—by one of royal blood. Uh, me, specifically."

"'Tis true," said Bert. "There are very few spoken spells that have any true power. Not enough to count on two hands. One is the Summoning . . . But another is the Binding. And even to have known the words to speak would have been a rare thing."

"But that would have been during the time of Artigel's rule," said Artus. "I never heard of Hugh or William in the Histories."

"Maybe these are the Histories that changed," murmured Charles. "The unraveling and reweaving the Morgaine spoke of."

"What happened next, John?" asked Jack. "Does it say?"

John quickly scanned the remainder of the passage. Suddenly his eyes grew wide and the blood drained from his face.

Artus gripped his friend by the shoulders in support, and finally the Caretaker Principia spoke.

"Bacon called out to them as they boarded the ship," John said hoarsely. "A ship with a large eye inset in the upraised prow, under the head of a great serpent."

"That's impossible!" Bert shouted, startling the others out of the subdued calmness they'd effected. "Impossible!" he repeated, shaking. "I won't believe it!"

"You recognize the ship?" asked Jack. "It sounds just like one of the Dragonships, but not one I remember."

"That ship," Bert exclaimed, "is the *Red Dragon!*"

"There's more," said John, who was still focused on the text. "Bacon cried out to them, and for a moment, it seemed as if the sound of his voice cleared away the mist that had settled over their minds.

"'We have claimed our inheritance,' Hugh replied to Bacon. 'Tell our father that, and this also: that we will pursue our own Crusade, as he did before us, and ours will be mighty, and rend this world from Heaven to Hades.'"

"That's our myth!" said Charles. "We—"

"There is more!" John exclaimed, standing and shaking his head from side to side. "But this can't be right."

He held the book closer to the lamp, then examined both sides of the paper. The dust on it was clotted, and well-absorbed into the paper. The book had not been opened in many centuries.

"It has to be a forgery," John whispered, to no one in particular. "There's no other explanation for this."

He turned back to the others, his disbelief almost tangible. "The last entry," John said slowly. "Hugh and William guided the boat back into the sea, then, as Bacon watched, they sailed it straight toward a great stone bluff, whose face split open to receive the ship.

"As it passed through, the ethereal whistling in the air became stronger, and Hugh's countenance grew cloudy again. But William turned and looked at Bacon with tear-brimmed eyes, and called out to him:

"'Tell Peter and Jamie I call Olly Olly Oxen-Free,' William said. And then the stone portal slammed closed, leaving not even a seam in the rock."

"'Tell Peter and Jamie,'" John repeated, almost choking on the words. "That's what William the Pig said. I think he was trying to pass a message to James Barrie and Peter Pan, by giving it to Roger Bacon seven hundred years ago."

PART THREE

THE SEARCH FOR THE
RED DRAGON

CHAPTER NINE
SHADOWS IN FLIGHT

THE FIRE POPPED and crackled as the chill of evening began to deepen throughout the cave.

The old man lifted his head and looked at the cave walls, which were covered with paintings. Most of the pictures were of animals, but several were of men, or creatures that resembled men. It was hard to tell.

Some of the images were ancient. Others were much more recent, and still glistened, wet, in the firelight. Those immediately opposite where the old man was sitting were so fresh that the paint dripped into a pool that had formed at his feet. There, the paint mingled with the blood that was streaming its way down his calves, and he realized with a sudden clarity that his blood and the paint on the walls were practically indistinguishable.

The cave was spartan in its decor. Other than the construct holding the old man, there were few furnishings: a couple of chairs, a great mirror with an ornate silver frame, and a battered old wardrobe covered in chains that were fastened with dozens of padlocks.

Nearer the back was something resembling an altar, and on it was a human head draped with a scarlet cloth. This didn't bother the old man, who had seen many heads in his time. What rattled

him was the fact that he had heard his captor *talking* to it before it
had been placed in the cave.

A clicking and popping noise—the sounds of thousands of
insects scuttling across the granite floor—told him that his captor
had returned and was approaching the mouth of the cave. The old
man's arms tensed against the leather thongs that tied him to the
frame. It was normally used for skinning animals, but it served its
current purpose just as well.

The clicking noises subsided, and a sallow voice echoed throughout the small cavern.

"Where did you send her?" his captor asked, as he had the night
before, and the night before that, but more insistent this time. "I
must know. It is in your best interests that I know."

"She's out of your reach, and that's all that matters," said the
old man. "Where she has gone, you cannot follow."

His captor responded with a sound that was half laughter,
half a contemptuous snort. "You don't think I know where's she's
gone? Or that I can't follow her as I choose?"

"Follow her?" said the old man. "You can't even enter this *cave.*
So I don't think you are as free as you think. Because if you were,
you wouldn't need *me.*"

The other speaker started to spit out a reply, then seemed to
acquiesce. "Well played. But I mean to find out, whatever it takes."

The voice became lower then, almost a purr, as a different
approach was tested. "Ah, you and I, Peter . . . We are old adversaries, are we not? But does that not also make us brothers, of a
sort? And can we not set aside old grievances and come together?
You could be first among my allies—my most trusted general.
What do you say?"

With the mention of his name, the old man's eyes widened in alarm, before settling into a resigned calmness. He smiled, and let out a short chuckle. Echoing off the cave walls, it sounded like the laughter of a child.

"You've finally made a mistake," the old man said. "I know who you are now. That has always been your problem—you simply can't bear for anyone not to know who's really pulling the strings, so to speak. I wasn't going to help you to begin with. But now—never."

"I could *make* you tell," his captor hissed.

The old man chuckled again. "Not likely. The pipes don't work on Longbeards."

"All right," the other speaker said, retreating a bit. "Perhaps if I offered you something you value more than power. If you will simply tell me where you sent the girl, and for what purpose, then perhaps . . . Perhaps I will allow you to return to the Well—one last time. . . ."

The old man laughed once more, but could not disguise the brief flash of longing that crossed his features. He blinked and pursed his lips.

"Thank you, no. I think I'll take my chances. Being old isn't as bad as I expected it to be. After all, you know what they say—you're as young as you feel."

He tipped his head back and crowed, and the sound was both mocking and triumphant. And then he smiled.

The sudden crescendo of insect noises told the old man that his captor was both livid and gesturing to summon his servants. In a moment several animals had filled the cave entrance. A few made snuffling sounds; one or two were growling. All seemed to be waiting for further instruction. One of them sneezed, then rubbed at its face with a grubby, five-fingered paw.

And then the old man realized they were not animals after all. They were children.

The wolf-child sneezed again. Irritated and distracted, the captor snarled a rebuke, and in that moment the old man saw his chance.

Quickly, he whispered a few words in an ancient tongue, and in an instant, his shadow had separated itself from his body and flew along the ceiling of the cave toward the opening.

His captor cursed and ordered the feral children inside the cave to kick sand over the fire, reducing it to smoke and embers—but it was too late.

The beast-children looked to their leader for the order to pursue this new prey, but he shook his head.

"Let it go. It isn't that important. It is only his shadow, after all."

Again he addressed the old man, who was hanging more slackly in the frame, but whose eyes were now glittering. "Let's begin again, shall we?"

"I can't believe it," said Jack, his voice echoing loudly through the halls of the Great Whatsit. "We're trying too hard to find meaning in meaningless things. You're seeing connections that aren't there, John."

"No, he isn't," said Bert, who had calmed down somewhat. "In fact, I think John is exactly right. I think William was trying to pass a message on. And Peter got it, which is why he sent Laura Glue to Jamie."

"Perhaps this was the *Liber* the Morgaine referred to," Charles offered. "It did reveal a missing Dragonship."

"Don't take this the wrong way," said Jack, "but what's the logic that holds this all together?"

"The ship," said a voice from the open doorway. "Father's right. The ship Bacon described wasn't just any vessel. It *was* the *Red Dragon*."

As one, the companions turned and looked at the speaker. Tall, with a more regal bearing than they'd remembered despite her rough sailor's clothing, Aven regarded them all coolly before lifting her chin and giving them a half smile.

"I must admit," she said, "I didn't think two of you would come, much less all three. But I'm very . . . I'm . . ."

Bert rushed to his daughter and wrapped his arms around her. She stiffened at first, then relaxed and returned his embrace. Aven looked up at the three Caretakers and gave them a sincere if weary smile. "I'm very pleased to see you. All of you."

One by one she gave each of them a brief hug, and kisses on both cheeks. Not an entirely informal greeting, but when she came to Artus, she gave him the same—no more, no less. Charles and John exchanged a puzzled glance, which didn't escape Artus's notice.

"You didn't tell them, did you?" he said to Bert.

"Tell them what?" said Aven.

"It's none of our business," said Jack, who had also noted the casual way she had greeted the king. "It's just that if we hadn't known better, we wouldn't have thought you were greeting your husband."

Aven looked startled. "Husband? You mean Artus?"

"O-of course," John stammered. "He's the king, and you're, uh . . ."

Aven lifted her chin and looked at them. "He is the king," she said. "But he is not now, nor has he ever been, my husband."

✦ ✦ ✦

"But—but," Jack started. "That's, that's . . ." He stopped speaking and just looked from Aven to Artus, dumbfounded.

"Aren't you the queen, Aven?" Charles asked. "I had the understanding—"

Artus cut off the discussion with a gesture. "She is, for all intents and purposes, the royal consort. In effect, she is queen. She and no other helps me to guide the affairs of the Archipelago. But if we had married—formally, as a matter of statesmanship— then she would have been expected to remain on Paralon. And that would not have made her happy."

"So you refused to marry Artus, just so you wouldn't have to be confined to Paralon?" said Jack.

"You misunderstand," said Artus. "I chose not to force her into a marriage that would have filled her days with sorrow and longing."

"Bear in mind," John said to Jack, "this is the Archipelago. Our conventions are not necessarily theirs."

"I'm just a bit startled, is all," Jack said. "I apologize, Aven, for saying anything out of turn."

"You didn't," said Aven. "But now you know. And despite my wanderlust, I always come back to Paralon. My family is here— both Artus, and . . ."

Her voice broke, and she pulled her vest tighter. She turned to Artus. "I've toured the entire northern perimeter of Paralon. Not a single ship escaped being torched. It's almost as if a signal was given to an invisible enemy, and all of them were destroyed in a single stroke. Have you heard any news from Samaranth?"

Artus hesitated, then shook his head. "The last report came just as we sent Bert for the Caretaker Principia. There's been nothing since then." He paused, considering. "Come to think of it, I haven't seen *any* dragons in more than a day. I wonder where they've all gotten to?"

"And the children?" asked Bert. "Are there any more missing?"

"From every village," Aven said. "The only ones who were spared were too small, or ill."

"One escaped," said Charles. "A girl with artificial wings, who called herself Laura Glue."

"Laura Glue!" exclaimed Aven. "Where is she? Is she here? What did she say?"

"Actually," said Jack, "we left her sleeping in a wardrobe at James Barrie's house."

At the mention of Barrie, Aven's expression darkened, but she only nodded in understanding. "That's who she *should* have gone to. Tell me everything."

After Artus, Bert, and the Caretakers gave her a hurried explanation, Aven sat at the table and looked over the book where they had found mention of a Crusade.

"Jamie didn't know what the message meant," said Bert. "'The Crusade has begun.' It meant nothing to him, except for a fragment of a memory."

"This is the fragment," Aven said, tapping the book. "The message is what tells me so. And Jamie knows more than he's led you to believe."

"Why?" John wondered. "What can possibly connect Jamie and the two men Bacon wrote about? And why wouldn't he tell us if he knew something more?"

Aven set her jaw and looked at John. "Olly Olly Oxen-Free

was the game Peter and Jamie taught all the Lost Boys. They invented it. It's not a coincidence that the game and its creators are mentioned in the same passage.

"The ship described in that book—the *Red Dragon*—has been seen firsthand only once in the history of the Archipelago. Everything else has been a story—the 'friend of a friend whose cousin once saw it' sort of stories. Even here in the archives, despite centuries of writing and record-keeping, there have hardly ever been any mentions of it at all."

"Precisely four," Bert interjected. "The first recorded sighting was when Ordo Maas built it from the wreck of the *Argo*. The second was during the first great battle between Arthur and Mordred. The accounting you just read would be the third."

"When was the fourth?" Artus asked.

Aven glanced at her father and hesitated. "It's in a book from Verne's personal archive. A future history that may or may not happen. And that's what concerns me—the *Red Dragon* seems lost not just in *space*, but also in *time*.

"The Morgaine said that the change that altered the course of history occurred seven centuries ago—but that the event that caused the change happened only nine years ago, because of something *you* did."

"Really," said John, "I've racked my brain trying to figure out what we did wrong, but I can't think of anything we did that wasn't necessary to defeat Mordred."

"Jules would say that nothing you did *was* wrong, young John," said Bert. "There are only choices that move us into the future—even if, at times, we seem to go back.

"It stands to reason that all of this is connected—and there was only one place you went to where Time itself could have been affected."

"The Keep of Time," said Charles. "Of course!"

"That's it, then," said John. "We're going back to see the Cartographer of Lost Places."

The companions each said good-bye to Artus, who already appeared apprehensive about the line of officials who had gathered outside the library with yet more documents and decrees that needed his attention, and began winding their way out of the Great Whatsit. As Jack turned to follow the others, Artus grasped his arm and pulled him over to a shallow alcove.

"I want to ask you something," the king said, his voice soft. "I want to ask if you will look after Aven. As a personal favor to me. And I'm not asking as king or anything. Just . . . me. Artus."

Jack started. He looked at the other man for a moment before answering. "Why are you asking me? Of course, all of us—"

"I know all of you will be looking out for one another," Artus interrupted, "but that's not what I'm talking about.

"I . . . I know how you felt about her, Jack. Before. I guess I've always known. So I hope you are not offended that I ask. To the others, she's a companion and a friend. But of all of them, only you would understand this request from someone who truly loves her."

Jack could see it in the young king's face. He did love Aven, deeply. And it took more courage to ask this of Jack, his onetime rival for her affections, than Jack believed he could have mustered had their positions been reversed.

"Of course I will, Artus."

"Thank you, Jack," Artus said, offering his hand.

Jack didn't hesitate to take Artus's hand and grip it tightly with his own. "I'll bring them back, Artus. Both of them."

It wasn't until he had walked out of the Great Whatsit toward where the others awaited him that Jack realized how much he meant the words he'd just spoken.

He did mean to bring back Aven and her son . . .

But not necessarily back to *Paralon*.

Aboard the *Indigo Dragon* once more, Aven instinctively slipped into command, as her father perceptively, subtly, stepped aside. The crew were accustomed to her, and indeed, seemed to step live-lier to their tasks under her direction.

Bert nodded contentedly and leaned against the forward spars as the airship lifted free from its moorings and rose into the air above Paralon.

The smoke had been mostly cleared by the easterly winds, but a light haze remained, and the moon rose, unfocused, into the first frame of its nightly show.

Charles, feeling a bit peckish, announced that he was going to go rummaging around in the galley below for something to eat. He was joined by Bert, who claimed to have learned a recipe from Tummeler for an exceptional millet and barley soup.

"Good old Tummeler," Charles said as he opened the door and began descending the steps. "I've often thought about having him for a visit to Oxford and London—I think he'd have a marvelous time. It's just that . . ."

"Difficult to explain a talking badger?" said Bert.

"Actually," confided Charles, "I was more worried about him getting wet. The smell, you know."

John stayed above, in part because he enjoyed the feeling of flight, but also to observe Jack. Since the trip had begun, neither he nor Charles had so much as mentioned Jack's turbulent feelings regarding the death of his friend in the Great War. Everything had been moving at such a breakneck pace that it seemed to have been overlooked that Jack's sleeplessness had begun long before the crisis in the Archipelago. There were larger beasts to be grappled with in his friend's soul, and John was worried that if no one was watching, they might eventually devour Jack from the inside out.

In their last voyage through the Archipelago, it had been John who was traumatized by the events of the war and who felt a profound loneliness at being separated from his wife. But then, he had been older to begin with, and had more life experience than Jack in the four years that separated their ages. So coming to the Archipelago as a Caretaker of the *Geographica* was cathartic. It compelled him to find strengths he barely knew he possessed.

But Jack had come there with a different set of perceptions—and then saw a friend die as a result of his own choices and actions. There was no way for someone else to gauge how that might affect a man, especially when yet another friend was later lost in battle, and there was no real family to return to, to ground oneself.

Without turning around, Jack chuckled. "I can feel your eyes burning holes in my back, John," he said. "I know you're concerned about me, but you needn't be. I can take care of myself."

"Of that I have no doubt," John assured him, sitting next to the railing. "But your friends are here to support you, Jack, in whatever way you need. And remember, I have some understanding of what you're dealing with."

Jack started to retort, then caught himself and grinned wryly. "Nine years ago I might have argued with you. But I've realized in recent years that I sometimes argue just for the sake of arguing. I wonder why I do that?"

"It's part of what makes you a good teacher," said John.

"Maybe," said Jack. "But with my students, I tend to win every time. It's not exactly fair."

John smiled. "You just need to learn the difference between arguing for arguing's sake and arguing when there's a point to be made. If it's the latter, then it won't matter if it's fair. Just if it's right."

Jack looked at his friend for a moment, then turned back to the sea and sky, watching.

The moon was fully above the horizon now, and it dominated the sky, turning the seas to cream and dispelling the last of the vaporous clouds that had obscured a sky of distant fireflies.

"It wasn't Warnie," Jack said suddenly.

"What wasn't Warnie?" asked John.

"It wasn't Warnie who began to call me 'Jack.' It was my own idea. Came to me in a dream when I was a child, actually. I just woke up and announced to my family that I was to be addressed as 'Jack' from then on. Sometimes it was 'Jacks' or 'Jacksie,' but Jack was what stuck, and Warnie was the first to pick it up. But I came up with the name myself."

John furrowed his brow and grinned wryly. "Then why tell us Warnie came up with it? What's the difference?"

Jack shrugged. "I don't know. I supposed I just felt ill at ease telling anyone about the dreams. Maybe more so after recent events. The dreams I had about Aven, and the Giants . . . Well, those were similar. But this time, no one was whispering that I should change my name."

"Well, if it's any consolation," John said, "I've never gone by 'John' in my entire life. I've always preferred 'Ronald,' but the military used my full name, and there were times when propriety required that I be introduced as 'John,' and so that's how Professor Sigurdsson came to know me. And then you fellows, of course. But there's no one else in the world who knows me as John."

"We're not really in the world, in case you hadn't noticed," Jack noted.

"Point taken."

"So would you rather we called you Ronald?" asked Jack.

John shook his head. "I don't think so. Being 'John' is something I've come to associate with the *Geographica* and our travels together, and it's almost as if I've become a different person here. So John is fine."

"How about you?" Jack said, turning to Charles, who had just emerged from the galley licking his fingers. "Anything you'd like to share about your name or names?"

Charles cleared his throat. "Well, I once wrote a play, starring myself, in which I assumed the identity of a great adventurer, modeled after Baron Munchausen, whose name was Brigadier-General Throatwarbler-Mangrove. I tried to coerce my friends to refer to me as 'Brigadier-General,' or at least 'TM,' but it never really took."

Jack's eyes goggled. "That's amazing."

John laughed and snorted. "How old were you when that idiotic idea crossed your mind?"

"It was last month," said Charles, looking slightly put out.

"Sorry," said John.

"You'd have been in fine company," Bert said as he emerged from the cabin with two steaming mugs of millet and barley soup. "Baron Munchausen wasn't his real name either," he said, handing a mug to Charles.

"Really?" said Charles. "What was it?"

Bert puffed his cheeks and blew on the hot soup. "Ramon Felipe San Juan Mario Silvio Enrico Smith Heathcourt-Brace Sierra y Alvarez-del Rey y de los Verdes. But we all called him Lester."

"Dear God." Charles shook his head. "I'm sorry I asked."

The night passed uneventfully, although Aven's expression grew darker every time she noted the lack of ships on the great expanse below them.

Bert, Aven, and the crew knew the way to the smaller archipelago, where the keep was located, well enough to make consulting Tummeler's *Geographica* unnecessary. This was a reprieve for John, who was hoping that his error in leaving the real atlas in London wouldn't come up.

"We're approaching the islands," Aven said. "We should give the center a wide berth—remember the steam, from the volcanic cone? That will play havoc with the airship."

"She can't quite bring herself to call it 'the *Indigo Dragon*,'" Bert said to Jack. "Still too attached to the old one, I'm afraid."

Aven tossed aside Jack's copy of the *Geographica* and snorted. "These children's books are more a threat than anything. They don't note things important to navigation, and they skip too many of the dangers in the Archipelago."

"Tummeler probably worried that it would be bad for sales," Charles offered helpfully. "It's the publisher's dilemma."

"We'd probably better keep to the original," Aven said, turning to John. "That's what it's for, after all."

"Ah, about that," John began.

"Oh, my stars and garters!" Bert exclaimed. "I don't think this is a problem that can be dealt with by reading the *Imaginarium Geographica.*"

The others crowded around the starboard side of the ship's railing to see what the old man was talking about. Just ahead, in the creeping light of morning, they could see the silhouettes of the necklace-shaped ring of islands amidst the ever-present steam.

The stone columns of granite were just as the companions remembered them—with one stunning exception.

"The Keep of Time," Bert said in astonishment. "It's gone."

CHAPTER TEN
THE TOWER IN THE AIR

THE LARGEST OF the islands, where the Keep of Time had previously stood, was stark and barren.

Aven piloted the airship in a lazy circuit around the island so they could take a better look. Where the tower had been were a few scattered loose stones, but no indication of the foundation. It was if the tower had simply been removed.

"It seemed perfectly fine when we left it," said Charles. "I don't know what could possibly have happened to it."

"I'm beginning to," John said slowly as he paced the deck. "True, it *was* fine—but that was the second time we left, remember?"

As one, the companions all realized what John was referring to, and suddenly the Morgaine's cryptic answers began to make much more sense.

The Keep of Time had been an immense tower, inside of which were stairways leading upward to a seemingly infinite number of doors. Each one opened into a point in the past, with those at the bottom leading to the times most distant in prehistory, and they advanced chronologically as one ascended.

Near the top, the stairs ended at a platform just short of the last door. That door opened into the future and was forever out of reach. Thus, the tower was constantly growing in tempo with the progression of Time.

The next-to-last door, behind which they found the creator of the *Imaginarium Geographica*, who was known as the Cartographer of Lost Places, was the only one that opened to the present. But behind the fourth door from the top, John had found he was only in the recent past—and indeed, had a conversation with his dead mentor, Professor Sigurdsson, there.

After John's encounter with the professor, and their subsequent meeting with the Cartographer, the companions had descended the stairway to find their adversary, Mordred, the Winter King, had arrived on the island as well.

And he had set the base of the keep on fire.

The companions had gone in the only direction they could—up—and as they climbed, Charles conceived of the plan that would ultimately save them all.

He proposed opening the door below the Cartographer's and escaping into the immediate past. And sure enough, the door opened into the entrance at the base of the tower—one hour before the Winter King arrived. The companions then simply boarded their ship and left.

Aven stared at the island in shock. "We left safely, but an hour later Mordred still came here, and he still set the fire."

"It never occurred to me that the Winter King might still have stormed the tower," said Bert. "I always assumed he'd looked for us, not found us, and simply begun to pursue us again."

"Same here," said John. "Everything came to such a head on Terminus that I didn't stop to think of what had gone before."

Charles was mortified. "You . . . you mean it's my fault the tower was destroyed?" His legs began to wobble and he sat heavily on the deck, his head in his hands.

Bert laid a reassuring hand on his shoulder. "You aren't to blame, Charles. Mordred's actions were his own. You were the hero—you actually thought of a way to escape, when no one else had an answer. Mordred had already started the fire. After we escaped, he simply did it again."

Bert's words had no effect on an inconsolable Charles. "I destroyed it," he murmured, disbelieving. "I destroyed the keep...."

He sat up straighter. "Worse! I destroyed *Time*. That's what the Morgaine were talking about. I actually wiped out an entire *dimension*."

"This really is some kind of extraordinary achievement," John said supportively. "Not many people can lay claim to having broken Time, and we did it purely by accident."

"Oh, I don't think it's as bad as all that," said Bert. "Time is sturdier than you'd think. But I do believe we've found the source of the crisis."

"Shouldn't there be debris?" asked John. "I mean, even if the tower was burned, shouldn't it have left a huge pile of rubble? A bunch of scorched stones? *Something?*"

"It wasn't an ordinary tower," Bert replied. "It was actually *made* of Time—well, and granite, and, er, ragthorn wood. But there's no telling how it would be affected."

As John, Charles, and Bert debated, Aven noticed that Jack was on the opposite side of the deck and hadn't been looking at the island at all.

"What are you looking at, Jack?" she asked. "You've been staring at the water since we got here."

"Look at this," Jack said, waving her over without taking his eyes off the sea below. "There, just below us, see? That dark impression in the water? Could it be some sort of submarine, like the *Yellow Dragon*?"

Aven squinted and peered down to where Jack was pointing. "It's not a ship—it's a shadow. See, where the airship is casting a similar shadow on the water, and how it changes position with the light?"

"Huh," said Jack. "Whatever's casting that is a great deal bigger than the *Indigo* . . ."

Jack stopped and swallowed hard. He and Aven looked at each other as a sudden realization occurred to them. Then, together, they looked straight up.

"Oh, shades," said Jack.

Charles was just starting to collect himself when Jack and Aven rejoined the others. They were both grinning like Cheshire cats.

"What?" said John. "What are you two smiling about?"

"Good news," announced Jack. "Charles didn't destroy the tower after all."

"Not all of it, anyway," said Aven.

"I'm confused," said Bert.

As if on cue, the *Indigo Dragon* circled around to a point opposite the island and the risen sun—and the broken shadow that split the sea to the northern horizon fell across the airship.

The companions and crew all looked upward and saw what was casting the shadow.

High above them, like a great gray comet frozen in its descent to Earth, was the Keep of Time.

"Oh, thank God," said Charles.

✦ ✦ ✦

As the airship began to ascend, it occurred to the companions more than once that what they were attempting would have been impossible with any of the other Dragonships—including the original *Indigo Dragon*.

In terms of distance, the tower was only perhaps two miles above them. But if that measurement were applied to the portion of the keep that had been consumed by fire, then it represented thousands, perhaps even millions of years of history.

The *Indigo Dragon* approached the lower part of the floating tower and confirmed their supposition. It was jagged and charred, and the damage rose several hundred feet higher, then stopped. At some point, something had stayed the advance of the flames, but the damage done was inconceivable.

Aven guided the ship higher, to a point considerably past the charred portions, and at Bert's direction threw an anchor line through one of the windows that opened into the stairway. Once secured, they maneuvered close enough to tether a rope ladder fashioned from the old ship's riggings ("We kept some of it out of nostalgia, you know," said Bert), and one by one they began to climb across.

Inside, the keep was exactly as they remembered it, save for the haze that obscured what remained of the lower levels.

"Watch your step," Bert warned. "Wouldn't be advisable to slip off the stairs."

"You're a master of the obvious," said Jack.

"You're the Caretaker Principia," Aven said to John. "Lead on."

Together, the companions began to climb.

✦ ✦ ✦

It took sustained climbing for most of the day to reach the uppermost doors. The tower was silent except for an occasional rumbling noise that emanated from below.

"Forgive the sentiment," said Charles, panting slightly, "but I almost wish the fire had burned up *more* of the place, so we wouldn't have quite so far to walk."

"I'm with Charles," said Jack. "I still don't understand why we couldn't just fly the ship higher and enter a window closer to the Cartographer's room."

"Because," Bert said, "the Keep of Time is also a judge of character. Remember how the last time the descent seemed to take less time than the climb up? That's because it did. And do you recall the door we stepped through for our escape?"

"Right," said John. "When we went through, it opened up down below only an hour earlier from when we'd entered."

"It took us where and when we needed to go," Bert affirmed, "because we earned it by our efforts. We could have flown higher, true—but I suspect it would not have shortened the distance we needed to climb."

As if on cue, the ceiling seemed suddenly closer, the stairway ended, and the next door bore the keyhole that marked the room where they would find the Cartographer.

"You're welcome," Bert said to no one in particular.

As before, the door was locked—but Aven, as queen, had a ring that bore the seal of the High King. A touch was all it took. There was a soft click as the lock disengaged, and the door swung inward.

The Cartographer of Lost Places was sitting at his desk, concentrating on a very elaborate map.

"If I've told you once, I've told you thrice," he said, irritated, "I haven't the faintest idea who killed Edwin Drood, so you can just stop asking. You wouldn't be in this mess if you hadn't started that dratted serial."

"Edwin Drood?" John inquired, stepping forward into the densely cluttered room. "I haven't asked you anything about Edwin Drood."

The Cartographer frowned and peered at his visitors over the top of his glasses. "Really? Aren't you the Caretaker Principia?"

"Well, yes, but . . ."

"Hold on a moment," the Cartographer said. He hopped off his chair and strode over to John. "You're not Charles."

"Ah, that would be me," said Charles.

"Really?" exclaimed the Caretaker. "How extraordinary. You used to be much more handsome."

"What?" Charles sputtered. "But . . . but I've only seen you the one time."

"Nonsense. You've been here plenty of times," said the Cartographer. "Although I wish you'd get rid of that apprentice of yours. He's a bad egg, that one. What was his name? Maggot something?"

"Magwich," said Charles. "And that's the first thing you've said that's made sense."

"Hmm," said the Cartographer. "You really aren't Dickens, are you?"

"None of us is," Jack put in.

"It's for the best," the Cartographer said. "He was a clever fellow, but he had terrible judgment when it came to apprentices. First Maggot, then that explorer fellow who snuck into Mecca. Just asking for trouble, the whole lot of them."

Bert moved in front of the others to try to get the mapmaker to focus. "Do you remember me, at least?" he asked.

The Cartographer tilted back his head. "Hmm. The Far Traveler, unless I'm mistaken, which is seldom. Yes, yes . . . I do know you. What year is it, anyway?"

"It's 1926," said Charles.

"Excellent to hear," said the Cartographer. "It's helpful to know Time keeps moving forward, even as the past vanishes into smoke and ash."

"Um, about that," Charles began before Aven stomped on his foot. She scowled and put a finger to her lips.

"We noticed there'd been a situation," said Bert.

"Situation?" the Cartographer exclaimed. "More like a catastrophe, if you ask me. Someone set fire to the keep and burned up an awful lot of history. It burned for nearly six years, you know."

"How did you finally manage to put it out?" asked Jack.

"Put it out? Me?" said the Cartographer. "*Hello*—didn't you notice the lock on the door? I couldn't lift a finger. Just had to wait it out."

"How *did* it go out?" asked Bert.

The Cartographer sat cross-legged on the floor and indicated that the others should sit as well. "I think it went out when it reached the doors that opened up to the end of the Silver Age, or the beginning of the Bronze," he said. "Around 1600 BC or thereabouts. That would have done the trick."

"What happened at the beginning of the Bronze Age?" Charles whispered to John.

"Deucalion's flood," John replied.

"Yep," said the Cartographer, winking at Charles. "Water out the ying-yang. It also put out the Thera eruption, so it could certainly douse a little tower fire."

"Well," said Charles, "at least it stopped the damage before it could take the whole tower out."

"Stopped?" the Cartographer said in surprise. "Slowed, maybe, but not stopped. The entire base of the keep is missing, or hadn't you noticed? The fire may be out, but the foundation is gone, and the structure is fatally weakened. Stones continue to fall into the sea, and door by door, the tower is still vanishing. What remains is only here because it's in the future—but our past catches up to us. It always does."

"What happens when it finally gets to the top?" asked John. "What will happen to you?"

"Well, only one thing is certain," said the Cartographer. "I'm finally going to get out of this damned room."

He stood up and dusted off the seat of his pants. "Now, you didn't come up whatever stairs are still remaining to talk about my health," he said wryly, "but anyone who's indifferent to the fate of Edwin Drood is okay in my book. So what can I do for you?"

The companions took turns relating the story until all of the events had been laid out for the Cartographer, who sat at his desk and listened without comment. When they had finished, he simply turned away and began to work on his map.

John, Jack, and Charles looked at one another, bewildered, but Aven stepped to the desk and tapped the mapmaker on the shoulder.

"Excuse me," she said. "But you might just be the rudest person I've ever met."

The Cartographer put down his quill. "Really? What a boring

life you must have led. I'm sorry—it was a lovely story—but was there a question?"

"About a million of them!" cried Jack. "Where have all the children been taken? And the Dragonships? Who's burning all the other ships? And what happened to change history seven hundred years ago?"

The Cartographer sighed heavily. "No doubt you came to see me because of the nature of the keep, but my knowledge and understanding of it is rudimentary at best. I make maps. I make very good maps. I am the best mapmaker who ever lived. So if you need maps, I'm your man. But it isn't my fault or responsibility that someone ruined a tapestry on Avalon, or wrecked history, or did whatever they did that has the Morgaine's knickers in a twist.

"I also don't have the slightest idea where the children are, or who is burning your ships. Sorry. And as to the missing Dragonships— the Morgaine already told you where they are, and I wouldn't be surprised if the answers to some of your other problems come to light when you retrieve them."

Even Bert looked puzzled at this, and the Cartographer let out an annoyed groan. "And you call yourselves Caretakers. The Morgaine said they were in the Underneath, guarded by the Chamenos Liber, did they not?"

"Sure," said John. "But—"

"But nothing," said the Cartographer. "The last time you paid me a visit, how did you find the Keep of Time to begin with?"

John blinked a few times, then his eyes grew wide and his face turned a deep crimson.

"I'd forgotten," he said.

"So," said the Cartographer. "The other shoe drops again."

"We don't have to go looking for Chamenos Liber," John told the others sheepishly. "We're already there. This chain of islands here was called Chamenos Liber in the notes in the *Geographica*."

"I remember!" declared Charles. "You'd set it aside as unimportant because it was a mishmash of Latin and ancient Greek, and all the notes about it were otherwise in Italian."

"Alighieri," said the Cartographer. "Now *there* was a Caretaker. Even came back from the dead so his sons could finish that little poem. You'd never catch *him* whining about Drood this and Drood that."

"So why did you call it that?" Jack asked the Cartographer. "Why Chamenos Liber?"

The mapmaker shrugged. "It wasn't named by me. It was named by someone much older—actually a granduncle of sorts, now I think about it. But if your Caretaker Principia had paid just a bit more attention, half of your problems might be over already."

"Why half?" asked Charles.

"As you've already noted, *Chamenos Liber* is mixed Latin and ancient Greek, and the meaning of Latin words can change with specific usage. *Liber* doesn't mean 'book'—it means 'boy.' Translated properly, *Chamenos Liber* means 'Lost Boys.'"

At the revelation, Aven stiffened, although no one noticed but Jack—and he couldn't tell if it was from dismay, or from shock like the rest of them.

"So the islands themselves guard the Underneath, whatever that is," said John.

"You're getting your wind, philologically speaking," observed the Cartographer. "The rest should be a breeze."

"The rest?" John said.

"And you were so close to having my respect," said the Cartographer. "The Underneath is an extension of the Archipelago—another chain of islands formed of circles within circles beneath the surface of the Earth. It's not recorded in the *Geographica* because no one really goes there anymore, so I never got around to making any maps for it. The Underneath is very, very old. Some of the islands even predate the Drowned Lands. And the last time I was there, I hadn't yet learned cartography, and I even had a name.

"Thus, most of what is in the *Geographica* that concerns the Underneath was added later, by various Caretakers. Only three traveled there with any frequency—although I know others from your world have made their way to it now and again."

"Who were the three?" asked Charles.

"Dante Alighieri, of course, and that Frenchman . . . what's-his-name, who planned that foolish trip to the moon . . ."

"You mean Jules Verne?" Bert guessed.

The Cartographer snapped his fingers. "That's the one. Verne. And the third was that young boy . . . a whelp. Can't have been more than twelve, at most. Awfully young for a Caretaker if you ask me, but you lot seldom do anymore."

"A twelve-year-old Caretaker?" exclaimed John. "That sounds pretty unlikely."

"That's what I told him," said the Cartographer. "But he had the *Geographica*, after all, so I had to take him at his word. I think his name was 'Barry' something."

Aven went white. "Barrie," she said, her voice breaking. "His name is James Barrie."

"What it is, what it is," said the Cartographer, waving his hands dismissively. "I can't keep you all straight anymore."

"How do we get to the Underneath?" asked Jack.

"That's simple," replied the Cartographer. "The portal is straight down, through the center of the volcanic cone, and the phrase that opens the passage is inscribed in the *Imaginarium Geographica*, so accessing and opening the portal should be no problem."

Reflexively, Jack, Charles, and Bert all looked at John, whose face began to turn several shades of red again.

Aven's eyes narrowed, and she took an accusatory stance as she realized why John was suddenly so embarrassed.

The Cartographer sighed. "Oh, bosh and bother, bother and bosh," he said, exasperated. "Now I remember you. Sigurdsson's student. The soldier who fancied himself a scholar. Misplaced it again, have you?"

John began stammering out an explanation about the *Geographica*, and Laura Glue's wings, and his car, and how they *did* have *copies* of the atlas that had been transcribed by a badger, which *might* have the information they need, and had started in on a half-hearted apology when the Cartographer held up his hands.

"No offense, but I don't care," he said matter-of-factly. "I can't really be more helpful here, and considering that there are four Caretakers present and no *Geographica*, I'd say the criteria for choosing Caretakers is rather more lax than it used to be."

"In a fashion, it actually *is* in the possession of a Caretaker," reasoned John. "The automobile is just down the street from James Barrie's house."

"Is that a defense?" said the Cartographer. "That you left it a world away, near the home of a Caretaker who actually walked away from the job?" He looked at Aven and raised his eyebrows. "Who are these people, the Marx Brothers?"

Aven smiled, resigned. "Anything you can offer us would be helpful," she said. "Anything at all."

The Cartographer regarded her carefully. "I remember you, too. You're the angry one. But not so much anymore, I think. Why is that?"

Aven looked startled by this sudden focus on her. "I—I couldn't say," she stammered. "Perhaps I just grew up."

"Maybe," said the Cartographer. "I think there's more to you than most people give you credit for. And I'll bet my last drachma that you're not through growing."

Aven didn't respond, but simply met and held the mapmaker's gaze. After a moment, he looked away.

The Cartographer went to his window and looked out at the passing clouds. It was his solitary view, and changed only with the onset of nightfall. When he spoke again, it was more somberly than before.

"I am truly sorry. I cannot be of more help to you. What you need is beyond my means. I can offer only this: What has happened to the Keep of Time was the sum of all the events that have gone before. It wasn't set into motion merely a thousand years ago, or seven hundred, or even nine, whatever any of you think."

This last was said with an understanding look at Charles, who nodded in acceptance and no small relief.

"There may yet be other consequences, other effects springing from the cause. The tower is failing, and it was the loss of the lower part that has permitted crossings into the past where none were possible before. The doorways were focal points, nothing more—and the pathways to which they led are now drifting freely throughout the world. That something has already been changed seven centuries ago means that someone, somewhere, has learned how to make use of this fact. And I tell you this now so that you are forewarned, O Caretakers of the *Geographica* and the Archipelago. Be wary. Be watchful. For Time is now in the hands of your enemy."

Charles moved around the desk and offered his hand. "I do want to apologize. Whether it was my fault or not, someone should tell you they're sorry."

The Cartographer hesitated, then shook the younger man's hand. "Thank you, Charles. But do not think too badly of Mordred, either. The course of his own history may have gone very differently if only one time, long ago, someone close to him had apologized, or at the least, stood by him when it would have cost little to do so. But no one did. And we shall all pay the price for that error, I'm afraid."

The companions each thanked the Cartographer in turn and left the map-covered room. He was back at his desk, working, before they closed the door.

The Cartographer of Lost Places scumbled lines on the parchment at a furious pace for several minutes before finally capping his quill and laying it aside. He removed his glasses and rubbed his eyes, weary, and not for the first time. He suspected, but did not know, not for certain, what was to follow in the Archipelago, and in the world beyond. But what was to take place in the Underneath was a complete mystery. All that he knew was that the Caretakers, particularly the one called John, must find their way through the maelstrom of events on their own. It would be the only way for them to be prepared when the imago finally arrived.

"So the end justifies the means, eh?" he murmured. "This is a dangerous game you play at, Jules. It's beyond me—and I was more than three millennia old before you were born. But one of them should have been told. He should know that he will not see the end of it. It's only right, only just. Isn't it?"

He waited, almost as if he expected a response, but none came. With a deep sigh, the Cartographer picked up his quill, dipped it into the inkwell, and resumed his work.

CHAPTER ELEVEN
CHÀMENOS LIBER

THE COMPANIONS EXPECTED an easier descent down the tower, but they soon realized it wasn't to be. The rumbling they experienced earlier had resumed at an increasing pace, accompanied by vibrations that nearly shook them from the stairs. They kept close to the walls and moved as quickly as they dared.

"I think it's the instability the Cartographer mentioned," Bert, in the lead, called over his shoulder. "More pieces of the tower are crumbling."

"I hope we moored the ship high enough," said Jack. "It would be a sorry mess to find it had drifted free because the wall it was tied to suddenly fell into the ocean."

"Don't worry," Aven said. "Her crew is good. They'll keep the airship close and will be watching for us."

"Good to know," said Jack, sounding less than reassured.

They were close enough to the bottom to see open sky below when a tremor struck and dislodged the entirety of the counterclockwise stair. It fell past, taking chunks of the clockwise stair with it, along with several doors.

"Glad we're not going up," Charles remarked. "Actually, I'm glad we're leaving altogether."

Bert stopped them, putting his arm out protectively. He looked at Aven, and her brow creased with worry. "We should have already come to the window where the *Indigo Dragon* was tethered," Bert said. "That we haven't only means that that part of the tower has already fallen."

They were thirty feet from the disintegrating base, and below that was open air. Above, there were sections of steps missing. They could go no farther down, but neither could they go back the way they'd come. They were trapped.

"What can we do?" asked Jack.

As if in answer to his question, a familiar whirring noise rose outside the nearest window, and the *Indigo Dragon* came into view. One of the fauns expertly tossed a line through the opening. Aven caught it and secured it through the bracing under the steps, then pulled over the rope ladder.

"You first," she said to Jack.

"I'll wait, thanks," he replied. "Charles?"

"Already over here," Charles said, waving happily from the deck. "I was motivated."

Bert went next, then John. Jack was about to cross when another violent shudder shook the tower, and the stairway collapsed.

Jack was halfway onto the ladder, but Aven had been standing on the steps. There was no time to shout. It was all she could do to flail about for some kind of purchase, and she managed to twist the anchorline around her wrist before she fell.

The other end was still tied to the bracing, which weighed several hundred pounds. Aven cried out with the pain and tried to reach up to Jack, but he was too far out of reach.

"Aven!" Bert screamed. "Jack, can you reach her?"

"I'm trying," Jack gasped. "Give me a minute."

That was more time than they had. The weight of the bracing was dragging Aven down—and pulling the *Indigo Dragon* dangerously close to the tower.

"Cut the line!" Aven hissed.

"Never," said Jack. "Hang on, I'm coming!"

He wound his feet through the ladder and swung backward, upside down—but it was no use. Her outstretched hand was still too far to reach.

The airship lurched sideways again, and the propellers screamed with the strain. It was a losing battle. Slowly, the ship was being pulled closer to the wall.

"Cut the line, Jack!" Aven said again. "Save the ship!"

"I'm not going to do that!" Jack yelled back. "I made a promise to look after you, and I'm keeping it."

The look in her eyes softened, but she saw the situation more clearly than he did. "I can't reach my knife to cut myself loose," she said. "Not like this. And we're all dead if the airship smashes into the wall! Cut me loose! It's the only way!"

Jack looked at her, only a few feet away, and stretched his arms in despair. Grinding his teeth, he called up to Bert. "Throw me a knife! Quickly!"

One of the fauns clambered out onto the ladder as the ship jolted close enough to the tower to scrape a propeller against the stone, sending a shower of sparks over them. He passed a short dagger down to Jack, who took a deep breath and looked at Aven.

"Cut the line, Jack," she said softly.

And with a single stroke, to the horror of his friends, he did. Aven dropped away into the mist without a sound.

"Jack!" Bert screamed as the shaken young man rushed across the ladder and onto the deck. "What have you done? What have you done?"

Jack ignored him and ran to the wheel. "We have two miles," he yelled to the crew. "Cut away anything that will drag us back, and dive! We can still catch her! Dive! Now!"

The crew responded instantly, shifting the rudder, spars, and propellers to alter the pitch of the ship. With a vicious jolt, the *Indigo Dragon* tipped downward and began to drop.

John, Charles, and Bert grabbed hold of whatever they could and braced themselves. The fauns, seemingly oblivious to the danger, were cutting off anything that created wind resistance: the anchor, gone; the rope ladders, gone. Even the extra casks of food and drink were quickly tossed over the railing, to disappear in the airstream above them, so they could gain more speed. Faster and faster the ship flew—but in seconds, it was obvious it would not be fast enough. The time it had taken Jack to get aboard again and take charge of the ship would cost them dearly.

"We have to go faster!" Jack yelled, looking around. "The balloon! It's creating too much resistance! We have to deflate it!"

"Are you crazy?" Bert shouted back. "It's what's keeping us aloft! It won't do any good to save Aven if we crash and die right after!"

"No one's going to die today," said Jack. "John! Take the wheel!"

John staggered forward and clutched at the wheel, while Jack leaped over his friend and grabbed Aven's sword from its place above the cabin door. Wrapping one of the guy lines around his wrist, he jumped into the air and the line snapped taut, holding him parallel to the rearmost part of the balloon.

With one long stroke, Jack split the center seam on the back of the balloon, and the gases inside escaped with a roar.

In an instant, the airship had become an air rocket, and it was hurtling even faster toward the water.

"I see her!" John shouted, pointing.

Below them, now free of the line and the stair bracing that had trapped her, Aven was attempting to slow her descent by spreading her arms and legs. It was working—between her push against the wind and the plummeting speed of the ship, they would overtake her in moments.

And moments later they would hit the sea with the force of an explosion.

The fauns took hold of the wheel and maneuvered the ship until it was angled to fall below Aven. With excruciating slowness, they met, matched, and exceeded her speed, and the airship came up underneath her. Aven slammed roughly into the now-deflated balloon, and Jack caught her with his legs and free arm.

"Now!" he shouted to the fauns, who had anticipated his order and had already redirected the propellers. The force of the sudden shift slowed their speed, but ripped off one of the guide wings with a strangled screeching of torn wood and metal.

John threw himself against the wheel and turned it to compensate for the lost wing. The wind roared in their ears, and the water stretched across the horizon. The second wing ripped away, and suddenly their speed increased, but the Dragon at the prow acted as a natural rudder, and suddenly they also had direction—still down, but also forward.

But it wasn't enough.

The ship hit the water at tremendous speed. It had pulled up just enough to avoid a straight-on impact, but it bounced off the surface of the water so violently that the rudder and both propellers were thrown off, and it hit thrice more before slowing down to a skimming glide, finally settling into the sea, and at last, stopping.

It was only by sheer luck that none of the companions had been ripped away in the barely controlled fall. They sat on the deck, too stunned to speak, as the perspicacious fauns began to clean up what still remained of the *Indigo Dragon*.

Aven, still breathing hard, looked at Jack and laughed. "The good old *Indigo Dragon*," she said. "I knew she wouldn't let me go."

"I helped too, you know," said Jack.

"I know," said Aven. "I knew you would. That's why I told you to cut the line."

"That was exhilarating," John commented from the foredeck. "And I never, ever, want to do it again."

"Incredible," said Bert, shaking his head in disbelief. "I can't believe it."

"Neither can I," added Charles, standing up and looking around. "The *Indigo Dragon* is a boat again."

It had been a miraculous rescue, but the damage to the *Indigo Dragon* was nearly total. There was no way to steer, no motive power, and the balloon had a twenty-foot-long gash in it.

"I don't mean to be a sour apple," said Charles, "but did you realize we're in the middle of the Chamenos Liber?"

"That's exactly where we wanted to be, isn't it?" said Jack.

"Yes," Charles replied. "But in case you hadn't noticed, it's awfully hot, and it seems to be getting hotter."

He was right. The cloying smell and thickened air were the result not of fog, but of steam rising from the volcano below.

"We still don't know how to open the portal," said Charles, "and I don't think we can afford to sit here for very long."

"If we can repair the balloon," said Aven, "we may be able to reinflate it. Then we could at least move a safe distance away to reassess our situation."

"Our situation may become a catastrophe, as a wise man once said," stated Jack. "Can't the *Indigo Dragon* motivate us out herself?"

"She may be float-worthy," said Bert, "but remember: She was rebuilt as an airship. She's not equipped to move about in the water anymore—not that freely, anyway."

"Those are our options, then," said John. "We try to repair her enough to get outside of the volcanic cone . . ."

"Or we get steamed to death," put in Jack.

"Or someone might come looking for us," said Charles, hoping to elicit a hopeful smile or two. But no one offered one. As the steam continued to swirl about the ship, the companions moved to separate areas of the deck and set about making whatever repairs they could.

They worked throughout the remainder of that day, and then long into the night. After assessing all the damage, a quick vote focused them on repairing the balloon itself as the most viable means to leave the Chamenos Liber. As Bert gently reminded the others, the only course they could follow after that was to somehow get back to London to retrieve the *Imaginarium Geographica*, and then return to open the portal to the Underneath.

What was unspoken but clearly on the minds of them all was just how difficult that would prove to be.

The only ones who knew where they had gone were Artus and Tummeler. And it would be several more days at minimum before either of them would begin to worry that something was amiss—and even then, what could they do?

All the ships in the Archipelago had been burned. There would be no way for any rescuers to reach the *Indigo Dragon*, or for the *Indigo Dragon* to reach safe haven, in less than a month at best. It was possible the dragons could help transport them across the Frontier and back—but again, at present, the *Indigo Dragon* was all but marooned, and her crew and passengers were being slowly steamed to death.

And all the while, precious hours were passing. Passing, while the children remained missing and an unknown adversary wreaked havoc with history.

Aven was supervising the repair of the balloon. The fauns were remarkably versatile and had plundered the blankets in the cabin below to use for stitching material. The work was slow going, but Bert cautioned that despite their urgency, it was better to ensure that it was done right the first time—or else they might find themselves in hotter water later on.

"Very funny," said Aven.

"Pun intended," said Bert. "If I can't joke about imminent death, then I might as well just resign."

"Resign from what?" asked Jack.

"Depends on the day," said Bert. "Aven, I wanted to ask—when the Cartographer translated the name of the islands as 'Lost Boys,' you reacted very noticeably. Why is that? What does that phrase mean to you?"

The fact that Aven didn't immediately reply was an indication of just how deeply she felt about the question. Finally she handed her tools to one of the fauns and stood against the cabin wall, her arms folded.

"Obviously it's also a reference to Jamie and Peter's Lost Boys," she explained. "It was the name that all the children who came to Peter's secret hideaway went by—but he wasn't the one who started using it. It began long before Peter's time. And I also didn't know it referred to a place—especially one that guards the Underneath."

"But why would that bother you?" asked Jack. "We've mentioned the Lost Boys several times, and you never blinked."

"It wasn't just mentioning them," Aven said. "I just suddenly realized that I might have actually *been* to the Underneath before. I think it's what Peter and Jamie called 'the Nether Land,' and I know another way to get there."

Jack started. "You mean a way other than the portal? That's wonderful!"

Aven shook her head. "There *is* a way, back in your world. But it won't do us any good.

"It . . . was meant to be a secret," she continued, with a hesitant glance at her father. "It's how Jamie was able to go back and forth to the Archipelago without using the Dragonships."

"Ah," said Bert. "I've often wondered about that. It was one of Jamie's great secrets," he told Jack. "He refused to work on any maps or annotations of the Nether Land, and he stoutly refused to discuss it when the subject came up. It was one of the first conflicts we had with him as a Caretaker."

"There is a wardrobe in London," Aven went on, "one of two

that originally belonged to Harry Houdini. He claimed to have built them himself, but Jules always suspected that he stole the principles behind them from the inventor Nikola Tesla."

"You mean 'borrowed,'" said Bert mildly.

Aven shook her head. "Stole. Tesla tried to have him arrested for stealing his papers, but Houdini ate the papers in question, then broke himself out of jail to ask the magistrate to release him for lack of evidence."

"I see. Forget I asked. You were saying?" said Bert.

"Houdini built two wardrobes for use in his stage act," said Aven. "He or a member of the audience could enter one, then instantly appear in the other, which was placed at the opposite edge of the stage. He pushed the limits further with every performance, moving one wardrobe to the balcony, then the lobby, and once even to the street outside, where a surprised volunteer emerged and was nearly run over by a carriage. Shortly after that, the trick was discontinued, and he never performed it in public again."

"The trick had lost its appeal?" Jack asked.

"Hardly," said Aven. "It was the biggest draw of the day. But he found a more useful application for it. Because of his skill as an escape artist, he was approached by both Scotland Yard and the United States Secret Service to work for them as an intelligence-gathering agent. His touring show was his cover, and in the rare event he did get caught by a foreign agency, he could simply free himself and walk away."

"Handy," said Jack. "Where do the wardrobes come in?"

"Houdini realized that the ability to instantly transport himself from any location would make him unsurpassable as a spy," said Aven. "So he would often arrange to have one of the wardrobes delivered to government offices, or royal residences, on the pretext that the delivery was a mistake. It was always returned to him, but in the meantime he could count on having an open door to wherever it was."

"And the other wardrobe could be kept in his dressing room for a convenient escape," said Jack. "Impressive."

"Exactly," said Aven. "There were the occasional sightings of him in places he wasn't supposed to be—but how can you bring charges against a man who was seen onstage only minutes later, by an audience of five hundred, in a theater a thousand miles away?"

"That explains something else," mused Bert. "Houdini and Conan Doyle used the wardrobes to avoid Samaranth, didn't they?"

"Yes," Aven said, suppressing a giggle. "They did. They were crisscrossing Europe trying to stay out of sight while you tried to talk sense into Samaranth. Giving up the wardrobes was part of the offer they made in exchange for his not roasting them whole."

"And he gave the wardrobes to the next Caretaker, who was Jamie," continued Jack.

"Right," said Aven. "That was around the time he first met Peter, who had learned a way to cross the Frontier on his own, using the wings Daedalus the Younger made for all the Lost Boys. Somehow they were able to place one of the wardrobes in the Nether Land, and they kept the other at Jamie's house, so that either or both of them could cross at will. I've used it more than once myself to get to the Nether Land."

"After a visit with Jamie in London, I'd assume?" asked Bert.

Aven blushed, and tried to frown, but couldn't quite manage it. "Yes. That too."

"That's why it was a surprise to you that the Nether Land might be in the Underneath," said Jack. "You've never traveled there any other way, have you?"

Aven shook her head. "It was one of Peter's rules. He wouldn't permit outsiders to know the way there—and I was an outsider. I haven't been back there in years, but I think Jamie's wardrobe is still in London."

"It is! I saw it myself. This is grand news," Jack exclaimed, clapping his hands. "If we can get back to London, we can simply enter the wardrobe at Barrie's town house and be sent right to the Underneath without the return trip."

Again Aven shook her head. "It won't work. When Jamie left, I wasn't the only one who felt betrayed. Peter kept the wardrobe but locked it so it couldn't be used."

"But he's the one who sent a messenger to find the Caretaker," said Bert. "Why didn't he simply send her through the wardrobe?"

"There's only one reason," said Aven darkly. "Because he wasn't able to."

At the other end of the ship, John and Charles had been sitting in the light of the cabin's oil lamps, dissecting their copies of Tummeler's *Geographica* for any scrap of useful information, but with little result.

John dropped his copy, kicking it across the deck—an action he immediately regretted, and he quickly retrieved it and buffed the cover with his shirtsleeve.

"I shouldn't be angry with Tummeler," he said to Charles, who had been watching from a nearby perch atop a broken section of railing. "He certainly can't be expected to have included every notation in the *Geographica*. It's quite an accomplishment that he recalled as much as he did. But it's not going to be a help. Not with this."

Charles nodded as he bit into an apple from the ship's stores. "You're probably right about Tummeler's *Geographica*. Then again, so was Aven—it's not so much useful as it is interesting. Did you notice on one of the spreads, he annotated the description so thoroughly that there's only room for one small corner of the actual map? I also hadn't realized how frequently he found an opportunity to include some of his recipes in and around the texts. Enterprising fellow, is our friend the badger."

"I just can't help thinking this is once again all my fault," said John. "I'm a professor now. A teacher. I'm well educated. And I'm one of only a few people in the world who is capable of using the *Imaginarium Geographica*—but I can't even manage to keep track of it when I really need it."

"Cheer up, old chap," said Charles. "From what I've heard, that Einstein fellow is redefining the scientific laws of the universe, but he can't make change at the market. Maybe it's the price you pay for being the best at something."

"You're not helping," John said morosely.

As they talked, the horizon was beginning to brighten from the dark of night's passage to the cobalt gray of dawn's arrival. One by one, the stars began to fade out, with the exception of a single bright point of light low in the western sky.

"That's heartening at least," John remarked, indicating the solitary star. "One of my earliest stories was about the morning star and an ancient myth.

"When I was a student, I read an Anglo-Saxon poem about an

angel called Earendel. It so impressed me, so inspired me as both an allegory and a literal representation of the light of faith, that I researched it for more than a year. I was certain I'd discovered an Ur-Myth—one of the original stories of the world.

"Earendel, or Orentil, as he was called in the older Icelandic version of the tale, was a mariner who was fated to sail forever in the shadowy waters of an enchanted archipelago," John continued. "I revised the mention of the star to represent his beloved, who drew him up from the darkness into the heavens. And the poem that resulted was the beginning of all the mythologies I've been working on ever since."

"And the beginning of your apprenticeship as a Caretaker," said Bert, who with Aven and Jack had approached them while John was narrating. "It was 'The Voyage of Eärendil' that first brought you to Stellan's—and my—attention."

"I didn't know that," said John, who was still watching the morning star. "It's an interesting foreshadowing to what followed, don't you think?"

"Maybe more than you realize," said Charles, who had risen from his seat and was gripping the railing alongside John. "Look," he went on, pointing excitedly. "Your morning star is coming this way."

He was right. The point of light that appeared to be a star was only growing brighter as the sun rose, and it wasn't moving in a straight line, but seemed to be bobbing and weaving.

"A bit erratic for a star," Jack said.

"Not erratic," corrected Bert, with tears in his eyes. "She's just following the signal."

The star dipped suddenly and came into full view in front of the cresting sun. Each of the companions gasped in turn, as they realized that John's star had *wings*, and the point of light was a fiercely shining Compass Rose.

It was Laura Glue.

Seeing the *Indigo Dragon*, she let out an excited whoop and flew directly toward them.

In one hand she was clutching the Compass Rose that had led her to them in Oxford.

And in the other she held the *Imaginarium Geographica*.

CHAPTER TWELVE
DANTE'S RIDDLE

DESPITE THE CIRCUMSTANCES, it was a glorious reunion. There are rare moments in human experience, Jack thought to himself, that fill one to bursting with emotion. Many are based on relationships, or personal experiences, and are too individualized to really be shared or explained. But there is one emotion that is universal, in which an infinite amount of gratitude may be felt with the smallest pinch of experience: the knowledge that one has not been forgotten.

Seized by joy, the companions passed the elated Laura Glue from one to another, hugging her tightly and laughing. All save for Aven—who seemed happy to see the girl, but was strangely removed from the reunion the others were celebrating.

"I knowed I could find you!" she said, beaming. "I told Jamie I just knowed I could!"

"And so you did!" declared John, who had rather delicately taken the *Geographica* from her grasp. "I can't believe you came, Laura Glue."

"I wanted to show Jamie my wings," she said. "So we went out to the autogobile where you'd put them, and that's when he saw the book, and boy, did he call you lots of names."

John reddened. "I'd imagine so. But how did you find us?"

She held up the Compass Rose. "Same way as before. Jamie knew how to remake the mark, and he said you'd be needing your book right away. So we had tea, and when it was night, we went to the park, and . . ."

Laura Glue paused, thoughtful. "He said that it was ap—apro—"

"Appropriate?" Charles put in.

"Yeah," she said. "He said it was appro'prate that I leave from where the statue of my grandfather is. But you know, it doesn't really look like him at all.

"So I started flying, and came through the black clouds, and that's when the Compass Rose brung . . . um . . ."

"Brought," supplied John.

"Right. That's when it brought me here," said Laura Glue. She looked around at the tattered remains of the *Indigo Dragon*. "Hey—who broke your Dragonship?"

"That was me," said Jack. "I had to rescue Aven."

"Excuse me," said Aven, "but there was more to the situation than just saving me. It's not my fault the tower was falling apart."

"Now, now," Charles said placatingly. "Let's not be placing blame. We should be looking to the *Geographica* to get out of here, should we not?"

Aven threw one last poisonous look at Jack before nodding her head. "You're right. Let's get back to our plan. I . . ."

Aven stopped. The moment Jack had mentioned her, Laura Glue fell silent, and had been staring at the queen with platter-shaped eyes.

"You," Laura Glue said reverently, "you're a Mother now, aren't you?"

"Yes," Aven replied, unsure what the girl really meant by the question. "But once I was your friend, remember?"

"I remember who you look like," said Laura Glue. "But you weren't a Mother. Not then."

Aven knelt before the girl and took her hands. "We used to play together, you and I. We had tea parties, and pretended we were wolves, and once I broke my arm, and you carried me to safety."

Laura Glue's mouth dropped open in surprise. She took her hands and traced the lines of Aven's face, then fell forward, hugging her and sobbing. Aven was startled, but after a moment, she hugged the girl back.

"Poppy!" Laura Glue gasped through a sheen of tears. "It's you, isn't it? You've come back at last, and . . . and you're a *Mother*."

"Poppy?" Jack said, looking askance at Bert, who shrugged.

"It's the first I've heard of it," said Bert. "Although as I understood it, all the children who went to the Nether Land chose their own names."

"We do," said Laura Glue, who had wiped her nose on her sleeve before Charles could give her a handkerchief. "T'anks anyway, Charles," she said, tucking it in her belt.

"Well, I don't know about the rest of you," said Jack, "but I'm rather anxious to get a look at this 'Nether Land' myself. Shall we get to it?"

"Of course," John said.

"Oh!" exclaimed Laura Glue. "I almost forgot!"

She reached inside her belt and pulled out a note written on a familiar cream-colored paper that seemed to be favored among Caretakers. Beaming, she handed the slightly crumpled paper to John.

The others crowded close as he unfolded it and read:

John—

    While our young friend Laura Glue was showing me her wings, we discovered something else that had been left behind in your automobile. I trust it has now come to you in a timely manner, and that you will find it helpful.

    The message she brought was sent by Peter, and thus must involve the Nether Land, and the Lost Boys. And these days, there is only one way in.

    The words to open the passage are on page 42.

    Godspeed to you all.

Sir James Barrie

John opened the *Geographica* to the spread of the page Jamie had indicated. "That looks awfully familiar," he said pensively. "Is this actually an island in the Archipelago?"

Bert pressed closer and peered over his glasses. "It must be, although I've never been there myself."

The island was shaped like a broad cup, wide at the top, narrowing to a tight neck, then widening again to a small base. The legend above identified it as "Autunno."

"Autunno," said John. "Italian, from a Latin base. Autumn. The island is called Autumn."

"Hm," said Bert. "I don't recall ever needing to go there, although Stellan may have. But it looks ordinary enough."

"It's Hell," said Charles.

"What?" the others said in a chorus.

"Hell," Charles repeated. "Or at least, Sandro Botticelli's version of Hell."

Bert snapped his fingers. "Beat me with a noodle—he's right. The cartographic image is that of an island, but the shape and topographical details match exactly the painting Botticelli did of Hell for Dante's *Inferno*."

"That makes sense," said John. "The Cartographer said that Dante was one of the only Caretakers who visited the Underneath."

"Fine," said Jack, "but how does it apply to finding the Underneath?"

"I think it *is* the Underneath," replied John. "The coordinates for Autunno are exactly the same as those for the Chamenos Liber. So it stands to reason that it is precisely where we've been told it is—Underneath, being guarded by the Chamenos Liber."

"Can't Autunno also be translated as 'Fall'?" asked Jack.

"I don't like the sound of *that*," said Charles.

"Mmm, possibly," said John. "I'm not as practiced with Italian, especially in this rough script. Give me a few minutes and I'll have all the text sorted out."

"Italian?" Jack asked Bert as John moved to the foredeck for privacy. "Dante wouldn't have written his annotations in Latin?"

Bert shook his head. "Remember that Dante, for all his faults, was also a communicator. Most of the poems of the time were classified as 'high' for the serious topics, or 'low' for the vulgar ones. He thought it was a mistake not to write about the grander themes in a language that was more accessible to the common people.

"So when he chose to write an epic about the redemption of man, a subject of utter gravity and great import, he shocked most of civilized society by doing it in Italian. His tendency to do the contrarian thing was probably one of the reasons he was selected as a Caretaker."

"Indeed," said Charles. "That's an exceedingly noble and Romantic notion. Romantic with a capital R, that is," he added.

"How so?" asked Bert.

"I believe that as human beings, we are all connected to one another, and in that way, largely dependent on one another for survival. A belief," he said, observing the fauns still at work repairing the balloon at one end of the deck, and John translating Dante's notes at the other, "that has only grown stronger during this adventure.

"I call the concept Co-inherence," Charles continued. "What that means is that each of our thoughts and actions has a bearing on others. And always, always, there is potential in us all for immense good, or incredible evil. But even then, despite the evil men do, there can still arise a measure of good."

"Yes," agreed Bert. "Remember the Cartographer said not to judge even Mordred too harshly."

"Exactly my point," said Charles, "but the reverse is also true, and even the best of intentions . . ."

". . . can pave the road to Hell," finished John, who had just approached them, cradling the *Geographica*. "I think I've translated all of Dante's notes. The solution to opening the portal to the Underneath is a riddle."

"Jamie couldn't simply tell us the words to open the portal?" Jack said.

"I don't think it's as easy as all that," said John. "There must have been some reason that we needed the actual *Geographica* here. And I think that reason is what the answer to the riddle will reveal.

"Dante wrote a lot about Autunno here," he went on, indicating the annotations in the atlas, "but he also included bits and pieces from his own writing, so he obviously expected whoever followed him to be familiar with his work."

"Typical author," said Charles.

"He refers to the portal as 'Ulysses' Gate,'" John noted. "Does that mean anything to you, Bert?"

"Of course," said Bert. "Ulysses was in *The Divine Comedy*, remember? In it he told the story of his final voyage, where he left his home and family to sail to the ends of the Earth."

"I think this would qualify," said Jack.

"Indeed," said Bert. "Ulysses valued nothing more than his belief in the pursuit of knowledge, and he thought that attaining knowledge was limited only by one's efforts."

"Admirable," said Jack. "So what happened to him?"

"God sank his ship outside of Mount Purgatory," Bert answered, "and he ended up in the Pit."

Charles raised his hand. "Anyone else thinking this is all a bad idea, and we should just focus on repairing the boat? No?" He lowered his hand. "Don't say I didn't bring it up when we get to the running about and screaming part."

"We already did that," said Jack, "when we escaped from the tower and I rescued Aven."

"Not that I'm not grateful," said Aven, "but I wish you'd stop bringing that up. I was perfectly willing to sacrifice myself so the rest of you could carry on."

"And what good would that have done?" Jack said indignantly.

"For starters," Aven told him, "the *Indigo Dragon* wouldn't have been wrecked. And you'd already have been halfway to Paralon to bring more help."

"And you'd be dead," said Jack. "I just couldn't let that happen."

"And I'm appreciative," said Aven. "But if our positions had been reversed, I'd have done the same."

Jack smirked and shook his head. "There wasn't time."

Aven stared at him. "What's *that* supposed to mean? *You* had time to save *me*."

"Of course I did," said Jack matter-of-factly. "I'm a man. We're made to think more quickly."

Bert had just enough time to exclaim, "Oh, dear," before Aven swung her fist and clocked Jack square on the chin, knocking him backward into the balloon, which was still under repair.

"Wow!" said Laura Glue. "You sent him ass-over-teakettle."

"Language," warned Bert.

"Sorry," she said.

Aven rubbed her knuckles and looked at the others. "Sorry about that. I might have stopped myself from hitting him, but I didn't think of it quickly enough."

"Not a problem," said Charles.

"If you're finished with the fisticuffs," John said, "can we please see this through?"

"Sorry," said Aven.

"Ulysses wasn't the only Greek hero mentioned in *The Divine Comedy*," said John. "In what Dante described as the eighth circle of Hell, he and his guide, Virgil, met Jason, the leader of the Argonauts, who had commissioned the building of the ship the *Argo*—"

"Which Ordo Maas rebuilt into the *Red Dragon*!" Charles exclaimed. "Brilliant, John! Well done!"

"That's another piece of the riddle, but it's not the whole picture yet," said John. "Let's assume that every reference Dante makes here that involves Jason or Ulysses is literal when applied to Autunno. It says that when Dante entered the ends of the Earth—referring to Ulysses' last voyage—it opened at his command with words that appeared in the *Red Dragon's* breath."

"Oh no," groaned Jack, who had rejoined his friends but was also keeping a respectable distance from Aven. "Does that mean we can only solve the riddle if the *Red Dragon* is present?"

"I don't think that's it," said John, peering more closely at the *Geographica*. "The handwriting is complicating the translation somewhat. But try this—what if Dante didn't mean the actual *Red Dragon*, but was simply referring to a red dragon? Say, Samaranth, or one of his companions?"

"Same pickle, different barrel," said Bert. "We don't have a way to contact any of the dragons from our present position."

"That's a dumb riddle," said Laura Glue.

"Not now, Laura," Charles said. "This is very important."

The girl stomped her foot. "I told you, my name is Laura *Glue*. And I said it's a stupid riddle because everyone knows what dragon's breath is."

"They do?" Jack said, crouching to look the girl in the eye. "What is it?"

She shrugged. "It won't do us any good anyway," she said glumly. "There aren't any volcanoes around here."

John and Bert looked at each other in surprise.

"The *Red Dragon's* breath," said Charles. "Red, as in hot vapors?"

"It's worth trying," said John.

Aven called to several of the fauns to bring over some of the cord from the balloon rigging. They fashioned a makeshift harness for John, then lowered him gently over the side of the ship that seemed closest to the sulfur that was venting from below the Chamenos Liber.

Carefully, John held open the *Geographica* to the pages that depicted Autunno and Dante's notations. The thick fumes made him cough, and his eyes watered, but sure enough—in seconds, something began to appear across the pages.

"Pull me up!" he yelled. "I have it! I have the answer!"

They hoisted John back to the deck, and he opened the *Geographica*.

"That's why Jamie couldn't just tell us the words," he said excitedly. "I think it's only possible to see the necessary words here, or wherever else there might be volcanic fumes."

"Lucky us," Charles said drolly. "What does it say?"

"It's an Opening," said Bert. "The third kind of spoken spell. Go ahead and read it, John—after all, you figured it out."

John traced the near-transparent letters with his fingers, then began to recite the words:

> *By knowledge paid*
> *For riddles wrought*
> *I open thee*
> *I open thee*

> *By bones bound*
> *By honor taken*

I open thee
I open thee

For life eternal and liberty gain'd
To sleep and dream, as kings we reign'd
I open thee
I open thee

John closed his eyes, then opened one and looked around quizzically. "Ah, Bert? What happens now?"

Bert raised his eyebrows. "Don't have a clue. I haven't done this before either."

For one minute, then two, the companions simply looked at one another, and at the water around the *Indigo Dragon*.

"All right," Jack began.

"Wait," said Charles. "Can you see that? Something's turning the ship around."

"That's not the ship," said Aven. "It's the water."

The sea within the Chamenos Liber was beginning to rotate. Slowly, but the motion was unmistakable now.

As they watched, the clockwise motion started to move faster, and then faster still.

"I think we'd better hold on to something," suggested Bert. "I have a bad feeling about this."

"Let's get you into the cabin," Jack said to Laura Glue.

"No!" said Aven. "If we capsize, it'll be safer on top."

"Good enough," said Jack, who wrapped one arm around the girl and the other around a stout section of railing.

The sea was making a noise like breakers crashing on the shore, but it was constant, and growing louder with the speed of the rotating water, which was forming a gigantic whirlpool. It opened in the center of the islands, and then spread rapidly outward until it caught up the *Indigo Dragon* against the crest. The current pulled the little craft over the edge just as the sound crescendoed to a roar, and the sides of the whirlpool dropped away to darkness.

"Dear Christ," said Charles. "It did mean 'Fall.'"

And the *Indigo Dragon* fell.

PART FOUR

INTO THE UNDERNEATH

CHAPTER THIRTEEN
CROATOAN

THE OLD MAN waited until he could no longer hear the clicking noises that indicated his captor's presence, and was certain that the beast-children who served him were also gone, before speaking.

"It's all right," he said into the darkness of the cave. "They've all gone now."

A pearlescent glow began to emanate from the large mirror opposite the frame where he was tied, and images that extended far deeper than the mirror should have allowed began to swirl into clarity.

Whether it depicted fog, or flame, or simply chaos swimming beneath the silvered glass, he could not tell—but eventually a single image sharpened and came into focus.

The mirror showed the head and shoulders of a woman. She was neither young nor old, but seemed to be an ideal combination of youthful beauty and mature experience. She wore a loose-fitting tunic draped low across her collarbone, and a single silver necklace. Her dark hair was pulled up in the back and fastened with silver pins.

Her eyes were deep-set and weary, and showed her to be much older than her appearance indicated. She looked at the old man and smiled.

"Hello, boy," she said. "How do you fare?"

"I've had better days," the old man admitted, "but I've had worse, too, so I suppose it all evens out eventually. Time will tell."

The woman hesitated. "So—there's been no word?"

"None," said the old man. "But I have hope."

"Based on what?" she said sharply. "You sent a child to seek the help of your greatest enemy. Don't you think that's an act of desperation?"

He laughed and shook his head. "That's not what I did at all. I sent my granddaughter, whom I trust fully, to seek the help of a Caretaker of the *Imaginarium Geographica.*

"That isn't a desperate act. That's a *plan.*"

The passengers of the *Indigo Dragon* didn't fall so much as they *descended*; they were still dropping with great speed, but it didn't feel as if the descent were unfettered, more as if the drop through the portal were being controlled.

Even so the impact was hard, and no one was conscious enough to hear the splintering of wood as their craft struck something much more massive, flinging them to and fro, and came to a stop.

It may have taken minutes or hours for the companions to awaken in the diffused light of the Underneath. But when they awoke, they might as well have imagined themselves to be near any common seashore in their own world. The shore was sixty or seventy feet below what they'd actually landed on: a great wall of wrecked, rotting, moldering ships. Hundreds of them, of every make and vintage, stretching away far into the distance; ships with names like the USS *Cyclops* and the HMS *Rosalie* and the *Spray of Boston.*

The companions all began to collect their wits, taking stock of the unusual scene they'd landed in. The sails (on the ships that had used them) had mostly rotted in the sea air, leaving a neglected field of masts pointing skyward, awaiting a harvesting that would never come. There were rafts and dinghies; pirate ships and tugboats; gondolas and even a Chinese junk. There were also other ships: great gray metal behemoths that were unrecognizable to them. And there were a number of aircraft as well, although many of these were also of an unfamiliar make.

Below the wall of ships was a narrow, sandy beach that was broken by shallow inlets ringed in a reddish stone. A short distance behind that was the tree line of a thick, old pine forest, and birdcalls could be heard coming from somewhere within.

A few hundred yards above them, where the *Indigo Dragon* must have fallen through the portal, was a vortex of water that receded upward as they watched. In seconds it dissipated into vapor and mist, as if it had never been there.

There was a yellowish light, but there was no sun.

And there was no sign of the *Indigo Dragon*.

John was quick to come fully awake and alert, and he did a brief head count. Charles and Jack were only a few feet away, on the foredeck of the large cargo ship they'd landed on, and Bert was wringing water out of his hat near the cabin. Aven was still unconscious but appeared uninjured and breathing, and she had her arms wrapped protectively around Laura Glue, who was nestled up against her chest, still clutching the Compass Rose.

None of them were aware of the eyes that watched them from inside the forest, nor did they notice that the birdcalls had changed.

Jack sat up, groaning. "I think I almost preferred life during wartime," he said testily. "At least at the Somme, all I had to worry about was not getting shot."

"Look here," Charles exclaimed, pointing. "What in heaven's name do you suppose those to be?"

The others looked to where he was gesturing and saw an extraordinary sight: massive white towers that stood on either horizon and stretched from beneath the surface of the water to beyond the clouds. The towers appeared to be some kind of stone but had an almost organic look to them. At such a tremendous distance, it was impossible to be sure. The sides of the columns were smooth and flowed upward with a graceful line that was practically sculpted.

John shaded his eyes with his hand and peered at the sky. "I can't see where they end," he said finally. "But there must be a ceiling to this place. We came through something, didn't we?"

"It was Deep Magic," said Bert, "Old Magic, that created that portal above. It was Old Magic that closed it again. For all we know, the sky above us here *is* the sea of the Archipelago."

"Can any of you tell where the light is coming from?" Charles asked, turning around. "It's almost as if we're, well, inside a lightbulb."

"I don't know," replied John, who had found the *Imaginarium Geographica* lying a few feet away against cargo boxes stenciled with the name SS *TIMANDRA,* and was busily dusting off the cover with his sleeve. "Maybe we've fallen into some sort of bowl-shaped world."

"Hmm," said Bert. "Now there's an interesting thought."

"That we've ended up in a bowl?" said John.

"May I?" Bert asked, indicating the *Geographica*.

John handed it over. "Be my guest."

Jack went over to Aven and Laura Glue to make sure they were uninjured, then joined Charles near the promenade, where he was making an impromptu catalogue of the vessels that comprised the great wall.

"Amazing," said Charles. "There must be hundreds, no, *thousands* of ships and aircraft here. Could all of these have come through the Chamenos Liber?"

"I doubt it," said Jack. "For one thing, they're spread out over an extremely wide area. I don't think the portal we came through is mobile—it's fixed in space."

"Then these must have come through by other means," Charles reasoned.

"Are there other means?" asked Jack. "We *wanted* to get here, and look at how much trouble we had."

"These are all wrecked, abandoned," stated John, coming up behind them. "I don't think their arrival was planned or voluntary."

"There are plenty of tales about the Devil's Triangle in the western Atlantic," said Charles. "Maybe the Underneath is what's, ah, behind those accounts."

"How they got here might be an interesting story," said John, "but what worries me is that none of them went back in the other direction."

At that moment, Bert came scurrying back to them, thumping the book in excitement.

"I think we've stumbled upon one of the greater mysteries of the *Geographica*," he said. "There are some maps that have excellent descriptions of the lands they depict, but little if any cartographical or navigational information. That's why we've had to make corrections and additions to the *Geographica* as the centuries passed—to try to make it more complete. And I think we already have maps of this place in the atlas!"

"And there's a map of an island shaped like a bowl, with no sun?" asked Jack.

"The Cartographer said the Underneath was formed of circles within circles," said John, "and that goes along with Dante's descriptions, as well as the map of Autunno."

"It's worth a look," said Charles.

John and Bert opened the *Geographica* on top of an orange crate and began to carefully page through it. Finally, Bert tapped a map with his knuckles. "Knew it. I just knew it," he said under his breath. "They *are* here. Damn your eyes, Jules. . . ."

Jack and Charles moved closer to see which maps Bert was referring to.

"The Underneath *does* have other names," explained Bert, "and each of the lands within also has its own name and identity."

"Like Paralon is an island within the Archipelago of Dreams," said Charles.

"Precisely," said Bert. "This place been called Skartaris by some, but most would know it as Pellucidar," he continued, pointing at an expansive map that bore a strong resemblance to central Europe.

"From Edgar Rice Burroughs's books?" Charles said contemptuously. "That's terrible—don't tell me *he* was a Caretaker."

"Close, but no cigar," replied Bert. "He has the imagination in spades but didn't care one whit about learning the languages needed—or having much to do at all with the Archipelago, save as a source of story material. Jules spent considerable time with him—apparently—and made every effort to accommodate his eccentricities, but to no avail."

"It's for the best, believe me," snorted Charles. "His prose is atrocious. Of course he couldn't master other languages. He's still working on *English*."

"Now, Charles," Jack admonished. "You have to admit, some of his publishers are very respectable. That American magazine that serialized his Ape Man stories, for example—they're first class."

"Granted," said Charles. "But the idea that he might have become a Caretaker is appalling."

Bert sighed. "What can one say? People do have their own ambitions, and most reasons for pursuing them aren't benevolent. Some accepted for the wealth, as Edgar did, and some for the fame."

"Did you do it for the wealth or the fame?" Jack asked Charles.

"I'm still trying to decide," said Charles, grinning. "If we ever make it back to London, that is."

Aven and Laura Glue had finally come fully awake and had chosen to leave the discussion of maps to the Caretakers. They had moved a short distance away and were playing some sort of game. Neither one seemed particularly bothered by the happening that had brought them to this place, Jack noted aloud.

"Of course not," said Bert. "They've both been here before—or somewhere like here, at least."

"Why aren't there more notes?" John asked as he thumbed through the previous few maps. "There ought to be more of—well, *something* written about this place."

"No one makes new annotations if no one visits," said Bert, "and since the last one here was probably Jamie, I'm not surprised by the lack of information."

"Skartaris," Jack mused, rubbing his chin. "That sounds very familiar, come to think of it. . . ."

"It should," said Bert. "That's the name of the mountain that cast a shadow across the entrance to the center of the Earth in Jules's book. Scartaris."

"So it was based on the Underneath?" John exclaimed. "And he never told you this?"

Bert shrugged. "He is a writer, after all," he said plaintively. "We do make things up on occasion, you know."

John was about to make another remark when his brow furrowed, and he leaned closer to the page he'd just turned to. Suddenly he gasped and then swallowed hard.

"I say, John. Are you all right?" asked Jack.

The others looked down at the Caretaker Principia. All the blood had drained from his face, and he was trembling so violently that the atlas was shaking in his hands.

"John?" Jack asked, concerned. "What is it?"

Wordlessly John stood up, then slowly walked away from the tree line back to the clearing where they'd awakened. He stood there, staring at the *Geographica*, then dropped it to the ground and looked up into the sky.

Aven and Laura Glue had noticed the others' concern and rejoined them from the fallen trees where they'd been sitting and playing their game.

"Is he all right?" Aven asked Jack in a low voice.

"I can't say," he answered. "He looks as if he's seen a ghost."

"Not a ghost," John said without turning around or lowering his gaze. "A Titan."

The companions crowded around the *Geographica* and examined the spread John had been looking at. It was one of the first maps, one of the oldest maps, which might have been made in the time of Ptolemy himself. And thus, much of what was written on it was in ancient Greek.

But it wasn't the writing that had so stunned their friend. It was the illustration.

It depicted a world within a world. And the smaller sphere was held aloft on the back and shoulders of the Titan Atlas. The drawing also showed him holding back the oceans above with his hands, so that the world within would not be flooded.

And together, they suddenly realized what the towers on the horizon were.

"Look," John said, tipping his head at the sky. "If you squint your eyes, you can just make out his hands."

John took charge of the group and declared that they'd be better off climbing down from the wall of ships and making their way to the beach to try and assess where they were. It was easier to do than any of them expected: The ships were accumulated in such a way that the wall formed a natural (if exceedingly large) set of steps. Within an hour, they were sitting on the beach just outside the tree line. John and Bert continued to study the *Geographica* while the others looked around for any other distinguishing landmarks they could use to identify the island.

"Distinguishing landmarks other than the giant skeleton holding up the sky, that is," said Charles. "If that isn't a Nether Land kind of sign, I don't know what is."

"This isn't the Nether Land," Aven declared. "I have no idea where we are."

Laura Glue's head bobbed up and down in agreement. "The sky is all right, but we don't have smelly trees," she said bluntly. Then suddenly she grew alarmed. "My wings! I've lost my wings!"

"They're probably just aboard the *Indigo Dragon*, wherever it is," said Jack. "I'm sure they'll turn up."

"Unless it sank," Charles said. "Do you think it was damaged that badly?"

Aven shook her head. "I doubt it. I think it struck the ship we landed on and may have rolled to the other side of the wall. Even if it ended up in the water, the hull was fine, and if we survived however far we fell, it should have too. I haven't seen any of the crew, either—so perhaps they've just moored her someplace to continue repairs."

The queen of Paralon sounded very sure—but the worried expression on her face told a different story.

John closed the *Geographica*. "That's all I can get," he said. "There's nothing else in here that can help identify where we are."

"Dante wrote about nine circles of Hell," suggested Charles. "Perhaps he based that on nine lands here in the Underneath."

"Dante wrote more allegorically than literally," said Bert. "There's no way to be sure, short of exploring the place on our own."

"I say," declared Charles, "perhaps we could just ask that lot over there at the trees."

The companions looked in the direction Charles was facing and saw nearly a dozen men standing just outside the tree line, watching them. The men were curiously dressed, wearing common-looking shirts and trousers, but also various belts and outer garments that were adorned with feathers and colored beads.

They were also heavily armed. Several held muskets loosely

against their shoulders, and all had either spears or bows and quivers of arrows.

"Oh, no," cried Laura Glue. "Run! Hide! It's Grandfather's enemies! It's the Indians! We have to run!"

Before the companions could process what the girl was saying, another line of men stepped out of the forest on the opposite end of the beach. They were dressed identically to the first group, and were just as well armed.

The companions were surrounded.

"Very odd Indians," Charles said to Jack. "They seem to be Europeans."

"Maybe she meant Eastern Indians," said Jack.

"Her grandfather's enemies, she said," John whispered. "From Barrie's book, remember? I think they *are* some kind of American Indian."

The two groups of men made no move toward the newcomers they'd encircled, but instead watched and waited. And then another man stepped out of the woods behind the first group and began to walk forward. Bert gasped in recognition.

"Oh, dear," said Bert. "Oh dear, oh dear, oh dear."

"What is it?" John hissed. "What's wrong?"

"These aren't just Indians," Bert said. "We've just delivered ourselves into the hands of someone who is supposed to be long dead."

"An enemy?" asked Jack.

"We'll find out in a moment," replied Bert.

The line of curiously costumed Indians parted, and a tall, broad-shouldered man wearing a feathered headdress walked toward them. He was not much older than the companions were, but there was a gravity about him that bespoke hard-won experience. The experience of decades, not years.

His brow was thick, and his cheeks were deeply scarred. His complexion was European, but his dress was a collision of Asian and American Indian, save for his boots, which were Dutch colonial. His manner was brusque, yet cultured—a definite enigma, thought John.

"As the official representative of the Imperial Cartological Society, I welcome you to Croatoan Island," the man said, "and even though you were not invited, you shall remain here as our guests."

"Thank you," John said evenly. "And whom do I have the pleasure of addressing?"

"My name," the man replied, "is Sir Richard Burton."

CHAPTER FOURTEEN

THE IMPERIAL
CARTOLOGICAL SOCIETY

THE MAN WHO called himself Burton made a series of quick gestures with his upraised hand, and suddenly the others rushed forward and held the companions fast. There was no mistaking their intent now.

Burton strode confidently to the group of prisoners and examined them one by one. He stopped at Bert, considering.

"I seem to know you," Burton said. "How would that be?"

"I have one of those faces," replied Bert.

"No," Burton said. "I don't recognize the face. But you *smell* like a Caretaker of the *Imaginarium Geographica*."

Those words sent a chill through each of the companions. This man was indeed their enemy. And he knew more about them than they did about him.

Close up, John was able to take in the strange appearance of their captors. Most of the men were indeed European, and fair-skinned, but several were also darker-hued, from a light reddish-tan to a deep, rich brown.

"Croatoan Island?" Jack whispered to Charles.

"The missing colony, from Roanoke, Virginia," Charles whispered back. "Sir Walter Raleigh's expedition."

"Precisely so," Burton said, wheeling about to face Charles. The man had the hearing of a fox. "To survive the first winter in the New World, they became a part of the local tribe of Algonquin Indians. Then, when the following year proved to be even harsher, the colonists persuaded the Indians to help them build new ships with which they hoped to return to England. That, as you can plainly see," he concluded, "didn't happen."

"So you're all Indians now?" asked John.

"There are full-blooded English here," Burton said, "and Dutch. Most are some combination of each. But we are nonetheless a tribe, and we look after our own.

"We are the Croatoans. And we are ourselves."

Burton instructed his men to tie the companions' hands together with thick twine, but he allowed Aven and Laura Glue to remain unbound.

"But," Burton added as a caution, "if either of them tries to flee, shoot the other one."

Laura Glue gulped and took Aven's hand.

Burton and his men marched their captives away from the beach and into the woods. The captors formed a ring around the companions, but Burton walked in front—and John noticed, as did the others, that he both kept and carried the *Imaginarium Geographica.*

They walked at a brisk but bearable pace for almost an hour before finally arriving at their destination. The eerie, cold light above was beginning to fade, to be replaced by the warm glow of firelight from the settlement ahead.

The village of the Croatoans was set in a small valley deep within the pine forest. It was bracketed by tall bluffs on two sides, and a shallow creek ran through it to the south. There were several dozen buildings of simple construction. Wood-and-wattle lodges, mostly—although there were shingles on the roofs of several buildings, and almost all of them had at least one glass window.

The tribe took little notice of most of the companions—as if marching a group of prisoners through the village were an everyday occurrence—but every villager they passed took special notice of Laura Glue.

This didn't go unseen by the girl, and she gripped Aven's hand all the tighter.

In the center of the village was a great circle of stones, like low altars, and adjacent to each stone was a fire that had been stoked to blazing.

As they approached, Bert couldn't contain the sigh of relief that escaped his lips.

In the center of the firelight was the *Indigo Dragon*. Not the entire ship—but the living masthead.

"Oh, thank goodness," said Bert. "At least they rescued *her*."

"Rescued?" said Burton. "Hardly. The *Indigo Dragon* was our first prisoner. We just went back for the rest of you."

"How did you know she's called the *Indigo Dragon*?" asked John.

Burton tipped his head at Bert. "Ask *him*. I'm sure he knows who I am."

Bert glared at their adversary, which was a surprise to John— Bert hardly ever glared at *anybody*.

"You've all heard of him, I believe," Bert told the others, "or at least have a passing familiarity with his writings. What you don't know is that Charles Dickens chose him as an apprentice caretaker, with Nemo's blessing. But it didn't work out, and he was dismissed."

"Was that before or after Magwich?" asked Charles.

"Does it matter?" said Jack.

"Good point," said Charles.

"He faked his own death and disappeared," Bert informed them. "No one expected to hear from him again."

"A fair enough assessment," said Burton. "I had made a fortune with my books and decided to create a new future for myself in the Archipelago of Dreams. I had been here again for only a short while when I became caught up in a terrible storm. When it finally passed, I found myself here, and my ship was destroyed. The Croatoans nursed me back to health, and as payment, I let them make me their leader."

The companions' heads were spinning with a thousand questions, but as usual, it was Aven who returned them to the matters at hand.

"I'm glad you rescued the *Indigo Dragon*," she said, "but what of her crew? There were more than twenty fauns aboard. Were any of them injured?"

"Not to begin with," Burton replied. "But they put up much more of a fight than you lot did."

"And so you killed them?" Aven exclaimed. "What a waste of life."

"Oh, they weren't *wasted*," Burton said. "In fact, they were *delicious*."

The companions were speechless with shock—except for Aven.

"Barbarian!" she exclaimed. "You're no better than a Wendigo!"

"Rightly so," said Burton. "We men of the West have always been more barbaric than our counterparts in the East. How much more so might we be, now that we're in the westernmost lands that exist?"

Near the ring of stone and fire was a large structure that appeared to be the central meetinghouse for the Croatoans. The companions were allowed to sit on mats that were laid along the center of the building, and they took in their strange surroundings.

The walls were lined with great carved chairs like the British Parliament, and the room was brightly lit with torches that were Norse, according to John. The mats on which they sat were Persian, as were the tapestries adorning the walls and draped over the chairs.

Burton took his place on a pedestal at the far end, and other officious-looking members of the Croatoans filed in and took the rest of the seats.

With pomp and flourish, Burton introduced the members of the Indian council as they entered. It was slightly disconcerting to the companions to see men dressed so strangely, and speaking in unusual tongues, introduced as Murthwaite and Kelso and Jiggs and Barnaby. There were more traditional Indian names as well, often attached to European ones, in an unusual but nearly seamless marriage of cultures.

"This is almost a textbook model of cultural democracy," whispered Jack. "I'd love to do an actual case study on how they came to implement it."

"It probably helped things along that they were trapped in the Underneath," Charles whispered back.

"Not necessarily," noted Jack. "They probably just ate anyone who disagreed with them."

Most of the Indian Elders sat cross-legged in the broad chairs along the walls, while two of them (whom Burton had indicated as his aides-de-camp) sat on the pedestal with him—though on noticeably lower seats nearer the back. The first, the man called Murthwaite, wore a broad mustache and thick glasses and was scrupulously taking notes on everything said and done.

"Secretary-general," whispered Charles.

"Indeed," said Bert.

The other aide was a dusky-skinned, full-blooded Indian Burton called Hairy Billy. He was naked from the waist up, save for several strings of beads and elaborate necklaces that lay on his chest, and had taken a curious interest in Aven. Aven, for her part, regarded him coolly but gave no indication that she noticed the unusual attentions.

"But he's bald," said Laura Glue. "Why do you call him 'Hairy Billy'?"

Burton smiled and crouched down in front of the girl. "Once, when he was much younger, he crossed the waters here to a forbidden island, where the children all choose their own names. And although he was rescued later, he insisted we call him by his new name—so we let him keep it. But we took something else."

He gestured at the Indian, who gave a wide, openmouthed smile in return, revealing the fact that he had no tongue. It had been cut out.

Laura Glue shuddered and shrank back from Burton, who grinned more broadly and stood up.

"Discipline," he said to no one in particular. "It's a harsh lesson to learn, but necessary. And lessons we learn through pain are seldom forgotten." This last he said while fingering the deep scars on his cheeks, before he snapped out of his reverie and turned to Bert.

"I suppose these are your apprentices, eh, Caretaker?" said Burton.

"Full Caretakers," Bert replied. "The very ones who defeated the Winter King."

At the mention of their old adversary, Burton's eyes glittered, and he took a renewed interest in the three young men.

"I have heard of you," he said slowly. "The three scholars who changed the course of the world's destiny. I suppose the prophecy would have been fulfilled sooner or later, else what's a prophecy for?"

"Prophecy?" said John.

"For another time," Bert said hurriedly. "What do you want of us, Sir Richard?"

Burton laughed. "The honorific is not necessary. At any rate, it doesn't apply here. The hierarchy is determined first by age, then by strength and ability. And I'm first among equals in both categories. You may address me as 'Elder,' or if you prefer, simply 'Burton.'"

"When we, ah, met, Burton," said Charles, "you introduced yourself as a representative of the Imperial Cartological Society. Is that an organization of the Empire? I'm afraid I never heard of it."

Burton swiveled around. "Indeed. It is of the Empire, and it was sanctioned by Victoria herself.

"After my enlightening but brief apprenticeship as a Caretaker with Dickens, I continued researching the history of the *Geographica* and the Archipelago on my own, and I made a surprising discovery: There had been *many* apprentice Caretakers throughout history who, like myself, were trained, then abandoned."

"For cause," Bert said mildly.

"An opinion," Burton shot back, "of one viewing the situation from a privileged position."

"Well, why were you set aside?" Charles asked.

"Because," replied Burton, "I disagreed with one of the fundamental rules of looking after the *Imaginarium Geographica*—that it, and everything having to do with the Archipelago of Dreams, must be kept secret from the world. Nemo and I had many violent arguments about it, but in the end, he left the decision to Dickens, and I was shut out."

"You don't think knowledge of the Archipelago would be too great a burden for the common man?" asked Jack.

"Knowledge is a responsibility," John said, nodding, "but most people don't know they aren't ready for it until they already have it—and by then, it's too late."

"Really?" said Burton. "John, isn't it? Isn't that how you came by the job? By having it thrust upon you?"

"He was being trained," countered Bert. "He has the temperament. Surely even you can see this. That's much different."

"Is it?" said Burton. "The only difference I see is that I have more faith in mankind's ability to bear the burden. I think they will be able to take it. More, I think it is their right.

"The world and the Archipelago were once one. It was only because of their separation that someone decided the Archipelago should be kept secret—and because of that one foolish choice, the world has been starved of treasures and resources we should have claimed long ago.

"So I took my argument to the queen, who sanctioned a private organization—the Imperial Cartological Society—to begin keeping records, making maps, and funding exploratory ventures that would not be hostage to the Caretakers."

"Private, eh?" said John. "Now who's keeping secrets?"

"A necessary function at the onset," retorted Burton, "else we'd have risked being discovered by those like yourself, and possibly losing our greatest resources."

"What resources?" Bert asked.

"We have our own apprentices in the society," said Burton. "And we wanted them as untainted as possible—or converted to our cause before you could reach them."

"I don't know," said Jack. "I was pretty young when I was recruited into all this."

"We get them younger still," said Burton, "so that if they're approached by one of you, they already believe in a different agenda."

Bert's eyes widened in horror as he realized whom Burton was referring to. "Harry. You mean Harry, and Conan Doyle, don't you?"

Burton laughed again, and it was at once mocking and triumphant. "How do you think the Winter King and his minions were able to track you so quickly?" he said. "They nearly caught you that night in London, didn't they?"

John felt the blood drain from his face. "How could you know about our meeting at the club in London, when you've been trapped down here?"

"I get reports from those who sometimes fall into the Underneath," said Burton, "as well as from books, newspapers, and diaries that come with the occasional ship. I read about the break-in at 221B Baker Street in a copy of the *Illustrated London News* that came down with a dory. And your adventures in the Archipelago became the stuff of legend fast enough, so I put the pieces together.

"And as to the Winter King—how do you think he was able to operate so easily in your world, if not for the help of those who shared his goals?"

"World domination?" John said wryly.

"No," said Burton. "World reunification."

Charles was still processing Burton's revelation. "So Harry Houdini and Arthur Conan Doyle were . . ."

"My apprentices," Burton confirmed. "I recruited them before you and that idiot Verne had the chance to." He gestured brusquely at Bert. "They were barely more than boys, but they had the minds for it—and the will to defy those who would keep this knowledge for themselves."

"So for decades now," said Jack, "there has been, what? A counter-Caretaker organization, run by the British Crown?"

"Victoria may have sanctioned the society, but the seeds of its founding were Elizabethan," Burton said, turning again to Bert. "Surely you know to whom I'm referring?"

Bert's face darkened. "That's apocryphal. There's no evidence of John Dee's betrayal—not that it has any bearing on us now."

Burton crossed his arms and began to pace, as if giving a lecture. "No? Then think on this: How many Caretakers have been formally enlisted throughout history?"

"Formally?" said John. "That's easy enough to guess—most of their signatures are inside the *Geographica*."

"Right," said Burton. "Three every generation or so, for several hundred years. But consider—how many more, like myself, were initiated into the mysteries of the *Geographica* and the Archipelago, only to be cast aside when they were deemed unworthy?"

"If Magwich is any example of one who was cast out," put in Charles, "then I'd say it was pretty justified."

"I can't argue with you there," Burton said. "But not all of those chosen were top-notch either. Cervantes is a good example of that. Can you imagine anything worse than a Caretaker who actually loses the *Geographica*?"

"I'm sure he had other good qualities," Jack said, trying not to look at John, who swallowed hard and blushed. "But setting aside Magwich, isn't it possible there were valid reasons the other, ah, apprentice Caretakers were rejected?"

"No!" Burton shouted. "It wasn't that they were unqualified, but rather because of the same inconsequential difference of opinion that cost *me* the opportunity! They each disagreed with the first fundamental rule of being a Caretaker of the *Imaginarium Geographica*!"

"Secrecy," said Bert.

"Yes!" Burton roared, eyes ablaze. "The damned secrecy! Keeping the wonders and marvels of the Archipelago of Dreams confined to the libraries and offices of a few secular scholars. Even the selection process itself is offensive. The Caretakers are supposed to be among the greatest, most creative thinkers of the world. But for centuries, the position has been reserved mostly for light-skinned Europeans, and even among them, mostly scholars from Oxford. That's part of what I founded the society to change."

He circled his captives, feral, hefting the *Geographica* in his hands. "It was my mandate from Queen Victoria herself," Burton said, "to acquire the *Imaginarium Geographica* and replicate it. To make copies of it, so that any man, woman, or child, whatever race, religion, or creed, could have a copy for themselves!"

Burton lifted the book over his head, and his voice rang throughout the small valley. "I intend to make this, the rarest of books, so common that it can be purchased on any street corner!"

The sound of Burton's proclamation rang and echoed throughout the structure, and to his surprise, the companions merely blinked and smiled.

"Uh," Charles began, "I really don't know how to tell you this, old fellow, because I don't want to dampen your spirits about something that obviously means a great deal to you—but it's been *done*."

Burton paused for a moment, then lowered the book and squinted menacingly at Charles. "What do you mean?"

"I mean," Charles continued, "you're a bit behind the times. An enterprising badger named Tummeler has been publishing copies of the *Geographica* for almost a decade now. There were several copies on the *Indigo Dragon*. It's in its fourth printing now."

"Fifth," said Bert.

"Pardon," said Charles. "Fifth."

The expressions on the faces of the other companions told Burton that Charles spoke the truth.

He looked closely at Bert. "And you agreed with this? You allowed it to be duplicated, for anyone to own?"

"Anyone in the Archipelago, yes," said Bert. "I still stand by my oath as a Caretaker—open knowledge of the Archipelago is too dangerous to be released into the world. Or," he added, "watched over by those who cannot be trusted to guard its secrets."

Burton's response was a look of fury and a brutal, openhanded slap across Bert's jaw.

Aven cried out in anger, and the council of Indian Elders rose to their feet with a clamor of shouts and harsh language. Murthwaite began blowing into a conch shell and calling for order, and Laura Glue crawled underneath one of the unoccupied chairs to hide.

With a gesture, Burton quieted the room, then turned back to the companions. The fury was not gone, but merely subdued.

"I've allowed my own desires to direct the tenor of our discussion," he said in a low, even voice. "We have brought you before the Council of Elders for something more important. And while it's likely that you will be put to death, I give you my word as a gentleman that it will be swift and painless if you answer my question, and answer it honestly.

"What have you done with our children?"

John visibly relaxed. Perhaps the fear and concern behind that question was the reason for their brusque treatment—and this might even give them an opportunity for a nonlethal resolution after all.

"Whatever our differences regarding the *Geographica* and our role as Caretakers," he said, "I think we are more alike than you know. The reason we are here in the Underneath is that we are seeking our own children. The children of the Archipelago— including her son"—he nodded at Aven—"have gone missing. Our mission is the same, Burton."

"Is that so?" Burton sneered. "Then how do you explain *her*?"

He was pointing at Laura Glue, still hiding under the chair. "If your children are missing too, how was she spared?"

"It was Grandfather," Laura Glue said defensively. "He knew how to keep me from the men."

"Which men?" Burton asked, still suspicious.

"The men with the clocks in their bellies," said Laura Glue. "They came to get us, and he sent me away. He put plugs of beeswax in my ears and said they would keep me safe."

"Beeswax?" Burton snorted. "Of what good is beeswax?"

"I suspect that the children were lured away somehow," offered Bert. "The beeswax may have been meant to block out the sound."

"Impossible," Burton said. "We Croatoans keep sentries, and they are well-trained. None of them heard any Clockwork Men— not a toot, whistle, plunk, or boom. We didn't see or hear the children being taken," he continued, "until it was too late—and I heard a single child, my own daughter, Lillith, cry out. When we got to the shore, we saw them running about in the darkness. They were all children, being directed by one they called Stephen.

"We rushed toward them, but it was too late. The children were being taken away in ships—living ships," he added with a snarl and a dark look at Bert, "and in moments they had vanished completely. And there is only one enemy we have had these many years whose army consists of children."

"The Lost Boys aren't an army!" Laura Glue said hotly, forgetting her fear and clambering from under the chair. "We're just children, and that's it and that's all!"

The surprise in Burton's face was surpassed only by the expressions of the Indian Elders. They were genuinely shocked, appalled, and even fearful at the child's mention of the Lost Boys.

Burton gestured to Hairy Billy, who moved with a swiftness that belied his bulk and in a flash had Laura Glue locked in his arms, immobile.

THE SEARCH FOR THE RED DRAGON   525

Burton stepped closer and sniffed at her like an animal, appraising.

"I thought you smelled familiar," he murmured. "You have the stink of the Pan, unless I miss my guess."

"Grandfather doesn't stink!" cried Laura Glue. "Except after dinner sometimes, but he pretends he's asleep."

"Grandfather, eh?" Burton said with a sideways glance at the Elders. "I think we now have something with which to barter our children's release."

"But we just explained to you," said Charles. "We didn't have anything to do with your missing children."

"And yet," said Burton, drawing a finger along the girl's cheek, "we found you on our shores, in possession of a living ship, accompanied by the progeny of our great adversary.

"I think someone is lying to me. And that is a very dangerous thing to do."

He barked a few curt words in a language none of them understood, and with that, the council was ended. Ignoring their protests and exclamations of anger, Burton took Laura Glue by the hand and Aven by the shoulder and led them both out of the lodge.

At Murthwaite's direction, several other burly men joined Hairy Billy in pulling the companions to their feet and marching them briskly out of the building and down a small path that led away from the main settlement.

As they marched, the companions realized that the guards were far enough away that they wouldn't be overheard, and so they immediately began to formulate a whispered plan of action. The first order of business was rescuing Aven and Laura Glue.

"Not to be a wet blanket," said Charles, "but we need the *Geographica*, too. There's too much in it we may yet need if we're to rescue *all* the children."

"I'm not leaving them to Burton," whispered Jack. "Especially Laura Glue. You saw how he looked at her when he realized her lineage."

"Of course," said John, "we won't leave her, or Aven, either. And we *do* need the *Geographica*. But we're outmatched, outnumbered, and have no real idea where we are or where we're to go if we can escape."

"Technicalities," muttered Charles, eyeing the silent guards around them.

"I don't think we *can* leave," Bert said suddenly. "The clues we've been looking for might be right here."

"Can't leave?" John exclaimed. "Good heavens, Bert, why in blazes not?"

"Two reasons," said Bert, his face darkening. "One—Burton referred to the ships that took their children as 'living' ships. So I think I know what's happened to our missing Dragonships, and to what use they're being put."

"Agreed," said Charles. "They're being used by this 'Stephen' rogue to kidnap children."

"That's what makes the second reason even worse," said Bert in a choked voice. "Much worse."

"Why?" asked John.

"Because," Bert said, turning to look at Jack. "The name of Aven's son, the kidnapped prince, my grandson . . .

". . . is Stephen."

CHAPTER FIFTEEN
HΛVEN

THE CROATOANS PUT their captives in a small lodge made of wicker and animal skins, but that nonetheless also had leaded glass windows. It might have seen other uses, but it was obvious to them all that this was now their prison.

The fires outside were allowed to burn down to embers, and eventually the settlement grew quiet as deep night descended on the Underneath.

In the lodge, the companions slept. And sleeping, they dreamed. Not dreams of their recent adventures (and ordeals), but dreams that seemed to be searching for the meaning that lay beneath all that had transpired.

John had no fear.

He had often wondered what it meant to be afraid of something, but in the years since the war, he had gradually come to realize that nothing made him afraid. He had witnessed the deaths of many friends and had seen himself placed in mortal danger. And he had emerged from those experiences changed—for the better, he hoped. But unlike the physical changes borne by those who had been wounded in some way, John's change was invisible; he was no longer afraid of death.

His new attribute showed itself, not through an irrational reck-lessness, but rather in a disregard for any personal price he might pay for a course of action. The best word he could use to describe this awareness was from India: satyagraha. It meant to do anything, give anything, sacrifice anything, to pursue what was right without harming another. And to do it without regard to self.

The only fear John had was for his children.

He had often dreamed of them falling from a great height, and just out of his reach. Falling, like Icarus flown too close to the sun, too far away for a father to save. Sometimes he dreamed that he could almost reach them, and once, when the dream was of his eldest son, he dreamed that he extended his hand and grazed the boy's fingers before he fell.

Thereafter, he determined that if the boy was close enough to touch, he was close enough to hold—and save. And that played constantly in John's thoughts afterward. Chopping firewood for the household stove, he sometimes imagined that a large split log was a child's hand, and he carried it from the woodpile to the hearth using only the tips of his fingers, holding on by the least, most tenuous grasp. He often lost the wood, as the splinters it left reminded him. But he grew stronger; and eventually he could carry a huge log between his fingers as far as he chose to walk, with-out risk of dropping it.

After that, he still dreamed of children falling—but he never again failed to save them.

Jack dreamed about desire. Not so much about the desire *for* things, or desire to *be* something, but about the *meaning* of desire. And in that way, he also dreamed of fear.

As a child, he once dreamed that he could leave behind the dreary life he saw ahead of him, and go to a place where he could be a child forever; and he knew that he desired it. But awake or asleep, he chose to smother his desire.

As he grew older, his dreams manifested themselves in action, and he followed his desire to be a hero and have a life of grand adventure—but his fears were also realized, and those close to him paid a dear price. And again, he put away his desire.

Now he was torn between what he wanted to do and what he knew he must do. And it seemed that the two were often the same; but he could never be sure. And, unable to decide, Jack ceased dreaming and slept fitfully the rest of the night.

Charles also dreamed. And in his dream, he could fly. And it was glorious.

Dawn, or whatever it was that passed for dawn in the Underneath, was still to come when the companions were awakened by someone poking at them in the darkness.

It was Laura Glue.

"C'mon," the girl whispered anxiously. "We've got to leave, now! It's almost morning!"

"What happens in the morning?" said Charles, still groggy from sleep. "And, uh, weren't you a prisoner, like us? How did you get free?"

The girl shook her head, almost frantic. "No time, no time! We have to go now!"

She untied Charles, who then helped her to free the others, and carefully they opened the door of the lodge. Outside, the two

stocky men appointed as guards were lying on the ground in poses
that suggested unconsciousness rather than sleep.

"We bonked them on the noggins," Laura Glue whispered.
"Took 'em right out."

"'We'?" said Jack.

In response Laura Glue pointed to two shadows standing at the
base of one of the bluffs that bracketed the settlement.

It was Aven, who was waving and looking around to make certain they were unobserved, and one other.

"Hairy Billy?" John said suspiciously as they approached. "Isn't
he Burton's toady?"

"Perhaps," said Aven, who was hugging her father. "But once he
was a boy called Joe Clements, who ran away from home to become
a Lost Boy. He was one of the last full-blood Algonquin among
the Croatoans, and they mocked him, calling him 'Injun Joe.' So
he went someplace where he could choose a new name—his own
name. With us."

"How do you know we can trust him?" asked Charles.

In answer, Hairy Billy pushed aside his ornate necklaces and
showed them a plain leather cord, looped through a silver thimble
identical to Laura Glue's.

The massive barrel-chested Indian turned and pulled something from a bramble bush that he handed to John. It was the
Imaginarium Geographica.

John started to stammer a thank-you, but Hairy Billy merely
smiled his openmouthed, grotesquely tongueless smile, then turned
and motioned for them all to follow.

Jack grinned. "Burton thought he was so clever with his secret society and covert agents," he said. "He didn't realize it works both ways."

In silence they followed the Indian through the underbrush of the pine forest for almost a quarter of an hour before finally emerging into a broad clearing. There ahead of them was the unmistakable rise of another island, and in between, nothing but a mile or so of moist sand. In the distance was a sound of thunder, which grew louder with each passing second.

"That's not thunder," Laura Glue said when she realized they were scanning the sky for storm clouds. "We have to hurry, please!"

Hairy Billy made several motions with his hands, indicating that he could go no farther with them, then squeezed Aven's shoulder briefly and disappeared into the trees.

Back in the direction from which they'd come, there arose a great hue and cry, and a roaring of fury that could only have come from Burton.

"Our absence has been noted," said Bert. "We'd best hurry along."

"To what end?" said John, scanning the expanse ahead of them. "They'll be on us in a few minutes, and then we'll be back where we started—only this time, there'll be no pacifying Burton."

"Listen to her!" cried Aven, grabbing Laura with one hand and Bert with the other. "Just follow us and try to keep up!"

With that the three took off at a dead run across the sand. John, Jack, and Charles had little choice but to follow.

It was when the companions were almost halfway across the expanse of sand that their pursuers burst out of the forest and onto the sand. Turning to gauge their pursuit, the Caretakers suddenly realized what the increasingly loud sound was.

It was not thunder. It was the incoming tide. And it was rushing across the sand with terrifying speed.

"Step in time, gentlemen," John yelled as he picked up his pace. Up ahead, Aven, Laura Glue, and Bert had nearly reached the nearby high ground, which, in just a few moments, would be an island.

The sound of the water was so deafening now that they could no longer hear the cries of their pursuers, but a stolen glance back told them that a number of Croatoans had indeed followed them out onto the sand.

The force of the water was pushing a wall of air before it that nearly knocked them off of their feet, and the spray from the foam had already soaked them to the skin before they reached the cluster of rocks where the other three were waiting anxiously.

John reached the rocks first, then Jack, and finally, the water crashing down at his heels, Charles. Just inches away, a flood of biblical proportions filled the expanse between them and Croatoan Island and as far as the eye could see.

The noise it brought was a sound of ragged beauty. The harmonies of a wall of water falling into a narrow space speak of chaos, and strength, and inevitability, and they are beautiful in their terrible splendor.

The Croatoans foolish enough to pursue them didn't even have time to scream before being swept away, while on the opposite shore, Burton and the rest of their pursuers had been completely cut off by the thundering waves.

"Mustn't we keep running?" Charles said to the others, who were watching the roiling waters rush by. "It's going to settle in a few minutes, and they'll just be after us again."

Laura Glue giggled, shook her head, and pointed.

Out in the water was one of the Croatoans, who'd been identified at the council as Jinty. He was nearly seven feet tall, and his great stride had allowed him to far outpace the others, trapping him in the onrushing tide. But instead of pushing forward, he seemed to be frantically trying to get back to the dry shore where Burton and the rest had stopped.

He was mere yards from safety when a great beast, which resembled a porpoise the size of a London bus, snatched him between jaws filled with needlelike teeth.

"That's jus' one of the *little* ones," said Laura Glue. "Until the tide goes out again tonight, no one's going to be chasing us."

In a flash the girl's expression shifted from triumph to one of misery. "Oh, no!" she exclaimed. "I've lost my flower!"

Jack placed a comforting hand on her shoulder. "It's all right, Laura Glue. We don't need it anymore—not while we have you. You saved us again, didn't you?"

He bent down and kissed her lightly on the cheek. "That, my dear girl, was a kiss," he said.

Laura Glue blushed. "Jamie's kisses are prettier to look at," she said, smiling, "but that was okay too, f'r a Longbeard."

The companions moved farther along the shoreline and began to explore the island the girl had led them to. It was not dissimilar to Croatoan Island, but it seemed . . . *older*. More ancient. The trees were more deciduous than evergreen, and they radiated a scent of antiquity, as if they'd always been there. As if they'd always *be* there.

But of all their reactions to this new topography, Aven's was the most profound. In direct contrast to their surroundings, she actually seemed . . . *younger*.

And it was then that her father realized where they were.

"This is it," Bert said, "isn't it? This is Jamie and Peter's Nether Land."

"I think so," said Aven, looking at Laura Glue, who was happily bobbing her head in agreement. "It feels right. I can't say for certain until we've gone farther inland."

"This way!" Laura Glue exclaimed, grabbing Aven and Jack by the hands. "Follow me! I know the way!"

With one last look across to the island where shortly before they'd been held as prisoners, the companions stepped into the broadleaf forest and disappeared into the Nether Land.

Laura Glue marched them through increasingly dense foliage, often taking pathways that seemed to the others to be illogically convoluted. But she insisted that the twists and turns and switchbacks were necessary, and Aven generally agreed.

"The Lost Boys have been at war with the Indians for a long time," Aven told the others. "Booby-trapping the forest is one way to fend off any attacks—or at least, slow them down long enough to warn us that enemies are coming."

"What kind of booby traps?" Charles said, craning his head around nervously. "And are they effective?"

"Effective enough," replied Aven. "Peter gave the job to two brothers, the Skelton boys, and just the initial tests were enough to keep the rest of us from tromping around out here without checking on where they put the traps."

"What happened during the tests?" asked Jack.

"That's when we gived the Skelton boys their nicknames," Laura Glue put in. "Stumpy and One-Eye."

"Sorry I asked," said Jack.

✦ ✦ ✦

It took most of the day, or the day's equivalent in the Underneath, for the companions to make their way through the forest. Occasionally they heard the sounds of birds, but they neither saw nor heard any other creatures. But every so often, they could feel something watching. Bert, John, and Charles exchanged concerned glances, but Aven, Jack, and Laura Glue seemed not to notice. Aven in particular grew more and more animated as the trees began to thin and the terrain grew more hillpocked.

"Look!" she exclaimed, jumping across a large boulder at the base of a huge oak. "It's my house! Father, look!"

There amidst the tangle of roots was a child-size set of furniture made of sticks woven together with reeds and sapling strips. There were remnants of what might have been a tea set scattered among the leaves and forest debris, and underneath the table she found a tarnished, twisted silver spoon.

"This is where I used to play, when I came here with Jamie!" she said excitedly. "He helped me build the furniture, and we had a set of spoons he'd brought with him from London. We were the envy of all the Lost Boys, having real spoons for tea."

"Fascinating," said Charles.

"There are imaginary houses and tearooms like this one set up all throughout the hills," Aven went on. "We're close now. We're very close."

With that, she carefully placed the spoon on the woodland table and turned to the others. "Follow us," she said, taking Laura Glue's hand once more. "We know the way from here—and there aren't any more traps.

"I've come home."

Laura Glue and Aven took off at a quick clip, and the men had to lengthen their strides just to keep them in sight. The forest continued to thin, with the mighty oaks giving way to slighter, paler aspens and stout, bushy cedars.

Eventually the trees stopped altogether, and there was nothing ahead but a high rise of colored sand. Aven and Laura Glue were atop it and waving at the companions to join them.

"There," said Laura Glue, pointing to the near horizon. "That's our city."

From a distance, what Laura Glue called a "city" looked like a fortress that fragmented into a cluster of volcanic flumes, rising high above multicolored but otherwise unimpressive dunes of sand and stone.

"Uh, is it behind the sand?" asked Charles.

"It's no use just looking for our houses," said Laura Glue. "You won't see them. Not yet, anyways."

"Why not?" asked John.

"Well," Laura Glue replied, "it's because here, in the Nether Land, our houses are the exact opposite of your houses in Angle Land. There you can see the houses in the day, but not when it gets dark. But here it's exactly the opposite. Our houses are the color of night, so you can't see them in the daytime, only at night."

"You mean your houses are black?" Charles asked.

Laura Glue scowled. "Of course not! Night isn't *black*, it's just *dark*. There's a difference, you know."

"Sorry," said Charles.

"The things that seem dull in the daytime are magic at night," said Laura Glue. "And that's where we live—in the magic houses."

"It is getting toward nightfall again," Bert observed, scanning the sky. "Will we see them soon?"

"Yes," said Aven, who was practically glowing with joy. "Just wait. And watch."

The light of the Underneath began to fade into slumbering pastels; and as it did, the city of the Lost Boys began to awaken.

It was indistinct at first: small pinpoints of light here and there. But as the sky darkened, the lights became brighter and more colorful. The warmth of lanterns sprang up in cultivated rows, and sparkling lights that moved with life spun in circular angles, as if someone had electrified giant spiderwebs and draped them over the stone towers.

As the lights appeared, the companions could see that it wasn't a desert at all, but an oasis filled with magic. There were pools of water reflecting the glittering homes above, and bridges connecting the towers that moments before had seemed only a mirage, a trick of the light.

It was everything a magic city was supposed to be. And it could only have been created by children, for there was no board or brick of it that would have been imagined by an adult—and when adults saw it, it was not with grown-up eyes, but with the eyes of the children they had once been.

"Well of course you can see it!" Laura Glue said indignantly in response to the exclamations of the others. "I told you it was here!

"We call it Haven."

At the edges of the city, set within broad stone walls, was a series of grates that were nearly covered over with WARNING and KEEP OUT! signs. Laura Glue ignored them all and marched straight to a grate with a sign that read SPEAKE THE PASSWORDS OR BE KILT.

Charles leaned toward the grate. "Alakazam!" he said loudly, to no effect.

"Nice try," offered John.

"Do you know the passwords?" Jack asked Laura Glue.

"Of course I do!" she exclaimed. "You all just got me discombobulated, is all."

The girl tapped her forehead for a moment and pursed her lips. Then she leaned in close to the grate and began to call out the secret words—and was answered in turn by the voice of a gatekeeper somewhere within.

"Apple core!"

"Baltimore!"

"Who's your friend?"

"Me!"

There was a gasp and a giggle, then the sound of a creaking, rusty mechanism being turned. Slowly the grate swung inward, and a light appeared in the tunnel below. A puckish face appeared, framed by an explosion of ribboned, light brown pigtails that stuck out in every direction.

"Laura Glue?" the girl with the lamp said, hesitant. "Is that be you, Laura my Glue?"

"Sadie!" Laura Glue exclaimed joyfully, running forward. "Sadie Pepperpot, it is be me! I be coming home, neh?"

"Neh," replied the girl, giving the evil eye to the rest of the group. "What you bring with you? You bring Longbeards to the city?"

Laura Glue shook her head. "Not Longbeards. Caretakers, like Jamie. We got to take them in, now!"

Still skeptical, the girl turned and trotted off down the tunnel. Laura Glue followed, and Aven went right behind her. The companions brought up the rear, and in a few moments the tunnel gave way to an opening of brick, which came up underneath a large stone fountain of Pegasus.

The fountain was in the center of a courtyard, and there, amidst a dozen children running about, a regal, thin-framed man with curly brown hair and a hawkish nose stood and spread his arms in greeting.

Laura Glue let out a shriek of joy and ran to the man, leaping into his arms.

"Uncle Daedalus!" she cried out. "I did it! I flew! I flew all the way to the Summer Country, and then I flew all the way back!

"And I brung the Caretakers," she added, "even though they're not Jamie."

"You did wonderfully, my little Laura Glue," said the man, hugging her tightly, then lowering her to the ground. "Why don't you see if there's room for a few guests at dinner, neh?"

Still cheshiring from ear to ear, Laura Glue ran off and joined another group of children. Additional shrieks indicated that her greetings were continuing. The man she called Daedalus shook hands with the companions as Bert introduced all of them one by one. When Daedalus got to Aven, he smiled and then kissed her on the forehead.

"My word," said Charles. "I don't think I've ever seen her blush before."

"You have been missed," Daedalus said to her. "It brings me joy to see you again, even though the circumstances be grim."

Before he could elaborate, Laura Glue came rushing back,

trailing a group of children the likes of which none of them had ever seen. There was a flurry of introductions as Laura Glue rattled off the names of her friends for John, Jack, Charles, and Bert. But again, it was Aven they were focused on, and they looked at her with something akin to awe.

"Is it true?" asked a lanky, towheaded boy called Fred the Goat, who had been caught midmeal and talked with his mouth full. "Are you really a Mother?"

"I am," said Aven. "That's why I've come back. We're searching for my son."

"Back?" asked the girl Laura Glue called Meggie Tree-and-Leaf, who in fact resembled a bramble bush. "When were you here before?"

"Don't you remember her?" exclaimed Laura Glue. "This is Poppy! She's come back to us at last!"

Fred the Goat's mouth dropped open and a half-chewed carrot fell out. "Poppy Longbottom? F'r reals?"

"Poppy Longbottom?" said John. "Hah! Did you really choose that yourself?"

"Oh, shut up," Aven said over her shoulder. She turned back to Fred the Goat. "Yes, I'm Poppy. At least I used to be. But you can call me Aven now."

"Hmm," mused the girl named Sadie Pepperpot, who had opened the grate to admit them. "Aven. That's a good Mother name."

"I don't believe her," said a small boy with a shock of black hair that stuck straight up from his head. "I think she's just another Longbeard, except, you know, without the beard."

"I'll have you know, Pelvis Parsley," Aven said, bending low to look at him an inch from his nose, "I am indeed Poppy Long-bottom, and I can prove it."

She reached inside her blouse and pulled something out of a pocket hidden in the lining. She held her hand in front of Pelvis Parsley's face, then slowly opened it.

Resting on her palm was a small silver thimble.

Pelvis Parsley's eyes saucered. "Holy socks!" he exclaimed. "You have a kiss from Jamie? Then you really *must* be Poppy!"

With that the boy let out a war whoop and began dancing around the room, pulling Aven along by the hand. The other children picked up the yell, and soon the din was overwhelming.

"You know," Jack said to Daedalus over the clamor, "Laura Glue was quite put out if we called her by less than her full name—but it doesn't seem to bother anyone else if she just calls them 'Poppy' or 'Sadie.'"

Daedalus grinned. "At one point in time, there were no less than five Lauras among the Lost Boys. And, as Laura Glue was the smallest of them, she clung very tightly to anything that would make her distinctive. In particular, her name."

"Hah." Jack laughed. "There's plenty more than just her name that sets *that* girl apart from the crowd."

"Indeed," said Daedalus.

The noise continued as everyone took their places along several long tables laden with dishes and plates—all of which were empty.

"Ah, is the food still being prepared?" asked Charles. "Or have you already finished eating?"

"Finished?" said Fred the Goat. "We barely got started. I'm only two courses in."

"How many courses are there?" asked John.

"Eleventy-seven," replied Fred. "Unless you count dessert. Then there's more."

"Good heavens!" Jack exclaimed. "That's a lot of courses. Who prepares it all?"

Laura Glue laughed. "We all do, gravy-head."

"You uses your 'magination, Longbeard," said Sadie Pepperpot. "That's what makes the world interesting, you know."

"I suppose you'd have to," noted Jack, "to have eleventy-seven courses."

"It all sounds grand to me," said John, "as long as I don't have to clean up afterward."

"That's the best part about an imaginary feast," explained Laura Glue. "You can simply imagine that all the mess that's left over gets cleaned up by an imaginary Feast Beast, and as soon as you do, it's done."

"Aw, they're just Longbeards," Pelvis scoffed. "I bet they don't even know how to use their 'maginations."

Bert leaned close to the shock-headed boy and wiggled his nose. "That's where you'd be mistaken, my boy," he said. "If imagination is your cook, then these three fellows will make the greatest feast the Lost Boys have ever seen."

And with that cue, John, Jack, and Charles smiled and began to think of the most extraordinary foods they could dream of.

And even Pelvis Parsley's usual sour expression could not hold back the shrieks of delight he uttered when the first incredible dishes began to appear on the tables.

CHAPTER SIXTEEN
ECHO'S WELL

EVEN IF IT had not been the most exceptional dinner they had ever attended, which it was, the companions would have stayed through to the end just to watch the children use their own imaginations to conjure up the Feast Beasts to clean up the leftovers. The creatures looked like large, furry rats, with great dark orbs for eyes and massive claws that were both threatening and delicate.

The Feast Beasts devoured all the leftover food, then gathered up all the dirty plates and utensils—and ate those as well before scampering away into one of the buildings.

Fred the Goat let out a huge belch and smacked his lips. "Mmm," he said contentedly. "Tasted almost as good coming out as it did going in."

John frowned in distaste, but Charles merely laughed, and Jack let out a belch of his own.

Sadie Pepperpot and Laura Glue implored Aven to go with them to see their garden, and the rest of the Lost Boys began playing a taglike game they called Monster and the Frogs while Bert and the three Caretakers retired to Daedalus's workshop to discuss the recent events that had brought them together.

The workshop was what might have been created if Thomas

Edison had been allowed to run loose in the British Museum with unlimited resources and a penchant for modernizing old artifacts. There were electrical generators and motors and steam engines wound in and around marble statues, stacks of parchment, and pieces of Roman chariots. Bronze Age armor lay in piles next to archaic telescopes and what appeared to be projection equipment, and in each corner of the expansive room was a brick oven over which hung bubbling cauldrons.

The inventor indicated that the companions should sit in several Greek chairs set near the center of the workshop, while he moved from cauldron to cauldron, inspecting the experiments that were evidently still in progress.

"Laura Glue told us you were Icarus's brother," said John. "Pardon my asking, but how is that possible?"

"The man you know as Daedalus had two sons," the inventor replied. "Icarus and Iapyx. As Caretakers, you are evidently well educated enough to know what befell Icarus, and if any of you are fathers, you can imagine the impact that Icarus's death had upon him.

"My father was one of the great inventors of history. He developed the art of carpentry, and with it invented the saw, ax, plumb line, drill, and even glue. Although," he added ruefully, "the methods of using wax as a fixative turned out to be less successful than he'd hoped."

"He was also a very talented artist, wasn't he?" asked Jack. "Many sculpted wooden figures that have been found throughout Europe have been attributed to Daedalus—it's even said that his works have a touch of the divine."

Daedalus the Younger nodded. "It's true, they did. And to some degree, he absorbed that from one of his teachers—a legendary builder named Deucalion."

"Our shipbuilder friend," Charles whispered to John.

"My father's problem," the inventor continued, "was pride. Daedalus was so proud of his achievements that he could not bear the idea of a rival—any rival.

"His own nephew had been placed under his charge to be taught the mechanical arts, and he promptly developed inventions of his own that humiliated my father.

"Daedalus was so envious of his nephew's accomplishments that when an opportunity arose, he *murdered* my cousin. And for this crime, my father was tried and punished."

"How was the boy killed?" asked Jack.

"Father pushed him from the top of a high tower," said Daedalus. "And as punishment, he was imprisoned there forever, never again to leave."

Imprisoned? In a tower? At this, John and Charles exchanged a startled glance, but Bert gave no indication that it was significant, and Jack was too involved in Daedalus's story to notice.

"And your name?" said Jack.

"I'd been the Healer for the Argonauts, then followed them to the Trojan conflict," said Daedalus. "I took the name as a way of honoring my father's memory, and then chose to continue his work as well."

"And improved upon his designs," Jack said, "if Laura Glue's wings are any indication."

"Thank you," said Daedalus, smiling. "I've had time to get them just so."

"How did you end up here in the Underneath?" asked John. "Or in the Archipelago at all, for that matter? We're a long way from Troy."

"A long way *now*," replied Daedalus, stirring one of the cauldrons. "But not *then*.

"In those days, the world was more unified. It was easier to travel to all the lands that exist. Many of the places that might be considered mythological by your world's modern standards actually exist—they just take longer to get to than they once did."

Daedalus finished tending to his experiments and took a seat alongside the companions, who proceeded to relate to him all that had happened to them since Laura Glue's arrival in Oxford. The inventor listened attentively, stopping them only briefly now and again to ask a question or clarify a point. And when they had finished, he steepled his fingers under his nose and leaned back heavily.

"I was not here when the children were taken," he said slowly, "so I cannot speak to the exact circumstances of their abduction. When I returned, Peter was also gone, and those few dozen children who had not been taken filled in bits and pieces, but, as children are wont to do, they did so imprecisely. So I can only speculate.

"As to the message Peter sent, I believe it was meant to tell Jamie—yourselves—who it was who was taking the children."

"You know?" exclaimed John.

"I can guess," said Daedalus. "In your world, 'The Crusade has begun' might refer to any number of events. But here in the Archipelago, particularly in the older parts, such as the Drowned Lands or the Underneath, the word 'Crusade' has only ever referred to one great journey—the original voyage of Jason and the Argonauts."

"How does that help us?" asked Jack. "Peter wasn't referring to that same Crusade, was he?"

Daedalus shook his head. "Doubtful, especially after what you found in the Library of Alexandria. No, I think he was referring to something entirely new."

The inventor thought for a minute more, then jumped from his chair and strode to one of the bookshelves set against the walls. He scanned the titles, then chose a large volume whose covers were of carved slate. The front was engraved with the Greek letter *alpha*.

Daedalus turned several of the pages, then looked up at the companions.

"Do any of you know the origin of the name 'Lost Boys'?" he asked.

Bert frowned. "It—it's never come up. I always assumed it was simply a term of convenience, used for all the children in Barrie's stories, based on the orphans Peter had taken in."

John shook his head. "It has to be far older than that. Chamenos Liber, remember? Lost Boys. Perhaps the name came from the islands?"

"No," said Daedalus. "The islands that guard the Underneath were named because of who came here in the beginning, not the other way around.

"Jason was a great hero, in many ways the archetype for all who followed after. He had a remarkable charisma and a fierce intelligence, and he managed to draw together heroes with more power, authority, and experience than himself. He traversed the world on extraordinary quests and saw his legend raised to immortality within his own lifetime. And that was his downfall.

"He let it go to his head. He saw himself as invulnerable,

invincible. There was nothing that Jason could not do, especially with the support of his Argonauts—the demigod Heracles, the musician Orpheus, even the great Theseus himself among them. And when Jason had achieved his greatest victory and captured the Golden Fleece of Colchis, he destroyed it all by betraying his own wife, Medea, without whom he would have failed."

"Yes," said Jack, "after which, according to legend, she slew his sons in revenge."

"According to *legend*," said Daedalus, tapping the book, "but not according to *history*. True history, which spun out *here*, in the Underneath."

Daedalus handed the book to John. "Can you read Ancient Greek?" he asked.

"Well enough," answered John, taking the book, "as long as it isn't mixed up with Latin."

He scanned the page the inventor had indicated, then the next, and the next. "Amazing," he muttered under his breath. He looked up at Daedalus. "I think I see what you mean."

"What is it, John?" said Jack.

"According to this book," explained John, "Medea never killed Jason's sons, but brought them to these islands in exile. They were left to fend for themselves and became very bitter—they blamed their father for being abandoned here—so they discarded their Greek names and chose new names for themselves."

"What did they choose?" asked Charles.

"You'll never believe it," said John. "They called themselves Hugh the Iron and William the Pig."

"Those are the men in Bacon's History!" Jack exclaimed. "The ones who stole the *Red Dragon*!"

"To them, they weren't stealing," said Bert, "but reclaiming their birthright."

"Just so," said Daedalus. "The sons of Jason and Medea are the original Lost Boys."

"That must be the right deduction," Bert said sadly. "William and Hugh must be the ones who have taken the children and caused all the destruction."

"They would have known the *Red Dragon* was once the *Argo*," reasoned Charles, "and they did tell Bacon they were claiming their inheritance."

"They also said to give a message to Peter and Jamie," said John. "At least William did. So perhaps he believed that only they would be able to understand the clue and help. What can they possibly have been thinking? How could they be on a crusade of vengeance while at the same time be sabotaging their own efforts by trying to do the right thing?"

"That's adolescents for you," said Charles.

"Satyagraha," John murmured.

"It's the basic conflict between the two halves of men's souls," said Jack, "but Charles is right. There's no way to determine what they were planning."

"You'd have to put yourselves in their sandals," said Daedalus. "Imagine yourself to be them. Imagine you have been abandoned, and you will never grow old—but you will never have anything more, because you are trapped, and all paths to the future are seemingly closed to you. What would you choose? How would you act, if the means for retribution were placed within your grasp?"

"How can I make a determination like that, when I'll never be faced with the same circumstance?" said John. "I *have* grown old. I *have* begun a family. I can guess what they have endured, but the recollections of my youth will be imperfect. So there's no way for me to know how I might have chosen, when I'm already on a path I can't retrace."

"Ah," said Daedalus. "But what if you *can?*"

Daedalus led the companions out of his workshop and down a cobbled path between the gabled towers to a brightly lit clearing where Sadie Pepperpot and Laura Glue had their garden.

There were rows of carrots and lettuce, clumsily arranged between clusters of beets, corn, and some leafy vegetables that none of them could readily identify. Laura Glue was excitedly leading Aven around from cluster to cluster and waved happily when she saw the companions approaching.

"Jack! Charles! John!" she called. "You must see my snozzberries! They're almost ready to harvest!"

"Snozzberries?" Charles said behind his hand.

"Third dessert course," Daedalus replied.

"Ah. Lovely," said Charles. "Show us the snozzberries, my dear girl."

"I'm sorry I left," said Aven. "I got caught up in a lot of old feelings. It's a very comforting place for me."

"No need to apologize," said Daedalus, "but you should come with us now. We're going to the Well."

The inventor didn't explain, but walked past the gardens and into a small orchard that stood on a grassy knoll. The children followed, circling the grown-ups like a whirlwind of paper cranes, and took turns interrupting one another in their haste to explain that the orchard was the reason Haven was built.

"This is Raleigh's Orchard," said Laura Glue. "It was planted when the Indian colony first came here to the Underneath. . . ."

"But there was an argument with the people on some of the other islands," added Sadie Pepperpot.

"And so the Indians moved to the other island," said Fred the Goat, "and we been at war with them ever since."

"The apples look very robust," Charles noted, tracing one of the heavy fruits with a finger. "Do you mind if we have a few?"

"The apples are for *everyone*," replied Laura Glue. "Friend and enemy alike. But you must never, *ever*, eat the seeds."

"What happens if you eat the seeds?" asked Jack.

Pelvis Parsley pointed up at the tree directly adjacent to them, and the companions realized that the apple tree . . .

. . . had a *face*.

Looking more closely, they could make out the shape of a human torso, and arms that had grown into branches. And it seemed as if the tree was observing them *back*.

"He's called Johnny Appletree," said Laura Glue. "A long time ago, he traveled across distant lands planting seeds, and apple orchards sprang up wherever he went. Then he got on a ship going to Angle Land, but it never arrived. Instead it came here—and he found out that apples are apples everywhere, but in the Nether Land, you mustn't ever eat the seeds."

"If it's all the same," said Charles, "I think I'd like apples from a different tree. It feels a little too much like taking someone's ear to eat fruit from a tree with a name."

"Why was there war with the Indians over the orchard?" John

asked. "Couldn't they plant trees of their own on Croatoan Island?"

"They didn't go to war over the apples," said Daedalus. "They went to war over Echo's Well."

The children led the companions down the hill from Johnny Appletree to a pile of stones that sat in a circle of grass.

They gathered around the stones, which were stacked several feet above their heads, and John realized that the stones forming the base were not actually stacked, but rose up out of the earth itself.

On one side was a broad opening, which dropped away into a deep hole.

"A well," John observed.

"Echo's Well," said Daedalus. "Look into it, but do not speak."

Hesitantly, John leaned over the opening and peered down. There in the darkness about a dozen feet below, a perfect reflection looked back at him. He leaned back and stepped aside so Jack and Charles could do the same—and he noted that Bert made no move toward the well at all, even for a peek.

"It is an old magic, from a time when magic was new, science was old, and vanity was all," Daedalus said, in a manner that was exceedingly reverent. "When the proper words are spoken into the well, it may allow you to become what you truly desire to be.

"If it is your wish to never age, you need merely speak into the well, and youth is restored. If it is your wish to become something other than what you believe yourself to be, then you may still get your wish—but may be no happier for it.

"So," Daedalus concluded, "this is your choice. To achieve your objectives at this critical time, to save those you have come here to save, you have to understand those who have come before. And to do that, you must *become* those whom you have been before. You must become boys who never grew up."

"Does it really work?" Jack asked.

"Yes," said Aven, "it does. I've done it myself."

"Yes, you have, Poppy," Daedalus confirmed. "Are you asking to do so once more?"

Aven paused, then reluctantly shook her head. "I . . . can't. I must admit, I'm tempted, but I think when we find my son, it needs to be his mother he sees, not another child."

"And you, Far Traveler?" Daedalus said to Bert.

Surprisingly, Bert not only declined, but took a step backward, away from the Well's opening.

"I don't know," John replied, noting Bert's reaction. "This has gone far afield of what I was willing to do."

"But think, John," said Jack. "Understanding William and Hugh's choices, and how Peter interpreted their actions, may be the key to everything going on. How can we decline, if this is the only way?"

"I'll do it," Charles declared, to the others' surprise. "I don't think I'd mind spending a little time as a child again. Just for the energy, mind you."

Bert shifted his eyes to look at Daedalus, but the latter took no notice. His attention was completely focused on the three young Caretakers.

Charles began to move closer, then halted. He took another step forward—and then two steps back.

"I—I don't think I can do this, after all," he said. "To be completely forthright about it, I'm a bit worried that what I'll become isn't what any of us expect."

"That's the talk of a lunatic," Jack exclaimed. "You are who you are. What else could you be?"

"I . . . I'm not really an Oxford man," Charles confessed. His level of distress at admitting this was evident by the nervous tapping of his fingers against his belt. "Not by any legitimate reckoning, that is."

Jack laughed. "That's nonsense, Charles. Of course you're an Oxford man. What are you playing at?"

Charles let out a sigh and sat down on a stump a few paces away from the Well. "I'm afraid all the playacting was done before . . . and when I thought better of it, it was too late."

"But when we met in London those years ago, you said you *were* from Oxford," protested John.

"No," Charles replied. "I said I was employed at the Oxford University *Press*, and that fool inspector Clowes made the mistake of thinking that meant I was at Oxford University. And considering we were being questioned about a murder, I wasn't of a mind to correct him.

"Actually," Charles continued ruefully, "I attended University College in London for a few years, and that's it and that's all. I've been to Oxford a number of times, certainly, enough to know the schools and the city. But a lot of common people—like the inspector—are oblivious to the difference between the press and the university. So I don't often clarify it for them."

"But then why not tell us afterward?" asked Jack.

"Because the both of you were Oxford men," admitted Charles. "And face it, Jack—I'm older than both of you. More so now than then, it seems. I'm a good writer, I think . . . but my true skills lie in editing and publishing. And I could tell very quickly the caliber of men you both promised to be. And . . . and I wanted you to respect me, Jack."

"Charles," said John. "I think you've already earned our respect, a long time ago. Really—don't give it another thought."

"There's just one thing," Charles added. "Please don't tell Tummeler."

Jack and John both grinned and clapped their friend on the back. "Don't worry," said Jack. "I don't believe Tummeler will ever think any less of you, as long as you don't take up a post at Cambridge, that is."

"So," said Daedalus. "You have made your choice."

"I'm afraid so," said Charles. "It's just not for me."

The inventor turned to John. "And you, Caveo Principia? Will you speak into Echo's Well?"

John shook his head. "One day, perhaps, I might feel the need to recapture my childhood. But today is not that day. Thank you, no."

Daedalus laughed. "The Well does not steal the years from you. Can you ever recall a time where your faculties were not fully engaged, where every experience of your life did not form a chain with all of the rest? This is merely another link in the chain—but it is a link forged long ago, and it will shape your current perceptions accordingly.

"You will remain yourself, however you appear to us."

"I'll do it."

It was Jack who had spoken.

"It makes sense. I'm the least encumbered of any of us. I have neither a spouse nor children. If something goes awry, at worst I'll have to wait out a few years to retake the exams at Oxford. I can do this."

Daedalus bowed and stepped back from the Well.

Jack stepped forward, then leaned in and looked down.

There was no source of light in Echo's Well, but like the sky of the Underneath, it glowed faintly with warmth. There was water not far below the rim, and Jack could see a reflection on the surface. It was his face—but it wasn't his reflection.

It was an image he hadn't seen in decades. It was himself, when he was a child. And so he said the only thing that made sense.

"Hello, Jacks. It's good to see you."

John and Charles gasped in surprise as their friend began to shift and change while they watched.

Jack was still there; he hadn't moved. But there was less of him. It was as if the winds of childhood had swirled around him and drawn off some of his substance.

His face was Jack's face, but the north wind took away the leanness and sharp angles, leaving new, softer geometries in its wake.

His body was still Jack's body, but the south wind had taken length, and breadth.

His hands were still Jack's hands, but the east wind made them smaller and more eager, as they once had been.

His voice was still Jack's voice, but the west wind took his words and transformed them into memories, and when he spoke, John and Charles felt a shiver pass through them and felt younger themselves for having heard him:

"Olly Olly Oxen-Free!"

PART FIVE

THE KING OF TEARS
AND THE
QUEEN OF SORROWS

CHAPTER SEVENTEEN
THE TUNESMITHS

THE OLD MAN'S face was ashen. His captor had not returned to the cave, nor had the children who were dressed in the animal skins. He hadn't been tortured or beaten—again, anyway—but nevertheless, he was dying.

To live, a man must have food, water, air, and shelter. Everyone knew that. But not everyone knew—or if they knew, believed—that it was also necessary to have spirit.

One's spirit can be gone for a time, to no ill effect. And it was possible for a man to reject his own spirit, although the ties are never completely broken. But if a spirit leaves of its own accord, then the man it belongs to is weakened. And the old man's spirit had already been gone for too long.

"It's no use," the woman in the mirror said. "No one is coming."

"Have faith, Medea," the old man pleaded. "It isn't over till it's over."

The woman in the mirror rolled her eyes. "Child's logic, Peter."

"That's the best kind," he replied weakly. "It allows you to believe what you need to believe despite all evidence to the contrary. Children do that all the time, and it works more often than you'd think."

"Not often enough, or else you wouldn't be here."

He chuckled. "Thus speaks the cynicism of adulthood. And you wonder why I gave it all up."

"Oh yes," she said, mocking. "That explains your gray hair."

"No," the old man replied. "I just finally found my balance. I have the advantages of being a Longbeard, but I didn't have to give up my child's point of view. That's what allows me to have hope."

The reflection in the mirror scoffed. "Your child's logic sounds a lot like faith to me."

At that he smiled. "Sure. What's the difference?"

"A belief in things not seen makes no sense, Peter."

"And yet," he replied, "a man with no shadow and a woman who exists only as a reflection in a mirror are being held captive by a creature who exists mostly as a disembodied voice. I wouldn't have believed in any of that, either. But it's happened."

"If you'd behaved more like an adult instead of living as a child, perhaps it wouldn't have, Peter. If you'd acted more like a father—"

"That's the only father I knew," said the old man, indicating the head in the back of the cave, "and while his example was imperfect, he was here when I needed him to be, and he gave me the knowledge I needed to survive. And he never left me alone, Medea. Can you say the same about your own children?"

But there was no reply. The mirror had already gone dark, and the cave lapsed into silence once more.

The only problem, John surmised, with depending on the judgment of a child to decide a course of action that would determine the fate of two worlds was that children, as a general rule, didn't care about the fate of the world.

They cared about running, as fast as they could run; they cared about climbing apple trees; they cared about telling terrible jokes, and laughing anyway. They cared about being children. Which was as it should be—except when, as John kept trying to point out, the fate of two worlds actually did depend on the judgment of a child. All of which he would have explained to Jack, if he could just manage to talk the professor-turned-boy down from Johnny Appletree.

"You are a teacher, aren't you, John?" said Charles. "Don't you have experience talking to children?"

"I teach college, not finishing school," said John. "Anyway, we've both got children, haven't we? This shouldn't be quite so hard."

Daedalus laughed. "I never said it would be easy."

John turned to Aven. "You have a son. Can't you get Jack to focus for five minutes so we can sort this out?"

"It's been some time since I could talk to my son as a mother talks to a child," said Aven.

"Why is that?" asked John.

"It happened very early on," Aven explained. "My boy decided he was a man who would one day be king, and therefore should do away with foolishness like a mother's coddling. He was five, I believe. He wouldn't let me kiss him anymore either. He didn't think it was appropriate to display affection in front of 'his people.' Of course, 'his people' usually just consisted of his playmates at Paralon, his tutors, and Tummeler. But he'd made his point."

Jack dropped out of the tree and landed clumsily next to Charles, who jumped in surprise.

"This will take some getting used to," said Charles.

"Why?" asked Jack. "I'm still your Jack, Jacksie, Jack-Jack. I'm still myself. I can still think, and reason, and remember—dear God, how I can remember!"

John grinned wryly. His friend had the energy of a ten-year-old, that was certain. Less certain was whether that viewpoint, both new and familiar at once, could give them the knowledge they sought.

"Tell us, Jacks," said Daedalus, "if you were Hugh and William, and you had been left here in the Underneath by your parents, what would you do?"

Jack pondered the question a moment. "I think I would build a tree fort." He leaned over to Aven and whispered behind his hand, "There are Indians about, you know."

"After the tree fort," prompted Daedalus.

"I'd look for food and potable water . . . ," said Jack.

"An adult's answer," said John.

"Then I'd probably have a pee," finished Jack.

"Oh, for heaven's sake," said Charles.

"Then what?" asked Daedalus.

"I'd have a good think," said Jack, "and I'd probably wonder why it is that adults make children do things they don't want to do."

"Maybe it's because adults know what's best for them," Charles suggested.

"That's good for the boilerplate," said Jack, "but too often adults do whatever they want to do, regardless of what the children want or need, and the adults never pay attention anyway, so why bother?"

Aven scowled at this but remained quiet. John and Charles looked at each other, unsure of what to ask next. Jack pretended to put an apple seed in his mouth—much to Daedalus's dismay—then, grinning, dropped it.

"What are you all so worried about?" said young Jack. "We should play a game. Do you know any games? I bet you do."

"Jack, really," Charles said, exasperated. "There are very important matters to discuss."

"I thought so too," said Jack, "but I now realize I was wrong. There's nothing as important as having fun."

"There are many things more important than having fun!" retorted John. "We have to rescue the missing children! We have to find out what's become of the Dragonships! There are many, many things that need to be put right!"

"Well," said Jack, who had climbed back into Johnny Appletree and was hanging from his knees, upside down, "isn't that what adults are supposed to do?"

"He has a good point," Bert put in mildly. "Are you starting to see the pattern?"

"Adults don't pay attention to what children say," John said, crestfallen. "And here we are, underscoring the point."

"Jack . . . I say, Jack," Charles began, walking around the tree. "Will you come down from there, so we can discuss this properly?"

Jack stuck his fingers in his ears. "Lalalalala!" he cried. "I can't hear you! I can't hear you!"

Charles scratched his head. "We're never going to get through to him if he can't even hear what we're saying."

John snapped his fingers. "That's it, Charles! That's the ticket!"

The Caretaker Principia turned to Daedalus. "When Laura Glue came to us in Oxford, she told us Peter had sealed her ears with beeswax. Why would he have done that?"

"It's an old trick of Peter's," Daedalus said, "that goes back to the origins of Haven itself. It's to prevent . . ."

He paused and put his hand to his chin, thinking. "It's to prevent one from being swayed by the persuasion of the panpipes," Daedalus said finally. "But why would Peter have put beeswax in his own granddaughter's ears? She wasn't at risk from him."

"What do you mean by 'persuasion'?" asked John.

Daedalus folded his hands behind his back and bowed his head. "It is something inexorably intertwined with the history of the *Argo*, the Lost Boys, and finally, with Peter himself," he said. "The pipes of Pan have always had the ability to influence, to persuade, and to enchant. But of all who have heard its charms, the only ones who cannot resist . . .

". . . are the *children*."

"It began with the old gods," Daedalus continued. "The Romantics civilized the stories and retroactively remodeled our images of what they were meant to symbolize. They were not toga-draped Caesars and Cleopatras; they were raw. Primal. And the one who most embodied that, who arose from Mother Earth herself, wrapped in root and loam, and who never truly scraped off the soil of his birth, was Pan.

"His exploits and mischief are literally the stuff of legends, but the most famous story of Pan involves the origin of his trademark panpipes," said Daedalus. "There was a beautiful nymph named Syrinx who was beloved by all the other dwellers in the wood, but she scorned them all. She believed they were lesser creatures than she, and as such were beneath her notice.

"One day, as she was returning from the hunt, Pan saw her through the trees of his wildwood, and he became enamored of her. She rejected his advances and ran away. He shouted words praising her grace and beauty, but she didn't stop to hear his compliments, and quickened her pace. He followed, continuing to pursue her until she came to the bank of a river. There he overtook her, and she had only enough time to call out to her kin, the water nymphs, for help.

"Just as the Pan laid his hands upon her, the nymphs turned her into river reeds, which infuriated the god. He stormed to and fro across the banks of the river, shouting his fury, when a slight, plaintive melody caught his attention.

"It was the reeds that had once been Syrinx. When the air blew through them, it produced music, and the sound was very pleasing to him. So the god took some of the reeds to make an instrument that he called a syrinx—the panpipes—in honor of the nymph he had pursued and lost.

"But Pan was not yet finished with the nymphs. One of those who had protected Syrinx was a graceful dancer who had a sweet, trilling voice. Her name was Echo."

"Like the Well," said Charles.

"Not like the Well," corrected Daedalus. "Echo *is* the Well—or at least, she is the water within.

"Like her cousin, Echo scorned the love of any man. This angered Pan even more, to have been turned away twice by those who were not respectful of his birthright as a god. In revenge, he instructed his followers to kill her.

"Echo was torn to pieces and spread all over the Earth, and all that was left was her voice. As punishment for what he had done, the gods, led by the goddess of the earth, Gaia, remade the nymph as an elemental and allowed her to exist as a pool of living waters. They also granted Echo the ability to reflect back the words spoken to her, and to give the speaker his heart's desire.

"The gods then took from Pan the one object he treasured most—the pipes he had made from the nymph Syrinx. And they gave them to a mortal who had been called on a great quest by the hero Jason.

"They gave the pipes to *Orpheus*."

"How did the pipes make their way from Orpheus to Peter?" Bert asked. "That implies that there are more connections to the time of Jason's Crusade than just the name of the islands."

"Correct," said Daedalus. "Under Orpheus, 'the Pan' became a title in and of itself. A designation of office, of a sort. Orpheus was the first 'Pan' to use the panpipes, and although he was skilled with the lyre, it was possession of a divine instrument that time and again saved the Argonauts.

"After Jason's betrayal of Medea, the Argonauts scattered to the corners of the Earth. Heracles was already gone, as was Theseus. Argos, the builder of the ship, was dead. And the others went on to lead their lives free of Jason's corrupted legacy. But of them all, only Orpheus maintained a relationship with Medea. He was a kind of uncle to her sons, and secretly helped her when she told him of her plan to hide them away from their father.

"What he didn't realize was that she intended to abandon them here. She never left them wholly ungoverned—she built a home for herself on a nearby island—but she seldom visited them, for fear that Jason might discover they still lived."

"What a wench," said Charles.

"More like a witch," said John.

"Well spoken, John," said Bert.

"She *was* a witch," Daedalus agreed, "in action as well as name. She enchanted the dragons that had guarded the Golden Fleece, and defeated the bronze giant Talos when he attacked the *Argo*. If she had not been a witch, the Argonauts would have perished many times over. She knew this, and it was at the root of her hatred for Jason's betrayal."

"Those poor boys," said Aven, who had been quietly absorbing all that was said. "To revenge herself against their father, she condemned them to a fate worse than death. A lifetime of loneliness."

"That's what Orpheus thought too," said Daedalus. "He pleaded with Medea to take them elsewhere, but she would not be swayed, and she was far too powerful for him to go against her will. And so, Orpheus chose a different route. He began seeking out playmates for the boys who could be brought here, to the Underneath."

It slowly dawned on John where the inventor was going with his story. "He used the panpipes, didn't he?"

"Yes," said Daedalus. "He went out into the world—to *your* world—and lured away children to become the playmates of Jason's sons. To become Lost Boys themselves. This is the origin of the legends of children being lured from their beds in the middle of the night by soft strains of music that no adult seemed to hear. It wasn't that they couldn't hear it—but it was not meant for them. And so the children simply disappeared, and no one knew to where."

"Orpheus concealed himself well," Bert huffed. "I know a great deal about the myths and legends of the world, and I've never before heard his name connected with the disappearing children."

"Not as such," said Daedalus. "But that was not the name by

which the children knew him either. They had their own name for him, and fashioned their own mythology. And in the whispers under the covers, and in the dark corners of the room, the children knew that if you heard music in the night, it meant that the King of Crickets was coming for you."

Bert paled, then sat heavily on the grass. "The King of Crickets," he said, his voice trembling. "He . . . he's a Pan?"

"Originally he was Orpheus," Daedalus explained, "but after him, others assumed the office of the Pan, and the mythology about the King of Crickets followed them, too.

"Ulysses had two sons with the enchantress Circe, and one of them became the Pan for a time before leaving the Underneath. A few poets from your world, and at least one painter, have held the office. And there came a time when the Lost Boys took it on themselves to find their own playmates, and thereafter the Pan was not an adult, but a child."

"And because of Echo's Well, he never needed to age," Charles concluded. "Ideal."

"So children were enchanted and brought against their will?" said John. "I like that not at all."

"Peter didn't believe in it," said Aven. "He believed that children should choose to come here if they wished, and not be forced to become Lost. Orpheus trained him to use the pipes, as he had trained Peter's predecessor, Puck, but Peter never used the pipes as the others had. He would find children and whisper to them in the night—and if they so chose, he would bring them here. But *never* against their will.

"Having seen the power of the panpipes, others among the Lost Boys—particularly Hugh and William—became uncomfortable with the idea that they could be compelled against their will to do anything. And so Peter came up with the idea of putting beeswax in their ears as a means of protection against the music. Because they were children, he even made a game of it."

Aven lowered her head and swore softly as memories began to flood back to her. John and Charles exchanged knowing glances with Bert, and almost involuntarily they all looked at Jack, who was running gleefully through the apple orchard with the other children.

"It's the first thing they learn here," said Daedalus. "The children imagine that the King of Crickets is coming for them, and they all pack beeswax in their ears and hide among the trees and the rocks. Peter would designate a 'safe' base, and one by one, the children would make their way 'home.' The first one there would then take the wax from his ears and shout at the top of his lungs . . ."

"Olly Olly Oxen-Free," John and Aven said together.

On hearing the words, all the children immediately stopped their games and crowed into the air.

"Hey!" Jack called out to John. "You win! Good show, John!"

"Peter saw being the Pan as a noble calling that would allow him to protect children," Daedalus said, "so that what had happened to Hugh and William would not happen to other children."

"That's quite an undertaking for a child," Bert pointed out, "and a very mature point of view."

"It is," Daedalus agreed, "but then, Peter is an exceptional being. In all these centuries, he was the first to come here of his own free will, and the only child ever to discover the Underneath of his own accord."

"I didn't know that," said Aven, "but I'm not surprised."

Daedalus grinned with the memory. "It was he whom I first made wings for, to help him fly," he said with no small pride. "His lame leg, remember? He had the spirit for it, and had done such a great thing in coming here, that I felt compelled to help him move as freely as the other children."

"And after that, you just kept making wings for the Lost Boys," said Bert.

"Well," said Daedalus, "you know how children are. Once they saw what one of them had, they all wanted them."

"Hey!" said Jack, running up to the companions. "Do I get to have a pair of wings too?"

Daedalus knelt down to look him in the eye. "That depends," the inventor said. "Are you Lost?"

In answer, Jack merely laughed and ran back to the other children.

John folded his arms and turned to Charles. "I think someone has the panpipes," he said. "That explains everything that's happened: Peter's caution with Laura Glue; the warning in Bacon's History; and especially, the missing children. If someone were using the panpipes against the children, they'd be unable to resist. And none of the adults would even know it was happening until it was too late."

"Peter was the last to have them, and the only one now living who knew how to use them," said Daedalus. "I can only assume he was taken when the children were, because we never found him—and he would not have gone willingly."

"Could he have been entranced as well?" asked Charles. "Since the pipes affect children?"

"Not all children," put in Charles. "Not if they had beeswax in their ears."

John snapped his fingers. "That's why the King of Crickets needed the Clockwork Men—to catch the children who couldn't be compelled to follow the piping."

"The children who couldn't be compelled," Bert said darkly. "*And* their leader."

"Peter hasn't been a child in years," Daedalus said, looking askance at Aven. "He decided, finally, that it was time to grow up. And he's never regretted that choice. He adores his daughter, called Alice Blue Bonnet, and even more so *her* daughter, Laura Glue."

"Then he was taken by force," stated Aven. "And his last act was to send Laura Glue for help."

"Then we've got to help him," said John, pounding a fist into his hand. "We must. And we have to start by finding the tunesmith who's causing the trouble."

"What are you thinking, John?" said Bert.

"I think if he can live for thousands of years," John replied, motioning to Daedalus, "and also Hugh and William, then others from that time may have survived as well. And we know of one trained to use the pipes, who had no issue with compelling children against their will.

"Orpheus. I think our adversary is Orpheus."

CHAPTER EIGHTEEN
SHADOWS OF HISTORY

AT DAEDALUS'S SUGGESTION, the companions and the Lost Boys left the orchard and returned to the more secure confines of Haven proper. The crenellated towers extended all around the orchard and gardens as well, but all of them felt an easing of tension at the idea of being within more closely built walls.

Jack had continued to evince further changes as a result of his transformation. It was as if he had forgotten being an adult, except when a point in the conversation required some arcane bit of knowledge that only he possessed. Then he rattled off details that made him seem exactly what he was: an Oxford professor in a ten-year-old boy's body.

On the walk up the path, they again passed by Echo's Well, where Daedalus asked John and Charles if they wouldn't like to reconsider, now that they'd seen that no harm had come to Jack.

"Thank you, no," said John. "I think one of us having the perspective of a child is enough."

"But as you can clearly see," Daedalus persisted, "he's lost none of his ability to reason, and none of his education. It's simply being filtered through a more youthful point of view."

"Sorry," John said again, exchanging a puzzled glance with a slightly concerned Bert. "I think I can keep my focus better as an, ah, Longbeard."

"Same here," Charles answered when the inventor posed the question to him. "I might like to return sometime, once the crisis has passed, and give it a go—but not this time around, I'm afraid."

"As you wish," Daedalus said, with the faintest of tension in his jaw. "I only thought it might help. There are still many questions to be answered."

"Agreed," said John. "Foremost among them is this: Why weren't all the children taken?"

Daedalus stopped and turned to him. "What do you mean?"

John indicated the children skipping around them in odd, loopy circles. "Pelvis Parsley. Meggie Tree-and-Leaf. Fred the Goat. All the children here. Why weren't they taken with the others?"

"Perhaps they had beeswax in their ears, like Laura Glue," Charles suggested.

"No," said Bert. "She told us the Clockwork Men came for them, remember? The beeswax would have protected them from the panpipes, but not from Clockworks."

"Oh," said Charles, crestfallen.

"Is there anything special about the children who were left here?" John asked Daedalus. "In the Archipelago, none were left. They were all taken. So for these children to have been left behind, there had to be something setting them apart."

Daedalus considered that a moment. "I cannot say. Perhaps the enemy had what they came for—Peter."

"That doesn't fit," argued Aven. "It isn't consistent with everything else we've seen."

"I agree," John said. "We . . ." He stopped and turned around. "Charles?" John asked. "What is it?"

The lanky editor had stopped walking and was standing about twenty feet back on the path. He was staring at the playing children with an odd look on his face.

"Charles?" said Bert. "What's wrong?"

"Oh, I don't think anything's wrong," said Charles, not taking his eyes from the children. "But has anyone noticed," he continued in a trembling voice, "that Jack is sporting an extra shadow?"

The others stared. Charles was right. When Jack darted around a large stone bench, playing Monster and the Frogs with the other children, his shadow followed as a shadow should—and a second shadow followed an instant later.

John craned his head around to look for another light source. "There's probably a very simple explanation, Charles," he said with the beginnings of a smile. "In our last outing together, Jack was the one who gave up his shadow. I hardly think he'd overcompensate by adding a new one this time."

"It's not a second light casting it," noted Bert, "or else all the children would have two shadows."

He was right. The other Lost Boys were playing in the same area, but only Jack had twin shadows.

Aven summoned him over, and he ran to the companions, panting.

"That was quick," said Charles.

"I was tagged out anyway," said Jack. "Do you want to play with me, Poppy?"

At the mention of her old Nether Land name, Aven blushed. "No thank you, Jack. When did you get the extra shadow?"

Jack looked at her and blinked, then looked behind him, turning around like a dog trying to catch its tail. "Oh, that?" he said, as if she'd asked him why he had two ears or a nose. "It began to follow me after I spoke into the Well."

"What do you think it wants?" asked John.

"Easy-peasy," said Jack. "It wants me to follow it."

"Follow it?" Daedalus said, surprised. "Why didn't you mention it sooner, Jack?"

"Because," Jack said, rolling his eyes in exasperation, "I wasn't *out* yet."

The companions retired back to Daedalus's workshop, bringing Jack with them. Of all the Lost Boys, only Laura Glue chose to come as well, rather than go to sleep.

"I don't need to sleep too often, 'cept after long flights," she said. "And my grandfather always said, 'He can sleep when he's dead.' I'm not sure what that means, but if it's all the same, I'd rather stay with you."

"Of course, dear girl," Charles said, taking her hand. "We wouldn't feel safe without our good-luck charm."

Jack's extra shadow continued to dart about at odd moments, as if it wasn't quite comfortable being attached to someone with a shadow already in residence. It didn't react when Bert or John tried to touch it, but it swiveled around completely when Daedalus tried to touch it as well.

"Hmm," the inventor sniffed. "I don't know if I should be insulted or not, that I repulse a shadow."

"Where does it want you to go?" John asked when they'd gotten settled into the chairs at the workshop.

"West," said Jack. "I'm pretty sure it's west. It's very curious," he added, stroking his arms in wonder. "It's a bit like the chill you might get when a ghost enters a room, except it isn't cold—it's warm. Very warm."

"What do you think?" Bert asked Daedalus, who had busied himself checking his cauldrons. "Is it a good omen or bad?"

"I don't think it's an omen at all," the inventor replied. "I think it's another message. And it's one that should not be ignored. To sever one's shadow is not a task for the faint of heart. If it is gone too long from the body, one could weaken, even die. So for someone to send it, here, now, to Jack—they must want to guide you somewhere very, very badly."

"What lies west of Haven?" John asked.

Daedalus turned, face lit by the vapors from his cauldron fires. "The rest of the Underneath. The path of Ulysses, and Dante, and Jason. And maybe . . . just maybe, the answers you are seeking, Caveo Principia."

The inventor handed John the book he'd read from earlier, there in the workshop.

"This is a History written by one of your predecessors," said Daedalus. "One of the oldest. It was written by Homer's son-in-law, the poet Stasinus, thousands of years ago, and it contains what you will need to know about traversing the districts of the Underneath.

"The primary name of these lands is Autunno, which refers to everything found here, but each of the individual islands has its own obstacles and oppositions to overcome.

"The tidal forces here can be immense, as you saw crossing

from Croatoan Island," Daedalus went on. "The inhabited outer lands of the first district are not themselves a true archipelago of islands, but the high ground that exists during the tide. When it's out, we can go anywhere we like—but when it comes in, as you've seen, it becomes impassable."

"Impossible?" asked John.

"Impassable," repeated Daedalus. "Others who have traveled here saw the tides as a river. Some called it the Styx, others, the river Lethe. Names have come and gone, but the tides remain."

"We say Atlas is shrugging," said Laura Glue.

"I wouldn't blame him a bit if he did," Charles said.

"At any rate," Daedalus continued, "the tides here do not shift with the moon, as they do in your world. They move by the calendar, each day. So when morning comes, they will go out again. . . ."

"And Burton and the Croatoans will be able to cross," said Bert. "Understood. We must leave before then."

"Croatoan Island and the land Haven stands upon comprise the first district," said Daedalus. "The second consists of the isle of Centrum Terrae, which is a kingdom of lakes and black forests. It has been the province of witches and sorceresses, now abandoned, but great beasts still roam there. Be cautious, and heed the History's warnings.

"Also in the second district is the pirates' island of Hooloomooloo," said Daedalus. "It must be traversed to reach the next district, but skirt the perimeter and avoid meeting any of the inhabitants if you can.

"In the third district you will find but a single isle—Lixus, the island of automatons. If you move through it quickly, there should be nothing to fear on Lixus."

At this, John and Charles exchanged curious glances, both of them thinking the same thing: automatons? As in Clockwork Men?

Charles began to say something but was silenced by a slight shake of John's head. Something was not quite right here. John just couldn't yet put his finger on what it was.

"The fourth district," Daedalus continued, "is also comprised of a single land—Falun, the Great Pit. In truth, it is less an island than a great rending in the earth, where ores are mined to provide the raw materials for the inhabitants of Lixus. You must go straight through the center. But be wary, for the way is filled with more perils than those physical.

"The fifth district contains the seventh and eighth lands. First is Aiaia . . ."

"Circe's island," stated Charles. "From the *Odyssey*."

"The same," Daedalus said with a hint of surprise. "If you know that much, you should already know of the dangers you may face there.

"Just apart from Aiaia are the Wandering Isles, which are the only other islands past the second district that are fully inhabited. The original settlers were Greek refugees, but centuries later a company of travelers seeking refuge from the Black Plague also came there during your Middle Ages.

"They greet wanderers as fellow travelers, and those with the ability to tell stories are accorded great benefits, much as if they were visiting royalty."

"So," John concluded, "if we can get through witches, pirates, mechanical men, the Great Pit, and Circe, we'll end up at a place where we will be honored for our storytelling. Grand, that."

"Look at it this way," said Bert. "After all that, we'll have no shortage of tales to tell."

"You've told us there were eight lands," said Charles. "But there was another indicated on our map of Autunno. What of the ninth land?"

Daedalus closed the book and shook his head. "I don't think you'll be going that far. What you search for is most likely found within the closer lands. To go farther is not something many before you have done, and I would not advise it now."

"I suppose you can make that decision later on," said Charles, "if circumstances warrant."

"I won't be going with you," Daedalus said with a curious halting in his voice. "At present, I cannot leave my experiments."

"Hah," Aven snorted. "That's a crock. Most of the children of Haven are missing too, or hadn't you noticed?"

"I . . . have other responsibilities, which require that I stay here on Haven," said Daedalus. "I am truly sorry."

Bert frowned, and Aven drew in a sharp breath, but John and Charles merely thanked the inventor for the book and the wise counsel.

Daedalus and Laura Glue went to a large storeroom and assembled some of the supplies the companions would need for the journey, while Jack remained with the others.

"I'm not sure I trust him entirely," John murmured. "Something's afoot."

"Nonsense," Aven said. "He's Daedalus—he's been a friend and protector to the Lost Boys for as long as I can remember. I trust him completely."

"I'm not certain either, daughter," said Bert.

"Why?"

"Because," Jack chimed in, "he's a Longbeard."

"So are we," Charles said, gesturing at the others. "Do you trust *us*?"

"That's different," said Jack. "You're only adults on the outside—but on the inside, you're just like me."

"Okay!" Laura Glue exclaimed as she and Daedalus returned to the workshop, laden with bundles. "We're ready to go save the world!"

It was decided that they wouldn't wake the other children, but would let them slumber as the companions left. John made the suggestion in part to hasten their departure, but also because he realized that leaving would be more difficult for Aven if she had to say good-bye to all her friends.

There had been some discussion as to whether Jack and Laura Glue should remain behind, in the safer confines of Haven, but Laura Glue insisted that she could be an invaluable guide, since she had been born in the Underneath. And Jack refused to stay on more practical grounds: The missing Lost Boys had been taken from Haven to begin with, and even Peter Pan couldn't protect them. The safest place for him to be was with the others whom Peter was depending on to save them all.

Daedalus hugged Aven and Laura Glue and walked with the group of travelers to the westernmost gate of Haven. He opened the gate but did not step through.

"Go ahead," John said to the others. "I want to speak with Daedalus a moment."

When the rest of the companions were safely out of earshot,

Daedalus folded his hands behind his back and looked questioningly at John. "Yes, Caveo Principia?"

"You *can't* leave, can you?" John said in a low voice.

Daedalus looked at him as if to say something defiant, then deflated slightly and shook his head, looking down at the edges of the stonework that marked the limits of Haven's foundation.

"You didn't take your father's name, did you?" John continued. "You *are* Daedalus."

The inventor didn't answer right away, but instead looked out across Haven and sighed deeply.

"After Icarus's death, Iapyx wouldn't speak to me," he said at last. "He believed it was my arrogance that had caused the death of his brother, and I cannot disagree. But I could not see it until it was too late.

"Daedalus, the self-obsessed instrument of his own son's death, could never atone for that sin. But another son of Daedalus, who takes the name of his father and continues his work out of respect for the values he once had, might restore honor to the family, if not to its patriarch. Do you understand?"

"I think so," John said after a long pause, "but I'm not sure what purpose is served by keeping your identity secret from Aven or the Caretakers."

Daedalus sighed again. "It's not so much that it's a secret," he explained, watching the others in the near distance. "Every child who comes to Haven takes a new name. To them it's a new beginning, an opportunity to start over, without being judged for who they may have been before. I simply wanted to afford myself the same chance."

"By masquerading as yourself?" asked John.

"By portraying myself as someone who chose to honor, rather than blame," Daedalus replied. "But even after all these years, after all the good I have done, my name is still remembered because I murdered my nephew and caused the death of my son."

John shook his head. "It isn't what I would have chosen," he said. "The fact that you pretend to be your younger son means that all of the good you have done isn't credited to you, it's credited to him. What good is atonement if it isn't yourself doing the atoning?"

Daedalus didn't answer but stared hard at John, then turned to walk back into Haven.

"Be well, Caveo Principia," he called out without looking back.

John watched as Daedalus disappeared into the spires of Haven, then turned and ran to catch up with his friends.

The light of the Underneath was beginning to change the sky from deep umber darkness to the colors of bruised fruit. In front, Laura Glue led the companions with a bronze lamp that cast a bright glow all about them. Jack, to his friends' slight dismay, skirted the edges of the light, jumping in and out of its gleam, delighting in the interplay of his two shadows. The companions moved in a straight line, due west, and as they walked, they discussed the events of the night.

"When Daedalus mentioned the King of Crickets," Charles said to Bert, "I thought you were going to be felled in a faint. What was it about the name that bothered you so?"

Bert suppressed a shudder. "It's another old story, one that proved too dark even for the Brothers Grimm," he said, "although it was Jacob who originally retold the tale in one of the Histories.

"The King of Crickets is the quintessential boogeyman," Bert explained. "The movement in the dark. The creature under the bed. The monster in the closet. He is Nightmare personified, and he is very, very real.

"There are many such monsters in the world. They have always existed, and probably always will. But what frightened me was the idea that the King of Crickets was also a Pan. That would explain how his legend grew among the children, more so than grown-ups."

"Do you think the King of Crickets and Orpheus are one and the same," asked John, "since the myth originated with him?"

"I hope not, lad," Bert said, shuddering again. "From what Daedalus said, Orpheus's only motivation in taking the children was to bring them here, to be playmates to Hugh and William. But according to Jacob Grimm's History, the children taken by the King of Crickets were never heard from again."

"Why is it that all fables and fairy tales involve children in peril?" wondered Charles. "Was there some great assembly of storytellers that decided the best tales to tell children should also frighten them to death?"

"It's the Longbeards who do it," said Jack, playing hopscotch with his own shadows. "They tell us those stories to frighten us into behaving, so that we'll value their protection. But we don't listen, because we know the one thing that grown-ups forget. . . .

"All stories are *true*. But some of them never *happened*."

CHAPTER NINETEEN
THE GILDED ARMY

UNLIKE THE CROSSING between Croatoan Island and Haven, which could be forded at low tide, the gulf between Haven and Centrum Terrae could only be traversed by bridge.

The west side of Haven ended in a high bluff, to which the bridge was anchored. It was constructed of thick cables and ancient wood, which, although weathered and faded, had once been painted in the colors of the rainbow. John recognized the architecture as being Scandinavian and was nearly too fascinated by it to cross.

"There are descriptions of a 'Rainbow Bridge' in some of the writings related to the Eddas," he said excitedly. "I wonder if this has any relation to those?"

"It's entirely possible," Bert said. "Stellan's specialty was Norse mythology, and there are several islands in the Archipelago that have deep roots in the Eddaic stories."

"I say," Charles commented, "wasn't the original compiler of the Norse stories, Snorri Sturluson, one of our predecessors?"

A quick check in the endpapers of the *Imaginarium Geographica* showed that Charles was correct: the thirteenth-century scholar had indeed been a Caretaker.

"Amazing," said John. "I wonder if Sturluson ever came to the

Underneath, then? There were tales about the great serpent—a dragon, basically—that stood guard at the roots of the world-tree, Yggdrasil. That bears a great similarity to the story about the Golden Fleece and the dragon that guarded it."

"Maybe there were clues in the Eddas that can help resolve this," suggested Charles. "What happened to the dragon and the tree?"

"According to the myth, the dragon was slain, the tree felled, and the world died in fire and ice," Bert replied.

"Oh, well," said Charles. "Never mind, then."

The bridge, while old, was sturdy and stable, and they were able to traverse it in a matter of minutes. What they found on the other side John immediately named an "ur-forest." A first-growth, dawn-of-man forest, with trees of such immense stature that every other forest in the world might have been only an image reflected in a child's looking glass.

It was dark, foreboding. And there was only one apparent path to take, directly through the center of the island.

"Oh!" Laura Glue exclaimed. "I almost f'rgot!"

She hastily unpacked her bundle and instructed the others to do the same. Inside were red cloaks with hoods, which she explained must be worn before they could enter the forest.

"It's part of the Law of the Forest," she said, fumbling with the tie strings.

"She's right," John said, flipping through pages in the History. "There's a caution here in ancient Greek, and it mentions the red hoods. It relates to some Spartan legends, apparently, and refers to the red hoods as 'shields.'"

"Humph," said Charles, who had wrapped the thin red cloth around his shoulders and was now helping Laura Glue with her own hood. "It doesn't seem sturdy enough to protect us from a drizzle of rain, much less shield us from anything."

Jack was scowling and examining his hood with a look of distaste. "This is a girl's color," he complained. "Don't we have one in green? Green would be best, but I'd even settle for blue."

Laura Glue shook her head. "Red is the Law color," she insisted. "No other color will work."

John, again consulting the History, concurred. Jack muttered a few more words of protest, but nevertheless did as he was asked. He draped the cloak halfheartedly over one shoulder and fastened the ties with a slipknot.

"All set?" Bert said, examining the others. "Then into the woods we go."

The children, that is, Jack and Laura Glue, wanted to take the lead, but Aven wouldn't hear of it. She scouted the path about twenty paces ahead of the rest of them, followed by Jack, Laura Glue, and Charles, with John and Bert bringing up the rear.

As they walked, none of them noticed that they were being watched from high within the canopy above, and by more than one set of eyes. They were focused on the path, which for all practical purposes neatly bisected the island. The path was uncluttered and had once been neatly lined with golden cobblestones, but most had been worn down with use and age, and only traces remained of the yellowish pigment they once bore.

Every little while they would find a spot that had been clear-cut, all the lumber having been taken out long before. There was no obvious evidence of the woodsmen who had cut the timber, save for something Charles glanced out of the corner of his eye. It was what seemed to be a figure of human proportions, some distance into the wood, away from the path. Statuelike, the figure's arms were upraised as if it had been frozen midswing and then had the ax taken from its hands.

Charles thought he caught a flash of metal underneath the vines that had grown up around the figure, strangling it from view, leaving little exposed except for the rictus of terror frozen permanently on its face.

None of the others had seen it, and Charles saw no benefit in pointing it out, so they moved on.

"The principal use of the History," John was explaining to Bert, "seems to have been to equip travelers against whatever dangers there were on the islands. And it always uses stories as examples, like parables."

He thumbed through several pages, and then stopped. Near the back was a section that seemed to have been ripped out.

"Maybe that's why Daedalus dismissed any talk of the ninth island," said Bert. "He had no reference materials addressing it— or the dangers that we might encounter."

"Or maybe he knew they were ripped out," suggested John, "and chose not to tell us."

"Quiet!" Aven whispered, holding her hands out to her sides. "Don't speak. Don't move.

"We're being tracked."

Slowly, carefully, Aven indicated with a slight nod of her head the dark masses up ahead that the companions realized were living creatures. Up ahead, coming closer, and, they realized with mounting horror, also coming up the trail behind them.

They were wolves.

Massive, shaggy behemoths that stood as tall as racehorses, and carried the bulk of bulls.

The wolves moved out of the trees, silent as a child's prayer. They did not look at the companions directly but slowly moved in widening circles until they had surrounded the small party completely.

There was nowhere to run. And there was no possibility of combat. The companions were clearly outmatched.

"You wear the Hoods," growled the graying wolf they all assumed to be the leader. "The Hoods of Law."

"Yes," Laura Glue said, emboldened by the creature's ability to speak and, seemingly, reason. "They are the right color, so you have to leave us be, growly wolf."

The wolf stared at her for a moment, then made a raspy chuffing noise and swayed its head from side to side.

The great creature, they realized, was *laughing.*

"Little Daughter of Eve," said the wolf, "I am Carthos Mors, and I obey the Law of Centrum Terrae, set down lo these many years between my great-great-grandsire and thine own ancestor, the Queen of Sorrows. You wear the Hoods. You bear the color. And we are sworn to protect thee."

As he spoke, Jack was hastily repositioning his cloak to cover himself as much as possible. Charles placed a steadying hand on his friend's shoulder, and John and Bert drew up more closely behind Laura Glue.

"Protect us?" said Aven. "Protect us from what?"

The other wolves had already begun to growl, raised their hackles, and looked skyward. The answer to Aven's question was above, in the trees.

The silence of the forest canopy was suddenly broken by a fierce chittering sound, as the huge winged monkeys dropped from the treetops where they had been tracking the companions' progress.

Snarling, Carthos Mors and the other wolves leaped to the attack, and the companions fled for cover.

Shouting, Aven directed the others to the remnants of a structure that was thirty or forty yards off the path. It had once been a house but had long ago been burned, and all that remained were the foundations and a few charred trusses. There was also a great stone fireplace and chimney, which Aven herded Jack and Laura Glue into, drawing her long knife as she did so.

John and Charles handed Bert the *Geographica* and the History, picked up stout branches, and took up defensive stances alongside Aven.

Laura Glue was more awed than frightened by the spectacle taking place before them. Jack, for his part, was thrilled, and only slightly distracted by the fact that their hiding place smelled strongly of burnt gingerbread.

From their vantage point, the companions were able to see the fierce battle. The monkeys were roughly the same size as the children, with wings that were broader than the men were tall. Their teeth gleamed, and their claws slashed out wickedly at the defending wolves. And most fearsome of all was the fact that the monkeys' eyes glittered with a fierce, feral, almost evil intelligence.

Carthos Mors and the other wolves took up a V-shaped formation that kept rotating fresh wolves to the front of the battle— which meant that only the thick ruffs of their backs were exposed to the cutting, slashing claws of the monkeys.

The monkeys' ability to fly gave them a huge advantage—in a

surprise dropping attack. But for sustained combat, against an organized opponent, it was soon clear they were outmatched. After a few minutes of fighting, the monkeys shrieked their dismay and abandoned the effort. In moments they had disappeared into the tops of the trees.

After assuring themselves that it was safe to break formation, the wolves dispersed into the shadows, except for Carthos Mors, who approached the companions. To their surprise, he again addressed Laura Glue, as if she were their natural leader.

"Daughter of Eve," the great wolf began, "thou should have no further fear from thine enemies. We have honored the Law. What else might we do for thee?"

"We got to cross your island and go to the next one," Laura Glue said. "We're supposed t' follow the path."

"Then we shall guide and protect thee," said Carthos Mors, bowing. Without another word, the wolf turned and began to walk down the path. Laura Glue followed him first, then the others, albeit a bit more reluctantly.

In the undergrowth, the companions could see the shapes of the other wolves, pacing them, protecting them.

Charles and Bert could not resist casting fearful glances at the sky now and again, but the monkeys did not reappear.

Inside of an hour, they exited the forest and found a well-crafted dock with a broad raft, and a cable strung overhead to guide the raft across the water to the neighboring island.

Carthos Mors bowed again, this time to each of them in turn before facing Laura Glue. She laughed and scratched the scruff of his neck. The wolf hesitated, then licked her, once, with a great pink sandpaper tongue.

"Fare thee well, Daughter of Eve," he said before disappearing into the trees.

Moving onto the raft, the companions unfastened the moorings and quickly moved away from Centrum Terrae.

Crossing to the next island was much less stressful than the crossing from Haven had been, or even the crossing from Croatoan Island to Haven. As Daedalus had said, the tides had indeed receded, leaving only a shallow track of water to guide the raft through. It beached some distance out from the approaching dock, and the companions were easily able to cross the rough, pebbled ground to the Hooloomooloo.

The pirate island existed in the same geographic space as the other islands they'd seen, but instead of being illuminated by the wan, omnipresent light from above, Hooloomooloo seemed mired in perpetual twilight.

There were wisps of fog drifting about, grazing at the edges of buildings before moving on to other pastures.

The entire island was built up in a shantytown of shacks and taverns. Every inch of arable ground was covered in hastily constructed buildings that looked as if they might collapse in a stiff wind. There were rings of docks lining the visible shoreline, and surprisingly, they were filled with ships.

Whatever or whoever had torched the ships of the Archipelago had obviously not done so here.

"Remember Daedalus's warning," Bert cautioned. "He said to skirt the island and avoid any contact with the inhabitants, if we can."

Moving under cover of the fog and mist, the companions

kept close to the docks, with the expectation of using the bulk of the ships for hiding places if they encountered anyone. But they never did.

There were a number of cats mewling about the docks, fighting over scraps of fish and offal and proclaiming their love for one another in screechy sonnets sung from fence tops, but those were the only living creatures they saw until they reached the far side of the island.

There, at a waypost, they found a single, solitary sentry. They would have taken pains to avoid him altogether, but the mists obscured their sight, and they were upon him before they had a chance to hide.

He was a pirate, grizzled, old, and garbed as they expected a pirate to be, with broad pantaloons, thick boots, a weathered captain's coat, and a tricornered hat. He also wore a patch over one eye and waved at them as they approached.

"Be ye friend or be ye foe?" the sentry called out. "Old Pew, he would rather you were friend, for I'm afeared that my fighting days be numbered, they be."

Unlike with the wolves, Laura Glue was frightened, and she kept hidden behind Bert and Aven. Jack eyed the pirate with a curious expression, though, and Charles and John both realized that a direct answer would be best.

"We are, ah, we be friends, yes," Charles stammered. "Aren't we, John?"

John stepped forward and handed the pirate a folded piece of parchment Daedalus had placed in his bag. "Yes, friends," he said.

Pew unfolded the parchment and gasped, then switched the patch to the other eye and looked at it more closely.

"You have Hook's Mark," he said with awe. "Ye may not be friends, I thinks, but ye be not enemy, either."

On the parchment was a black spot. But it was apparently enough of a passport to allow them to move through unhindered.

Pew took off his hat, exposing a nearly bald pate covered in the thinnest of gray hair, and bowed deeply, pointing.

Just past the end of the dock was a large, flat stone, rising almost a foot above the water. Through the fog, they could see that it was only the first of a line of stones, arranged as if to facilitate crossing, and heading west.

"Cross if ye be inclined," said Pew, "but best be a'hurried, afore the tide return and cover the Devil's Spine."

The companions murmured their thanks and quickly moved down the dock. Charles stepped over first, and, finding the footing to be solid, helped the children, Aven, and Bert to the stone.

Only John paused on the dock.

"Might I ask a question?" he said to Pew, who shrugged.

John took that as assent. "How many of you are there on Hooloomooloo?"

"What, pirates?" Pew said, a note of surprise in his voice. "Why, not long ago, we be thousands. But now, only old Pew watches the ships. Old Pew, and his cats."

"Where did the others go?" asked John.

"Take'd," Pew replied. "Take'd, and used up, and kilt. The Crusade, men say. The Crusade of the King of Tears, takes a man and uses him up. They left on the ships with the eyes of fire, they did. Left old Pew, and none returned, nor will they."

"Why not?"

"Because plunder and pillage, that's what men do. And God

permits. But a Crusade be like Babel, and an offense to God. And they be struck down, and lost.

"Seek those whom ye may, but do not pursue a Crusade—only death will follow after."

The stones were evenly spaced, and they led the companions to the next district and the next island in little more than an hour.

The mist was thinning and the sky was brightening as they moved farther from Hooloomooloo. Not far from landfall, Bert noticed that the water level was rising against the stones—the tide was returning.

"It's too early," Charles said. "It shouldn't be coming in again until tomorrow."

"Different district, different rules," said Bert. "I don't think we can count on anything being as we expect it to be from here on in."

They stepped off the last stone onto a granite shore just as the incoming waters covered it over with a rush of sea and foam.

"Just so," said Aven. "Heaven is with us."

"We can hope, daughter," Bert called over his shoulder, as he followed Jack and Laura Glue, who began playing a game along the shore. They were skipping stones across the surface of the water, and in a moment Aven had joined them. John and Charles sat on the ground and took stock of their bundles.

"You're so worried about something that I think your eyes are going to cross," Charles said to John, squeezing his shoulder supportively. "What's got you in such a bother, old friend?"

John rubbed at his temples and grinned wryly at Charles. "I'm not certain it's anything at all. But some of the things Daedalus told us don't ring true."

"Really?" Charles exclaimed, surprised. "I thought he was very forthcoming."

"That's part of what worries me," said John. "He was very prepared for us. He wasn't surprised when we arrived, and he even knew which History we would need to take to traverse the different districts of the Underneath."

"If I may interject," said Bert, who had moved closer to the two men, "I'd thought the same thing. But wouldn't he have been expecting, or at least hoping, that Laura Glue would return with Jamie? Or a Caretaker, as she did?"

"How would he have known to expect that?" said John. "He claimed he wasn't nearby when the children were taken, and Laura Glue told us Peter sent her on the mission as the Clockwork Men were attacking. How would Daedalus have known?"

"This makes no sense," Charles said flatly. "I think you're worried about a dilemma that doesn't exist."

"Don't be so sure," said Bert, who had grown more and more worried as John talked. "I think he's right."

"So do I," said John. And with that, he explained what he and the inventor had discussed in private before the companions had left Haven.

"So Daedalus isn't Daedalus the younger after all?" said Charles.

"No," said John. "Daedalus is the original Daedalus, not his son pretending to be Daedalus."

"If he can't leave Haven," Bert pointed out, "then he had to have been present when the Clockworks attacked."

"Which means he did know about Peter sending Laura Glue to find us," said John. "So then when we came, why did he lie to us about not being there when it happened?"

The question, more an accusation, hung in the air. But no one had an answer.

John began reading through the History and what it said about the island, which Daedalus had called Lixus. It was the color of cobalt, and nearly barren. In contrast to the heavily wooded islands they had come from, there was no visible foliage, and only great towers of stone ahead.

"Occupied by automatons, Daedalus claimed," said Charles. "Do you think it's possible this is where the children were taken?"

Bert scanned the island and shook his head. "I can't see why. The Clockworks must have been under Orpheus's direction, and so I'm clueless as to what could have brought them here, of all places. John?"

John frowned and bit his lip in frustration. "It has a great deal here about Lixus, and some notations made by Pliny the Elder around the first century, but it isn't making sense."

"Did you feel that?" said Jack. "My stomach jumped."

"Not now, Jack," Charles told him. "We're trying to decide how to move forward."

"Isn't that my decision too?" said Jack. "There," he added. "There it was again." He crouched and placed his hands flat to the ground. "Don't tell me you can't feel that."

But this time they had. There was a tremor. Then another, and another.

A worried look came over Aven's face, and Bert and Charles each took a step backward toward the water. John was too absorbed in the History to notice that anything was amiss.

"Yes," he murmured, pacing. "It's starting to become clearer.

There's only one tree left on this island, and it's in the center of those towers of stone. It may even have been the tree where the Golden Fleece once hung."

"The one guarded by the dragon?" Charles asked as another tremor, stronger now, shook the ground. "Fine by me. I'd love to see Samaranth right about now. Or even a little dragon. Really, any dragon would do."

Another tremor struck, this time strong enough that Laura Glue was nearly knocked off her feet.

"Hmm," said John. "The automatons are Clockworks. It's they who guard the tree, but there's still an inconsistency here. . . ."

Another tremor struck, and this time there was thunder with it.

"I think I have it!" John cried. "The problem isn't in the translation . . ."

The ground shook, and the island echoed with the boom that followed almost instantly.

"It's a misunderstanding of scale," John finished.

Laura Glue's scream interrupted any reply that was forthcoming from the others, as a towering figure moved into view.

A great bronze statue, nearly a hundred feet high, stepped over the companions and bestrode them like the colossus it was.

"Talos, the Bronze automaton of Crete!" Bert said breathlessly. "I'd never believed he really existed."

"In the stories, Medea helped the Argonauts defeat him," John exclaimed, "but it looks like he's recovered."

"I hate to tell you this, old boy," Charles stammered, his voice shaking with sudden terror, "but he's not alone."

In the distance, several more gleaming giants moved into view. It was an army—an army of golden mechanical giants. The shaking of the ground was constant now, as was the thunderous din of their footfalls.

"Run!" Aven yelled, pointing at an opening between the towers. "We can't stay here in the open! We need cover!"

A great bronze sandal crashed down in front of them, throwing the companions to the ground, and one of the giants seized their bundles before the companions could reach them. There was no offense they could mount, but the giants were slow. Escape was possible.

John, Charles, and the others dashed between the giant's legs and headed for the stone towers. The other giants had closed in and encircled them, but they were too ponderous to move with any speed, and their stature was so great that there were huge gaps between their feet.

The first giant, which Bert had called Talos, reached down with a massive hand, fingers grasping, and nearly had Laura Glue—but she was nimble and slipped through.

The towers of stone were close enough to delay the pursuit of the giants, and the companions ran between them, not pausing for a breath, or for more than a passing glance at the great, solitary tree that stood in their center.

The island was small, and they ran until they reached the far side. By then the tremors had stopped, and there was no sign of pursuit.

Laura Glue, however, was frantic and sobbing.

"It's all right," John said, reassuring her. "We've escaped. They don't seem to be following us now."

"They don't need to follow us now!" Laura Glue cried.

"What do you mean?" John asked. "They got our bundles, but we managed to keep the History and the *Geographica*."

"John, you don't understand," said Aven. "It's Jack. They took *Jack*."

CHAPTER TWENTY
THE CITY OF LOST CHILDREN

IN HIS DREAMS there had been giants. But they were not golden, and they had not taken notice of him, as had Talos and his fellows. The fingers of the giant automaton had formed a cage from which he could not escape, and the crashing footfalls had made it impossible for Jack's friends to hear his cries.

He was a prisoner. He was alone. And he was only a child. But he still had his mind. He was still himself, still Jack. And he still had his scholarly training. Passive observation, not panicked action, was what was called for here. And so he waited, and kept quiet.

Once Talos realized that his small captive was not going to struggle or try to flee, he relaxed his grasp enough for light and air. Jack looked between the giant's fingers at the ground below—which was a mistake. His stomach twisted and turned, and finally he retched, spilling his last meal from Haven across the broad golden palm. The giant never noticed.

Jack decided that whatever else he was in for, he ought to at least not make himself ill on top of being terrified. So he closed his eyes, sat back, and tried to think of more pleasant things.

Thus calmed, it was only minutes before the boy professor fell asleep.

✦   ✦   ✦

Despair.

That was all the companions could feel. A dull, throbbing ache of despair.

Despite all they had come through, all they had endured, they seemed no closer to discovering what had happened to the children of the Archipelago, or the missing Dragonships, or Aven's own son. And now they had lost their friend to an incomprehensible foe.

"I can't bear this anymore," John said miserably. "Every time we've come to the Archipelago, it's to fail. To come up short. Every time, we run as fast as our legs may carry us, and fight with every last breath in our lungs, and it's never enough."

"But it is enough," countered Bert. "Don't you see, John? It is enough. Remember what Stellan told you, in the tower?"

As if in answer, an enormous granite block fell from the sky and crashed into the water, close enough to drench them all with the spray. A moment later it was followed by an oaken door, which slapped the surface like a stone, skipping once, twice, then stopping.

It was one of the doors from the Keep of Time.

"You mean *that* tower?" Charles said gloomily. "The one I wrecked, that's literally falling down around our ears?"

A closer examination of the shallows near the beach revealed that a number of the large blocks had fallen there, and lazily spinning in the water were several of the doors.

"Look," Charles said, pointing to one of the doors. "A rising sun is carved into that one. I think it's Hittite."

"That means the tower is still crumbling," said Bert. "The effects of scattered Time may be worse here. We must be on our guard."

"You mean on our guard enough so we don't lose any more children?" John asked bitterly.

"Quiet, all of you!" Aven said, her tone making it clear that she wasn't asking for debate. "Don't you see you're scaring her to death?"

Sitting nearby, huddled into a ball on the sand, was Laura Glue. She hadn't said a word, but tears were welling in her eyes, and it was obvious she was very, very frightened.

John and Charles felt like idiots.

Both men knelt and consoled the small girl. "We're sorry, Laura Glue," said John. "Sometimes adults get scared too. And we say things we don't really mean."

Laura Glue looked up and sniffed. "So . . . so you're not ascared after all?"

"Scared out of our wits," Charles admitted, "but that doesn't mean we can't keep our wits about us. And it doesn't mean we're going to leave Jack to the mercy of those awful machines."

"It doesn't?" she exclaimed, eyes shining. She reached up and took each of their hands. "Are we going to rescue Jacks?"

"We are indeed," stated Charles, with a furtive look at Bert and Aven. "How can we fail, with our good-luck girl Laura Glue guiding us?"

John examined the History to discover the next steps they needed to take, while the others scouted the beach. It was decided that building a fire would be too risky, since it might draw attention to them, and at the moment they had no idea where the army of golden giants was.

Laura Glue told them that the giants were not the same as the

Clockworks her grandfather had warned her about, the ones they believed had taken the Lost Boys. This was both reassuring and troubling at once. It meant that there was an additional mystery to be solved, but also that there might be another adversary to be dealt with.

Bert calculated that a stone from the keep was falling about every hour, which meant that every three days or so another intersection crumbled, and another door fell too. So every three days, another entry point into the past became unfocused, uncontrolled, and loosed upon the world.

"Stay close," Bert cautioned. "Jules and I have had no small experience with Time, and if there are any 'soft places' about, I don't want any of us to step into them by accident."

"Look for a horn," John said suddenly. "Somewhere here on the shore should be a horn to summon a ferryman."

In short order, Aven called out to them from an outcropping just to the north. There, on a tripod of ash, bound with a silver cord, was a conch shell.

"I think this is it," said John. "Do any of you know how to use it?"

Without replying, Aven lifted the conch to her lips and sounded a long, clear note that echoed across the water.

In moments, as if from nowhere, a long, flat boat appeared, propelled by a ferryman using a tall black pole.

He was dressed in a black leather coat and wore his hair cropped short. His skin was pale and his hair so white it was devoid of color, but he seemed no older than John, and his face was expressionless. He wore round black glasses that hid his eyes, but as the boat approached he raised a hand in greeting.

Charles gulped. "Are . . . are you Charon?" he said hesitantly.

The man nodded once. "I was called as such, long ago. Charon, Methos, Morpheus . . . These were all my names, once upon a time. But now I am simply called Kilroy. Have you a coin for the passage?"

John looked at Aven in alarm. Talos had taken the bundles, and with them anything else Daedalus had included to aid in their passage between the islands.

"What kind of coin?" Charles asked suddenly.

"A silver talent is traditional," replied Kilroy, "but any silver coin will do."

Charles fumbled around in his pockets for a moment, pulling them all inside out until finally he found what he was looking for. "Aha!" he said triumphantly. "Will this do the trick?"

"An Irish punt?" John said in surprise.

"It's my lucky coin," said Charles.

"I'm not so sure it works," John said wryly.

"That's why I hadn't mentioned it before," Charles admitted, "but on the other hand, I've got it now, and that's lucky enough, isn't it?"

He handed the coin to the ferryman, who didn't so much as glance at it before putting it inside the black coat. Kilroy moved back and motioned for them to step onto the boat.

The companions took their seats, and with no apparent effort, the ferryman pushed off with the pole and the boat slid smoothly into open water.

Jack woke in darkness.

Feeling his way around, he discovered he was in a small stone room, approximately ten feet wide and twelve feet long. The ceiling was high, and the walls had brackets for candles, but there was no other decoration in the room, which was obviously a cell of some sort.

The door was stout, and near the top, higher than Jack could jump, was a small window inset with iron bars.

There was just enough ambient light out in the corridor for him to see once his eyes had adjusted, but only just. And it was far too little to tell if he still retained his second shadow.

"Hello?" Jack called, hesitant. "Is anyone there?"

An unexpected answer came drifting through the small window. It was a song. A child's rhyme, sung by a child's voice.

> *Ring a ring o'roses,*
> *A pocket full of posies,*
> *A-tishoo! A-tishoo!*
> *We all fall down.*

Jack shuddered. It was the song made up by children during the time of the plague in London. It was an older version than the one he himself had known as a child—the first time he was a child—but authentic. "A-tishoo! A-tishoo!" told him so. Sneezing was a common symptom of plague victims—before they fell down dead by the thousands.

He called out again. "I'm Jack. Who are you? Who's there?"

The singing stopped abruptly. Then, hesitantly, a girl's voice answered. "Abby. Abby Tornado. Why be you here, Jack?"

"A giant golden Clockwork captured me," Jack replied. "And when I woke up, I was in this room."

"A golden Clockwork?" said another voice, a boy this time. "I should have liked to seen that, I should. I were only taken by a common-variety Clockwork, neh?"

"Are you the Lost Boys?" Jack asked. "Is this where you were taken?"

"Some of us are, and some of us aren't," said Abby Tornado. "There be lots an' lots o' children here. Some of us be from Haven, and some from elsewheres."

"I'm from a place called Prydain," said the boy. "An' I want to go home."

Prydain. In the Archipelago of Dreams. Jack had found some of the missing children, at least.

"Why were you brought here?" said Jack. "What is this place?"

"It was supposed to be a great game," the boy explained. "That's all it was—just a game.

"A boy like us, but who wore a golden coat and the head and horns of a ram, came to us and told us that if we played a game with him, we would be taken to a place called Pleasure Island, where we'd never have to go to bed, and we could eat cakes and sweets, and no one would tell us what to do, because there are no grown-ups on Pleasure Island, none at all."

"What was the game he asked you to play?"

"We were to sneak out of our beds after dark," said the boy, "and were to go to the docks. Then, as the clocks struck midnight, we set the ships on fire."

"Why would you do that?" Jack exclaimed.

The boy hesitated, then answered in a voice that said he was uncertain himself. "I—I don't know. The music told us to, so we did. And after we set the fires, we waited for the King of Crickets to pick us up in his Dragonships, and they were supposed to take us to Pleasure Island, but they brung us here instead."

A chill settled over Jack. The King of Crickets. Orpheus. That explained a great deal.

"Did the ships bring all the children here?"

"No," said the boy. "Some of us he kept on the ships, and some of us he left here."

"No one has been back for days," Abby Tornado said. "We're all hungry. You didn't bring any food, did you?" she asked hopefully.

"I'm sorry," said Jack. "I didn't."

"Oh," said Abby. "Well, do you want to play a game?"

"I don't know many games," Jack admitted.

"I want to play Olly Olly Oxen-Free," said the boy. Then, in a smaller voice, he added, "I want to go home."

"Be brave," said Abby Tornado. "Olly Olly Oxen-Free."

"Olly Olly Oxen-Free," the boy replied, as did another, and another girl, then another boy, and more, until the sound was a quiet hum of children that echoed throughout the corridors of their dark, dank prison.

It began as a game, Jack said to himself, *but it's become a means of survival for them, hasn't it? And for me, too, it seems.*

Olly Olly Oxen-Free.

Kilroy the ferryman took the companions to the next island, called Falun, which stood in the fourth district.

The ferryman was not verbose, but he answered any questions they asked, simply and without hesitation.

The children, Kilroy said, were most likely being taken to the seventh island in the Underneath. There was a fortress there that had often been used to keep prisoners—sometimes for centuries. And children were not excepted.

On the pebbled shore the boat slid to a halt, and Kilroy bade the companions farewell. Charles thought to ask him something more, but as the ferryman bent to adjust the rudder, Charles got a glimpse behind the dark glasses.

Kilroy had no eyes, and where they were supposed to be were rows of sharp ivory teeth.

Charles stepped quickly away from the boat and did not look back.

Falun, the sixth island, was nothing more than a great rending in the earth; a huge cleft, which glowed with the redness of the mythical Pit it inspired.

"Dante following Beatrice?" said John.

"Just so," agreed Bert, indicating a series of steps that had been hewn into the walls. "Lead on, Caveo Principia."

"Thanks a lot," said John.

As with the crossing from Haven to Centrum Terrae, the opening at the bottom of the rift was connected to the next island by a bridge, although this one was not nearly as trustworthy as the first. It was made of thick, ropy strands of what could have been a spiderweb, and their feet stuck wherever they stepped. As they crossed, it became more and more of an effort to move easily, and they were all relieved when they finally set foot on solid earth once more.

"Remember," Bert cautioned, "this is also Circe's island. It could be more dangerous than all the rest combined."

The island, which the History said was called Aiaia, looked like any island in the Mediterranean. There were olive trees and short, scrubby bushes, and here and there they could see scorpions lying in the warm sand.

And ahead was a great, foreboding building. It was a fortress, in every sense of the word.

The structure was not ostentatious by any means, but the various battlements and towers gave testament to what lay underneath. The towers were capped with steeply pitched roofs, and the outer wall was ringed with archways of sculpted stone. At the wall nearest the companions were three great metal-reinforced oaken doors, each with a small window inset about ten feet off the ground.

"Do we knock?" Charles asked. "What does it say in the History, John?"

"It doesn't," John replied. "So I suppose knocking is as good an idea as any other."

"Then again," said Charles, "what if it brings out more hostiles? I'd rather avoid a battle, if we can help it."

Aven rolled her eyes and rapped her knuckles firmly on the door.

"That settles that," said Charles.

There was no response, so Aven knocked again. Finally a panel in the window slid back and a meek voice spoke.

"What do you want?"

The companions looked at one another, and Aven gave John a nudge.

"Ah," John began, "we're looking for a friend of ours. A small fellow, called Jack."

"Hmm," the doorman said. "No Jack here, I'm afraid. No, all we've got here is children. Sorry I couldn't help you." And with that, the panel slid shut.

"Hey!" Aven yelled, pounding on the door. "Jack is a child. Let us in!"

The panel slid back again. "Well, why didn't you say so? I can't be expected to know a 'Jack' is also a child. I've got responsibilities, you know. Can't keep track of everything."

There was a clomping noise, followed by the sound of several bolts being thrown back. The door creaked open, and instead of the near giant they expected, they saw that the doorman was only four feet tall.

The curious creature had a hunchback, a carapace like a beetle's, and six arms. There were two disks on his head, which looked as if they'd been horny growths that had been filed down. One eye was rheumy, the other an empty socket, and his face was sullen.

"Where's Jack?" said John. "Can you take us to him?"

"I'm sorry," the six-armed creature said plaintively. "There have to be forms. I can't release anyone until you've filled out the proper forms."

Charles stepped forward and raised a finger. "I can handle that," he declared. "I'm an editor. I know how to deal with paper-work."

The odd little creature led them down a series of corridors, talking all the way. Apparently he didn't get many visitors, and so was taking full advantage of the opportunity to get acquainted.

"I'm called Asterius," he said without looking back, "and I assure you, anything you've heard about me certainly isn't true."

"What would we have heard of you?" Bert asked.

"I can leave whenever I want," Asterius replied, "I just choose not to. I'm also of noble blood, did you know? Could you tell? Yes," he continued, answering himself, "noble blood. It's obvious."

Charles looked at John and twirled a finger at his temple. John grinned and nodded.

"I don't usually mix with commoners, not that I have any time to," Asterius said. "There's always so much to do here."

"Where is 'here,' exactly?" asked John.

"My house," Asterius said, surprised. "Didn't you know? You came to see me, after all."

"Actually, we came for Jack," Charles said mildly.

Asterius deflated slightly. "Oh yes, that's right. Well, paperwork," he said.

"You have a very large house," Bert observed.

"As well I should," the creature replied. "It is as big as Creation, after all."

"That big?" said Charles.

"Oh yes," said Asterius. "Maybe bigger."

"Do you have many visitors?" asked Bert.

"No," Asterius answered. "Not many. Oh, every nine years or so someone comes along who wants to fight, but that's about it."

The corridor opened into a broad room filled with shelves, old bones, and papyrus rolls. The little creature positioned himself on a high stool and began to shuffle through a sheaf of documents.

"Yes," he continued, somewhat mournfully. "Ever since that brat Theseus put my eye out, I've been stuck here at . . . at . . . a *desk* job. I should be out wandering the countryside, spreading fear and terror wherever I roam. . . ."

Asterius sighed. He looked at Charles with a wan eye. "You don't believe me. You don't think I'm capable of spreading fear, do you? I never get any respect."

"Oh, I assure you, you're considerably fearsome," Charles said, elbowing John.

"Oh, yes," agreed John. "Fearful. Terrifying. I wouldn't sleep for nights if I even got a glimpse of you on the horizon."

"Really?" the little creature said, eyes brightening. He sat slightly taller (as much taller as the carapace would allow) and seemed to puff out his chest. "Well then, now that's been established, what can I do for you?"

"Jack," Aven said, exasperated. "We're here for Jack."

"Hmm," said Asterius. "All I have here is unsuitables. Is Jack unsuitable?"

"Unsuitable for what?" said John.

"To fight," said Asterius. "To fight in the Great Crusade. Those who were suitable went with the king, and those who were unsuitable came here. You really are rather unlearned, aren't you?"

Having found whatever documentation it was he needed, Asterius led the companions back into the great labyrinth of halls and corridors, still talking all the way.

"Here we are," he announced, hefting the lamp to a short pedestal to better light the spacious room they had entered. "The Aedificium."

It was a great octagon, but, their strange guide explained, it appeared from a distance as a tetragon.

"Why is that significant?" asked John.

"It's a Christian conceit," said Charles. "The tetragon is supposed to be the perfect physical expression of the permanence and solidity of the Kingdom of God."

"The Abbey of the Rose!" Bert exclaimed, snapping his fingers. "Stellan knew of it. He once said that the design of this place was based on the original plans for the library of Babel, although whether he meant before or after the Great Confusion, I'm not sure."

All the shelves in the Aedificium, or sacred library, were heavily laden with Bibles. There were incunabula from centuries past; leatherbound Bibles from recent decades; and hand-bound, illuminated manuscripts that had been lovingly, carefully illustrated by the monks who had once resided in the abbey.

In his conservative estimate, John calculated that the room contained twelve thousand Bibles.

"The other papers are in order, so if you'll just choose the Bible that opens the gate," said Asterius, pointing to an impassably solid wrought-iron door, "then we can go retrieve your 'Jack.'"

"Which one do we choose?" asked John.

"I'm not doing this for my health, you know," Asterius complained. "There are covenants, and there are bindings, and I've already extended courtesies to you regarding the discrepancies in the paperwork, but if you don't even know how to get in . . ." The little creature let the words trail off into silence, as the companions looked around in despair at all the books.

"Here," said Bert, pointing to letters engraved above the gate. "Perhaps this will give us a clue."

"Could it be a riddle, like the one outside Samaranth's lair?" asked Aven. "Or a magic word?"

Bert shook his head. "The monks of the abbey would have

eschewed any use of magic words. A riddle is possible, though. Can you read what it says?"

"I can," said Charles, taking the lamp from Asterius and holding it high to illuminate the lettering. "It's Hebrew."

He looked over the letters for a moment, lips moving silently, then turned to the others. "I think it *is* a riddle," he told them, "but I don't know what it means, because the phrase itself is no mystery at all."

He turned back to the riddle and began to recite: "The wolf also shall dwell with the lamb, and the leopard shall lie down with the kid; and the calf and the young lion and the fatling together; and a little child shall lead them."

John looked startled. "You know it?" Bert asked him.

"Yes," John said. "It's from the Old Testament. Isaiah, unless I miss my guess."

"You didn't," said Charles, "but what does it mean?"

"All along," mused John, "we've made mistakes and missteps because we were thinking like adults instead of like children. We haven't even paid enough attention when we knew it would be important to do so.

"I think this means exactly what it says. We must be led by a little child."

They all turned to Laura Glue, and Charles knelt in front of her. "Laura Glue," he said gently, "our good-luck charm. Can you help us?"

"I'll try," she replied cautiously.

She looked at the books, then slowly began to circle the room. She passed the illuminated Bibles John would have chosen, and the incunabula that would have been Charles's preference.

Finally she stopped and withdrew a small, battered Bible from the shelf. It was an old German Bible, and it was small enough to easily fit in her hands. A child's Bible.

Inside was an aged slip of paper, with the outline of two tiny hands.

"Albert's hands," Asterius said, taking it from her and nodding. "The ghost tracings of a child long gone are still totemic and still bear power. You have found what you need."

Nimbly Asterius folded the paper into a key and inserted it into the lock on the gate, which instantly popped open.

The companions stepped inside a dark hallway lined with doors and lifted the lantern. From the darkness beyond, they could hear children's voices, and among them a familiar voice calling out "Olly Olly Oxen-Free."

It was Jack.

When he heard the voices of his friends, Jack called out with joy, and it was only a few twists and turns down the corridors to the cell where he was being held.

There were happy hugs and handshakes all around, and the light of the lantern showed that not only was he unharmed for his experience, but the second shadow was intact as well.

Hurriedly Jack told them what he had learned from Abby Tornado and the others.

"Well," said Aven, "now we know what happened to the ships in the Archipelago."

"We aren't going to leave the children here, are we?" said Jack.

"Of course we aren't," John said firmly. "They'll be coming with us. All of them."

"No!" Asterius protested, wringing his hands. "There's been no paperwork to allow it! It simply can't be permitted!"

The companions' only answer came from Aven, who drew her long knife and pointed it at the small creature.

Asterius sighed.

"You see?" he said to Charles. "No respect."

In moments the rest of the cell doors had been opened, and the corridors that had been black and silent were ablaze with torchlight and the joyful laughter of children.

PART SIX

THE NINTH CIRCLE

CHAPTER TWENTY-ONE
SHADOWS AND LIGHT

THE OLD MAN had become fevered, and with the fever came delirium. So he began to speak, to tell stories, for it seemed as if no help would be coming after all, and all that remained for him was to tell stories and, finally, to die.

"This is a story," he began, his voice weak but clear, "about the secret of Perpetual Youth. Not Eternal Life, for there is an ending to all things. But to live one's span with the energy and vigor for life that one has as a child is a treasure worth seeking. And seek it I did. But when I found it, I realized it was not so much a secret as a terrible, terrible truth—and truths, once learned, can seldom be unlearned.

"The secret is a great *lie*. For there is no such thing as Perpetual Youth. It is only an illusion.

"Illusions can be kept. Illusions can be cherished. But they can never become real. And to choose to see oneself as a child forever is only that—*illusion*.

"All things grow. All things change. And eventually, all things must pass. It is the way of life. To stay young is to remove oneself from the motion of the world. But to grow up is to take hold of that motion, and use it, and shape the world for those who come after. It is not a choice. It is a responsibility."

"You're ill, Peter," said the woman in the mirror, "and that's merely a collection of useless platitudes, not a story. You should be quiet, and rest."

"A story?" the old man said. "I know a story. Once there were two children, a brother and sister named Phrixus and Helle, whose stepmother was a witch. She was a great beauty and had seduced their father into marriage.

"She hated her husband's children, and often wished there were some way to rid herself of them. And so on the anniversary of her marriage, she had an idea: She constructed a house deep in an ancient forest. Its walls were made of sugared bread, and sweet wine flowed across its floors. Its roof was made of almond cakes, the windows were framed in boiled licorice root, and inside, cooking over the fire, was a cauldron of a confection she called Turkish delight, which smelled of winter, spring, and summer all at once.

"Children were drawn to the house, as all children would be, and one day, so were Phrixus and Helle. But they saw her for what she was, and saw what she was trying to do to them, and they forced her into the oven she intended for them and burned her to a crisp. Then they escaped by flying away on the back of a magical golden ram, and they lived happily ever after."

"You have it all wrong," the woman in the mirror said. "They escaped on the ram long before I ever built the cottage on Centrum Terrae, and it wasn't for them that I built it. It was for my own children. And I never meant to harm *them*."

The old man chuckled, then coughed. "I'm getting my stories confused again, aren't I? I was confusing that tale with the story of Medea."

The woman in the mirror seemed to withdraw, then the image

clarified again. "They're the same story," she said, her voice subdued. "You just have the details wrong, Peter."

"How could I have forgotten how Jason betrayed Medea?" the old man said. "Or how she followed him to the ends of the Earth, and beyond, and then farther still. And finally she took upon him the revenge she had so long sought."

"She paid the price for her choices," the woman said. "A far greater price than she ever expected, and so did her husband. He is but a shade, and she a reflection. So why, after all this time, can they not be forgiven?"

"Because," replied the old man, "it is her sons who paid an even greater price than that. A price they continue to pay. A price they will always be compelled to pay, until the day they forgive themselves."

"But they did nothing wrong!" the woman in the mirror exclaimed. "Nothing!"

"And never telling them that, Medea, is the sin you cannot repent of."

It was difficult to count the number of children the companions freed from Asterius's labyrinth, because they wouldn't stand still long enough to be counted.

At Charles's best estimate, there were between one and two hundred. The majority of them were Lost Boys, and so there were many happy embraces and reunions with Laura Glue and Aven.

The rest of the children, perhaps thirty of them, were from various islands in the Archipelago of Dreams.

Bert, John, and Charles decided that while Asterius was harmless enough, there was still a very real possibility that the stories of Circe were also true, and none of them wanted to meet the enchantress—especially with hundreds of children in tow.

"She also tended to turn her visitors into swine," added Charles, "so I'm for leaving here, posthaste."

"Agreed," said John. He gestured out over the water. "It's low tide still, and the next islands are close, in the same district as this one. So I think we can actually walk across."

Charles clapped his hands. "That's right! These are the Wandering Isles, where they greet travelers like royalty! What are we waiting for? Let's go!"

Charles and the two-shadowed Jack took off at a trot across the shallow water, splashing other children along the way. Soon all the children were running and splashing their way across the narrows to the eighth group of islands.

"I think if we had any illusions about this being a stealth operation," Jack said to Bert, "they've pretty much been shattered *now*."

The Wandering Isles were very similar to Aiaia, and the heritage of the inhabitants was obvious from the architecture of the Grecian houses and temples that dotted the nearby hills.

The shore was open and well cultivated, and there was evidence of fishermen having been there recently. A large number of chickens bustled about pecking at insects and scorpions.

"That's a sign of civilization," said Charles. "A society with well-contented chickens is a well-contented society."

"You're a very odd man," said Bert.

"I get that more often than you'd think," replied Charles.

"What next?" Aven said to John. "Does the History say where else we need to go, or what we need to do?"

John shook his head and showed her the book. "The pages after the ones about Aiaia have been ripped out. We're on our own, I'm afraid."

A peal of thunder rumbled through the air, and several of the children squealed in response.

For the first time since the companions had come to the Underneath, storm clouds began to gather overhead. Black, foreboding, they were an ill omen, and Bert pulled his collar tighter and shuddered as he watched the clouds rolling in.

"This is no ordinary storm," he said to Jack. "Aven and I have witnessed its like before. This is a *Time Storm*."

He pointed skyward, just to the east. "Up above us is the Keep of Time, and as it crumbles, more and more portals into the past are being loosed," he explained. "They are colliding here, intersecting, with no boundaries and no control. And I believe the center of every crisis we have encountered is here, in this very spot."

As Bert spoke, the air above them began to shimmer, as if they were viewing a mirage. Suddenly an airplane burst into view, engine screaming.

It was a large silver twin-prop plane, of a make that John didn't recognize. It roared past, just skimming over the surface of the water, and close enough they could see the face of the woman piloting it and that of her navigator sitting behind her.

A stencilled name on the fusilage identified the plane as a LOCKHEED ELECTRA, but that was all they managed to make out before the pilot pulled up, gained altitude, and vanished to the east over the towers of Aiaia.

"That's not good, if that was who it appeared to be," Bert said darkly, "although it's nice to know she wasn't actually lost in the Pacific."

"Who was that?" asked John.

"It doesn't matter," said Bert. "What does matter is that the plane came from somewhere in the future—around 1937 or so. Time is starting to fracture."

"Look," Charles said, pointing to the east. "Here comes another one."

They looked, but it wasn't another plane that was dropping rapidly out of the sky toward the beach.

It was the *Indigo Dragon*.

The decks were manned by the Croatoans, and an all-too-familiar man was at the wheel.

"Greetings," Burton called out with a wave. "We meet again, Caretakers."

Before the companions could respond, the Croatoan warriors, all heavily armed with knives and spears, had leaped over the sides of the airship and encircled them on the sand. Once more they were captives.

"You planned to use the airship all along, didn't you?" John said.

"Of course," said Burton. "The chance to gain both an airship that could finally take me out of the Underneath, as well as a Dragonship that could cross the Frontier back into the real world, was too good to pass up. Besides, your crew had done most of the repairs, anyway."

"You mean before you ate them," Charles spat. "But how did you find us?"

In answer, Burton merely smiled—and held up Laura Glue's Compass Rose.

Bert groaned. It had still been attuned to seeking the Caretakers. All Burton had to do was follow the glow.

Aven pieced together something else. "We didn't really escape from you, did we?" she said coldly. "You allowed us to escape, just so you could follow us."

Burton nodded and grinned more broadly. "That I did," he replied. "And you are far too trusting, you helpless wench. Just because Billy could show you a shiny trinket, you thought you could trust him. And you were wrong."

From the foredeck of the *Indigo Dragon*, Hairy Billy smiled— but it wasn't the smile he'd shown them before, the smile of a friend and collaborator. This smile was cold and cruel. He took off the silver thimble he wore around his neck and dropped it to the deck as if it were trash. In that moment the companions realized the full extent of how they had been manipulated and betrayed.

"But why, Burton?" said Bert. "What purpose did it serve?"

"You wouldn't willingly tell me where you'd taken our children," replied Burton, "so we had to let you think you'd escaped so we could follow you. And from the looks of things," he added, looking around at the children playing in the sand and surf, "it was the right decision.

"Now," he said, as he stepped closer and a more threatening tone crept into his voice, "where are our children? And where is my daughter Lillith?"

None of them knew how to answer, or to even say anything that Burton might believe.

At least, John thought to himself, none of the children had yet realized what was taking place there on the beach.

None, save for one—*Jack*.

Burton didn't know one of the children was actually a Caretaker.

Quietly Jack was moving among the children, whispering to them, and several had already begun running toward the *Indigo Dragon*.

Burton realized that they were about to be overwhelmed with children, and he barked a series of harsh commands to the Indians who were still aboard.

The rest of the Croatoans climbed out of the ship and began to herd the children toward the nearby fishing cottages—which was exactly what Jack had intended to happen. He was hiding under one of the small fishing boats, and his expression told John that he needed to keep Burton's attention, even if only for a few more moments.

"I'll tell you where your children are," John said, much to the others' surprise, "if you'll answer a single question for me."

"Fair enough, Caretaker," agreed Burton, still fingering the spear that he had loosely cradled in his arms. "What is your question?"

"Why are the Pan and the previous Caretaker enemies?"

Charles's jaw dropped, and he stared at John in amazement. That was not what he had expected him to ask of an avowed enemy of Peter Pan's.

The reaction of the Croatoans was different. They looked at one another and nodded, as if this were one of the common stories of their people. Even the expression of the one called Murthwaite seemed to shift to one that was more respectful as Burton began to answer.

"Well asked, Caretaker," the explorer said, a soft burr in his voice. "The Pan and his friend-now-enemy were as brothers once. They met here in the Archipelago, and it was here that the Pan showed his friend the secret of how to never grow old.

"Then," he continued, "they met a maiden, and she gave them each a kiss. The Pan rejected his, for he thought that keeping it would make him grow old, and he feared this most of all. But the Caretaker kept his kiss and fell in love with the maiden, and together they began to grow up.

"However, the Caretaker had fears of his own, as well as reasons that compelled him to return to *his* world—and so he gave her a choice. He would leave the Archipelago and abandon his duties, and her as well. Or she could come be with him, grow old with him, raise a family with him—but at the price of never returning to the Archipelago."

Aven was silent, but the tears streaming down her cheeks told her friends that what Burton said was true.

"I never knew," Bert whispered. "I never realized that was the choice she had."

"Ah, Aven . . . ," Charles said, his voice low.

"The old Caretaker, your predecessor, and the Pan have been enemies ever since," said Burton. "Now—I'm losing my patience. *Where* are our children?"

John's mind raced for some kind of an answer, whatever he could say that wouldn't make the situation worse—but suddenly Burton was distracted by something more pressing. The other Croatoans' shouts caused him to turn and gasp in surprise as he watched the *Indigo Dragon* lift away from the beach and rise swiftly into the air.

At the wheel, a smiling Jack waved, and in moments the airship was out of reach of the Croatoans' spears and arrows. Without a backward glance, Jack piloted the ship over their heads, pointed it westward, and vanished.

Burton howled in fury and turned to John. "You'll pay for this, Caretaker. I promise you that."

He pulled his knife and was about to strike at John when suddenly the sky turned black and the island vibrated with thunder. Over the water, the air had begun to shimmer again. Something else was coming through one of the rifts in Time.

It was not an airplane this time. It was a ship. Large, of a familiar design, it was a graceful, majestic vessel, and it slid smoothly through the air and water until it solidified in the shallows just footsteps from the Croatoans and the companions.

Aven let out a shout, and Bert's mouth dropped open even as his eyes welled up with tears.

It was the *Argo*.

The long-missing *Red Dragon* had appeared at last.

Burton's eyes blazed with recognition. To him, the appearance of another Dragonship, here, now, only confirmed his suspicions— which meant the two men at the helm, as young as they appeared to be, were his enemies.

The men had the appearance of brothers and were dressed in a manner similar to the Lost Boys. They were speaking in loud voices tinged with Greek accents. They were Hugh the Iron and William the Pig. Jason's sons. The original Lost Boys.

John's eyes widened in realization, and he looked at Bert, who nodded frantically. He realized the same thing John had about the two young men who were waving a greeting and coming ashore, not realizing that the Croatoans were preparing to attack.

"Go back!" John yelled. "William! Hugh! Get back on the ship! You must get away!"

"What?" one of the young men called, waggling a finger in his ear. "I can't hear a thing with this cursed beeswax Peter put in our ears, can you, Will?"

The other shrugged and tapped the side of his head, then, with the other hand outstretched in friendship, walked toward Hairy Billy.

Instead of taking the proffered hand, the Indian lifted his spear and impaled the boy on it.

"No!" Aven and John screamed together.

Hairy Billy merely smiled wickedly and drove the spear deeper into the bewildered boy. The boy called Hugh cried out in horror and leaped to his brother's defense, but the other Indians were already moving to the attack.

This new spectacle was distracting enough to the Croatoans that Aven caught one of them off guard, throwing him to the ground and snatching away his spear. Quickly she stabbed the Indians holding Charles and Bert, while John coldcocked the one who been behind him and caught Aven's knife.

The Croatoans were now being pulled in two fronts, but they were still focused on the weaker opponents with the Dragonship. Burton turned to face the companions and was knocked brutally off his feet by Aven.

"Being called a wench I can live with," she said, "but no one calls me 'helpless.'"

In a flash, Burton was back up and sparring with her, while Charles and Bert were busy with their own opponents. Only John tried to reach the two young men who had arrived in the *Red Dragon*. But he was not fast enough.

The Croatoans fell on them, swords ripping and tearing at their flesh with the spears and knives. William made a valiant effort to defend himself and was obviously skilled with weaponry, but he could do little more than fend off the attackers until he and Hugh could stagger back onto the ship.

In seconds the living Dragonship had pulled away from the shore and was gaining speed back toward the rift in Time.

"No!" John shouted. "Don't let them go! Charles, we have to stop that ship!"

But it was already too late. The *Red Dragon*—the *Argo*—was already far away from the shore, carrying the battered bodies of William and Hugh with it.

The air around the islands began to tremble, and again the sound of thunder split the air. And suddenly the ship was gone. It had vanished back into Time.

John dropped to his knees and pounded the sand with his fists. "We could have stopped it," he exclaimed. "We could have stopped it all. But now it's too late."

Even the Croatoans had paused in their attacks on the companions, realizing that something was amiss.

"What are you talking about?" said Charles, still brandishing a spear at one of the Indians. "What's wrong?"

"Don't you see?" John said. "William and Hugh were unharmed before Burton fought with them. He's the one who set this in motion—and now they've disappeared back into the ripples of Time itself, where they are wrecking on the shoreline where Bacon found them seven hundred years ago!"

John stood and marched to Burton, grabbing him roughly by his jacket. "If only you had listened!" John shouted. "If only you had trusted us, this would all be over. And now it's all gone wrong! You fool! You arrogant fool!"

"Look!" Bert shouted, pointing over the water. "It's coming back!"

The thunder was constant now as Time shuddered, and once more the *Red Dragon* sailed into view. But this time it wasn't alone. Behind it, with the sole exception of the *Indigo Dragon*, all the other Dragonships—White, Orange, Yellow, Green, Blue, and Violet—were falling into a well-ordered formation.

On the foredeck of the *Red Dragon* stood the two young men they had seen on the beach just minutes before, but they had *changed*.

These were not boys, but men, who were battle-hardened and cold. And they were not entirely human, not any longer. The exposed metal on their arms, torsos, and faces showed that their bodies were at least partially mechanical. And even at that distance, the companions could hear the ticking emanating from their chests.

These were the Clockworks Laura Glue had warned them about—the abductors of the Lost Boys.

And behind them, filling the decks of the seven Dragonships, were hundreds and hundreds of children. Some were dressed in animal skins, some in armor. But all of them were fitted for battle.

The companions and the Croatoans stood mute as the armada came to rest in the shallows of the island. Then the leader of the army climbed over the *Red Dragon*'s railing and jumped to the sand. He was a dark-skinned, blue-eyed young man, and on his head and shoulders was his mantle of command—the unmistakable head, horns, and pelt that comprised the Golden Fleece.

"Dear God," Aven whispered, her eyes locked on the golden warrior at the forefront of the army now leaving the ships. "That's Stephen.

"That's my son."

CHAPTER TWENTY-TWO
THE THIMBLE

WITH ONLY A gesture from their leader, the Children's Army streamed over the sides of the ships and through the water. In minutes all of the adults, Caretakers and Croatoans alike, were surrounded. A group of the children went to the nearby fishing cottages and captured the Indians there as well, and also the children who had been freed from the labyrinth, and who seemed more confused than anything else.

It was only then that the thunder subsided enough for them to hear the soft melodies being played by the pipes.

A tall, emaciated figure, cloaked and hooded in black, stepped off the *Red Dragon*. In his hands were the panpipes, and he played a tune that resonated strongly within everyone who heard it.

But with the children, the effect ran more deeply. Every one of the children who had been on the ships wore glazed, entranced expressions. The piper was controlling them all.

"The King of Crickets," breathed Bert.

The music stopped. "The very same," purred a voice that trembled with hate. "But you may call me the Piper."

Aven was still too fixed on her son to notice or care what the tall man was saying. Stephen would hardly look at her. To him, she was simply one of his prisoners.

"He's only a child! He's not yet nine years old!" said Aven. "How can he be this . . . this . . ."

John suddenly realized what had rattled her so. This Stephen who commanded an army and wore the Golden Fleece was a teenager, fourteen, perhaps older, and already had the manner and bearing of a man. Whatever else he had become, he was no longer a child.

"He *was* a child, when I claimed him," said the Piper. "He and many, many others who serve me. They have traveled many places, and the journeys have taken several years to complete."

"But it's only been a few days!" Aven cried.

"To you, perhaps," said the Piper. "But our Crusade has been in progress for a long while, and will go on longer still. We have returned here only to deal with a few loose ends."

There was a cry of pain and surprise, and the companions were astonished to see Burton lying on the ground, bleeding from his mouth and sobbing.

Standing above him with a clenched fist was a girl, who was dressed like the Croatoans. It was Burton's missing daughter, Lillith. He had seen her in the throng and rushed to embrace her—and was met with a blow to the face that belied her size.

This wasn't a girl any longer, but a warrior, as her father had just discovered to his great sorrow.

"I almost feel sorry for the bugger," Charles whispered. "He does all these awful things just to find his own child, and she's as entranced as the rest of them."

"I'm not that sorry," Bert whispered back. "Much of this is his fault."

"What is it you want, Orpheus?" John said, feigning boldness. "Why are you doing all this?"

"Orpheus?" the Piper said in surprise. "You think I'm *Orpheus*?" He tipped back his head and laughed, long and hard. "Oh, my dear Caretakers, you have surprised me, when I thought there were no surprises left in this world. It was worth returning just to hear that."

"Not Orpheus?" John whispered to Bert. "How could we be so mistaken?"

Bert shook his head. "I don't know. If the Piper isn't Orpheus, then I'm at a loss."

"How did he know?" wondered Charles. "How did the Piper know we were Caretakers?"

Before John could answer, several of the soldiers started to blink and shake their heads. Apparently, without constant reinforcement, the mesmerizing effects of the Piper's music could not hold sway over them.

The Piper again raised the pipes to his lips and began to play, and instantly Stephen, Lillith, and all the rest of the soldier children straightened, their eyes glazing over once more. Then the tune took a wicked turn, and the Indian girl Lillith drew a long knife from her belt.

She advanced toward the companions, and it became clear that the Piper was compelling her to kill them.

Aven rose to her feet and took a defensive stance. John may have been a soldier, but she was better at hand-to-hand combat. The girl was smaller, but the knife was lethally sharp, and it was obvious she could wield it with skill.

All along the outskirts of the group, the children from the

labyrinth huddled together in knots, terrified that something beyond their understanding was happening—and even more terrified that it was beyond the grown-ups' understanding too.

"John, look," Charles hissed between clenched teeth. "The Piper is playing, but it isn't affecting Laura Glue or the children of Haven at all."

About fifty feet away, their little friend was putting on a brave face, but she was obviously scared to death—and utterly unmoved by the Piper's music.

"She had beeswax in her ears," said John. "Didn't she?"

"It's not the beeswax," argued Charles. "It's got to be something else that's shielding them from the spell."

Charles was right. The Indian girl Lillith was completely entranced and was circling Aven, feinting and lunging with the precision of a cold machine—but Laura was still crouching at the base of the rocks, a terrified expression on her face.

"None of the children from any of the Dragonships were able to resist the music," whispered Charles. "And Lillith succumbed again the minute he began to play. So what is it that makes the others immune?"

"I don't know," said John. "It must have something to do with Haven, maybe something peculiar to all the children who were there. . . ."

John's breath suddenly caught in his throat when he realized the words he'd just spoken.

Something unique, that only they possessed.

Something peculiar to the children in Haven, and the other children in the labyrinth who had been deemed "unsuitable" to enlist in the Crusade.

Something that made them immune to the effects of the Piper's music.

And suddenly John's heart began to race, and he realized what it was, what it *had* to be. But how could he use the knowledge to their advantage without getting everyone killed?

His train of thought was broken by a scream. Lillith had at last found an opening in Aven's defenses and struck a wicked blow to her side. Aven dropped to her knees in pain, her left arm falling useless as her tunic turned crimson with blood.

Lillith quickly moved forward for a killing strike but was halted by a trilling harmony from the Piper.

"No," he said. "Not yet, anyway. Defeating her is enough. There is no one who might stop us now."

Aven struggled to her feet as Lillith moved to take her place at the Piper's side. "No," Aven said, her voice a rasp of agony. "It's not over."

"Oh, but I think it is," said the Piper. He again put the pipes to his lips and played a discordant tune, and suddenly Stephen strode forward and, with a kick, forced his mother roughly to the ground. He placed a sandaled foot on the back of her neck and pushed her face into the abrasive sand. All the while, his face was empty—only the music, and the illusion it painted in his mind, mattered.

The notes changed, and Stephen lifted his foot and turned to face the Dragonships.

"Shall I tell you about your son?" the Piper said, his voice cruel and mocking. "Shall I tell you of all the atrocities he will commit, and the death he will bring to the world? Do you want to know all the evil he has already done?

"Do you want to know the best part?" the Piper went on, his voice growing softer, but still dripping with wicked glee. "He knows. Deep inside, somewhere within, he is still the child you remember. And as he goes forth at my command, at the head of my army, bringing destruction to the world beyond, he knows what he is being compelled to do—and there is nothing that can prevent it. He is mine, now and forever."

Aven did not move, but wept into the sand. "My son is truly lost to me," she murmured dully. "Lost. My lost son."

Lost son, thought John. *Lost Boys*. It *had* to be. Peter had known. He had *been* the Piper once—so he had to have known too how to defeat the Piper's spell. And Jamie had to have known as well, or else why send Laura Glue for him to begin with?

"'Abandon all hope, ye who enter here,'" quoted the Piper. "It was prophesied, inevitable. And now," he said, raising the pipes to his lips, "we shall have an ending, and go forth to the Great War that we have been building for seven hundred years."

"Stop!" John called out in what he hoped was a forceful-sounding voice. "Show mercy. At least let her say her last farewell. Let her say good-bye to her child."

Aven looked up at John. The fatigue and pain masking her face was not enough to hide her astonishment. What was he playing at?

The Piper tilted his head and smiled cruelly, as if sensing an opportunity for further torment. "Farewell to her child," he purred. "Let it not be said I am without mercy—to a point."

He gestured with his hand, and Stephen spun about on his heel and stood above the battered figure of his mother once more.

It was all John could do to keep his expression placid, and his voice steady. "Aven," he said, "accept the Piper's mercy. Say good-bye to your son. Say good-bye . . . and give him one final kiss."

Please, thought John. *Please, Aven. See this. See this connection. For the sake of us all, see this in my eyes, and know what you must do.*

Aven saw it.

She looked up at the Piper, showing him a pleading, already grieving mother, needing, wanting this one small thing. "May I?" she asked. "May I give my son a kiss?"

The Piper preened at the plaintive, almost desperate tone in her voice.

"Yes," he whispered. "For this, the last time you shall ever see your son, I shall permit a kiss."

Aven tilted her head slightly in acknowledgment of the act of mercy. She stood shakily, weak from loss of blood, and slowly, painfully, walked to her son.

Stephen looked indifferently at his mother, his arms crossed. His gaze was not dead, but it was passionless. There was no spark, only drive. He was a tethered life that lacked his soul, and it showed in the vacancy of his eyes. And in moments his master was going to use him to start a conflagration that would consume the world.

Aven choked back a sob.

She leaned in, as if to kiss Stephen's cheek—then, masking the motion with her crippled left arm, she swiftly reached up with her right hand and pulled something out of her tunic.

She kissed him, and at the same moment slipped the small silver thimble into his hand.

For an instant it seemed as if nothing happened. Then Stephen's eyes went wide, and he began to shudder.

The Piper's eyes narrowed. Something was amiss.

Aven watched a myriad of emotions suddenly flowing across her son's face, and he made a small noise, as if in pain. And then his eyes cleared. They widened, focused, narrowed.

And Aven's son smiled at her.

"Mother," he said softly. "You know I don't like being kissed in front of my people."

The Piper snarled and lifted his pipes to his lips.

Before she could react, Stephen thrust Aven behind him and in the same wheeling motion hurled his long knife at the Piper.

It struck him in the throat, before a note could be sounded by the pipes, and he let out a choking scream.

There was a thunderclap, and a shattering across the sky. And the figure of the Piper exploded into shards of darkness.

Guided by the shadow that had sought him out and bound itself to him, Jack steered the *Indigo Dragon* past the last of the Wandering Isles into the sixth and final district of the Underneath, to the last island.

The Ninth Circle, according to Dante. The center of Hell. Not someplace one might choose to go willingly. But Jack did, not because he was compelled by the shadow, but because he felt its need. It needed help, and it had sought *him* out. Not one of the adults. Jack. *Young* Jack. It trusted him, and he could not betray that trust.

Incredibly, the ninth island was small and unremarkable. All that it appeared to hold were a few stunted trees and a tumble of stones that appeared to be a cairn, or perhaps the entrance to a cave.

Jack tilted the guidelines of the *Indigo Dragon*, spun the wheel, and headed for the island.

The pieces of darkness that had formed the Piper's body were thousands upon thousands of crickets, which scattered into the crevices and under the rocks, the better to escape the light. But what remained behind had nowhere to go.

It was a shadow. And *only* a shadow.

When its body was destroyed, the pipes fell to the ground and cracked apart. They would not be easily repaired—and the effect of their breaking was obvious and immediate.

The children began to awaken.

The long enchantment they had been under was over.

As their eyes began to clear, they became themselves again. Those who were armed dropped their weapons. Those with friends recognized them and embraced them in a happy, bittersweet reunion—for to some of the children, it had been only a few days since they'd parted. For the rest, it had been years.

Even Burton was sobbing, as his daughter dropped to her knees and embraced him. "Ah, my Lillith, my Lily-girl," he said. "I've missed you so."

"I missed you, too, Papa," said the girl.

The shadow hissed and rose into the air. "You may have destroyed my form," the former Piper hissed, its words like acrid smoke. "But I have not come here alone."

Hugh the Iron and William the Pig, the half-Clockwork Lost Boys, were still under some kind of compulsion. The destruction of the panpipes seemed not to deter them at all. They marched briskly to the *Red Dragon* and removed from its deck several large paving stones, which they laid end to end in a path that led from the ship to the clearing where the shadow of the Piper still hovered.

Then one last passenger calmly climbed over the railing of the *Red Dragon* and, careful to step only on the stones, walked toward the astonished companions.

It was Daedalus.

"You gave your word the children would not be harmed," the inventor said to the shadow.

"And none of them have been," the shadow hissed. "Yet. You said you would deliver all the Caretakers to me as children, yet when I arrived, I find them fully grown."

"They wouldn't look into the Well," replied Daedalus. "Only the one, Jack, and I don't see him here."

"One is not three, Daedalus," the shadow said. "Had they been children, I might have entranced them with the pipes, and we would be done with this."

Laura Glue cried out in happiness and ran forward to embrace Daedalus, not realizing what was actually taking place. Charles reached out and caught her, then pulled her close.

"What is this?" Aven exclaimed. "What have you done, Daedalus? What have you allied yourself with?"

"He was against us all along," said John. "That's why he wanted us to look into Echo's Well, and that's why the History is missing the last pages. It was all a trap."

"Try not to think too badly of me, Aven," Daedalus said, as Hugh and William continued to remove stones from the ship and lay them around the clearing. "I simply did what I must, as we all do. You were motivated by love of your son. While I . . . I simply wanted to get out of that damned city of children. That accursed tower where I've been trapped for all these centuries."

"So much for repentance and redemption, eh, Daedalus?" said John.

"Spare me your Christian balms," said Daedalus. "My nephew had humiliated me, and while it wasn't my intent to kill him, I couldn't let his offense simply pass."

"And what of Icarus?" put in Bert. "What of your own son?"

Daedalus started, then regained his composure. "Regrettable. I never wanted it to happen. My designs were not perfected then, so it really wasn't my fault. It was an accident, that's all. An accident."

"You have to be the *worst* father I've ever heard of," said Charles.

"You're forgetting Jason," said Bert, with a sorrowful look at Hugh and William.

"Peas in a pod," Charles stated. "Both despicable."

"Enough talk!" spat the shadow. "Honor your bargain, Daedalus. Destroy them."

"I hate to deflate your balloon," said Charles, "but the panpipes are broken. You no longer control your army of children, and those two"—he gestured at Hugh and William—"are no match for all of us."

"Fortunately for us," Daedalus replied, "Hugh and William are not the only servants at my command."

Daedalus raised a hand and made a complicated gesture with his fingers, and an instant later the companions heard a thunderous noise, followed by a tremor.

"Is that thunder?" said Burton, looking up at the dark skies.

"It isn't thunder," declared Charles. "It's the sound of a master chessman making an excellent move."

The sounds were echoing across the islands with a regular rhythm now, and far to the north, Talos and the other bronze Clockwork giants moved into view. They would be upon them in minutes.

"Check," said Daedalus. "And mate."

The shadow laughed, and all John could think was that it sounded nothing at all like crickets.

The entrance to the cave was guarded by a dozen children, all dressed in dirty animal skins. Of the beasts he could identify, there was a fat boy in a bearskin, three girls dressed as foxes, two smaller boys dressed as possums, and one boy who had unsuccessfully clothed himself as a skunk and who stood a distance away from the rest.

As Jack approached, the children jumped to attention, raising crude, handmade stone and wooden weapons, but they relaxed immediately when they saw it was a child like themselves.

"Did you bring us anything to eat?" one of the foxes asked. "The King of Crickets keeps f'rgetting, and he hits us if we ask."

"I'm sorry, I didn't," said Jack.

"Drat and darn," the girl said. "I'm tired of standing guard. I want to play a different game."

"You're playing a game?" Jack said.

"Yes," one of the other girls said, nodding. "Do you want to play? I'm Boo Radish. Who be you?"

"I be—I mean, I'm Jack," said Jack. "What kind of game?"

"There's a monster inside," said the skunk boy. "He looks like a normal Longbeard, but he's a monster just the same, and we have to keep him here, in the cave."

"So you're the frogs, then?" asked Jack.

The second fox clapped her hands. "You do know the game! Why didn't you say you were a Lost Boy?"

The fat bear puffed out his chest. "If we guard the monster, we get to be Lost Boys too."

"I only just found out I was one," said Jack. "Can I go in?"

The beast-children moved aside deferentially, and Jack and his two shadows stepped to the mouth of the cave. Not far inside was a frame to which the "monster" the children guarded had been tied.

"I think I have something that belongs to you," said Jack.

"Thank you for bringing it back," answered Peter. "Did Jamie send you, then?"

"In a manner of speaking," said Jack. "I'm one of his replacements. I came with Laura Glue."

"That's my girl!" the old man said. "So, Caretaker . . . would you like to play a game?"

CHAPTER TWENTY-THREE
UNRAVELED

THE BRONZE GIANTS were nearly upon them, and the children had begun to panic. The adults were doing their best to maintain order, but it was impossible—there were too many children, and there was no way to organize any kind of defense against so massive an enemy. All the while, Daedalus and the Piper's shadow merely watched the chaos taking place around them.

Only John kept his wits about him.

"There are no coincidences," he shouted to Bert over the din. "Even with the Time Storm, we had to have come here for a reason! There has to be a purpose to all of this!"

"What are you thinking, John?" asked Bert.

"This! Look at this!" John said, pointing to the illustration of Autunno in the *Geographica*. In the very center was an image of a chariot, drawn by two dragons.

"Medea's chariot," said Bert. "What of it?"

"Look at the names inscribed underneath!"

Bert looked, and his eyes widened in shock and surprise. One of the dragons was Samaranth, and the other was a green-gold beast called Azer.

"And look at the shape!" said John. "Look at the entirety of the Underneath! What does it look like to you?"

"Rings within rings," Bert gasped, as what John was driving at dawned on him. "It's a giant Ring of Power!"

"Will it work?"

"Where do you think the kings of the Archipelago got their authority?" said Bert. "It had to begin somewhere! Why not here, where the original legends of heroes began? It's worth trying!"

But it was nearly too late. With thundering footsteps, the bronze giants began encircling the shore, towering above the companions and the children.

Quickly John grabbed Aven and Stephen and explained what he wanted them to do. Then he showed the prince of the Archipelago the Summoning for the dragons and told him to read it aloud.

The giant Clockworks were nearly upon them, trapping them all. There was no escape, either to the hills or to the ships. Unless they did something then and there, there would be no battle.

"Read it!" John instructed Stephen, thrusting the *Imaginarium Geographica* at him. "Read it!"

Stephen nodded and knelt, bending protectively over the book.

By right and rule
For need of might
I call on thee
I call on thee

By blood bound
By honor given

I call on thee
I call on thee

For life and light your protection given
From within this ring by the power of Heaven
I call on thee
I call on thee

As he finished, the last of the giant bronze automatons moved into place. They were surrounded.

The bronze giants were all that was necessary to turn the frightened children into obedient, subdued drones once more.

Children know when the threat of violence is real and cannot be defied. And so when William and Hugh began to herd them onto the ships, it was in silence and order.

Daedalus had ordered the adults, both Caretakers and Croatoans, to kneel in the sand.

"It was an excellent effort," Daedalus said, "but ultimately futile." He turned to Aven. "Don't worry. None of the children will be harmed. Whatever you may think of me, I'm not without feeling."

"What will you do with them?" asked Charles.

"Those who choose to return to our Crusade will come on the ships," said the Piper's shadow. "The rest will be returned to the Minotaur's care on Aiaia."

"Imprisoned in the labyrinth, you mean!" Charles said.

"It's better than death," said Daedalus, "as I'm afraid you're about to learn."

"What are you waiting for?" Burton whispered to John. "Don't bother denying it—you, the wench, and the old man are all watching the skies. What are you expecting to happen?"

"I don't know," John replied. "A miracle, perhaps."

"Well, I'm not going to simply die kneeling in the sand," said Burton. "And neither will the Croatoans. But . . ." He hesitated. "If you do have some miracle planned, will you do what you can to save my daughter as well? Please?"

John drew back and looked at the leader of the Indians. His face was open, sincere. He had made a request but had also meant it as an apology.

"Of course," John finally said. "If it is in my power to do so, I'll save your girl."

"Thank you," said Burton.

"What in Hades is that?" the Piper's shadow exclaimed.

John and the others looked to the sky. The dark clouds continued to roll and churn, but there, to the west, something else was approaching.

"The dragons?" exclaimed Bert. "Is it, John? Did the summoning work, after all?"

But it wasn't the dragons moving beyond the clouds. It was something much, much bigger.

Jack had found Peter Pan, the man who had summoned them to the Archipelago, and he carried with him Peter's shadow, which had guided him to the last island in the Underneath, and all of this had been done under terrible circumstances and against impossible odds. But there was one more obstacle Jack could not seem to overcome.

He could not enter the cave.

A peal of laughter sounded from somewhere behind Peter, and

Jack could just make out the image of a beautiful woman in an ornate mirror that hung on the cave wall.

"He doesn't know, Peter," she said. "He doesn't realize what he has to give up to come in."

"He is a Caretaker of the *Imaginarium Geographica*," said Peter. "I'm sure he understands sacrifice."

"Sacrifice?" Jack said, taking a step back. "What do I have to sacrifice? Why can't I enter the cave?"

"This is the center of the Underneath," said Peter. "One of the oldest islands that exist. And nothing can come into the cave that isn't real."

"I don't understand," said Jack. "What isn't real?"

"Tell me," said Peter. "Who are you? Who are you really, Jack?"

"How did you know my name?"

"We've met before," Peter told him, "which is how I know this isn't really you. Now tell me," he said again, "who . . . are . . . you?"

"I—I'm just Jack."

"No," said Peter, "you aren't. You can't be, if we're to save your friends."

"I know what you're asking of me," Jack said dully. "It—it's just difficult to give it up."

"I know," said Peter. "Perhaps better than anyone. But you can't stay a child forever. To choose to speak into Echo's Well is to choose illusion. To choose to avoid the responsibilities of being an adult. The real trick—the real choice—is to keep the best of the child you were, without forgetting when you grow up.

"It is the best of both worlds, Jack. Being a child is to believe in magic everywhere. . . .

". . . but even Peter Pan had to grow up one day."

✦ ✦ ✦

It may have taken minutes or hours for the massive apparitions to come clearly into view in the diffused light of the Underneath, and the clouds of the Time Storm were still floating thickly in the air. But when the clouds finally began to dissipate, and the companions could see clearly once more, they saw *giants*.

The great creatures were almost incomprehensible: They were chessmen that aspired to be continents, and they moved with the tectonic grace that their smaller mechanical counterparts lacked.

There was no booming tremor with the footsteps of the giants, which towered over the Clockworks as if the automatons were toys; just motion and coiled energy.

"Is that what we summoned?" asked John. "Stephen called giants to us instead of dragons?"

Bert spoke in a hush, awed by the sight. "The giants were the architects of the Rings of Power. I didn't know they still existed, much less that they could be summoned."

The giants were almost shapeless, having only a vaguely human form. They had no faces, but only a single circular eye, which glowed in the center of their foreheads.

Daedalus shouted in dismay and gestured for Talos and the automatons to attack, but the machines were more than outmatched.

The giants turned their gaze to the bronze Clockworks, and a great booming horn sounded: the language of Titans.

As the companions watched, the automatons stopped in midstride and slowly turned to stone.

The giants turned their gaze to the sea, and John counted

seven of them as they moved past the island, stepping over it in a single stride. A few more steps to the east, and they were already over the horizon. In moments they had disappeared completely.

"Decide, Jack," said Peter. "You cannot return my shadow unless you enter the cave. But you cannot enter the cave without deciding who you really are. And if you cannot, I will die."

Jack was struggling. He had been a child again for too long, and he was uncertain what to do.

"It's no use, Peter," said the woman in the mirror. "He'll never be able to do it. After all," she added scornfully, "he is only a child."

"But that's just it," said Jack. "I—I'm *not* a child."

The beast-children stood back in mixed wonder and fear. Something was happening to the strange boy who'd flown there in the living ship.

Having not just thought the thoughts but actually spoken the words, Jack grew taller, and his features lengthened, thickened. He was becoming older before their very eyes, adding days, weeks, then faster, months. . . .

And then months became a year—a terrible thing for a Lost Boy to contemplate. . . .

"I do know who I am," Jack said. "I'm an Oxford scholar."

One year, two years, five years, ten . . .

"I'm a Caretaker of the *Imaginarium Geographica*."

Ten years, and five more . . .

"I know," said Jack, with the surety and confidence of a fully grown man. "I know what needs to be done."

Peter nodded. "And that, boy, is the difference."

Jack stepped into the cave. Instantly the second shadow

detached itself and flew across the floor, attaching itself to Peter.

As Jack watched, the color rose in the old man's cheeks, and his eyes, dull a moment ago, glittered with life. He took a deep breath, then another, and another, and then lifted his head and looked at Jack. He was smiling.

Jack motioned to the beast-children. "Come on," he said to them. "This isn't a monster. Let's get him freed, neh?"

And the Lost Boys nodded their heads and did as he asked— not because he was an adult, who must be obeyed, but because they knew the boy called Jack was still somewhere inside the Longbeard, and Jack could be trusted.

"Let's get you into the light," said Jack. "And then let's go rescue your granddaughter."

The Piper's shadow screamed in fury. And Daedalus was at a loss. In a single move, all their plans had been turned to dust.

"That's what you call a checkmate," said Charles.

"I'm not defenseless," snarled Daedalus. "I still control Jason's sons, and they're more than a match for any of you."

"No, you don't," said Stephen. "Perhaps you did, but you built them to follow my commands, not yours. And they're not doing anything else you say."

Daedalus trembled with anger but realized he was beaten. Carefully he began to back toward the *Red Dragon*.

"Will, Hugh," called Stephen. "Stop him."

The two brothers moved swiftly behind the inventor and picked up several of the stone blocks. Daedalus stopped. "What are you doing?" he cried. "Put those back!"

Stephen turned to his mother. "He was condemned to stay

forever in the tower where he murdered his nephew," the prince said calmly, "but he figured out a way around that."

"That was the deal I struck with the King of Crickets," said Daedalus. "If I helped him with his Crusade, he promised to have the prince of the archipelago free me from my imprisonment."

"You were willing to sacrifice all these children merely to get out of a just punishment?" asked Charles. "What kind of monster are you?"

"I gave them wings!" said Daedalus. "I did more for these children than they deserved. And I deserved something in return. If some of them paid the price for that, it wasn't my fault!"

Stephen walked over to the inventor and looked at him appraisingly.

"I release you from your bondage," he said, and he reached out a hand . . .

. . . and *pushed*.

Daedalus screamed as he fell away from the stones and burst into flame. In seconds, there was nothing left of him but ash.

Aven looked horrified. Her son had changed in the years he'd been gone. He was no longer under the Piper's control, but the experience had changed him nonetheless.

With Daedalus's death, both Hugh and William finally seemed to come to themselves and, realizing they were no longer entirely human, began to weep.

The Piper's shadow flitted back and forth above their heads, hissing.

"What do we do about him?" asked Charles.

"If you don't mind," a voice called from above, "I'd like a word with him myself."

It was Peter. He and Jack were flying above in the *Indigo Dragon*.

"Now," Peter said to the shadow, "let's finish this, shall we?"

The shadow vibrated with hate as the airship landed and Peter climbed out. "You're an old man now," it growled. "What harm can you do to me?"

"Why don't you come down here and we'll find out?" said Peter. But the shadow stayed where it was, hovering just out of reach.

Aven looked both nervous and relieved to see Peter, who caught her eye and winked.

"We thought it was Orpheus," John explained, "but it only laughed at us."

"Of course it isn't Orpheus," said Peter. "This Longbeard killed Orpheus and left his head in the cave to taunt me.

"No, this fellow and I have a long history as enemies," Peter continued, circling the shadow warily. "He may be only a shadow now, but I'd know him anywhere.

"Oh, we've had great battles, he and I. We are old adversaries. He's the original specter of the Archipelago. He's the Sinner King. He's the *Hook*. But of all his names, you may know him best . . .

" . . . as Mordred."

"Mordred!" John exclaimed.

The shadow circled them. It seemed to know it had been named—and in the naming, it had lost most of its power over them.

"You have nothing that can harm me," Mordred said to Peter. "I cannot be defeated!"

"I have what you lack," said Peter. "I still have my body."

The shadow growled and suddenly lunged at the old man. But

Peter was prepared for the attack and reached into his tunic. He flung a handful of glittering dust at the apparition, and with a scream that rent the air, the shadow spread out, then vanished, leaving only the ringing echo of its cry.

"Is it gone?" said Jack. "Did you kill him, Peter?"

"I doubt it," Peter replied. "That was powdered silver—fairy dust. It's enough to dissipate him, for a time. But I don't think it can destroy him. After all," he added, winking at Jack, "a shadow is a pretty sturdy thing, if you treat it right. But is is still just that—a shadow.

"That's why he could never enter the cave. In Plato's cave, all shadows are cast by real things. But a shadow cannot cast itself. He couldn't enter the cave without revealing who he really was."

"Oh no!" John exclaimed. "Look!"

While Peter and the companions had been occupied with Mordred's shadow, Burton and the Croatoans had quietly commandeered and lifted off in the *Indigo Dragon*.

"Farewell, Caretakers," Burton called out from the aft deck. "And—thank you."

"Well, I'll be damned," said Bert. "That's almost as surprising as Mordred."

"I'm sorry," said Charles. "One of us should have been watching her."

"It's all right," Bert reassured him. "Burton won't damage her. He knows her value. And besides, we have all the other Dragonships now.

"For the first time since they were created, all of them are together. And all the children have been saved. All in all, I don't think we could have asked for a better ending to this adventure."

"Maybe you spoke too soon," said John, pointing over the beach. The Time Storm had continued to boil, and one more patch of air was shimmering. Something was coming through.

"Father!" cried William the Pig. "It's father!"

"Christ above," said John. "I think that's Jason."

From the portal of Time, a group of weary-looking wanderers dressed in ancient Greek attire walked slowly across the sand.

The leader wore a haggard expression, and his face was deeply creased, more with living than with age.

They approached the companions, ignoring the throngs of children who were watching their passage.

"We seek two boys," Jason said to John. "My sons. Have you seen them?"

"Father, please," said William the Pig. "We are here! We are right here in front of you!"

Hugh the Iron began to sob. "Will . . . it's no use. I—I don't think he knows we're here."

The shade of Jason made no indication that he heard or saw his sons, but merely turned away from John and stared out across the waters, his face racked with sadness and loss.

"He can't see them!" John said softly. "He can't see them at all!"

The ghostly procession passed around them, even through them; a parade of spirit that hardly acknowledged them, if indeed they even knew anyone was there.

William and Hugh fell to the sand in sorrow and grief. And after a few more moments, Jason and the others who followed him walked past the companions and vanished back into Time, still searching for Jason's lost sons.

"This is what Dante was warning mankind of in his writings," mused Bert. "He said that the hottest places in Hell are reserved for those who in time of great moral crises maintain their neutrality. I think what we just witnessed happening with Jason is precisely that."

"Remember Milton's caution also," Charles whispered. "'The mind is its own place, and in itself, can make a heaven of Hell, and a hell of Heaven.'"

CHAPTER TWENTY-FOUR
SECOND STAR TO THE RIGHT

IT WAS AN organizational nightmare, but within a day, the companions were able to get all the children aboard the seven Dragonships for the journey home. They had planned to go directly to Haven, but William and Hugh made a curious request, which Peter and the Caretakers chose to grant. And so their first stop was Aiaia.

They moored all the ships and accompanied William and Hugh to the labyrinth, where John explained to Asterius that the brothers had requested to live there with him in the Abbey of the Rose.

For his part, the odd creature protested mightily, but the broad smile on his face told them that he was very pleased to accommodate their request.

"They didn't want to come back to Haven," Peter explained to the companions. "They felt they were deformed. I tried to convince them otherwise, but they wished for this—and actually, they may find their calling here."

"Interesting children you've chosen to succeed you, Herb," Peter said when they returned to the ships. "Especially that one, John."

"He has the talent to make connections where none are evident, Peter," said Bert. "He has the rarest of abilities—to retain a practical head about him without losing the ability to imagine. He's really quite extraordinary. Do you know that as a child, he invented his own languages? And more, he invented etymologies, and histories, and even mythologies to accompany them?"

"Impressive," Peter commented, scratching himself. "His Histories will make for interesting reading."

"Oh, I don't think that's John's path," said Bert. "He's not built to write straight accounts, as Bacon did, or even to really fictionalize his adventures the way Jamie and I have. No, John's an inventor, pure and simple. It's what first attracted Stellan's attention. John has within himself entire realities that he's going to create and share with the world. And to be honest, I think his legacy is going to eclipse us all."

"See?" said Peter. "That's the advantage of having never learned to write. I don't have to worry about things like legacies."

"Hah!" Bert said. "This from the great Pan? Your legacy is already carved in stone." He paused. "Actually," he added, reconsidering, "it's in bronze. In Kensington Gardens."

"Yes," said Peter. "I've seen it. It's awful. Makes me look like a prat. I told Jamie that if they were going to put up a statue, it should at least be one of the ones that pees on people."

Bert chuckled. "Like the one in Bruxelles?"

"Who, Christoph?" said Peter. "He isn't a statue. At least he didn't start out as one. He was one of the first Lost Boys, who learned a valuable lesson from Medea.

"Don't piss on a witch's front door."

◆ ◆ ◆

On Haven, with a sense of responsibility and no small regret, the Caretakers claimed the Histories that had for so long been part of Daedalus's collection in his workshop.

"He did do a lot of good things over the centuries," said Peter as he passed through to check on their progress. "If nothing else, try to think well of him for that."

"He's a very forgiving sort, isn't he?" said Charles. "I don't know that I could have felt the same way about someone who'd betrayed me so greatly, if I were in his position."

"I think I understand why," John said. "I've been reading in the other Histories, and I've come across a story that explains a great deal about the Pan. You both know the story, and quite well. We just never knew the full extent of it until now.

"There was an old tale, about a European village that was overrun with rats. The village elders held a meeting to decide what to do, and a stranger stood up and declared that he could lead the rats away to the river to be drowned by playing a tune on his magic pipes. The town agreed to pay whatever price he named if he could indeed do this thing, and so that very night, he did.

"He told the villagers to shut their doors and windows tightly, and to stuff rags in the cracks and crevices so that they could not hear the tune he played. And sometime in the night he performed his task, for when they awoke the next morning, all the rats were gone."

"I know this tale," said Charles. "*The Pied Piper of Hamelin*. Jacob and Wilhelm Grimm wrote the story in one of their books. As it went, Hamelin refused to pay the Piper's fee, and so the next night he played a tune that entranced the children in the same way he did the rats. But instead of leading them to the river to drown, he led them to the sheer face of a mountain, which split open to receive them, and they were never seen again."

"Jacob learned of it from travelers in the Archipelago of Dreams," said Bert, "although I'm certain he never came here to the Underneath, or else he'd have learned the truth of it."

"The children *were* seen again," John continued, "just not in Europe. They were brought here, to the Underneath, where they were sorted out by Mordred posing as the Piper."

"The Time Storm," said Bert. "He was using the openings in time caused by the crumbling Keep to cross back and forth in history and recruit his 'soldiers.'"

"Wasn't there one child who was unable to follow?" put in Jack. "One who was lame, and couldn't reach the opening in the mountain quickly enough?"

"Exactly so," said John. "That boy, who had a crippled leg, was tormented by the enchanted melody that in all of Hamelin town only he remembered. And he mourned the loss of his friends, and saw the anguish of their parents, and he determined to do something. He decided that he would find them and bring them home."

"And did he succeed?" Charles asked.

"In part," said John. "After many years of searching, he finally found the lost children. But he never returned home. Instead, he became lost himself."

The Caretakers went to look for Peter, to say good-bye before leaving for the Archipelago. They found him with Laura Glue in Raleigh's Orchard, near Echo's Well.

"You'll be able to cross back into the Archipelago with the Dragonships," said Peter. "It's part of their nature—to cross magical barriers. They needn't be able to fly, although we won't tell Burton that," he added with a wink at Laura Glue.

"And what of you, Peter?" asked John. "What do you plan to do?"

"Why, what I'm already doing," he answered. Peter walked past them and looked into the Well. It reflected back the aged lines of his face, the white shock of hair. But it didn't change.

"Olly Olly Oxen-Free," he called, grinning. Nothing about his appearance changed.

"See?" he said to John. "I didn't change, because I found who I really was, who I really am. Who I want to remain. I'm Laura Glue's grandfather."

"I suppose if you ever wanted to retire as the Pan, you could just choose a successor," said Charles. "Not that you need to, of course," he added hastily.

"But I *did* choose a successor," said Peter. "A child of the right temperament and age, who, if he had chosen differently, might have come to the Nether Land and remained a child."

"How can you decide if a child has the right kind of temperament?" asked John.

Peter grinned puckishly. "Because if he didn't, he wouldn't have been able to become one here," he said, looking at Jack.

"Me?" Jack said in surprise. "When did you ever choose me?"

"Long ago," said Peter. "I came to you in the night and listened to your dreams. And then I whispered stories to you about the Nether Land, where you could become whoever you wanted, and even take a new name, Jack, Jacksie, Jack-in-the-Green. . . . Why do you think you were the one who was able to share my shadow, if not because we are the same, you and I?"

Jack went pale. "It was you," he whispered. "You're the one who called me Jack."

But Peter only winked, and spryly moved away to play with the children, his limp barely noticeable.

"It's never fully healed," John observed. "It was Peter who inspired Daedalus to resume his old experiments in flight. He wanted Peter to be able to move about freely in the air, since he could not do so on land. It may have been the single most redeeming thing the inventor ever did."

"The child in Hamelin," Charles exclaimed. "The one who went searching for his friends—it was Peter, wasn't it?"

"Yes." John nodded. "I believe it was. I don't know who he truly was before he came here, but once here, he became Peter Pan. And he always will be, forevermore."

As they said their good-byes to Peter, a tearful Laura Glue, and the rest of the Lost Boys, Peter had one parting gift for them—if it could truly be called a gift.

It was the padlocked wardrobe, the only thing he'd chosen to remove from Plato's cave, where it had been kept ever since his falling-out with Jamie.

"We know how to make and repair Daedalus's wings," Peter said, "and we have plenty of dragon feathers with which to make more. So we don't really have to have this.

"And besides," he added, "I don't really feel the need to go to London that much anymore."

He embraced his granddaughter and thumped the wardrobe.

"Find a good place for it, won't you?"

✦   ✦   ✦

"Well, gosh," Artus exclaimed. "What a handsome wardrobe."

They placed it in the Great Whatsit. There wasn't a better place for it in the entire Archipelago, John decided.

The reunion with Stephen and Aven made Artus happier than they'd ever seen him, and he declared that there should be a celebration across the entire Archipelago. Aven and Stephen left to make preparations, and the king was left with the Caretakers, who told him everything that had happened.

When they were finished, Artus sat back and looked pointedly at each of them. "I know you want to ask it, so ask."

"All right," said John, rising. "Where are the dragons?"

Artus nodded. "I knew it would come up sooner or later, but I was rather hoping for later. I sent them away, back to where they'd come from, past the Edge of the World, beyond Terminus."

"Why?" asked John. "They have always been the strength of the Silver Throne."

"Yes," said Artus, "and that's what troubled me. We—I—did not want to depend on brute force in order to rule. And I'd already decided that a monarchy may not be the best way to run an entire Archipelago. But if there were no king who was able to manage the dragons, it would be even more unwieldy to expect a Parliament to do it.

"So I decided. And as of today, my work is clear.

"Before another year has passed in the Archipelago, I will have begun the dissolution of the monarchy."

When the others had left, Jack hung back to speak with the king in private.

"Artus, I have something to ask," said Jack. "Something very personal, I'm afraid."

Artus nodded as if he'd been expecting the question. "You've been wondering about Aven, and our son."

"Yes."

"He's a good boy," Artus said. "I couldn't be prouder if he were my own flesh and blood."

"Then he isn't . . . isn't yours and Aven's?"

"I know you have eyes," Artus replied. "I have hair like straw, and I'm so fair-skinned when I'm out in the sun too long the freckles on my arms turn green. He has his mother's eyes and cheekbones—but he gets his handsome complexion from his father."

The pieces fell into place. "That's how your son can be nearly nine years old, even though it's only just been nine years since you met his mother," Jack guessed.

"Yes," said Artus. "Aven and Nemo had been closer than she admitted to anyone. And even he wasn't really able to convince her to settle down. She was—is—happiest on the seas, piloting a ship. So when I asked her to marry me, she said yes—and then I backed down after I saw how unhappy she'd become. She'd agreed at first in order to help me become accustomed to running a kingdom, and I thought she wanted it because of the pending birth of her son. But as it turned out, neither one of us needed a marriage for the reasons we thought we did, so we didn't."

"And yet," Jack went on, "you call Stephen your son and have raised him as such."

At this, Artus looked taken aback. "Of course. Why wouldn't I? There's a lot more to being a father than whether or not I'm the one who started the process. It's seeing it through that counts."

"That's very admirable," said Jack. "I don't know if I'd be capable of that—raising another man's child as if he were my own. I don't know if I have the strength of character for it."

"Stephen is Aven's son," said Artus. "That was enough for me. She knows I love her, and our arrangement, while it might be a bit strange to some people, works for us. And isn't that what matters?"

"It isn't for me to judge," Jack replied. "I've sometimes wondered if I'll ever get married at all. I watch John and Charles, and at times I envy them. But I can still relate. How you've done what you're doing is just beyond my understanding."

Artus clapped him on the back. "I'm sure if the situation arises," he said, "you'll be able to find the joy in it, as I have. And if you ever need advice, you know where to come to."

Aven and Stephen looked up from the table in the hall and waved. Jack and Artus waved back.

"Kids," said Artus. "They grow up so fast. It seems like just yesterday he was only nine."

"It was last week, actually."

"That's just as bad," said Artus.

The celebrations in the Archipelago lasted for a full day and a full night, as the peoples of all the lands came to Paralon to reclaim their lost children. Still, all the happiness over the successful return of the children couldn't mitigate the frustration the Caretakers felt over the dilemmas that would still have to be dealt with in the near future.

The *Indigo Dragon* was still in the possession of Burton and the Croatoan Indians. The Keep of Time was still crumbling and would continue to do so. And there could be rogue Caretakers back in their world who were actually working for the Imperial

Cartological Society. Basically, Charles declared, the entire adventure was still a catastrophe.

"Not a catastrophe," said John. "More a eucatastrophe, I think. It was all grim and terrible to a point, but things seem to have worked out in the end."

"Jack," said Charles, "he's making up words again."

"Yes," Jack replied, "but he's getting better at it, don't you think?"

"You're forgetting the most frightening loose end of all," said Bert. "Our great adversary still exists.

"Your shadow may be separated from you—may be captured, or imprisoned, or twisted and manipulated—but it cannot exist without you."

"Cannot exist?" said John. "As in, your shadow will not outlast your death?"

"Correct," said Bert. "And if that truly was Mordred's shadow we faced, then our old adversary, the Winter King, is still alive."

It was time to return home. There were matters there that needed tending to, and the companions felt that for the moment, they had done enough.

"After you," John said to Jack.

Jack looked at Charles, who also nodded that he should be first, and with a last smile at Bert, Jack stepped into the wardrobe.

One by one, they pressed the furs aside and emerged from the wardrobe onto the fourth floor of the town house near Kensington Gardens. First Jack, then Charles, and finally, John. They were greeted by a beaming figure holding a tray.

"Welcome back," said Jamie. "I've made tea."

EPILOGUE

ON AN ENCHANTED *island at the Frontier of the Archipelago of Dreams, a cave stood empty. Where once there had been weavers, and a loom, only dust remained. And where a great tapestry that was as big as the world had once covered the walls of the cave, there was only a cobweb, woven by a spider that had only that day taken up residence in the cave.*

Seven hundred years earlier, or just yesterday, Roger Bacon, the Caretaker Principia of the Imaginarium Geographica, pulled his cloak tighter to ward off the chill drafts that passed through his small alcove. The only light came from the tallow candles mounted upon his table, and there were no sounds save for the ticking of the timepiece he'd been given; a gift from the Frenchman.

Bacon carefully dipped his pen into the inkwell and continued writing the Histories to which he had devoted a considerable part of his life.

In the year 1212, a boy named Stephen, who claimed to be directed by Heaven itself, called upon the Sons of Adam and Daughters of Eve to rally around him in a great Crusade against the infidels and heretics in the East.

Thirty thousand children chose to follow him, and together they boarded seven great ships—and were never seen again in the world beyond. But they were not lost—

Stephen brought them to the Archipelago, where he joined with the Great Shadow and the Sons of Jason, and together they began a Great War that devastated all the lands that are.

As he wrote these words, the ticking suddenly stopped, and the wind was stilled. Then, as he watched, the words on the page began to shift and change, and suddenly he could not remember writing what had been there before, but only what appeared there now, in ink still glistening:

Thirty thousand children chose to follow him, and together they boarded seven great ships—and were never seen again in the world beyond. But they were not lost— Stephen brought them to the Archipelago, where he and his master, the Great Shadow, were defeated by the bravery and wisdom of three scholars, and the power of a mother's love.

But the Great Shadow escaped, and the ships vanished with him into Time's embrace. And the Great War that was to be waged in the Archipelago may yet take place far in the future, in a conflict referred to by the Frenchman called Verne . . .

. . . as the Second Great War of the World. . . .

And as he closed the book, the ticking began again, and the breeze, warm now, flowed around him even as Time itself continued to ripple and shudder around the old scribe. . . .

AUTHOR'S NOTE

After *Here, There Be Dragons* was published, and the real identities of John, Jack, and Charles became common knowledge, I realized that the challenge I faced with *The Search for the Red Dragon* was to be able to continue their story and still keep characters (who were based on well-known and much-beloved authors) fresh and interesting. And the best way I could do that was to broaden the mythology I'd created for the *Imaginarium Geographica* and focus on John's predecessor, Sir James Barrie.

I had alluded to Barrie's role as a Caretaker in *Dragons*, but I knew that bringing him to the fore would give me the opportunity to fold Peter Pan into the story. I had already stated that the *Red Dragon* had been made from the rebuilt *Argo*, and so making the mythological Jason and Medea's sons into the original "Lost Boys" gave me a direct line back to Peter Pan.

Orpheus, as the inheritor of the Greek god Pan's pipes, gave me a connection to Peter (Pan) and opened up the opportunity to tie in the Pied Piper of Hamelin. Adding the stories of Daedalus and Echo simply strengthened the connections I wanted to establish with the classical Greek mythology.

The Piper's story, and luring away the children, was something that could be woven into the tales of the Children's Crusades, which are, tragically, historically accurate. This was also the source for Hugh the Iron, William the Pig, and the child who led them (in one version of the Crusade stories), Stephen.

It was a passion of J. R. R. Tolkien's to try to find the oldest versions of the world's stories. So using that conceit as a template, I was able to write early versions of "Hansel and Gretel" and even wink at "Snow White" with Medea's mirror.

Harry Houdini and Arthur Conan Doyle were friends in real life and had, quite famously, attempted to prove the existence of fairies and other magical creatures. Houdini in particular is a perfect example of a Caretaker who was not also a writer—even if his tenure was short. And again, that he was a great illusionist who would have loved the concept of the transporting wardrobes segued nicely into an inspiration for Lewis's most famous work, as well as echoing the recent "revelations" about Houdini's secret life as a spy.

Richard Burton was an infamous explorer, who seemed to be exactly the sort of person who might stumble across a lost expedition like the Roanoke colonists—and the temptation to explain what "Croatoan" meant while in the same stroke establishing a basis for the Indians in Peter Pan was too hard to resist.

The names of ships forming the great wall in the Underneath will be familiar to anyone who may have read stories about the Bermuda Triangle. I threw in Amelia Earhart just for good measure.

It should be noted that while many of the stories and characters are based on real people and historical facts, I have taken liberties where it best suited the story to do so. Nothing here should be taken as definitive truth—but then again, all of us change and grow, and alter how we relate to the world as we do. I have tried to instill this quality in my characters as well.

And finally, as all the best villains do, the Winter King/ Mordred returns to the stage, though not in the form readers might have expected, nor is he presented in an entirely negative light. And a careful reader might note that his whole story has not yet been told. . . .

James A. Owen
Silvertown, USA

ACKNOWLEDGMENTS

Here, There Be Dragons began its life as an uncompleted ten-page outline, which was my last presentation to the last producer I met on an interminably long trip to Hollywood. It was that producer who worked with me as I shaped the story over the next few months, and who suggested that I begin approaching publishers with the intent of turning the story we intended to become a movie franchise into a book first. The book you are holding would not exist if it were not for the interest, advice, and encouragement of Marc Rosen, and the support of David Heyman.

The Search for the Red Dragon was easier to begin than its predecessor but was harder to finish, for all the right reasons. I have been overwhelmed by the support and goodwill extended to me by the many people who have assisted me in this process and been supportive of these books.

The home team at Coppervale International has been the foundation of all the work that I do. My brother Jeremy runs the Studio, which allows me to focus on doing my best work, and our Senior Apprentices Mary and Lon never failed to lend a hand when it was needed.

My representatives, including Craig Emanuel, David Schmerler, and Julie Jones at Loeb & Loeb, Ben Smith (formerly of ICM), and Ellen, Julie, Lindsay, Julie N., and Eddie at the Gotham Group, put together excellent deals, and have supported my work and career in many, many ways.

The team at Simon & Schuster has always included world-class people, and it has been my pleasure to work with them all. David Gale, Alexandra Cooper, and Navah Wolfe have been the most ideal of editors for me, and managing editor Dorothy Gribbin and copyeditor Valerie Shea made all of the work we did look even better. Lizzy Bromley and Laurent Linn have been just as ideal to work with in book design. Rick Richter, Rubin Pfeiffer, and Elizabeth Law are no longer there, but helped shape the best work of my career, and I am forever grateful to them. Carolyn Reidy, Jon Anderson, and Justin Chanda have been creative and tireless in their support of my books, as has Paul Crichton, who also knows where to get a really awesome steak in New York.

My friends, family, and close colleagues are the ones who make all of my efforts worthwhile, and make this life so very worth living: Brett, Shawn, Russ and Bekki, Daanon, Kevin and Rebecca, Victoria, Heidi, Kristin, Homer and Effie, Jeff at Cox Printing, Grampa John and Grammie Val, Tracy and Lisa, my mother Sharon, my brother Jason, and Cindy, Sophie, and Nathaniel.

All of you made these books possible, and I can't express my gratitude enough.